THE CORNISH DIARY

An absolutely breathtaking psychological thriller with a stunning final twist

ELEONOR SAMUEL

Joffe Books, London
www.joffebooks.com

First published in Great Britain in 2023

This book is a work of fiction. Names, characters, businesses, organizations, places and events are either the product of the author's imagination or are used fictitiously. Any resemblance to actual persons, living or dead, events or locales is entirely coincidental. The spelling used is British English except where fidelity to the author's rendering of accent or dialect supersedes this.

Cover art by Nick Castle

ISBN: 978-1-83526-018-0

Tim,
Here's to Helvellyn.

PROLOGUE

2019

"In here. Ssh." The soft groan of a door opening. The gentle roll and creak of motion, a lullaby. Rain against window glass.

"He's twenty months now, and he's just the cutest. Honestly. You won't believe . . . See."

See? Not much. A tuft of tousled hair, somewhere between honey and starlight. Soft milky skin. A muslin blanket. The ear of a love-grubby blue elephant clasped in a closed fist.

"Oh, look, he's sleeping. He was shattered earlier, with all the excitement. Just look at him. Like I told you. The cutest."

"Hannah?! Hannah are you down there?"

"It's Mum. We'd better go back up now, Livs."

Red balloons, glowing like embers in the August evening half-light, bobbing in the stairwell, an unsteady dance. A breeze from the deck. Footsteps on fibreglass, the last few heralding an explosion into festivity, chaos, festoon lights. Rubies and champagne flutes. Music. Wine flowing faster than conversation; a glass pushed into my hand.

A yacht. An actual yacht. Trust the Rainworths. Hannah's parents always did have more money than sense.

Thankfully, it seems to have stopped raining, although the summer sky is pregnant with clouds. Everyone is drunk. I'm holding my glass, looking around at the ruby faces of the Rainworths' ruby wedding anniversary guests, and trying not to think of Dad's gaunt cheeks because it's their night, not mine, and no one wants to see me cry.

The wine makes me feel a little better, and so does Hannah's lively arm linked through mine. There's a swing dance, and we're dancing like idiots, which makes it easier to forget, until I lose her into the exuberance, and find myself faltering.

"Livia. Livia!"

Blinking fractures the festoon lights into coloured strands. I've drunk more than I realised.

It's Kristopher, and he's drunk too. Snapping an off-centre shot on his phone, lurching towards me through the confusion. I've never seen my little brother drunk. Surely he's too young to drink? But no, he turned eighteen in May. I turned twenty-two in April.

"Dance with me, Livia." He's tall and rugby-player bulky, and even less co-ordinated than usual, now he's drunk. Neither of us are dancers, that's for sure, and he almost knocks me into the railings at the yacht's bow. The tune changes and our swing-less dancing flounders gracelessly, searching for the new time signature.

"Livia? Sweetheart." It's Leanna Rainworth, Hannah's brother's wife. She gives me a quick peck on the cheek. Her arms are overflowing with expensively wrapped gifts that she's carrying to her parents-in-law like a sacrificial offering.

"Livia, be a darling. Pop and get Hannah, and ask her just to check on Toby, will you? I thought I heard him crying."

"Sure."

I extract myself. I can't find Hannah. I search the deck, but she isn't there. Bloody Hannah. I stagger back the way I came. I don't have sea legs. Not even harbour legs. The water splashes loudly against the side of the boat. The sound fills my ears like a persistent whisper, somehow more intrusive than the babble of the band and the tuneless crooning of small talk. There's something blue in the water, pale, a sheet of paper or a rag, floating. It looks like cloth; it ripples with the currents, swirls, and then disappears out of sight.

Disappears. Just like Hannah. I still can't find her.

I can remember the way to the room myself, so I give up on Hannah and descend unsteadily below deck on my own. It's actually a relief to be out of the crowd. The quietness soothes my ears as I lurch between the luxurious cabins in the semi-darkness. I can't hear crying. I can't hear anything, much. Someone has spilled water on the carpet. Someone else must have come below to use the bathroom. Or maybe it was Hannah, and she already came to check.

The door to Tom and Leanna's cabin is ajar, and I push it gently, remembering the creak. A night-light plugged into a socket by the bed casts an azure electric glow over the empty pillow.

I stop.

The vibration of feet down the stairs and through the maze of cabins behind me seems to resound like thunder. I reach out to steady myself, my fingers tightening on the edge of the panelled door.

Suddenly, I understand slow motion.

"Livs?"

I can't reply. My eyes are scouring the darkness on rewind/fast-forward.

"Livs, did you come down already? Leanna said she'd asked you to find me, to check on Toby."

My breath seems to have jammed in my throat. It won't move up or down. In fact, I can't seem to make my body respond at all.

"Livs, is Toby—"

The door moans and swings wide. My stomach rolls with the boat as Hannah stumbles into the dark room and stops too.

Rain against window glass, a new burst, a gust of wind that throws the vacant shadows into sharp relief. A split second has never lasted so long. Hannah is frozen too. Even the boat has stopped moving.

At last my legs free themselves, and I fall over the end of the empty bunk to reach the porthole. Look out at the encircled fraction of the Solent beyond. Look out at darkness; absolute, lapping, beckoning darkness.

Something blue.

I remember, and my gaze travels downwards. Down, in time to see the muslin blanket fold in on itself and succumb to the sea.

And then I hear Hannah scream.

CHAPTER 1

2022

I never really understood the term *ghost town*, until I arrived in Porthtrevelen. I've never been superstitious or believed in the preternatural; if anything, my mother has always reproached me for my cynicism. But as I ease my car up the picture-postcard streets, something's wrong. A shadow, a presence, that sends shivers the length of my spine.

Rain runs in torrents over the windscreen. I try not to look at the dark shop windows, the boarded-up ice-cream huts, closed arcades. Hooks that once held buckets, spades and holiday promises dangle limply outside closed shops, waiting. The whole town's waiting, the wind whistling down the alleyways and swinging the occasional residual chalkboard and pub sign in wild abandonment.

I turn a corner into the last road, and the car almost stalls in protest. I'm nauseated, carsick. Is it possible to have made myself sick with my own driving? In the postcard pictures, these houses are a hundred colours of summer: pinks, whites and yellows, the cobbles bright, the sky blue. But the reality has no colour; I'm starting to suspect the postcards are Photoshopped. There's nothing here but pebbledash and desertion, in varying tones of grey. No blue sky. No welcome. No going back.

I wind down the window. Carsick. Really? I haven't been carsick since I was ten.

I slow the car to a crawl to check the numbers of the buildings. I don't even know what my new home looks like from the outside. I picked up my key from the estate agent in the last town nearly an hour ago. The drive down the high-hedged country lanes has taken its toll in time as well as energy; there can't be many hours of barely existent winter sunshine left.

It was still dark when I left Nottingham, squinting a final bleary-eyed goodbye to the filmy windows of my student terrace. The echo of traffic, trams and lecture theatres still hasn't quite faded from my ears. But Porthtrevelen is a lifetime away from the urban academia and alcohol excess that have defined the last six years of my existence.

I scour the vista ahead for something that fits the estate agent's description: twenty-nine to thirty-three Sunnyside. Sunnyside? Right. I let my gaze scan over the uneven rooftops. The flat I signed for is a sparse studio in a rambling converted building that was once a row of fishermen's houses. I didn't even have the chance to look around: just a virtual tour courtesy of Google, and an awkward three-way telephone conversation.

For the first time in an hour, my phone buzzes on the passenger seat. At least the place has signal. A message pops up on the fading backlight.

Good luck, Livs.

I swallow. Kris made fun of the Porthtrevelen plan. *All surfers, artists and fishermen. And eccentrics. You'll fit right in.*

Will I?

Artists and fishermen sound okay to me. At least that would mean habitation — real live people to drive out the ghosts from these eerily quiet streets. Three hundred miles didn't seem so far on the maps.

I draw a deep breath and glance up. My reflection in the rear-view mirror looks ghostly, too. Red lips in a white face, wisps of dark hair escaping across high cheekbones and serious, over-sized Prussian-blue eyes. I brush back the strands of hair, pausing to regard my reversed self for an uncertain moment.

29–33. I glance back out of the window just in time. There's an empty hanging basket jangling beside the door, and three parking spaces. I change down a gear and grind to a halt on the wet cobbles. My belongings settle with a sigh in the car behind me: cases, boxes, canvases, my battered easel. *You'll fit right in*. I hope that Kris is right.

Three hundred miles. There's not a single person in sight. Not a single living thing, with the exception of a glaring seagull perched on the eaves, looking at me down its red-spotted bill with one angry eye as I fight to open the car door against a squall of wind.

I fumble in my pocket for the key-ring. Number thirty-one. It was pretty much the only place available in my fraught three-week house-hunt; it seems that affordable long-term lets in Porthtrevelen are hard to come by. Overpriced weekly-rated holiday homes make up the majority of the town's picturesque streets. At least that made choosing easy.

I can do this. Right?

Right. I try my key in the outer door. It grates as it turns, and the door swings wide, moaning on its hinges. The hallway is narrow, the stairs spiralling upwards at an unlikely angle on one side, an old rustic wooden dresser on the other, arranged with numbered pigeon-holes for mail. Wind is howling around the corner of the building, assaulting the windowpane with driving rain and blasting past me to fleck the red floor tiles with bitter drizzle. The door rattles on its hinges. I falter.

Rain on window glass. A gust of wind—

The wail dies down abruptly, leaving me in silence. And, as it does, something else reaches me. A tingling of salt, the faint tumbling rush of waves, the plaintive lofty cry of a gull. A reminder of what persuaded me to come here, to leave everything and everyone — or everyone that's left. To take the internship with Lorchann McLeod despite my better judgement and every word of well-meant advice.

Three hundred miles.

The door slams. I forget the bags, the car, the rain; pocket the key and start to walk uphill. The road peters out, becomes an alley, the alley becomes a footpath. The houses transition to closed bed and breakfasts, *No Vacancies* on every board, and end in a final crooked ascent to a desolate promenade. I cross it, slip between two weathered wrought iron benches to reach the metal railings at the far side, and catch my breath.

I was wrong about the colour. There are more colours here than I've ever seen. A gradient from black-grey to blue-green, iridescent, lustrous and alive. Too many to describe; not even my father would have had enough words to capture them all. White-topped waves crash into the cliffs, water and foam swarming around the jagged rocks, a merciless and breathtaking onslaught. The air is so fresh that it hurts. I take a few desperate gulps, and let my hands close around the railing.

He would have tried. I can picture it. The start of a novel; a handwritten prologue penned in deep blue ink. *All it takes is an idea, Blackbird. And an eye for what's real, and what's beautiful.* Not once in twenty years did he ever type his drafts. In my mother's bedroom, every idea he ever scrawled is stacked in plastic crates and starting to gather dust.

It's time to forget.

I dash a hand over my eyes.

To my left, the promenade descends back into the tiny fishing town, to the smooth sand of a perfect beach that's gold and blue in summer but white and grey today, a newspaper-print version of the postcards. Boats and ropes and lobster pots are lined up on the sand, salt-stiff fibres, beaten wood, bare masts. I pause to paint them with my mind. *To forget.* That's why I've come. I let the weather wash over me, swamp me, and sweep away the seven hours of car journey, six months of uncertainty, and five years of bad memories.

A ghost town. Porthtrevelen. Inhabited by wraiths, smugglers and spectres of the sea. Oh yes, and me. Livia Rose Frost, the new intern. Would-be artist, not-quite architect, and newest occupant of number thirty-one.

* * *

I slam the car boot and trip up the kerb, banging the outer door open with my elbow so hard that it ricochets off the wall and rebounds into me. My rucksack slides off my shoulder and falls, wrenching my arm. First floor. I'm panting by the time I reach the top. Getting the key into the stiff new Yale lock is harder than it looks.

"Come on." I jiggle it, impatient. "Come *o*—"

It gives so suddenly that I fall. I stumble into my new home, and stare half-wittedly into the silence as I ease my load to the floor. In an instant, the extent of my possessions seems pitifully small.

The space is big, and empty. The wooden floor is worn smooth, and looks original. L-shaped, the depth of the room is in front of me, stretching vacantly towards the draughty single-glazed bay window that takes up most of the far wall. A rickety wrought iron bed is pushed against the faded wallpaper on the left, with a bedside table holding an alarm clock that might be left over from World War Two. Opposite it, a writing desk is abutted to an antiquated dressing table holding the biggest triad of oval mirrors that I've seen in my life. I gaze for a dizzying moment at my face in diminishing perspective, an endless series of ever-dwindling reflections, before I step away.

It's a relief to discover that the kitchen is more modern than the furniture. I open and close a few crisply creaking cupboards. The bathroom's cunningly hidden, barely accessible beside an extraordinarily ugly bookcase. There's no shower curtain on the metal rail, and the bath taps are labelled *cold* and *cold* as an extra test. I leave the door open in an attempt to disperse the lingering smell of decay.

The kitchen ends in an open space, the dual aspect of the room with another draughty window, a small folding-leaf table and a single spindly straight-backed chair. Homely.

There's a reason no one else has taken this flat.

Stop it, Livia. I move to the window, and scowl at myself in the glass. If my father's outlook was always half-full, mine has ever been half-empty. Even before the day he called to tell me he was dying. Even before the Solent. I run my fingers over the white-painted wooden struts that segment the cold window panes. Outside, the gaps in the crooked rooftops reveal a tantalising glimpse of the hazy blue horizon: an unclear distinction between sea and cloud. I'm starting to shiver again. I hope the heating isn't contemporaneous with the decor.

The rain's getting harder as I descend to my car. I fight my way back inside with my arms full of bedding, preoccupied with the idea of getting warm.

"I lend you help with that?"

I jump, violently. The heavy Yale-locked door shuts itself in my face, and the wilting bundle of duvet and pillows slips through my arms. There's a man on the other side of the dusty communal landing. How I didn't notice him, I just can't fathom. He's tall and substantially built, ageless beneath a bushy grey beard and corduroy cap.

"I'm sorry." Shrewd, crinkled blue eyes assess me over the central banister, travelling with an air of calm perception from my dishevelled tumble of hair to the bedding that half covers my leather ankle boots.

"I did not mean to cause fright." His accent is difficult to place, his gaze sharp as he holds out a creased, warm hand over the banister.

"That's okay!" I give up on the duvet, and kick my way free of it to reach his proffered hand.

He smiles. "Niklavs."

I blink. Eastern European? Russian? I've never had much grasp on languages. Or geography.

"Livia." I clear my throat and take his hand. He shakes it.

"Number twenty-nine A." He nods downstairs. "I hear your arrival few minutes ago."

Oh, yeah. The door. I chew my lip.

"Sorry about that," I mumble.

"No, do not apologise." The glimmer of laughter in his blue eyes obliterates my embarrassment. "It is very nice to meet you, Livia."

"You too." At last, I smile back.

"Good." He raises his eyebrows. "Now, can I help you with that?"

"Oh . . ." My cheeks are burning. "No, thanks. I couldn't—"

"Well, at least I can hold door?"

"Okay," I relent. "Thanks."

True to his word, Niklavs takes charge of both doors for me as I ferry the next two loads: suitcases, towels, my box of paints. He vanishes as I retrace my steps to the car, then reappears with a wedge of wood as I regard the final few items. My easel, a roll of canvases and my boarding case: a sturdy remnant of my school days. The battered metal trunk moved me in and out of my dormitories at school reliably for eight years, was dragged up and down the country by my uncomplaining father every start and end of term, before it finally accompanied me to university.

I stare at it. I'd definitely forgotten how big it is, jammed with books, pots and pans, every other kind of leftover possession. I'm starting to wish I'd gone for a ground-floor flat. I lift the easel out of the boot to try and clear my access and think of a strategy for moving the trunk that doesn't involve having brought Kristopher with me.

"Wait. One moment." Behind me, Niklavs kicks the wedge under the door and descends the steps with alarming speed. "Stop!"

"Sorry?" I glance up, trying to balance the easel.

"I think this is not good idea." He takes the easel from me and leans past me to test the handle of the case. It doesn't budge.

"Look at size of this." There's stern appraisal in his raised brows. "You will break back."

"I'll be fine." I bite my lip. "Maybe if you take the eas—"

"I do not think. No." Niklavs glowers at me. "How in name of God did you get it in car to start with?"

"Oh, uh." I shrug. "I don't know, Kr— Wait!"

He's put the easel to one side, and is pulling at the case with both hands. It slithers inexorably to the back of the boot and my car groans.

"Wait!" I grab the handle, inadvertently knocking the easel over with a clatter. Niklavs catches it with one hand.

"I used to be fisherman." His voice is firm. "I have hauled much heavier. But you, you are what? Hundred-pound ballet dancer. You have never lifted case in your life."

"That's not true!" I smile, sheepish.

"Is it not?" Niklavs is smiling too.

"Well," I concede. "My brother helped me get it in the car. But I'm definitely not a dancer."

"Artist then?" He props the easel against the back of the car. "How about I take case, and you take easel?"

"Oh, no. I—"

But with a grunt of effort, he's swung it out of the boot and towards the open door. I grab the easel and follow.

"Really." I'm not sure why I'm still arguing, when he's already through the door and halfway up the stairs. "Let me—"

Niklavs glances back over his shoulder at me, panting. I stare, mortified, as he manhandles the case up the last step. Surely he must already be drawing his pension? I flush.

"Next time," Niklavs tells me between breaths. "You bring brother with you."

I hasten past him to open the flat's door. Between us, we manage to shove the case in, sliding it over the worn boards. Niklavs glances around at the empty walls and rickety furniture.

"Nice place you have here." He turns to me, straight-faced. Then a grin tugs at the weathered corners of his mouth.

"Yeah." I can't help grinning too. "I know."

"Homely."

I snort. And suddenly we're both laughing. I kick the trunk, to try and persuade it even an inch further into the room, and only succeed in denting the toe of my boot, making Niklavs double over with laughter. The easel collapses with a resounding crash that makes the dust fly up from the floorboards and a few floating flakes of ceiling paint settle like snow onto my belongings. As I sink to sit on the edge of the case, I can hear Kris's voice in my head: *all artists and fishermen.* I erupt into a fresh fit of giggles that border on hysteria.

"Why you laugh?" Niklavs wipes his eyes. "You have broken toe, perhaps? It is good thing you are not dancer."

"Oh . . . oh . . ." I hold onto the edge of the case, trying to get a grip on myself. "No . . . Nothing."

"I was not making insult. About flat." Niklavs is still fighting with his smile as he picks up the alarm clock from beside the bed to inspect it. "It is good. Has potential. You know, I once had clock like this." He replaces it on the bedside table and rescues my easel from the floor, lifting it onto his shoulder to move it. "So, Livia. You have travelled long distance today?"

"From Nottingham." I jump up to help him. "About seven hours."

"Nottingham." He nods. "Robin Hood, I think. And D.H. Lawrence. The thief and the novelist, interesting combination. Where you would like this?"

"Oh, uh . . ." I follow him the length of the kitchen. He positions the easel beside the window, without me even needing to reply.

"There's great. Thanks."

"Perfect, for painting sea. Or perhaps, more often, cloud." Niklavs squints to regard the view through the raindrops on the thin glass.

"Yeah." I smile.

For a moment there's silence. The first real silence in days — months — without traffic or sirens or people. I remember myself.

"Do you want a drink?" I offer politely.

Niklavs raises his eyebrows.

"Do you actually have cup? Or kettle?"

"Um . . ." I glance down at the trunk.

* * *

29A is bigger than my flat, with doors to a separate bedroom and bathroom, a kitchen table and a real log fire with fireside chairs. I sit gingerly as Niklavs brews a percolator of coffee so strong that the smell of it gives me palpitations. He pours it into two cups and sits down too.

"Nottingham." He passes me one of the cups, and I eye it with suspicion. "There you were . . . student?"

I nod. "Yeah. I graduated last summer."

"Not student anymore." Niklavs nods too. "So, you have come here for work, or for art?"

I pull a face. "Work, sadly."

"But you make choice for art, I think." His blue gaze is shrewd. "Porthtrevelen has little to offer in winter. No work until it is tourist season, and then only if you are waitress."

"Kind of." I wrap my hands around the cup, slightly unnerved by how close to the mark he's come. "Actually, I've got an internship. With a project architect from Oxford who's working at Trethallyan Hall."

Niklavs raises his eyebrows.

"Estate of Gordon-Heyers. Impressive."

"Yeah." I look up quickly. "Do you know it?"

"Very beautiful place, but isolated. I see it from distance, when walking cliffs once or twice. Well hidden in trees. There was rumour he had plan to sell it, after wife taken ill."

"Oh." I glance down into the murky depths of the coffee. "I don't know. I'm only here for a year. Less, if the work finishes sooner — but I'm hoping it doesn't."

I'm definitely hoping it doesn't. I skimmed over that part when I explained the job to Kris. Lorchann McLeod are based in Oxford. A relocation remains an inescapable possibility.

"You will like Porthtrevelen, Livia." The creases around Niklavs' eyes deepen. "I move here from Latvia for six months forty years ago, and I never leave."

I sip the coffee and don't quite manage to stop myself coughing. Niklavs chuckles.

"You want sugar? Milk? You are like my daughter. Ruining good coffee. Even now — she is doctor, in Newcastle — still she does this. Ruins coffee." He moves to the fridge to pass me the milk.

"You remind me of her when you arrive, and bang open door." He grins. "I think for a moment it is her arriving."

His teasing melts my nerves. I can't help but smile back.

"How old is she?" I try not to slop the milk.

"Oh, she is older now." Niklavs sits down again. "Too old to bang door." He laughs wryly. "She has husband and job. Very busy with work. Too busy to come here. But she also once loved to paint. Like you."

"Oh." I look down, not sure what to say.

Niklavs sips his coffee. "You will be busy, too." The smile around his eyes doesn't fade. "Be careful. Do not lose it."

"Lose what?" I glance up, unnerved by the gentle emphasis in his gruff voice. Niklavs shakes his head.

"The passion."

* * *

I have to remember to forget.

It's dark. Darker than I remembered it could be. It was never dark in Nottingham. But it's dark here.

Niklavs' easy company worked wonders for the forgetting thing. We talked for hours. After the brutal coffee, there was brutal coffee with whisky, and then even more brutal whisky without coffee. Then I realised that in not so many hours I not only have to be sober, but refreshed and ready to put in an appearance at Trethallyan Hall.

I feel my way unsteadily up the crooked staircase. I can't even find the light switch as I tiptoe into my flat and pause, wary of colliding with the boarding trunk. The pixelated darkness rotates around me. I'm drunk.

After a brief search, I manage to switch on the light and locate the boiler. I turn on the heating and make the bed, fighting the urge to crawl under the covers. With nightfall, even the seagulls have lost their voices, and it's oddly uncomfortable. A gust of January wind rattles the windows in their frames, dispelling the silence like a myth. I move to pull down the blind and draw the heavy damask curtains, sobering up rapidly in the chill draught.

The job details are still in my satchel. I search them out and stare one more time at the glossy advert. *Lorchann McLeod Associates RIBA Chartered Architects was established in 1991 by senior partners Charles Lorchann and Peter McLeod . . .*

I scan over the punchlines: design solutions, heritage projects, 'Keeping the art in architecture'. The job description's at the back. *Intern to project architect. Location — varies.* I don't need to read it. I've done that a hundred times already.

I shift my focus from the text to the clear-edged, artfully angled photos. A scaffolded church conversion, a drawing board and scale. A young, slim, red-headed girl presenting a slideshow. Three men in suits, an across-boardroom-table handshake. It's the girl's eyes that capture mine, though. Somehow, the focus on her is different: her serious, tightly closed lips, her penetrating stare. For a moment, I have the disturbing feeling that she can see right through me.

Do I know her from somewhere? I stare, unnerved. There's something terrifying in her expression, something sinister and captivating in the vacuous depths of her eyes that just won't release me. I feel like I must. But no . . . I blink. It's the whisky, or the exhaustion. How could I?

I study her face for a moment more: the dusting of freckles on her nose, the pointed chin, red lipstick, gleaming straight auburn hair. She reminds me of someone, that's all. Of something.

Something I'm not sure I want to remember.

CHAPTER 2

2015

"Sophia . . . ? Sophia!"

Her eyeliner was smudged. She pouted at her reflection in the over-sized, over-pretentious mirror at the foot of the stairs. She didn't have time for this. She was going to be late. But it had to be right. She was going to see him this evening. She knew she was. He knew, too. She felt sure of it.

"Sophia!"

"What?" She glared at the mirror, as if it could reflect her anger back through the wall into the kitchen, and judiciously applied a bitten fingernail to the stray black line. She dropped the kohl into her pocket.

"Didn't you hear what I said?"

"I've gotta go, Mum." She snatched up the strap of her schoolbag from the bottom stair.

"Don't be late. The table's booked at sev—"

"I told you." She pulled open the door, sullen sunlight staining through the red and blue glass. "I'm not coming."

"*Sophia*!"

"I've got to go, Mum." She stepped out into the brisk March air.

"Sophia—"

The door slammed.

The old arrangements had suited her just fine. The days when Mum didn't leave the poky downstairs bedroom before twelve, and usually retreated back to it before six; the days before Leon and this stupid attempt at a second-time-round, before Mum started baking and talking about Jesus.

"Christ." She slumped against the inside of the bus stop, out of the wind. Fiddled with her brand-new smartphone. It was starting to rain. Her freedom had evaporated overnight. The mother she hadn't had for three years was back with a vengeance, and it was suffocating. She exhaled a steamy cloud of breath into the bus stop. Nothing was sacred. Her room. Her clothes. Her time.

An X2 cornered awkwardly into sight. Sophia pushed herself to her feet and found her bus pass. She was late. It was full. No one from school was left to catch it; even the last-minuters would have caught the one before. She pushed her way to the back, and wedged her way in beside three suitcases and a big woman wearing perfume that hit the back of her nose, when she inhaled, like glue. She pulled out her earphones and pretended to be listening to music so that no one would talk to her, and if they did, she wouldn't have to answer. *Anna Karenina* was getting tattered from repeated bus-ride abuse; she unfolded the book in her lap, inhaling the old broken smell of the pages, folded her legs under her, and sank into its welcoming depths.

She counted the stop-bells, not the minutes, from her earbud-muted reverie. By the time she looked up, her neck was aching. Sophia slid the book into her bag and rose in one movement, managing to make it to the front with un-stumbling grace as the bus lurched and slowed. She felt a little sick as she murmured her thanks and the door hissed closed behind her, and had to spend a moment recovering on the pavement before she walked through the gates.

"Stanley!"

She didn't pull out the earphones.

"You're late, Stanley. You missed chapel."

"That's not my name."

"Isn't it?" Michaela Allen was on form. "It's what they kept calling at register when they couldn't find you. Maybe you want to check that. Seen your dad yet, Stanley? He was in the paper yesterday."

Sophia pretended to turn up the volume of the non-existent music, and drowned her out. She didn't actually dislike school. Just the people that came with it. She sidled into maths in silence, and sat in the last seat, right at the front. In all honesty, she would rather have been reading *Anna*, because she'd finished the algebra coursework two weeks ago and being there while everyone else caught up seemed pointless. But it could have been worse. At least she had time to plan. There was a change of clothes in her bag, although he'd seen her in school uniform last time at the office, when she'd noticed him noticing, so really the pretence was pointless.

She skipped lunch and read her book in the courtyard behind the chapel, confident in the knowledge that no one else would brave the rain. Maybe, if Mum married Leon, she wouldn't have to put up with this Stanley crap anymore. Maybe they would both take Leon's name and she'd shake it off forever. Maybe they'd move.

Sophia wasn't sure that she wanted to think about moving. This was her home. And, after all, it was the Stanley money that was paying to keep her at a decent school. Not Leon's money.

It had stopped raining by last period. She dragged her feet as everyone else hurried for home, and walked the other way unnoticed; changed in the toilets in M&S, and balled up her blazer in her bag. Her pulse quickened as she brushed out her hair in front of the mirror. The corset top Mum hadn't wanted her to buy looked good with jeans, heels and an unzipped hoody; she felt the blend of admiring and disapproving glances as she slipped out into the street. The shops were closing, and she walked for a while before she made the right turn back towards Christ Church, her eyes scanning upwards as she passed the building where her mother wasn't working today.

Six twenty-five. He was there, on the bench, finishing a cigarette, like he always did when he left work. She made a pretence of standing in the bus stop, checking the time on her phone, starting to shiver. He turned his head, and she lowered her gaze to the screen, then glanced up and pretended to notice him looking.

"Hi," he said.

Her heart beat a drumroll. She was right. She knew she was right. She flicked her hair out of her eyes.

"Hi," she breathed.

There was a pause. He got up from the bench, and crossed the road, stubbing his cigarette out with his foot.

"You look frozen," he said.

"I'm okay." She wrapped her arms around herself. "I missed my bus." She gave him a little smile, the kind that offered to find out whether he was playing. He was.

"I've seen you before, at the office. Haven't I?"

"My mum works there."

"I know her?" He didn't miss a beat.

"Maybe." She shrugged, in an attempt at nonchalance.

He was perfect. In a dazzling film-star sort of way. He'd started in January, at the desk opposite her mum. She'd noticed him straight away, on the first day of term when she'd had to finish her *Othello* essay at Mum's desk because Mum had met Leon for lunch and owed time back.

"What's your name?" He leaned against the end of the bus shelter.

"Sophia."

Another pause. They both knew he already knew. He was looking at her in a way that made every muscle in her belly clench. The air crackled with static. This time, she didn't have to pretend to shiver.

"You really do look frozen." He raised an eyebrow. "It's an hour 'til the next bus. You want to go get a drink somewhere?"

She smiled. *Yes.* Just like that.

"Sure." She slid the phone into her pocket.

"Are you old enough to drink?"

"Probably." She lowered her eyes for one second, two seconds. Looked back up from under her lashes.

He smirked. "Come on, then."

* * *

She knew a place she'd be able to get served, but he knew somewhere better. He ordered drinks, and they sat in a booth where they could pay lip service to being able to see the X2 stop through the window. The strawberry cider was sticky on her lips, and over-sweet, like cough syrup. She drank it slowly and looked at his suit, wondering how old he was and whether it would matter.

There had been a copy of *Notes from Underground* on his desk that day, as she assessed him from her mum's desk. She'd noticed that straight away, too. Dostoevsky. With a breathless thrill of excitement, and after a few measured minutes of considering whether she'd look like a complete fool, she had quietly unpacked *Anna* from her bag, and laid her down, like a gauntlet. After that, any attempts to concentrate on her schoolwork had been doomed; her eyes had been elsewhere. She'd never written such a bad essay in her life.

Sophia watched as an X2 drew to a halt outside and the passengers got off: an old man, a skinny woman with a screaming child. The LED letters flickered as the bus swung back out into the road, passing the pub with a judder and rattling the windows like a ghost.

His eyes still hadn't left her. She could feel his scrutiny over the table; she in turn had spent enough time looking that the cider had made the pounding in her chest into a giddy, anticipant bubble. It was dark outside. Mum and Leon would be eating by now at their table for three.

"Do you always catch the bus?" His voice asked a different question than his eyes. She hesitated.

"Whenever Mum's not working."

"You don't drive?" He gave a little smile, and she glanced at the cider, conscious of the potential contradiction.

"No." She squeezed her feet around her bulky schoolbag, remembering the blazer, and that he must already know.

"Smoke?" He held out a packet to her, and jerked his head towards the garden. She didn't, but she nodded, took one, and got up to follow him anyway. The garden was empty. The bars of the radiant heater above them illuminated the attractive contours of his face. He reached into a pocket for a lighter, struck, and lit hers for her first as she held it in her lips and tried desperately not to cough. He took a drag of his own cigarette.

"Nice hair." He toyed with the purple dip-dyed ends. A thrill ran down her neck.

"Thanks." She shifted her weight so that she was an inch nearer him and lowered her cigarette to hold it at her hip. He curled her hair around his fingers and blew out a cloud of smoke over her shoulder. Close up he smelt like aftershave. Close up, suddenly, she wasn't quite as brave as she'd thought she was. Sophia dropped the cigarette and tried to scrub it out with her foot. What if he kissed her? She'd never kissed anyone — except Harry Davis at the year eight disco, and that hadn't even been a real kiss, just an awkward pre-pubescent attempt that, at the age of thirteen, had indelibly stamped her one-way ticket into social suicide.

The smoke had made her feel sick. She took an indolent step back and looked up through her lashes.

"Nice suit," she breathed.

He chuckled. "You like it? I hate it." He jerked at his tie until the knot loosened, then slipped it off and undid his top button, releasing a faint, enticing scent of bodywash and sweat that made her knees go weak.

"You know, there're a lot closer X2 stops you could've chosen." He was looking at her bag. She looked down too. The crested end of her school tie had escaped from the zip. Shit. She flicked back her hair from her face.

"I know."

He laughed under his breath.

"You know what? Forget the bus." He rolled the fabric of her hood between his finger and thumb, examining the laced front of the corset top with his eyes. "I can give you a lift. Do you want another drink?"

She nodded. They went inside, and she kicked the bag under her seat, out of sight. He drew a card out of his wallet and went to the bar. Surreptitiously, she slid the wallet across the table, the leather warm under her fingertips, and flapped it open.

His greyscale picture looked up at her from his driving licence. 12/12/1988. She counted backwards in her head and closed it again quickly. He was so good-looking. Painfully good-looking. And he liked reading, serious reading. Already, even through their minimal conversation, she could sense a kindred spirit.

"Here." He pushed a bottle at her across the table. She pulled her knees up to sit cross-legged on the chair, without thinking, and took a sip. He folded his arms, somehow amused.

"You could have spoken to me at the office."

"Not on a day Mum was there." The cider was making her bolder.

"No." He nodded. "Won't she be wondering where you are?"

"She's not at home. She has a boyfriend. They've gone out."

"Right." He gave a lopsided smile that made her mouth dry out. She took another sip of cider quickly. A boyfriend. A boyfriend? She looked at the open neck of his shirt, and the sultry smile on his lips. That word would never work for him. He wasn't a boy; he was a heart-stopping rock star of a man, and she wanted him to want her.

His car was parked a couple of streets away, not far from the office. His hand hovered behind her waist, keeping her spine rigid with anticipation the whole way, until he unlocked the car and she climbed into the passenger seat amidst a cascade of litter. She threw her schoolbag into the back and told him the second half of her postcode so that he could program it into the satnav. The car, although untidy, was new; it still smelt like factory plastic, and it had leather seats. Neither her mum nor dad — nor Leon — had ever had a car with leather seats. She smoothed a hand over them. He instructed her to pick some music, which she did, fiddling with the controls until he reached out to help her, and their fingers touched.

The effect was unbearable; the heat pooling deep in her abdomen, the rush of blood as he moved to change gear and they sped out along the country lanes. He steered with one hand, and rested the other on the gearstick, breathtakingly close to her.

It only took twenty minutes; he didn't seem to pay much regard to speed limits except where there were cameras. Her street was full of parked cars. Mum and Leon couldn't be back, because the drive was empty and the house was in darkness. Sophia let out a slow breath.

"This one." She half-gestured as they passed it. He stopped the car a couple of doors down, and turned off the engine.

"Thanks for the lift." She tossed her hair over her shoulder, popped the door latch, and hesitated, not sure if she should get out.

"Any time." He undid his seatbelt, and she thought he was going to reach the bag from the back seat for her, but he didn't. He leaned across her and pulled the door closed. His left hand slid over the leg of her jeans and she stiffened in shock. His gaze moved downwards.

She froze. This was it. The moment that she'd imagined in so many different ways — just not this one — and it was happening, right here, in his car.

The assault of his lips was decisive, lusty; she jolted instantly upright as his fingers closed around her thigh, his teeth grazing her lower lip, forcing her mouth open. She gasped, tasting his tongue, and he moved his hand suddenly upwards, along the seam of her jeans, making her eyes fly open as if lightning had struck her.

He laughed, softly. Released her, and picked up her bag from the back seat, wrapping the school tie around his fingers. Her pulse was rushing in double time in her ears. The taunt in his eyes was hot and calculated.

"Now you should probably tell me how old you are," he said.

She pulled the tie from his hand, and shoved it quickly away in her pocket, heart hammering.

"Sixteen," she lied.

CHAPTER 3

2022

It's not so much an ache as an incessant grating, a jarring that sets my teeth on edge. I stare, disorientated, at the cracked plaster for long, hungover moments.

Cornwall. Not a dream. The seagulls are just starting to bicker. The room is bitterly cold. I roll over and squint to make out the time on the antiquated alarm clock. Seven forty-five. My eyes hurt. After several uncomfortable hours I'm pretty sure my bed needs the judicious application of an Allen key.

Seven forty-five?

I blunder out from under the covers and snatch my hooded running top from the bedpost to sling around my shoulders as my teeth chatter into motion. Porthtrevelen. Lorchann McLeod. *Trethallyan.* At eight thirty. Shit.

I need coffee. I baulk at the bare boards and flinch my way across the cold floor into the kitchen, before remembering that I don't have a kettle. I come to an abrupt halt. Shit.

It's a relief to establish that one of the taps in the bathroom is definitely hot, as I switch to plan B and cajole the shower into life. I strip, and stand gratefully underneath the scalding water, steam curling around my electric-lit surroundings. My mouth is prickling with apprehension. Maybe I can do without coffee after all. My pulse probably doesn't need an accelerant.

By the time I get out, I've reached a point of numb calm. I dry and braid my hair and fumble for the map in my leather satchel; my car's too old to have a satnav and the phone signal is patchy. When Niklavs said isolated, he wasn't joking. I squint to make out my own pencil marks: a right turn, a private road. If I find it on time, it's going to be a miracle.

In physical size, Porthtrevelen is barely more than a village, although it takes longer to navigate the twisting town-centre streets in my protesting car than it does to cover the next two miles on the coast road. The temptation to slow and digest the scenery is torturous. I open the windows to let in the squalling sea air. All I want to do is stop and soak up the view; after six years of cityscapes, brick walls and painting from photographs, my imagination is weak with starvation. In my mind I'm painting a colour chart, a series of strokes: *Idanthrene, Cerulean Blue, Phthalo Turquoise, Davy's Grey.*

Somewhere behind me a church bell strikes eight fifteen, the chimes blasting with the breeze through the open window. I drag my attention back to the road. Half a mile more, and it starts to curve inland. Trethallyan. A right turn—

I've missed it. I decelerate, looking for somewhere to turn around. I'm going to be late. Without question.

Second time lucky, I catch sight of the white fencepost. The track is uneven and treacherously muddy; I feel the car wheels spin and clutch the steering wheel with both hands. Up, down again — the track undulates wildly — plunging into trees, a thicket of conifers that makes a dark stain against the shimmering backdrop of not-so-distant sea. Then suddenly it evens out; there are islands of tarmac infiltrating the mud under my tyres. And there, in front of me, is a set of gates.

My pulse beats a drumroll. I gaze up at the towering once-white-now-flaking ironwork, too afraid to reach out of the window and press the buzzer.

Eight thirty. There isn't time for a loss of nerve. I push the button.

"Hi, who is it?" A disembodied voice, a woman's voice, crackly and distorted.

"Livia Frost." The wind snatches the words out of my mouth. I'm not even sure that they've carried as far as the receiver. I hesitate. With a grinding creak of objection, the gates scrape into life, opening inwards. My palms are sweating as I shove the car into gear and almost stall on a cattle-grid. The gates groan closed behind me.

It's a house from a Bronte novel, a high-budget period drama, or a murder mystery: three storeys of crenulated grey granite, a patchwork of eras making up the remaining wing of this impressive memorial to wealth and status. When I was fourteen or fifteen, my father briefly indulged a phase of writing historical fiction, and for two years I dutifully accompanied him to every stately home in the north of England. But in all that time, not one of them equalled this: so bleak, so dark, so breathtaking in its austerity.

The gravel drive is flattened and riddled with weeds. I open the car door with a clunk and climb out. Wind and salty drizzle rip my scarf from around my neck; for a moment I stand, rooted to the spot, staring up at the stonework. What now? Do I knock? My car's the only one in the drive. There's nobody else here.

A spasm of shivers overcomes me. Of course there's somebody here. Someone opened the gate.

I flounder beside the car. The entrance in front of me really doesn't look like the right place to knock; the imposing pillared porch doesn't seem like the kind of entrance that people use anymore. I tiptoe a few careful steps to where the gravel disappears around the corner of the house. Set back is a low wall, a new addition, and a patch of grass so clipped and green that it looks artificial, laced with rain that's collecting in the plastic bucket of a yellow toy digger. In front of me, the body of the hall steps back, a solitary light glowing from one of its single-glazed windows. To my right, the drive sweeps round to once-stables, now garages, their doors the same weathered white as the gates.

I suddenly feel like an intruder. I stumble back towards my car, clenching my chattering teeth together.

"Hi!"

I jolt in shock. My satchel slips from my arm and plunges into the wet gravel.

"Are you alright there? Can I help you?" His voice carries clearly over the elements. He comes into sight, descending the steps between the stone pillars from the front door, and surprise displaces my nerves. He's familiar — a disordered interview-day memory, perhaps — I recognise him straight away: the same muscular six-foot-plus physique as my brother, rugby-club good-looking, with short light-brown hair, and a wide, dazzling smile. He's wearing a gilet over his checked shirt, drizzle clinging to his sleeves and to the shaped stubble of his beard. Instantly, I'm blushing.

"Um." I try to remember the lines I've been rehearsing in my head for exactly this moment. But they're gone. "I'm Livia."

"*Livia* . . . Livia Frost?" His hand is held out before he's even down the last step. "I'm Ryan. You're Sean's new intern?"

I nod, mute, as he reaches me and grasps my hand in an unsurprisingly firm handshake. I'm pretty sure the blush is radiating from every inch of my skin. Not Sean. That much should have been obvious to me. I'm not sure whether I'm relieved or disappointed.

"It's great to meet you, Livia." Ryan's voice is warm. "Well done with the interview. You made quite an impression."

"Oh." I rediscover my voice. "Thanks."

"Seriously." Ryan's attention falls on my rattling teeth. "Let's get inside, come on. We shouldn't be talking out here."

I don't argue. I expect him to show me up the steps, but instead he leads me across the gravel away from the house.

"This way. Sorry." He shoots a quick glance back at my scuffed leather boots as they sink into the grass. "I should show you the cabin; it's just here. It's where everything is."

Our feet scrunch in unison as we reach another gravel path between the dripping rhododendrons. I half run the last few steps, as Ryan produces a key on a blue-and-white lanyard from his back pocket. The building in front of us is a decade or two old, bigger than the house I grew up in, and clad in birch that's starting to weather, with a pitched tiled roof and a quadruple set of French windows looking out over a sloping expanse of lawn. Ryan strides around the corner to unlock another door, and gestures me inside.

"After you." He stands back.

I find myself in a sizeable open-plan room, set over two levels and flooded with grey daylight. Three ultra-modern fibreglass desks have been parked, slightly at odds, on the lower expanse of wooden floor. Towards the back, a flight of five steps leads up to a mezzanine at my shoulder height, railed off in pine and stainless steel. Natural light spills from the skylights above it, over two drawing boards and an impressive array of set squares and scales. Beneath the mezzanine, a kettle and a mug tree are perched precariously on a narrow pine work-surface, with an afterthought water dispenser.

The door closes behind us with a muted sigh.

"What do you think?" Ryan springs past me up the steps as I spin to take in the details of my surroundings. "It used to be the summer house, but Graham and I've turned it into a studio as a base for you and Sean and Katie while the work's being done. There's another room back here—" He crosses the mezzanine to depress a brushed steel door-handle at the back, revealing a glimpse of a smaller room beyond. "And a toilet through there." I don't even see which way he points. He descends the steps in a bound.

"You must have loads to ask. I'm sorry." He gestures for me to sit down, and perches on the desk opposite me. I open my mouth and then close it again. I'm already at a loss.

"Oh . . ." He pauses. "I should have told you to start with, Sean's not going to be here today. He's had to go to Oxford. I only found out when I called him first thing. I'm sure he'll get you . . . up to speed . . ." I don't miss the slightest lift of his eyebrows ". . . tomorrow."

Not here? I catch myself biting my lip and make myself release it. Up to speed?

"It all . . . all looks amazing." I have no idea what to say.

"I guess there won't be much for you to do before then. Although . . ." He slides to his feet, and reaches one muscular arm around me to open the desk drawer. "We *could* set up your laptop and make sure everything's working. Here—" He pulls out a slimline case with a blue-and-white logo on it. "Sean asked me to sort it. I'm no IT whizz, but I've got the permissions and it should work. I made your login your surname and the first letter of your first name. Password's the same the first time you sign in — it'll hopefully prompt you to change it. Can I get you a drink, Livia? Should I call you Livia, or are you a Liv?"

Coffee. I really want coffee. My head's still aching without the caffeine and Ryan's rapid pace isn't helping. I glance at the mug tree and the suspect looking jar of own-brand instant.

"I'm okay, thanks," I murmur, shy. "People usually call me Livs."

"You look like you could use a coffee, Livs." Ryan flashes me a conspiratorial grin. "I'll call Claire and see if she can bring some proper stuff." He glances at the jar too. "The stuff down here's shit."

"Oh. Thanks." I bite my lip. My cheeks are still hot. I try not to watch him as he walks away, and open the laptop instead. *Frostl.* I tap the six letters into the keyboard and the screen brightens, a monogrammed company emblem burning itself into the digital wallpaper: *LMLA.*

Lorchann McLeod. The drizzle, granite and rhododendrons are a far cry from the state-of-the-art steel, glass and repointed sandstone offices in Oxford where I had my interview. Not that I can remember much of the interview; it's all a blur, a blip in the pre-Christmas rush of shopping, train journeys, clinic appointments. I was discharged the day before the interview. I remember that.

This job doesn't make sense. That was everyone's reaction when I told them: Kris, my housemate Jen, my mother. At the other end of the country, hours away from anyone, completely cut off from any kind of support, after everything that had happened. I'd never even heard of Lorchann McLeod until I googled them that night when I got home, after the meeting with my old tutor. But he had put the advert in my hand, me specifically. The project was for the family of an old alumni, and the pay was unusually good. I'd be working one-to-one with a talented architect from a successful Oxford firm — Sean Lorchann, the senior partner's son — the guy had already won awards. It was too much of an opportunity to pass up.

It wasn't really the opportunity, though. Or the project. Or the pay. It wasn't until I opened the pictures of Porthtrevelen and the surrounding North Cornish coast that I made my decision, and I made it instantly. Won over by romantic images of cliffs and dramatic seaside sunsets, I stopped considering anything else.

I sigh and turn my attention back to the empty room. I have no idea what I'm supposed to be doing. I fight the urge to root in my satchel for the job description. I can hear Ryan on the phone in the back room, but I can't help the uncomfortable feeling that he also has no idea what I'm supposed to be doing. In fact, it occurs to me that as he clearly isn't an architect, I don't have a clue why he's actually here at all.

"Here." He rematerialises as if on cue. "Sean left this. Claire's just on her way down."

I take the proffered A4 envelope, searching my brain for the explanation that I must have missed. Claire?

"My wife." Ryan smiles, and pushes his phone back into his pocket. "Graham Gordon-Heyers is her father."

Wife. What did I expect? For some reason my cheeks and the tops of my ears are burning.

"We moved back from Dubai last year when her mother had her stroke, to help Graham out while the renovations are going on. He spends a lot of time at the hospital these days."

"Oh," I mumble. "Sorry to hear that."

"Oh, not at all." Ryan shrugs. "It's good to be back on British soil. Good that we can be here for Graham. And there's a hell of a lot of potential here." He gestures outside. "Sean's really got his work cut out."

"Yeah." I nod, lost.

"He's been splitting his time between here and Oxford for over a year." Ryan strides to the French windows to look out across the lawn. "He'd already redesigned the Gatehouse with Peter — Claire and I are living there now. But Graham has ambitions for a lot of the estate — I mean, months and months' worth of work — the stables, the head gardener's cottage and outbuildings. It's all just been sitting and rotting. Even once the plans and permissions are done, it makes sense to have someone based on site to manage and co-ordinate the builds."

"Are you helping?" I weigh the envelope in my hands.

Ryan laughs. "Not exactly. Sean would probably just call it meddling." He fiddles with the tail end of the lanyard dangling from his pocket, and for the first time, I notice the lettering in the fabric. "But since Covid I do most of my work from home, and I do know a little bit — I worked for Lorchann McLeod for a while once — so I muck in where I can. Besides, these days Graham needs someone who can handle the financial and logistical side of things. I'm glad I've been able to take it on for him . . ."

I look at the lanyard, confused. He doesn't work for Lorchann McLeod? But I definitely met him at the interview . . .

"He's very much for keeping things in the family. Always has been."

I frown. In the family?

"Hi!"

The door behind us has opened. I spin.

"You must be Livia!" The newcomer is smiling, her cheeks dimpled. She isn't much older than me, with silky brown hair spilling onto the shoulders of a demure dress that accentuates her generous hourglass curves perfectly. I try not to notice my own, disappointingly slight, figure reflected next to hers in the French doors as I stumble gracelessly to my feet.

"You're Sean's new intern? I'm Claire Lorchann." She sets down the shopping bag she's carrying and holds out her hand.

Lorchann. Claire Lorchann. His wife. The last jumbled piece drops into place. I glance nervously from her to Ryan and back again. *He's* a Lorchann. *In the family.* I take Claire's hand tentatively.

"It's great to meet you!" She abandons the handshake and leans forward to peck a kiss in the air beside my cheek. "I'm so glad you found us. I'm sorry Sean's not here. Has Ryan shown you where everything is?" In an instant, she's retrieved the shopping bag and is unpacking coffee and milk onto the worktop.

"We'll have to introduce you to Dad this afternoon, once he's back from the hospital. Katie should be here later, too — you'll like her — she's a surveyor and she lives in Porthtrevelen. I went to school with her."

I nod, mute. It's happened. I've reached the point of information overload. I watch Ryan move to join his wife.

"Sugar, Livs?" he asks.

I shake my head. "No. Thanks." Maybe the caffeine will help. I take the improbably large mug from Ryan.

"I think Sean's put copies of a lot of the most important current stuff in there." Ryan lolls against my desk and prods the envelope. "Essentially, now the Gatehouse is done, and the two cottages that have already sold, I think the plan's really to focus on the site of the old chapel on the clifftop."

"Trethallyan Edge is really pretty." Claire joins us, hands wrapped around a very floral-smelling cup of tea. "We played there as kids all the time. We always used to say the chapel was haunted."

"Don't listen to any of that crap, Livs." Ryan laughs. "It's not haunted. It's just a crumbling old wreck. I'm not quite sure why Graham's set his heart on it, but Sean's really excited about it — for Sean." Again, the upward flicker of the eyebrows that I can't quite fathom. "He's bet me that if he does a good enough job of the build, Graham might just change his mind and finally consider moving out of the Hall. He *has* always loved that view."

The sudden, subtle shift in the air is undeniable. Claire puts down her cup.

"I think that's enough about that."

There's an awkward pause.

"I'm going to call Katie. Back in a sec." Claire pulls out her mobile and slices a finger across the screen as she walks away. Ryan and I watch her go.

"Now I'm for it." He flashes me a sheepish smile. I chew my lip. Should I ask? Probably not.

"Graham's pushing eighty," he explains anyway. "He was fifty when Claire was born. Neither of them want to admit it, but he's not going to cope in the old Hall forever. He'd be better off converting it into apartments and going to live in one of the new-builds. We all know it, but no one's brave enough to say it. Anyway, I shouldn't talk about it. I'm sure Sean'll take you up to the chapel tomorrow."

"Does Sean have to go to Oxford a lot?" I scrape the toe of my boot on the floor, trying not to sound like I care too much.

"Sometimes. More since he hasn't had help down here."

Oh. Suddenly I can't curb my curiosity. "There was an intern here before?"

"Not for a few months." Ryan pushes himself to his feet. "Here." I can't help the unsettling feeling that he's changing the subject. "I forgot. Your key. For the cabin. It's stiff — if it won't turn, pull the door towards you. The code to the main gate's one two one two."

"Fab!" Claire' s back. "Katie can meet us at two, Livia. I just need to make sure I get away in time to go and pick up Finbar at three twenty. How does lunch sound?"

I look up, at her perfect clothes and dimpled cheeks. At the frank, cold rain that's now running in torrents over the

French windows. It's going to be fine. I fight to suppress a new burst of shivers. In a week from now, I'll have forgotten the fear. It'll be an irretrievable memory, a lip service to nervousness. Nothing more.

"Lunch sounds . . ." I clear my throat. "Lunch sounds great."

* * *

It's a relief to climb out of the mute air of Claire's showroom-tidy car; it's low tide, and the harsh wind hurts my throat. After a morning spent achieving nothing whatsoever, she insisted on driving us into town. I wish she hadn't. Five minutes of her driving, in combination with the narrow Cornish roads, has made me queasy.

I follow her from the damp grey car park onto the old flagstones of the harbour front.

"This is where I first met Ryan and Sean." She gestures around at the mismatched collection of craft galleries and trendy seafood restaurants through the drizzle. "When we were kids. It's changed a lot since then. This was a fish market." She waves a vague hand. Her comment has taken me by surprise.

"When you were kids?" I echo, aloud.

"They used to come here every summer. They'd camp, not far from ours. Charles and my father met out walking."

Charles? Charles Lorchann. I frown as I skirt the sea wall, unable to stop myself from glancing down at the still-life of ropes and lobster pots on the wet sand. Soon. Soon I'll be driving home through the enticing salt spray, unpacking my paints in the empty window—

"One day we stopped here to give Charles and the boys a lift back up to their camp. We've been friends ever since. I played with Sean and Ryan every summer — I used to look forward to July coming even more than Christmas. That's why my parents went to Charles when they decided to renovate the Hall, and sell off some of the estate. Here." She changes direction suddenly and I almost trip. "Oh no!"

With a forewarning blast of icy wind, the heavens have opened. Huge droplets of rain strike my face as Claire darts for cover. I stumble after her. We end up running the last two hundred yards along the narrow, cobbled shopping street, and burst through the doors of the café in dripping unison.

The place is eerily empty, devoid of life bar one angular man steaming milk at a hundred decibels, his outlandish collection of ear-piercings glinting in the artificial light. The walls are wood-panelled and whitewashed, and the counter is half-full of scones and cakes, spot-lit like sculptures behind the glass.

"There she is!" Claire squeezes between two tables, and I blink. The place is not completely devoid of life, after all. There's a woman in the corner, enshrouded in swathes of cashmere scarf. She folds away a laptop as we approach.

"Katie!" Claire repeats the ritual of hugs and air-kisses. I wait a step behind her, uncomfortable, as Katie extracts herself from the hug and turns to me. I can't tell how old she is. Her skin and sleek hair are young, but the tiny perpetual frown between her hazel eyes isn't; it's older than me, and Claire. It's a frown that suggests seriousness and not necessarily approval; that, perhaps, has seen this show before and remembers how it goes.

"This is Livia!" Claire steps back to gesture me forwards. For an agonising moment, neither of us commits to a hug or a handshake. Under the thrust of Claire's hand, we collide mid-decision, stumbling out a mortified greeting.

Silence. I feel myself turn crimson. Then Katie's eyes crease with laughter. A helpless smile pulls at my lips.

"Nice to meet you," I breathe.

"You too." She grins. "I'm Katie."

"Yeah." I grin back. "I figured."

"You're our new architect?" Her gaze has fixed on me.

"Almost." I shrug, shy again. "Postgrad. I haven't passed my last exam yet."

"So, you're working with Sean?"

Claire sits in one of the mismatched chairs. "Sean's not in today," she interjects.

"Oh." Katie nods. "Sure." I can't help noticing the way her gaze darts to my face. I sit down too, and stare studiously at the menu. First Ryan, then her. Could I feel worse about this?

"I'm going to get drinks," Claire declares. "What can I get you, Livs? Coffee? Latte?"

I nod. "A latte would be great, thanks."

"Katie?"

"Tea, thank you." Katie unwinds her scarf. I can feel her scrutiny across the table. I lay down the menu without having read it.

"So you just graduated?" Katie picks up the menu and toys with the pages. "Where were you studying?"

"Nottingham." I look back up at her. Something in her air of calm interest is reassuring.

"Nottingham." She nods slowly. "I'm pretty sure that's where Ryan graduated from. I guess you must have met Ryan by now?"

"Yeah." I smile, fleetingly. Katie smiles too. The milk steamer erupts into life with a vociferous sputter, and I give up on any further efforts at a reply. I glance down. The envelope Ryan gave me is poking out from the top of my bag, soggy and rain-spattered. I ease it out to look at it. The damp glue has come unstuck, giving a tantalising and now slightly dog-eared glimpse of the sketches, maps and pages of documentation underneath. I stare at it, scraping together my courage.

"Have *you* worked with Sean at all?" I blurt out.

There's a pause. I look up. Katie's eyes don't quite meet mine across the minefield of empty table-top.

"Occasionally." She shrugs. A little too casually. I feel myself frown.

"Is he . . . What's he . . . like?" I make every effort to keep my face impassive.

"Oh . . . um." She shrugs again, gaze fixed carefully on the menu. "Sean's . . . Sean." She hesitates. "He's very talented. And he's done a lot for Claire and Ryan . . ."

But? I look down too, at the envelope. Unmarked. Not giving anything away.

"He can just be . . . well . . ." She shakes her head. "You'll understand when you meet him."

"Oh." I press the flap of the envelope closed, suddenly reluctant to examine its contents. A knot has tightened in my abdomen. There's silence as we both search for a way back.

"You're here for a year, aren't you?" Katie asks. "Claire said."

I glance up. "Yeah. If I last that long."

It must only be a shadow. But for a split second, the strangest expression crosses Katie's face, and it makes my blood run cold. It's gone almost instantly, a placid mask falling back into place above her suddenly uncertain smile.

"One latte—"

I jump violently.

"And one tea!" Claire presents the tray with a flourish and unloads the drinks. She sits beside me. "How was the dress fitting, Katie? Have you brought pictures?"

I feel myself fade out as the conversation turns to the escalating costs of wedding photographers and table favours. For some reason, I'm shivering. For a first day, I already seem to have accumulated an awful lot of unanswered questions. I finger the envelope. Looking at it prompts an uneasy sensation in the pit of my stomach.

I order food at their example, and let their voices wash around me as I pick at a salad I don't really want. *You have to eat, Livvy.* I can picture my father, the sternness in his emaciated face. He never stopped coaching me, even when he was dying. *You won't be fit for the Fairfield Horseshoe if you don't eat. Come on, Blackbird. You know how hard I had to work to make your mother agree to let me come and watch you.*

I force a few more mouthfuls in.

You can beat our one hour fifty-five this year, I know you can . . .

"Oh, gosh!" Claire turns to me suddenly, snapping me out of my daydream. "Livia, what's the time?!"

I glance up, alarmed. Claire looks over each of her shoulders for a clock. There isn't one. I pull my phone out of my bag.

"Three." I stab the button and watch the backlight fade.

"Oh my goodness." Instantly, Claire's flushed. "I need to go. Fin'll be finished in twenty minutes, and there's going to be *nowhere* left to park! I'm so sorry, have you finished? You'll have to come with me. Unless—"

"I can give Livia a lift back to Trethallyan," Katie interrupts her calmly. "You go and get Fin."

"Are you sure?" Claire's expression relaxes into relief.

"I'm sure." Katie doesn't flinch. "Go."

Claire doesn't argue. The bell on the door jangles as she leaves, and I watch Katie finish her drink.

"You'll find she can be . . ." Katie replaces her cup in its saucer and turns to me, eyebrows faintly arched. "High maintenance, at times."

"Oh." I can't help but smile.

"Are you ready to go back?" Katie picks up her scarf. "I told Ryan I'd drop off some reports for Sean, so I need to drive to Trethallyan anyway."

She holds the door open for me as we make our way out into the empty cobbled street and along the harbour front. My attention drifts to the rusty colours and contours of the coiled chains and fishing nets.

"Have you met Graham yet?" Katie falls into step beside me, pushing her hands into the pockets of her duffle coat. I shake my head.

"Not yet. Just Ryan."

"Have you been to Cornwall before?"

"Once." A feather, the same grey and white as the sky and the wave tops, blows into my legs, and I stoop to pick it up. "Newquay. When I was a student."

"Trethallyan's beautiful," she observes. "You'll love it, when you get used to it." We reach a bright yellow Mini parked in one of the seafront bays, an old one, with white stripes on its bonnet and age-dulled round headlamps. She stoops to unlock the door. "Are you living in Porthtrevelen?"

"Yeah. I'm renting a flat." I climb in at her direction. Rain flecks the windscreen as we set off, the wind buffeting the tiny car with such force that Katie has to hang white-knuckled onto the wheel.

"That's good." She's frowning in concentration as we reach the peak of the gradient. I push the grey feather into my pocket.

"Do you?" I glance at her. "Live in Porthtrevelen, I mean?"

"Mmm. For now." She nods. "But I'm moving in April, after the wedding. Craig lives in Truro. We've bought a house there."

She flicks the indicator stalk, and we turn sharply onto the track. The Mini rattles over the bumps. We draw to a halt at the gates, and Katie strains out of the window to punch the four-digit code into the keypad. Ryan's still in the cabin when we get there, sat with his feet on one of the desks and a laptop on his knees.

"Hi, Livs! Katie." He dispenses with the laptop swiftly. "What've you done with Claire?"

"She's gone to get Fin." Katie crosses the cabin to prop something on the furthest desk. "I'm going to leave these here for Sean, if that's okay?" She winds her scarf back around her neck. "It was good to meet you, Livs. I'll see you soon. I should be here later in the week."

"See you." I'm tongue-tied. I wait until the door closes behind her before I start back towards my laptop. My desk? I sit down tremblingly and tip out the contents of the envelope. Ryan swings around on his chair in a way that reminds me startlingly of Kris.

"You went to Nottingham, didn't you?"

"Yeah."

"Me too." He flashes me a boyish grin, folding muscular arms across his chest. "Okay, most important question . . ." He assesses me, eyes narrowed. "Ancaster . . . ?"

"Nightingale." I shake my head, smiling despite myself. I consider him for a moment. "Hugh Stu?"

"How did you know that?"

"I didn't." I look down, cheeks pink.

Ryan shakes his head, too. "God, it's been a long time." He swings back in his chair. For a second his eyes meet mine. "Do you miss it?"

I think of campus, and the workshop, and learning to ice skate. But all the memories are confused, tied up with other things: Dad's coffin, Verity House, the graffiti under the railway bridge, waking up in Wollaton Park to the circle of concerned faces, the inside of A&E. I blink hard, and think of cliffs instead, and fishing nets.

"Not anymore," I tell him.

* * *

There's only one working street light in Sunnyside, pale and weary, and it casts more shadows than it does luminance. I clamber out of my car into its meagre glow, unlock the outer door and let myself into the hallway. The downstairs flats are in darkness, apparently deserted. I almost trip over a box outside my door.

"Crap—" I fumble to switch on the landing light.

The offending article is wrapped in brown paper, and someone has written something almost illegible on the top right-hand corner. Something about knocking if I need to borrow a cup.

Niklavs. I can't help smiling. I persuade my door open, and take the gift inside, tearing off the paper with a lump in my throat. A kettle. For a moment I'm not sure whether to laugh aloud or dissolve into tears. Seriously? I sit down with a bump on the battered lid of my boarding trunk, and pull out my phone.

Kris Frost 16:23
iMessage
slide to reply

Oh, crap. I was supposed to call him last night to tell him I'd arrived. I flick the message open, and toy guiltily with the touchscreen, unsure how to reply. I hit the call button instead.

"Livs!" He sounds less pissed off than I expected, and the artificial proximity of his voice makes the threat of tears dangerously imminent. I swallow hard a couple of times and make myself smile, as if he can see me.

"Hey, Kris."

"You were supposed to call me!"

"Sorry."

"S'okay, I kind of knew you wouldn't. You okay? How's the flat?"

"Yeah, it's good." I scrape at the bare boards with the toe of my boot.

"Met any crazy artists yet?" His voice is teasing.

"No." I grin reluctantly at the phone. "Just fishermen."

"Hah." There's a scuffle on the other end, and I realise for the first time that there are voices in the background.

"Sounds good, Livs. What's the architect like?"

"Mmm." I scuff my foot back the other way. "He's good."

"Really?"

"I don't know. I'm meeting him tomorrow. He wasn't there today."

"Right." I can hear his raised eyebrows. "Look, Livs, I'm really sorry but I'm going to have to go. We're just about to start."

Monday night. First Fifteens. I forgot.

"Give me a call later, right? Or drop me a text, at least?"

"Yeah." I nod. "Okay."

"Look after yourself, Livs." It's meaningful. I grin.

"Stop bossing me," I tell him.

"Stop making me."

"You're my *little* brother remember?"

"Yeah. Tiny." Kris laughs. "Shut it."

"Bye, Kris."

"See you, Livs." His voice muffles and cuts off. I hang up.

Look after yourself. He's right. Heartened, I scramble to my feet.

* * *

The walls look better with pictures, the floorboards less barren with the rug from my boarding trunk laid out. I spend an hour lining up cups and plates on shelves, unbundling cutlery and unloading utensils. I order pizza off a menu I found in the hall, and pick at it in between boxes. The paints I leave until last, positioning the worn wooden box beside the easel as an incentive to finish. My mind is on the seascape as I tackle the final items, turning the last few keepsakes out of my boarding trunk and kicking it under the bed, shoving the toiletries that have amassed on the dressing table to one side, and laying out my small collection of mismatched treasures in front of the triad of mirrors. A wooden cat, curled tight in a ball, the carved letters in its back worn smooth now with age: *Best friends always, Hannah.* My parents, arm-in-arm in a silver frame. A not-quite-gold medal on a red and white ribbon: *Fairfield Horseshoe 2020 01:53:29.* I swallow and feel for the top drawer of the dressing table. Some things are better out of sight.

"Ow."

The drawer won't open. I graze my fingers on the grain of the old wood. It's stuck. I jiggle it.

"Oh, come on."

I tug at the handle and something shifts inside. Intrigued, I kneel to get a better view. There's definitely something there, something too deep for the drawer — it's fouling against the top. I jam my fingers into the tiny crack and ease them forwards, feeling for the edge. Cardboard, paper. I manipulate it carefully, and pull.

The drawer flies open with such force that I stumble backwards, the bottles and brushes on the dressing table all falling over with a crash. Adrenaline spikes through me.

A book.

I take a sharp breath in; a bottle of body lotion rolls past my foot in a sullen arc. The thing that was jamming the drawer is a book.

Andrew R Frost.

I stand frozen, staring at my own surname on the silk-coated paper. For seconds, minutes, I can't move at all. Of everything that I could have found in my new room, this? My father's parting words greeting me from the inside of a poor-quality antique dresser? At last I breathe out, letting my fingers trace the contours of the embossed lettering and painfully familiar artwork. *Mercy's Child.*

It was a bestseller, overnight. The press response was massive, the sales unequalled, although maybe that was the posthumous label. Whatever the reason, the truth is I've never been able to bring myself to read past the first page. The scenes from my own childhood, spelled out in mass-market ink, are too agonisingly raw. And the blackbird on the front cover still makes me cry every time I look at it.

Steeling myself, I pick it up. Turn it over to read the dust-jacket blurb for the hundred-thousandth time.

Heart-warming, soul-shattering — a triumphant story of discovery and redemption.
Andrew R. Frost's final, sweeping bow.

I pause. My reflection in the mirror frowns back at me over the reversed cover art. Something feels wrong about it. The weight, the thickness, the binding. I run my thumb along the dip in its spine. The dust-jacket doesn't fit the book inside at all. Oddly curious, I flip it open.

A loose page slips out and swishes to the floor, making me start. I stoop to pick it up. Notepaper. It's notepaper.

I thumb through the pages, mind racing. Not my father's story. Not a bookstore blockbuster, not a novel at all. It's a notebook full of writing: in fountain pen, someone's journal, pages and pages of it, disguised in my father's book-jacket. Underneath the paper sheath, the inside of the cardboard cover is monogrammed — in the same blue homework-assignment erasable ink — with a tiny, elegant bird.

My hands tighten on reflex, my fingernails biting into the paper. The rush of my pulse in my ears drowns out my thoughts. A blackbird . . .

But no. I exhale in a rush. It's not a blackbird at all. I trace the shape with my index finger. It's a swallow — or a swift — a graceful curve, a forked tail; I try to remember the difference between the two, and can't. I open the front cover.

What makes a story?

The words stare up at me from the white paper. I blink, unnerved, and sit down on the edge of my bed.

Swift
31/05/21

What makes a story?

What's in a book that makes you turn the pages? Keeps you up all night, makes you late for work. What compels you? Completes you? Fills your mind so full of possibilities that there's no room for reality?

What is it, in a story? The fight? The passion? The pain?

You see, life's all about the stories. The good ones, the bad ones. The ones that wake you, sobbing, sweating, praying for them to end.

What's your story?

This is mine.

CHAPTER 4

Breathe in, lengthen the stride, count out—

It's not light yet. The windswept remnants of the gorse and the short, hardy grass are stiff and white with frost. I'm starting to feel the stretch in the backs of my legs, the burn at the base of my lungs. *In, lengthen, out.* Eyes on the crest, and it doesn't matter if there's another rise beyond it. One peak at a time . . . Lengthen. Out. I flick tracks, music crescendoing from my earphones, and tap my phone to check, careful not to break pace. Three miles. I've judged it okay. Five will see me back to my front door.

I chose the clifftop even though I can barely make out the path. Away from Trethallyan, up, high above the sea into the biting beginnings of a clear day. I've always been sure-footed. Before boarding school, I spent my childhood in Coniston in the Lake District. My father, aside from being an author, was an avid climber and fell-runner. I was eight the first time I went with him. Even at uni, I went back every weekend I could spare. Running was precious. It was our time.

Two years. Hard to believe. I barely even visited that house after he died. I couldn't make myself go into his room, not since the day of the funeral, not once. Not even when they cleared it; I watched Kristopher help load the removal truck from the silence of the empty guest room. My mother lives in Manchester now. The past is gone.

My breath steams in front of me as I adjust my strides to a more sustainable speed. Today is going to be better. I've promised myself that. I've never passed up a challenge before. I'm not about to start now.

I tug my Lycra sleeves over my smarting hands. *Eyes on the crest.* Even the sea is calmer this morning. Only a few of the rolling waves break to thunder their complaint to the gulls: shades of shifting grey against a dark sky. There are no shapes or sails on the water today. Nothing but nothingness. Empty space.

Two years. The thought recurs, sharp and unwelcome. Two and a half since the Solent. Since Toby Rainworth drowned, a few metres off the stern of his grandparents' yacht.

I grit my teeth and fix my eyes on the horizon. *In, lengthen, out.* I'm starting to tire. Too much daydreaming; I've outpaced myself. Forty-five minutes. There are signs of habitation, and dawn, on the horizon. Around the headland, Porthtrevelen levels back into view: benches, railings, a blur. The route ends downhill, and I sprint the last two hundred yards over the flagstones, until my chest is bursting and my eyes smart with the merciless assault of the wind. I pluck the headphones from my ears, tinny music spilling out into the deserted street, and press my hands to my knees, gasping.

"Good morning."

I raise my eyes to Niklavs' face, too breathless to make any kind of sensible response.

"Quite impressive run." He nods in the direction of the cliffs, and stoops to pick up the glass milk bottles from the doorstep.

"Oh," I pant. "Thanks. I mean . . ." I straighten, brushing the sweat-soaked wisps of hair back from my cheeks with my sleeve. "For the kettle. Thanks."

"You are welcome." Niklavs holds open the door for me. I stop at the foot of the stairs.

"Next time," I tell him, "I'll make *you* a drink, right?"

Niklavs smiles, amused. "Perhaps," he says. I can't help but grin at his lack of enthusiasm.

The sound of my door is becoming familiar. I let myself into my flat and hop across the floor, peeling off my leggings and base layer. I glance at the book on the dressing table as I tug my hair out of its ponytail to drag a brush through it.

What's your story?
This is mine.

The dust-jacket is still beside it on the dresser-top; I pick it up, fold the silk-coated paper and slide it into the drawer with the photo frame. Out of sight. As far out of mind as I can get it.

I've never felt so awake, as the cold water hits my skin. I cringe away from the shower, relishing the energised ache in my muscles. Better. Today's going to be better.

It's early when I arrive at Trethallyan. So early that the sun is barely up beyond the trees. I have to hang precariously out of the car window to reach the keypad, and as the gates grate open in front of me, I can't help but notice a chill in the crisp air that runs deeper than the bite of the January morning. The hall is charcoal against a pink watercolour sky, and its expectant hush is disarming. Either there are no inhabitants beyond the grand, decrepit doors, or whoever resides inside hasn't risen yet; not a single shard of light breaks out through the multitude of heavy sash windows as I climb out of my car and pick my way across the half-frozen grass.

The cabin's still locked; I let myself in tentatively with my new key. The door seals itself behind me and I pause in the stillness of the strange wooden room, breathing the smell of pine needles and salt. I catch myself walking on tiptoe to my desk and slip off my jacket, somehow reluctant to turn on the computer.

So. This is it. I perch on the edge of my chair, suppressing an unexpected burst of shivers. What now? I read — or tried to — the contents of the mysterious envelope, mostly photocopies of legal paperwork and survey drawings, last night. I open the envelope and arrange the paper-clipped piles on the desk. Re-examining them doesn't tell me anything new. I fidget on the chair. Alone in the abandoned studio, I feel like a child, out of bounds. My gaze drifts to the mezzanine and the steps, the drawing boards, the tantalising suggestion of rolls of paper and modelling textures that someone has organised meticulously underneath. Real modelling, not just CAD.

I slide to my feet.

The wooden hand-rail is surprisingly warm as I run my fingers along it; the last stair creaks as I reach the top. Above my head, the clouds beyond the skylight are brightening. The desk is immaculately tidy, a clean sheet of A2 exhibited like a promise on the nearest drawing board.

Growing bolder, I reach out and flick on the desk lamp, flooding the vast table with brilliant white light that refocuses even the blank paper into high definition. A thrill of excitement clenches in my abdomen. I trace my fingertips over the rulers, across the incline of the drawing board, feeling the quality of the paper. The other side of the desk is flat and more untidy, out of keeping with the rest of the room: a sprawl of Stanley knives and pliers, scales, scalpels and set squares. I take a step back, drinking it in. This is where I belong. There were mornings, not so long ago, when I regularly woke stiff and aching with my earphones in my ears, to find myself still in the university workshop, my eyes burning with tiredness. Mornings when I made the walk home on little or no sleep, dizzy with exhaustion and inspiration.

I pick up one of the drafting pencils, 0.7 mm, from the table and turn it in my fingers. Feel its weight, balance, precision—

"Are you looking for someone?"

Shit.

I gasp and start so violently that the pencil falls from my hand, hits the desk and rolls onto the floor with a clatter.

I didn't hear the door close, or even open. Didn't hear the soft, deliberate fall of footsteps until his shadow fell across the drawing board. He's tall, poised, utterly unsmiling; his dark brows are lowered in appraisal over even darker eyes, an inscrutable frown playing on his forehead and hardening the handsome, stubborn set of his jaw. I stand, immobilised, as he comes to a halt. He's staring. I stare back.

For long seconds, neither of us moves. Neither of us speaks. His gaze travels over me, sizing me up without any kind of effort to hide it, and I feel my pulse quicken. Finally, he shrugs off his coat to reveal a suit jacket over his Levi's, and the unbuttoned collar of a sharp designer shirt.

"I'm sorry." His voice is quiet, dangerously assured, the residual lilting hint of a Gaelic accent the only remnant not squeezed out of it by a public-school upbringing and Russell Group education. "*Who* are you?"

He scans over me again, and I falter under the intensity.

Say something. Anything.

"Livia," I manage to choke out at last. "Frost." It sounds strangled. I clear my throat. "Intern."

Shit, he's young. Too young to be who he's about to say he is. He moves past me to the window to jerk open the mutinously murmuring blind, casting cold January light in a clear pool over both of us. His dark eyes reach my face.

"Sean." It's cool, brusque. "Lorchann. Architect."

I hold his gaze, despite the flush that creeps into my cheeks at his poorly disguised mockery.

"You started yesterday," he speaks again, before I can.

"Yes." I find my voice. "I—"

"We probably need to talk." In a single stride he reaches the door to the back room and depresses the handle. I make out a glimpse, beyond, of a small meeting room set out with one long table and a lifeless projector screen that ripples with the backdraught of the door.

"I don't have time now. I have to take a call." Sean doesn't wait for me to respond. "After that, I don't know . . . Nine thirty?" He shrugs. "I won't have long. I don't really have time. I have a lot to do, and a site visit from English Heritage this afternoon."

What? I stare at him, stung. The smouldering of apprehension in my cheeks has become an indignant blaze. I grip my hands together behind me.

"Nine thirty." I nod.

"Great," he says curtly. For a split second, I can't tell whether he's being sarcastic. Then he disappears through the doorway, without as much as a glance back. The door closes with a click. I flounder beside the drafting table, uncurling my fingers from my smarting palms and trying to slow my breathing. I glare at the door, mute. *Up to speed?* Ryan's not-so-subtle hints from yesterday dance across my mind. So much for my optimistic start.

I crouch to retrieve the dropped pencil. *Sean . . . Lorchann . . . Architect.* I can almost hear the accompanying swagger. I screw the pencil into my fist and stalk back to my desk.

Why didn't I listen to Kristopher? I should have taken one of the safe-option jobs in Nottingham or London. I should never have come here. I lay down the pencil with a click.

"Morning, Livs!"

A blast of cold air washes in from outside. I look up. Ryan grins.

"You decided you were coming back, then?" He stamps his feet and pulls off a thick pair of gloves. His cheeks are red with the cold.

I force a smile. "It looks that way."

"Anyone else here?" Ryan flicks on the lights and glances tactlessly at the discarded black wool overcoat draped over the mezzanine rail.

"Yeah." I focus my gaze on my laptop and punch the power button. There's an expectant silence. "Sean," I add, under my breath.

"Sean's here?"

I don't miss the significance in his question.

"He said he'd meet me at half nine." I shrug it off.

"Right." Ryan nods. Silence again. I count the ticks of the wall clock. "I just came down to see if you needed anything. I saw your car in the drive."

"Oh, no." I smile again, brightly. "I um . . . think I'm okay. Thanks."

I study him for a moment. In appearance, it isn't immediately obvious. But something in Ryan's confident stride, level stare and polished self-assurance — although they are poles apart in most ways — bears a striking resemblance to Sean. All that's missing is the scathing, dark-eyed disapproval.

As if on cue, the back-room door opens. I jump.

"Hello. Sean Lorchann."

The voice is soft, and very close beside me. I sense his movement past me, catlike, balanced and athletic, and look up despite myself at the back of his shoulders and his steely grip on the phone he's talking into. He strides to the furthest desk and swipes up the folder Katie left there last night.

"Of course. What do you need?" He adjusts his hold on the phone to thumb through the ring-binder, and a shiver runs through me for no good reason. I keep my eyes locked on my screen as he passes back again. I breathe out slowly. Never pass up a challenge.

Except that's definitely in the list of unhelpful rules and assumptions they made me write out during the three weeks in Verity House and at my weekly clinic appointments, like a kid at school copying lines. Negative self-evaluations. At-risk situations. I've learned all the buzz words. I'm a fast learner. That's part of the problem.

I open the email browser and squint at the bright screen. Clinic is a long way away now. A long, long way. The at-risk situations, on the other hand . . . the triggers, the temptations. They're never far away.

It starts off so insidiously. So innocently. The buzz of perfectionism, the slight tightening of self-control: maths, measurements, fine detail. After the Solent, after Dad died, it spiralled. So easy, so cathartic. I never realised until it was too late; to me the reflection in the mirror never changed — not really — it only clarified, a testament to self-discipline and success.

I never told my mother. At the time, I thought that it was the last thing she needed: to know, to be afraid for me, on top of everything else. But in hindsight, she's always known. And my non-disclosure has driven its way between us like a wedge. Kristopher is the only person I've ever told. Kristopher was there, that night in A&E. And Kristopher didn't want me to come here.

Screw Kristopher. I pick up the drafting pencil and roll it in my fingers, watching the way the aluminium catches the light. And screw Sean Lorchann. I've come here to achieve something, to learn something. To find something: a dream, a reality, *the passion.* Niklavs' voice echoes in my ears. I pull up my feet to sit cross-legged on my chair, and fold my hands around my beaten brown ankle boots.

I spend a long time fiddling with the email settings on the laptop, trying to make it work, then turn my attention to accessing the cloud so that I can import my own portfolio. Outside, the sun has come out. There's a bird pecking at something on the path. I think suddenly of the book. *Swift 31/05/21—*

"Livs."

A little breath rushes between my teeth. I look up. I'd forgotten Ryan was even there. He's working on a spreadsheet of complicated-looking figures. Prices. My eyes widen. That's some serious money. I struggle to keep my face impassive as he wheels around in his chair.

"I think Sean's off the phone." His words hang expectantly in the silence.

"It's quarter to ten."

Shit. I glance at the clock, fear spiking in my gut. I stumble to my feet.

"Thanks," I whisper.

The steel door-handle's cold, the door surprisingly heavy. I push it open and stop in my tracks.

He's standing at the far side of the room, looking out of the one sizeable window, hands plunged carelessly into his pockets, the crisp silhouette of his shoulders tense and unforgiving in the hard white sunlight. A laptop, identical to mine, whirrs quietly on the table. I take a nervous step forwards and clear my throat.

"Did you still want to meet?"

Bad question. Sean Lorchann turns, and the answer in his face is undeniably *no*. I swallow. His expression is all shadows, no smiles, level, concentrated and inscrutable. He draws one hand from his pocket to gesture stiffly at the table.

"Sure." He nods.

"Okay." I make myself let go of my hands and fold them behind my back. Neither of us sits down.

"Why don't you have a seat?" It's short, to the point. I don't move. He approaches the table and pauses, fingers resting idly on the closed lid of the laptop.

"I'm okay, thanks." My mouth is unreasonably dry. *Jesus Christ, Livia.* I curl my fingernails into my palms. *Pull it together.*

"Right." His eyes narrow. I can't reply. My throat has tightened too much to speak; apparently forewarned wasn't forearmed. And, for all their poorly hidden hints, no one warned me about the sarcasm. Or the devastating good looks. Or, funnily enough, the general level of contempt that seems to have established itself in the gaping silence between us.

Sean drums his fingers lightly on the laptop.

"You got the details I left?"

I nod.

"This project is big. You know that." Abruptly he moves, striding away from the table to close the door, and something in the action shreds the remnants of my self-possession.

"Just to get some things clear," he turns back to me, "before we start. I didn't want an intern. I didn't get any choice."

Suddenly, the room seems very small. I suck in a deep breath, but he carries on before I can formulate a reply.

"Not very long ago, I was you." His arms are folded across his chest. "So I've been there. I know what it's about. You're green, naıve, full of unrealistic enthusiasm. I get it."

Outside the window a cloud has half covered the sun, casting darkness across us. I force myself not to look down. To keep my eyes trained on his face. *I get it.* Really? Does he? I grit my teeth.

"This isn't the place to be any of those things. This place is one wrong step away from a fuck-up. Every detail matters. So, yes, I know you have boxes to tick. I know you have exams to pass." Sean doesn't look down, either. His scrutiny is merciless. "But you need to get them out of your head. This isn't a tick-box exercise. You're not a student anymore; you're not living the dream, you're living the reality, and average doesn't cut it. You're going to have to work at my pace if you're going to do this, and you're going to have to be able to keep up."

If? I feel the muscles clench in my abdomen.

"I can see that." My own words startle me. Sean's eyebrows lift a fraction.

"Good. Because I don't do average. You need to understand that. I'm not afraid to push for what I want. And I'll push you." His gaze travels over me once, slowly, from my smarting cheeks to my leather boots and back up again. "Hard."

I swallow. His eyes on my face are dark, forbidding. I hold the stare. For a moment we stand, locked in silent calculation.

"You'll tick your boxes," his voice is dangerously soft, "but you'll tick mine, too."

I make a conscious effort to uncurl my fists. So much for introductions. For the dream. *You're not living the dream, you're living the reality.* The stark, dark-eyed reality.

"That's great," I murmur. "Thanks."

He turns away. I still don't move. I can see his reflection in the window, dark eyes burning, jaw clenched.

"Your visit." At last I claw back my ability to speak. "This afternoon. What time is it?"

"Huh?" He spins.

"English Heritage. I can show myself around the site if you're busy." Outwardly, I'm resolute. A millimetre below the surface, I'm quaking. "But I need to know what time they're coming, and where to meet you."

For a moment, he stares at me. I face him with more audacity than I feel.

"If you want me to 'keep up', then I need to be there."

Sean's eyes narrow. For a moment there's absolute silence. Awkward doesn't even touch it. It's a painful, razor-toothed silence that slowly expands to suck the whole room into its depths. I dig my fingernails into my palms.

"Why not?" His teeth are gritted.

I let out my breath. "Okay."

"Two o' clock. Trethallyan Edge. The chapel." Abruptly, he's moving, jerking open the door. "You know where it is?" He stands back to let me go out first. I try not to notice his crushing grip on the brushed steel, or the involuntary acceleration of my own heart rate. I step through quickly.

"I'll find it."

* * *

What's real, and what's beautiful.

For a moment I pause my ascent and let myself drink in the angles and contrasts of the dizzying drop beside me, the moody colours and contrasting textures of the vegetation against the sea. Claire said pretty. That's not the word I would use for the exposed footpath that winds its way to Trethallyan Edge. I'm sure my father would have had a hundred other descriptors; there isn't so much difference between writing and painting, except that I prefer to capture in oil what my father would have portrayed in ink. *What's real, and what's beautiful.* He always did tell me it was the most important thing in the world.

Sand and salt spray blast against my face. I grip my notepad in my hands and resume my climb, deafened by the wind as the path starts to curve inland. It turns out that whoever drew up the map in the envelope-of-all-knowledge hadn't paid much attention to scale. I seem to have been walking forever. If I'd realised just how far away this place is, I'd have driven.

Like everyone else has.

I come to a halt, blinking in disbelief. A hundred yards ahead of me, where the cliff softens, there's a steep track that cuts in from nowhere. There's a black Defender parked on the stone chips, and a silver executive car that's struggled to make it over the gradient. At the mid-point of the cliff, I can make out two figures. Levi's, suit jackets, clipboards. The indistinct outline of a building, half-hidden over the contours that lead down again towards the sea.

Not the dream, the reality. I brace myself. They're both watching my ascent. Sean Lorchann closes the cover of his tablet with a snap.

"Livvy." His voice is infuriatingly soft. He gestures to the stocky man beside him. "This is Mr Reye from English Heritage. Mr Reye, this is Livvy Frost, an intern architect who's just started work with us." His tone doesn't change as he steps between us, cutting short my half-offered handshake. I stiffen.

"Liv*ia*," I correct him under my breath.

Sean glances back.

"Liv*ia*," he echoes. The velvet quietness of his voice makes my jaw clench.

"Mr Reye and I were just discussing the possible promontory fort, which undoubtedly you will have read about, and whether it's going to affect any building we want to do here."

Promontory fort? What the fuck's a promontory fort? I screw up my face against the wind. I haven't read as much as a mention of a fort. I swallow.

"Cliff-castles. Scheduled monuments." The stocky English Heritage man turns to me, with a sympathetic look that I could do without. "They date back to the Iron Age. The banks and ditches here have been looked at very closely, but we don't have definitive evidence either way."

I look down, noticing for the first time the contours of the not-quite-thawed grass, and the odd ridge of granite poking up from the hard ground.

"I think we've just established that the chapel's not on the site of interest anyway," Sean remarks coolly. Without another look back, he's moving. I hesitate, then scramble downwards a few paces after him, over the gradient of the cliff. The descent is gentler than it appeared from a distance, a curving decline towards the rocks and white-gold sand of a concealed beach. I pick up speed, my feet skidding in the sandy, stony soil. The lines have disappeared. Sean halts halfway down. I slither to a stop behind him, and snatch my breath.

What's beautiful . . .

The view is unspeakable. Indescribable. An indefinite expanse, wild and unconquered. Crashing waves, gathering clouds, windswept bracken and thorny, sparsely flowering gorse. A secluded cove, not far below now, its expanse of wet white sand gleaming like treasure—

I forget that my eyes and nose are streaming. Forget that my cheeks are on fire from the cold and the wind. Forget that Sean Lorchann despises me, and look up at him by accident, straight into the blaze of unsmiling excitement in his dark eyes.

For a split second, he doesn't even seem to see me. He's squinting against the sun, his improbably handsome face tight with concentration, and I can make out the slightest movement of his lips. A thrill runs down my spine.

There's a building behind him. Not as old or as majestic as I might have imagined; it's small, plain and somehow faded, as though it's been cut from a sepia photograph and stuck onto its surroundings in error. The lintel over the door is granite and inscribed with a date, but the walls are brick and render, and most of the windows are boarded up. Sean turns without a word. I watch as he strides over to the ruin, and paces out the distance from wall to wall. I follow cautiously, bracken and last year's brambles snagging around my trouser legs. There's one remaining window in the far end, its diamond panes a multicolour of stained glass. I look up at the distorted, not-quite picture, remembering suddenly what Claire said about the chapel being haunted. For some reason, the hairs are standing up on the back of my neck.

"What do you know about converting consecrated buildings?" Sean snaps around.

"I um . . . don't—" I take a sudden step back, and trip on the brambles. He regards me dispassionately. "I mean—But I can—"

"Forget it." He leaps smartly over the foliage and starts back the way we came.

"Excuse me?" I'm not sure what's worse, running after him, or letting him disappear into the distance. I spring quickly up the incline, suddenly very thankful for my upbringing in the fells.

"Forget it." He shakes his head, pauses to face me. Mr English Heritage is barely out of earshot at the top of the rise.

"Wait," I screw my fingers into my palms. "I . . . haven't worked on any. But—"

"It's like I said," Sean speaks through gritted teeth. "You're not a student. I don't have time for hand-holding."

"I don't need my hand holding." I'm scowling openly. "But if that's what you think, then why did you even bother to let me come?"

"I don't know." He glares at me. "I'm living to regret it."

I stare at him, speechless.

"This isn't fair." My cheeks and the tops of my ears are flaming. Anger is overtaking my humiliation. "If I'm supposed to be working with you—"

"That's a point of contention."

I freeze. He's started to walk again. A point of contention? My fists clench.

"Well, either way!" I have to run to draw level with him. If he thought I wouldn't catch him up, he has another think coming. Not many people can outrun me.

"You can't expect to see any talent if you don't let me *do* anything. I won't be ticking anyone's 'boxes' that way!"

Sean stops abruptly.

"Fine." His cool gaze meets mine. "Plot out the site. Find out everything there is to know about the chapel. Go speak to English Heritage and the National Trust, and the fucking royal society for the protection of seagulls or whoever else is going to screw this up. Go back through the outline permission, the conditions, the historical restrictions and prove to me this is watertight. *Then* we can talk about it."

* * *

My story. I don't promise that it's going to be good. I'm no hero, no unfortunate protagonist. This is a story of finding myself. Not self-discovery. I lost myself a long time ago. I've come here to look. I've been putting myself back together for four years, but there are pieces missing. I've come to find the pieces.

Perhaps you know this place. Perhaps you don't. If I told you about it, would it make a difference? The blind cord rattling against the single glazing, the sound of the sea. The tone of the dying sunlight in the tri-fold mirror. Have you ever stopped to think what happens, when you hold up a mirror to a mirror? Here in this room, there's no choice. Look too deeply, and you'll be lost, to the reflection of a reflection, the shadow of a shadow . . .

Do I know this place? Not yet. Did *she*? The person whose writing is becoming as familiar to me as my own? I can see my grip on the notebook reflected in the mirror, white-knuckled, once, thrice, infinite times as I get to my feet. How do I even know she's a she?

I walk to the window and put down the journal, trying not to think about Sean Lorchann and promontory forts. The dusk outside is thick with descending fog; the sounds of the sea reach me through the old, brittle panes and the plastic end of the blind cord is tapping out a tattoo on the glass. I reach quickly to catch it and stop it, overcome with shivers.

The noises the gulls make sound like cries for help. The air smells like rain. I'm going to try and tell you the truth, I think. Will you turn the pages, if I do? Even if it's not great, or good. My truth? Even if there aren't any heroes?

A draught trickles over the windowsill, teasing at the edges of the pages, fresh with rain and briny sea-mist. I pull the blind cord sharply, the wrong way first, making it clatter upwards, and then down, covering the blue-black glass.

If I tell you, maybe I'll understand, too. Perhaps there could be a kind of absolution, that way.

Is that what makes a story great? The hope of redemption? The fight? Or is it only the turmoil that makes us read on? The parallels that strike us a little too close for comfort? The flaws that we can't quite disown?

Here goes.

I frown. Pick up the book from the sill, something catching my eye. Someone has stood here before, where I'm standing. Breathed the air I'm breathing. And they've scratched something into the wood.

Apus apus.

The parallels that strike us too close for comfort. For seconds, minutes, I stand, teeth chattering and watch the letters fade as the light dies. It's strange, a little unnerving, to think of someone else in my room.

I think of Trethallyan Edge instead. The noise of the waves. The dark threat of gathering cloud, the golds and whites of gorse-flower and wet sand: Cadmium Orange, Mixing White and Ochre. The wind through the bracken. The most important thing in the world. If only my father had known how right he was. The most important thing; the only thing. The only thing that got me through the self-loathing, the fear, the weekly clinic weigh-ins. The loneliness. *A kind of absolution.*

The floorboards are cool under the knees of my pyjama trousers as I kneel beside the easel. I unlatch the lid of the wooden box, swinging it open, running my fingers over the tubes of oils. I inhale again deeply, drinking in their smell.

Close my eyes for a moment. *Idanthrene, Davy's Grey* . . . Even with the blinds down, I can see the uncharted misty outline of the Porthtrevelen skyline.

For a while I was unable to paint places. Not from within the hospital curtains or the blank walls of the Verity House inpatient unit. A week of bed rest, and three more behind closed doors, repressed every landscape memory I had, dead-ending each creation in brick walls, fluorescent lights and concrete. The images beyond were too distorted, fragmented, broken down into nothing more than ideas and snatches. Empty shells that weren't quite people. Unformed thoughts that only lingered long enough to conceptualise in colour.

And then, one day, I painted the Solent. And I painted it again. Once more, twice more. So many times that I can't remember. It never helps. The water is always empty, and it's always raining. No matter how many shades of sunlight I mix on the palette.

It's more than a year since I last spoke to Hannah. More than a year since *Mercy's Child* posthumously hit the top of the UK bestseller list. I haven't seen Tom or Leanna since Toby's memorial. Since they moved away to live with Leanna's family in Kent, I've heard more rumours than truths. The kind of rumours that aren't worth listening to.

I've kept the pictures. Each and every one. The porthole, the beckoning water. What else can I do with them? It's not possible to destroy a memory. However much you might want to.

I close the lid. Beside me, the journal stares up from the floor, Swift's handwriting a spidery sea of pen-strokes. I pick it up, and click on the light. The sixty-watt bulb swings gently to the imperceptible electric buzz of its own lullaby.

Like I said, there's not so much difference between painting and writing. Not really. Whatever way, we tell our own story. Me, my father, Swift. Even if there aren't any heroes.

With a sudden feeling of certainty, I turn over the page.

Green

I pause on the word, uncomfortable. Naıve, full of unrealistic enthusiasm. I get it . . .

Like the dandelion stems,
yellow hair aglow in the sun,
she dances her dance—

no one else's dance:
it is all hers, this crisp-apple air,
that willow tree with
its fingers that reach
to brush her youth.
She sings her song

no one else's song:
not even the star-flecked thrush
can replicate her freedom

because, at seven o'clock
when she will be a child again
and taken away to bed,

the thrush will fly away.

And tomorrow when
she opens her eyes, grown,
the sun and the willow

and the thrush and the youth
will be gone forever. She just
doesn't know it yet.

I crouch down and pick up a brush. *Sap green.*

Who needs heroes? The scent of the paint washes over me. I swallow. Then in one first, bold stroke, I sweep the brush across the canvas.

CHAPTER 5

2015

"Hi."

Friday afternoon sunshine reflected in the dark-blue paint. The windows were open. He was making the most of the first wave of warm April weather. Music was trickling from the speakers.

"Hey." The latch clunked as Sophia pulled it. She dropped her bag into the footwell and climbed in. Outside, everyone else was holding up the traffic, crossing the zebra crossing to the jam of waiting cars. Somehow, he had got the best space. He leaned over to plant a kiss on her mouth and her pulse sped up in rebellious excitement.

"Good day?" He started the engine. She plugged in her seatbelt.

"Shitty," she replied.

He steered out into the road with one hand, and reached around behind her with the other to tweak the collar of her blue school blouse.

"Nice shirt." He grinned.

She smiled coyly. "You like it? I hate it." She tugged at her tie and slipped it off. He laughed.

"Touché."

He wasn't wearing a suit today. He must have changed at work. They swerved down a back street and he sped up, jolting them violently over the speed-bumps. She pressed her legs tightly together and held on to the sides of the seat, breathless with anticipation. He hadn't said where they were going. She didn't even know where he lived.

It had become routine, on days when Mum wasn't at work. The bus stop at St Aldates, the layby outside school. Once, twice, she had even skipped Thursday afternoon games to meet him — she hated hockey anyway — and they'd driven out to the riverbank at Sandford Lane and eaten lunch in his car. Rumours were already creeping around at school. For the second time in a year, she'd found herself an object of interest, but this time there was a gratifying shade of jealousy in the eyes that followed her down the corridors, and the whispering in the changing rooms. Jessica Lancaster had even seen her getting out of his car yesterday afternoon, while everyone else was at match tea.

"I thought we could get some food." They pulled up at traffic lights, and he looked over at her, his gaze hooded and hot.

She caught her breath.

"I need to get changed," she said. Her voice sounded husky.

He smiled lazily. "I guess you do." The light turned green and they glided back into motion, his hand brushing her knee as he changed gear. He glanced sideways at her pleated skirt, rolled shorter than she used to wear it, and the collection of leather bangles around her wrist.

"You painted your nails," he said.

She had. Black. Completely school-illegal, but no one had noticed, or if they had, they hadn't done anything about it.

"I like them."

"Me too," she breathed. She raised her eyes to look at him. Oh God, he was so hot. Nothing and no one had ever had this effect on her. Ever. Just being near him made her almost incoherent. But it was so easy, to be near him, to be with him; they could sit for hours in his car, and she could tell him things, things she'd never dream of telling anyone else: about herself, about school, about Leon and Mum. Even about the Dad thing. She'd never talked to anyone about the Dad thing.

They stopped at McDonald's, and she changed in the toilet while he ordered. He was waiting by the door when she came out, holding the scrunched-over top of the paper bag in one hand. He held the door open with the other.

"You look good," he murmured against her ear. His breath was warm, and smelt like spearmint and smoke. They got back in the car, and she cradled the sweating bag of food in her lap.

He drove to Sandford Lane a different way than normal. The tyres scrunched on the grit as he parked, threads of river glistening between the trees. He undid his seatbelt, and she sat cross-legged in her seat to eat, watching him between mouthfuls. He leaned to reach a carrier bag from the back.

"Drink?" he offered. She nodded. He flipped off the lid and passed it to her, sickly pear-drop cider bubbling over the top. She sucked the foam away quickly and took a swig. They finished their food, and he turned up the radio. The car windows had misted up. He rolled his down, and lit a cigarette.

"Still up for going out tonight?" He lounged back in his seat to look at her. He wasn't drinking. But, she supposed, he had to drive.

"Uh-huh." She nodded. "Where?"

"You'll see." He grinned. "Later."

"Have I been there before?"

"I doubt it." He flicked the cigarette butt out of the open window. "Hey, don't worry about it." He laughed under his breath. "You'll like it. I promise. Do you want to take a walk?"

They crossed the river and walked to the lock. There was a pub on the other bank; it was starting to get busy. Half past six. The smell of cooking food drifted over the water. She felt a little tipsy from the cider. His hand touched the back of her waist.

"How's the bitch club?"

She smiled despite herself. Ever since she'd told him about Michaela and the others, he'd adopted the term. It had stuck like glue.

"Oh, you know." She shrugged. "Bitchy. Same as ever. How's work?"

He shrugged. "Same as ever."

He never spoke much about work. Probably because Mum worked there too, and the connection was awkward. He was strolling with his hands loose by his sides, the metal lighter still curled carelessly into his palm. Tentatively, she reached out and touched it, and he glanced across at her through his lashes. He had such long lashes. Such beautiful eyes. He dropped the lighter into his back jeans pocket, and took her hand.

They walked for a while in silence.

She looked at the water. "Did you know J.M. Barrie's son died here?" It looked surprisingly calm on the surface, but underneath she knew the current must be deadly. "The author of *Peter Pan*."

He didn't reply. She looked down at her black school shoes, thinking of Michael Llewelyn Davies. A suicide pact. If you had to die, she supposed, it would be so much less scary not to do it alone.

Her mother had gone through a phase of wanting to die. For almost three months, Sophia had censored the house for everything sharp or potentially lethal; had cut up food with butter knives; thrown out every packet of painkillers she came across; and dispensed prescription medication once a day from her own locked bedroom drawer. But then Leon had arrived on the scene, devout and dutiful and full of pious goodwill — because, after all, Jesus forgives everything — and the old Mum had been gone, and instead it was Sophia who was harbouring disposable razors with not-quite-brave-enough intent in her bedside drawer, like a warning to herself of what things could turn into, if she let them.

"You really are too clever for your own good, aren't you?" He rolled her fingers between his, sending a bolt of heat up her arm and down her spine.

"What do you mean?"

His smile was teasing. He ran a finger through her hair to touch her neck, and she shivered helplessly.

"You. I'm not sure if there's actually anything that you don't know." He wrapped his fingers through hers, and pulled her hand with his into his pocket. Suddenly, she was breathing fast. He pressed his lips to her ear.

"You really are a fucking tease, Sophia," he murmured fondly. "Smoke?"

She shook her head. He took another one, and they looped back the way they had come, the slightly aniseed-smelling smoke lingering in the twilight around them. By the time they got back to the car, it was almost dark. He unlocked the doors from a hundred yards away and they got in. It was colder, now. She closed the door quickly and twisted in her seat to look at him.

"Where are we going?" she asked.

"Into town." He leaned one arm on the steering wheel to look at her. She glanced at her reflection in the vanity mirror.

"I need somewhere to get ready."

He laughed. "Get ready here."

Why? She narrowed her eyes at her reflection. She knew he lived in town — what was the issue?

He read her mind. "My brother's at my flat. He's staying until Monday. I don't especially want you to have to meet him."

"Why?" She frowned.

"He's a bit of a prick." He shrugged. "Look, I'd rather see you alone. Can't you get ready here?"

"It's dark." Even as she said it, it sounded petulant. He reached above her head, and punched a button with one finger, lighting the interior of the car with a smooth yellow glow.

"Now it's not," he pointed out. For a second, his face gave nothing away. Then he grinned at her, and she released her breath, dazzled by his smile. She picked up her bag from the footwell and took out her hairbrush and make-up purse. It was weird, having him watch her, but she managed a passable job in the vanity mirror with a much less steady hand than normal, and finished by brushing out the achingly straight tresses of her long hair.

"Very nice." He leaned in to kiss her, his lips travelling along her jawline to her ear. A thrill ran down the back of her neck. "You smell good."

"It's . . . just shampoo . . ." Her voice wouldn't come out right. He was looking at her in a way that she couldn't comprehend. Calculating. Hungry.

She gasped. Without as much as a warning shot, his hand was inside her skirt. Sophia froze. He slid his fingers along the inside of her thigh, upwards. She stiffened. He smiled.

"What's the matter?" he whispered. She was paralysed in her seat. His fingers hadn't stopped moving, finding their way in. A tiny involuntary noise happened in her throat, of pleasure and fright; she jerked backwards, her fingernails sinking into the upholstery.

"You like that?" His voice was gravel-rough. She couldn't reply. She squirmed, trapped in the seat, shocked and breathless.

"Oh, Sophia . . ." His lips trailed a scorching line from her ear to the nape of her neck, making her back arch. "I could do so much more for you than that, you know. If you'd let me." He kissed her mouth slowly, and withdrew his hand. Picked up a bottle from his footwell and popped the lid.

"Here. Drink up. You need to finish it before we arrive."

"What?" She wasn't quite coherent. "Arrive where?"

"Into town. Like I said." He slipped the key into the ignition. "We can't stay here, Sophia." There was a meaningful smoulder in his smile. "Because I wouldn't be able to resist for much longer if we did."

Oh fuck. She pressed her knees together, rigid with the realisation. He had started the engine, wrenched around to look over his shoulder as he reversed, one muscled arm slung over the back of her seat.

He took her to a bar. She put on heels, and wore a hood that covered most of her face, but it didn't matter because no one checked for ID anyway. He went to get more drinks, and she scanned the cocktail menu nervously in the dim light, deafened by the slow pulse of the music. Sophia put down the menu quickly before he came back and saw her looking. She'd never had a cocktail, and she wasn't exactly sure how much more she could drink. The sudden thought that she might be sick or pass out scared her, and she pushed the menu away to the other end of the low-slung sofa.

It was warm in the bar. She wriggled out of her coat, just in time for him to reappear. He said something, but she couldn't hear what, then grinned and slouched back beside her.

She drank her drink slowly, trying not to think about what had happened in the car. But she couldn't. She couldn't not think about it. His body was close against hers on the sofa; they had sunk so far back that her feet barely reached the floor, and his hand was on her knee. Every now and then, he would lean in to whisper something, or to meet her eye, and she would veer dangerously close to being persuaded. Eventually, she had to get up to use the bathroom, and his eyes followed her across the floor. She stared into the mood-lit mirror dizzily as the door closed behind her. *More*? He wanted more. She was dazed, nauseated with apprehension.

He was waiting outside the door when she came out, leaned against the wall, legs crossed. He pushed himself to his feet as he saw her.

"Took your time," he commented.

"Yeah." She tried for nonchalance. His arm moved around her waist.

"Do you want another drink?"

She hesitated. She still felt quite definitely sick. Whether it was the anticipation or the alcohol she couldn't tell, and she didn't want to find out. Her legs felt unsteady.

"No thanks," she murmured.

"Mm." For a moment, his face was against her hair. "I wish my stupid fuck of a brother wasn't there." His other hand slid to the hem of her skirt. "I'm going to fucking have to call you a taxi." He kissed her mouth, and she savoured the taste of his lips. Then he broke off, and felt in his pocket for his phone.

"Wait." Irrational panic had tightened her throat. She looked up at him, wide-eyed. "When will I see you?"

A tiny smirk played on his lips. "When do you want to?"

"I—"

"Think about what I said, Sophia," he whispered it against her cheek. "I'm free Monday."

* * *

Monday. Mum didn't work Mondays. He'd known that when he said it. She had ridden the taxi home in a blur of overly heightened sensation; he'd paid the driver when he hailed it, and all she'd been able to think about as the dark hedges flashed by the windows was the look, *that* look, the one she shouldn't remember. She'd let herself in through the back door and tiptoed to her room, lain on her bed for hours and hours, until it got light outside. *More. Think about what he said.* She hadn't slept. She'd heard Leon get up, then Mum, and had pretended not to hear when they called her.

Monday. It came slowly, but much too fast. She had a headache by the time she got to school, and put up her hand in maths to ask to be excused, no longer especially bothered by Jessica and Michaela's whispering as she left the classroom under the pretence of going to the sanatorium for painkillers.

She put on her coat to conceal her uniform and walked into town instead. She didn't even know where to start, and skirted the racks of lingerie like a thief, convinced that someone from school or the office would spot her. She knew what she thought she wanted. What he wanted. *I wouldn't be able to resist for much longer if we did.* Her own power terrified her.

It was raining by the time she walked back and re-joined her form between classes. English was slow and, for the first time in her school career, she hadn't even attempted the homework. She tried to fade into the background, left behind in the set text and unable to answer a single question, her mind elsewhere. R.E. was even worse, and as the chapel bell hit four, she almost ran out of the building, her pulse bounding in her throat.

As she crossed the courtyard, she remembered her black nail varnish and the bitch club, and the solace in his lopsided smile, and suddenly she didn't feel as nervous.

His car was parked around the corner from the gates, where she knew it would be, smoke drifting indolently from the driver's window. He stubbed out the cigarette as she opened the door.

"You're early." His rock-star grin melted the rest of her uncertainty instantaneously, and she climbed in, suddenly acutely aware of her new purchases under her clothes.

"I skipped detention," she fired back. He grinned.

"I reckon I can take your mind off it."

"Do you?" She looked up at him through her lashes, but blushed despite herself. She fiddled with the air conditioning as he pulled away, weaving perilously through the traffic. The sky was thick with stifling clouds. He cut off the main road onto a series of back streets, a new development by the railway line, a semi-circle of identical houses culminating in a car park, by a three-storey new-build of flats that backed onto the main line. A freight train groaned into motion, its wheels clattering reluctantly on the tracks. He stopped the car, and there was a momentary silence, until the heavens opened, April rain drumming deafeningly onto the metal bodywork and bouncing off the pavement as they made a run for the door.

Afterwards, she would always think it was strange, the level of detail she remembered. The shade of the carpet on the stairs. The precise time on the clock in his hallway. Exactly what he was wearing: the size and shape of his cuff buttons, the smell of aftershave on his collar, the watch on his wrist that was a lot more expensive than the crumpled black polyester bed sheets and translucently thin curtains. His thumb penetrated the knot of her tie, teasing it deftly apart and pulling it undone.

"Did you?" It was an undertone.

"Huh?" she gasped.

"Think about it?" His eyes were on hers. His hand closed lightly around her knee, his fingernails picking out the tiny ladder in her tights. Did she think about it? As if she could have stopped thinking about it. Anticipation held her breath like a frightened captive in her chest. Slowly she nodded.

"And?" His fingers were working their way higher, skimming their way to the hem of her skirt, so that she was giddy, almost sick with nerves.

"I don't know," she whispered.

"Don't you want to find out?" He was whispering too. The dusk-darkness buzzed around them, heavily expectant. He had paused at the hem of her skirt, toying with the pleats. "You liked it the other day." He seized her wrist suddenly. "This is how much I want you, Sophia." He thrust her hand against his jeans. Jubilation and shock stabbed in her belly.

She inhaled sharply. *He wanted her.* He let go, but she didn't withdraw her hand. He wanted her. Now. Her new underwear was uncomfortable and scratchy under her school uniform. Her throat was dry from breathing too fast. Outside, another train thundered past, shaking the building to its foundations. The clouds were so dark that the streetlights had come on in the car park; one was shining orange through the curtains. Her blazer slipped to the floor with a rustle as he shifted to put his arms around her, the mattress dipping under his weight, almost making her lose her balance.

"Relax." His lips were against her ear. "Why don't you let me try?" The buttons of her blouse were stiff; he was undoing them with one hand and guiding her to his belt with the other. She fumbled with the buckle, barely thinking. Her blouse was undone; his touch made swathes of goosebumps rise on her skin, and his hands reached her shoulders, pushing her backwards. She could have resisted, but she didn't; she let him ease her down onto the musky-smelling duvet, his knees holding her thighs apart as he took off his shirt. There was a strange sensation in her legs, and she wasn't sure if it was desire or terror. He unzipped his jeans.

He had a tiny scar on his chest; she reached falteringly to touch it as he positioned himself above her. A slow smile spread across his lips. Very deliberately, he hooked a finger into the fabric of her tights and pulled, rending a hole, shredding the flimsy 10-denier until it came apart in his hands.

If she was telling the story, that's where she would end it. She would fade the rest out, like the mute black screen between movie scenes where there's only inference. The reality wasn't muted, but it was oddly wordless. It wasn't like in films or books. His weight was heavy, and his hands were more eager than gentle. And it hurt, so much. She wanted to tell him to stop — to stop just for a moment — but she couldn't because her voice wouldn't work, and he wanted her, *he wanted her* and that was what mattered. Fireworks popped in her head; she gripped the duvet with both hands and gasped through her teeth, tears squeezing themselves relentlessly from the corners of her eyes until it was over.

And when it was, when the last groan had faded from his lips, and he had fallen back in the sweat-damp covers beside her, she opened her eyes to his dazzling face, and tried to convince herself that it was what she'd wanted, too.

CHAPTER 6

2022

> *So, it's morning. Another day. Another beginning. Except it's not like they say. Things never look different in the morning.*

The cabin door bangs shut and I look up, shoving the book into my bag.

"Livs!"

Not Sean. I let my breath out in a rush. The black Defender was parked in the drive when I arrived an hour ago, but I haven't seen him yet. In fact, I've barely seen him all week. Behind me, the door to the back room is closed. I haven't been able to will myself to open it; I have no idea whether he's there or not. Judging by the pattern of the week so far, it seems that, despite the presence of his immaculately tidy desk opposite mine, Sean Lorchann doesn't work in company.

"How are you?" Katie comes to offer a friendly hug. "How's everything? Are you settling in?"

"Oh. Yeah." I muster a smile. "Busy. You know . . ."

"Trethallyan Edge." Katie's looking at the desk. "Did Sean get the ancient monuments thing sorted?"

"Yeah." I drop my gaze to the chaos of maps and notes.

"That's good." She makes a beeline for the spare desk and starts to unload things from her briefcase. "Did he get the stuff I left him okay?"

I nod. The cabin door opens again, letting in a gust of rain and wind. Ryan slams it behind him, peeling off a sodden waterproof.

"Is he still planning to meet with Graham tomorrow?" Katie slides the world's smallest laptop from her bag and opens it, glancing back at me as the screen powers into life.

"I don't know. He hasn't really told me."

Anything. He hasn't told me anything; we've barely exchanged a sentence since Trethallyan Edge and English Heritage. So much for supervision. So much for *I will push you*. Yeah, right. Over a cliff, perhaps.

I grit my teeth. In the last week, I haven't once left the cabin before seven. I've memorised every detail; I know the background of the site down to the nanometre. Boundaries, accesses, ancient monuments and their historic relevance, ecological surveys, ground investigation, services and connections, the exact route of the public footpath that transects the plot. I know the year the chapel was built in and by whom, the footprint of the building that was there before; that there's a cellar underneath which was used in the war as an air-raid shelter, that it was only consecrated afterwards. I can suggest three different ways of making it work to the development restrictions, and two different ways of getting around every problem.

Ryan shrugs. "Welcome to the club," he tells me from the doorway. I blink. He shakes his head, amused. "He doesn't tell me much, either."

"Right." I smile, and tap the keyboard to stir my computer back into life. The screen brightens, then freezes. I glower at it. The invigoration of my early-morning run has quickly faded. The glare of the screen is already threatening to make my head ache. I fiddle with a strand of my hair, forcing myself to turn my focus back to my work.

"I set up Fin's trampoline yesterday." Ryan grins boyishly at no one in particular. "Awesomest thing ever."

"Nice." Katie nods her approval without looking up.

Fin. Another question I have, as yet, failed to ask. Their son, presumably. Sean's nephew. I look up at Ryan, putting together the words, but he speaks first.

"Is Sean here?" Apparently, he can no longer refrain from mentioning the elephant that isn't in the room. Katie glances up and I feel my face turn red.

"Uh. Yeah. I think so." I keep my gaze fixed studiously on the laptop and hit CTRL-ALT-DEL a couple of times. The screen turns black and I jab the *on* button angrily. There's a crackle of static.

I clutch at the edges of my chair.

There's a bird. There, on the screen. Black-brown, sharp-billed. My arm shoots out on reflex for the mouse, and in a split second it's gone. Almost fast enough that I could have imagined it.

I let out a tremulous breath. The logon screen has loaded as normal. I depress the *f* key with my index finger, unreasonably shaky. Ryan hasn't noticed. He's crouched down thumbing through the filing cabinet in the corner. No one has noticed; Katie is immersed in her work. On the computer in front of me, the LMLA emblem monograms itself into the digital backdrop. I move the cursor gingerly. Nothing.

I definitely saw it. It was a photo; either I'm crazy or it's somewhere on the computer. According to the clinic, I'm not crazy. They were convinced enough to discharge me. Defiantly rational, I click through to the C-drive and open the search bar.

"Quickly!"

My hand jerks on the mouse.

"Inside, go on!"

For a third time, the door bangs, the accompanying scurry and scuffle jolting me back to reality. Cold air swirls through the open doorway, heralding two sets of hurrying feet. Raindrops scatter across Katie's desk.

"Go on! Don't stop in the . . . There we go. Don't forget to wipe your feet. Hi, everyone!"

I look up in time to see Claire throw back her hood and stoop to plant a kiss on Ryan's lips as he straightens. Beside her, the small, accompanying, blue-cagouled figure stumbles and stops. Water drips from the child's coat and onto the carpet.

"Hi, Katie. Hi, Livs!" Claire's a whirlwind of flawless skin and immaculate clothes, all modest smiles and dimples, oblivious to the lingering tension in the muted air. Or perhaps it's only me that's tense. She steps back and crouches down to unzip the child's cagoule, unearthing a shock of blond hair and a glimmer of pale skin. The raincoat falls to the floor with a rustle. She gathers him into a brief, untidy hug, and kisses the top of his head as she stands. "Say hi, Fin!"

Fin doesn't say hi. He doesn't say anything. He slips free of Claire's hold and crosses the room.

"I can't believe he's four already." Claire is bursting with pride. "I thought I'd bring him to meet you, Livs, before we go to his appointment, while he's not at school."

"It's nice to meet you, Fin," I say . He doesn't seem to hear.

"What time does he have to be there?" Ryan turns to frown at her. "Don't you need to go?"

I'm not really listening. My eyes follow Fin as he reaches Sean's empty desk, and clambers adeptly onto the chair. He's a beautiful child, in an insubstantial sort of way. Sunshine fair, ethereal, vague: the wandering inhabitant of a daydream. I watch as he leans forwards precariously onto the smooth, empty table-top, studying something at the back of the desk, the computer chair threatening to wheel out backwards from underneath him. I shift anxiously.

"Oh—" Claire notices, before I feel obliged to intervene. She hurries over and catches the chair.

"I don't think Uncle Sean's working at his desk today, Fin." She helps him down and takes him by the hand to lead him back towards Ryan. "He must be busy in the other room. We'll have to see him later. Would you like that?"

Fin nods once. He doesn't speak.

I look at the swinging computer chair, uncomfortable. Not working at his desk today? So he does, usually?

I fiddle with the loose button on my shirt cuff. Usually, except for the last four days, and the three that he hasn't been in the cabin at all.

"Oh." Claire pauses. "Do you think I need to take the appointment letter? Maybe I should pop back up to the house and get it." She tries unsuccessfully to usher Finbar in the direction of the filing cabinet. "Fin, show Daddy what you did this morning, while I go back to the house. What did you write?"

"What did you write, dude?" Ryan deposits his armful of files onto the top of the cabinet. But Fin isn't looking. He's let go of Claire's hand and drifted away, turning in a full circle to take in the details of the room. He wraps his arms around himself tightly.

"Hello, Fin." Katie's voice is warm. "How are you?"

Fin regards her uncertainly. Stops turning, and stares, arms hugging his chest. Katie smiles at him. He doesn't react.

Claire shakes her head.

"Sorry. He's had a bit of a rocky morning. I'll be back in a second."

I blink as the door closes behind her, realising suddenly that I must have been staring, too. Finbar is standing statue still. I'm probably not much of a judge, but he seems very small. So slight, like there's nothing to him. His blond hair is dishevelled, haphazard, a wispy, flyaway nest of pale gold that sticks out in all directions from his head. His chin is pointed, his lips very red. And his eyes . . . there's something unusual about his eyes. They're startlingly dark brown in contrast to his milky skin: distant, distracted, and full of dreams. He seems focussed somewhere else entirely. Very slowly, he unwraps his arms. Then he glances down at his fingers, as if his own action has surprised him.

"Fin!" Ryan holds out a hand at waist level. "Dude, come on, high five. Did you go on the trampoline without me?"

Fin starts and looks up, turning wide, oddly lucent eyes on his father. For a moment he doesn't move. Then he holds out one skinny arm, and claps palms with Ryan.

"That's the one!" Ryan grins. "Here," he fetches Sean's empty chair for Fin to sit up beside him. "You want to see what I've been doing?"

Fin shakes his head. He hugs himself again, unblinking and silent. I watch him chew his bottom lip. He's wearing school uniform, royal blue and grey, the sweatshirt at least two sizes too big. I try to think what I remember from being four years old. Not much. Jumping in puddles, the school bookcase, Kicking King and Curly Cat. Sunny Saturdays. Finbar doesn't look like he's ever jumped in puddles.

"Okay. Fair enough," Ryan laughs. "Go on then, why don't you go and say hi to Livs?" I glance up, surprised at the mention of my name. Ryan leans forwards to whisper, not very quietly, in Fin's ear.

"You know how you just started at your new school? Well Livs has just started at her new work here. And she doesn't know anyone, either. So it would be really nice of you if you'd say hi to her." He holds up a hand, fingers close together, and gestures a wave.

Fin's gaze travels solemnly from his father's face to my seat, assessing me dubiously. I freeze.

"Go on," Ryan encourages.

Fin takes a single step, and then stops. I smile, awkward.

"Hi, Fin," I offer quietly.

Silence. Fin's eyes narrow a fraction, reminding me for an absurd moment of Sean's forbidding scrutiny. For some fathomless reason, I'm holding my breath.

He releases his lip from his teeth. Hesitates. Looks down at himself, at the embroidered logo on his blue jumper. The inhabitant of a dream, about to be captured in a classroom. A character from *Peter Pan*, a Lost Boy . . .

I remember *Peter Pan*. My father read it to me when I was the same age as Fin. And I read it back to him when he was too weak to read, too tired to write, left with barely enough energy even to imagine. When only a few, numbered heartbeats stood between him and his Neverland.

Fin looks back up at me. Up, before I'm ready, at the uninvited prickle of tears in my eyes. He frowns.

My breath has stuck in my throat. There's something in his expression. Something too solemn, too appraising for a four-year-old. Something that sends a chill along my spine. Very slowly, he moves forwards and holds up his hand. I can feel them watching, both Ryan and Katie. No one's speaking. For some reason, my throat is dry as I hold my hand out, too. Fin's palm contacts mine with a stinging smack.

"High five," I croak.

Fin's fingers press into mine, small and slightly sticky. I swallow.

"Alright, matey." Eventually, Ryan comes to join us, ruffling Fin's golden hair affectionately. "We need to find your mum. You're going to be late if she doesn't get back down here soon."

Fin looks at his jumper, pulling it to examine the logo on the front again as Ryan turns his blue cagoule the right way in for him and zips him back up.

"Say bye, now." Ryan spreads out his fingers and waves goodbye. After a brief hesitation, Fin copies him. Then they're gone.

For a moment, the room falls quiet. I look back at my screen, eyes still smarting. I dash a hand across them, trying not to look like I'm blinking too hard. Katie's voice makes me jump.

"Well, *someone* hit it off with Fin."

"Hmm?" I glance up in surprise.

"He really liked you." She leans back in her chair, regarding me thoughtfully. "That's pretty good going, for Fin."

"Oh." I'm blushing, awkward. "I don't know why." I look down at the laptop quickly, picking at the corner of the keyboard. "I'm no good with kids."

"You say that from experience?" Katie raises her eyebrows.

Livia, be a darling . . .

The muscles in my abdomen clench.

All I can think of is an open window. The second star to the right, and straight on 'til morning. Never growing up.

"Kind of," I whisper.

* * *

Today, for the first time since I came here, the sun rose. For the first time in a long time. I walked along the seafront in the dawn. There's a different kind of air at dawn.

I said I'd tell you everything. I guess I've been deliberating over where to start. The beginning was, by all accounts, completely unexpected, in a hospital car park, two weeks before Christmas. There was snow on the ground; I've always loved snow. I was an only child. I never learned to ride a bike. I went to an all-girls' school, and played the clarinet badly. I could run faster than the boys in my road. I always had an irrational fear of enclosed spaces I still have to close my eyes when I ride on the Underground. My parents split up when I was thirteen. It's amazing, how quickly you learn not to be a child. I learned to study, instead. I learned to close doors. I learned that, without an outlet, a soul is a terrifying thing. So I tried to live without one, for a while. I traded my innocence to try and fill the space. I thought I'd find something to live for. But you can't live without a soul.

Yesterday, I got ID'd for buying razor blades. Who gets ID'd for buying razor blades? Children and crazy people, I think. I'd like to tell you that I'm nearer the former, but I'm too old now to get ID'd for razor blades.

It's taken a long time to start opening the doors. But against all odds, here in Porthtrevelen, I'm learning to breathe again. In the dawn light, in this journal. Whatever I write, papercuts don't leave lasting scars. Evidently the pen is mightier than the blade.

It's so hard to choose, isn't it? Between the pleasure and the pain. And oh, it hurts. It hurts so perfectly. You can't turn on a light without casting shadows. But if you keep the light ahead of you — just keep walking — your shadow will only ever fall behind . . .

A shadow has fallen over my desk. I feel it, rather than see it. Katie left an hour ago, and I thought I was alone.

But I'm not alone. A shiver runs the length of my spine. I shut the journal.

Sean Lorchann crosses the floor with a tread so soft that it's almost soundless. His eyes alight for a moment on my screen. I close down the search bar and turn. His arms are folded.

"The chapel." He scans the strewn-out pages of my untidy handwriting from a distance. I nod, mute. He unfolds his arms. He's lost the suit jacket today. I glance over my shoulder. Scrub that; I can see it through the doorway, hanging on the back of his chair in the back room, where he's been working instead of at his desk.

Are you avoiding everyone, or just me? The words are on the tip of my tongue. I bite them back. I have the uneasy feeling that I already know the answer. Sean comes to a halt beside me.

"Those are the survey drawings?"

"Yes." I clear my throat.

"Good." He reaches to flick the plans out from under the rest of the melee of paperwork. His dark eyes skim over the mess to my face, and stop. I withdraw my hand from the top sheet quickly.

"Don't waste your time doing any more." His gaze rests briefly on my smarting cheeks. "I'll take it from here."

What? I suck in a slow breath.

"I've just spoken to my father. There's an intern opening in Oxford. With Peter McLeod." He turns the paper over to look at the back of it. Not at me. "One fifty a month more than you're getting here. It would have been very competitive, but they haven't advertised yet and Peter's agreed to take you without re-interviewing."

Outrage knots in my abdomen. I hold the breath deep in my lungs, incapable of reply, and try to blink away the vision of bracken, sunset, sand. The half-finished painting in my bay window. Sean hasn't moved. He's waiting. For what? For me to thank him? To put Trethallyan Edge in his hand, and relinquish, just like that? Because he can't stand me? Screw that. I draw myself up straight.

"I didn't apply to work in Oxford," I say.

There's an uncomfortable pause.

"I'm sorry?" The edge in his voice is unmistakable.

"I don't care about the money." I look up, straight into his unforgiving stare, and lose my voice. "I . . ." It emerges as a whisper. "I thought you said I didn't get to be average."

A conflict of expressions crosses his face. The silence widens between us. Sean's jaw clenches. He lays one hand lightly on the desk and I glance down, despite myself, to see his fingers drum once on the fibreglass. My pulse is racing. He picks up the plans.

"Fine." His voice is quiet, articulated: it cuts through the air like a whip. I look up at his face in disbelief. For a split second, he looks back at me in absolute silence. Then he turns on his heel and walks away.

I wait, frozen, as the door to the back room closes. Fine? I'm shaking. What does he mean, *fine*? The plans are gone. The rest of the notes are still spread unapologetically across every inch of my desk.

"Hey." I didn't hear Katie get back. She stops in the doorway to shake off her dripping umbrella. "Are you okay, Livia?" She must have caught sight of the look on my face.

"Yeah," I lie. I stare at the notes for a second more. "I just need to get my lunch from my car. It needs to go in the fridge." I slide to my feet. Make for the door and duck outside, rain striking the side of my face and running down my neck. I don't have any lunch in my car. Clinic rules 4 and 6 are both out the window. *Make a meal plan. Don't lie about food*. I stride out between the rhododendrons with my hands clenched hard in my pockets. It hasn't even got properly light. I push my way through the bushes, and almost trip over a stone slab.

I stoop, parting decades of ivy with my fingers. There are three stones sticking up from the damp earth. *Marly*. *Chief*. *Rigger*. Graves, three graves. I trace my index finger over the weathered writing, a hollow sadness catching me off guard as I think of Dad's old pointer, Tess, and those last few weeks after the funeral, before Kris and Mum made a final trip to the vet to end her misery. For some reason, my throat is hurting. I walk on quickly.

By the time I get back to the cabin, I'm drenched. The rain's getting harder, bouncing off the roof tiles and raging into the gutters. Katie is scribbling furiously as I let myself in, her phone tucked under her chin. She gives me a tight smile as I head for my desk. I get halfway, and then realise that I don't have anything to do. I walk purposefully to the water dispenser.

"Why is this such a problem to you?"

I glance up. The door to the back room is closed, but Ryan's muffled voice is unmistakable. I take a plastic cup, trying not to listen.

"It's not." Sean, his voice clipped and short. "I'm dealing with it."

"Seriously?"

"I told you. I said I didn't want another girl. Especially not someone so fucking young. I don't know why I bothered."

A snort. Ryan.

"Livs is a graduate. She's only five or six years younger than you."

I freeze. Stare at the door, motionless, cup in hand.

"Well, it matters! What exactly are you trying to pull, Ryan?"

"Not me. It's nothing to do with me, is it? She's Lorchann McLeod's. It was Peter's call. You might be everyone's blue-eyed boy at the moment, but it's him that has the say so, Sean. And he said so."

"I need talent on this, someone who can pull their weight. Not—"

"Not what? You know Livs will soon be as qualified as you are."

"Huh." It's scathing. "Qualified. Not experienced."

"Experienced?" I hear Ryan's smirk, and shove the cup forcefully under the water dispenser, willing it to fill faster as sullen bubbles rise and glug to the surface. My face is on fire. I'm suddenly not sure what would be worse, walking back to my desk under Katie's watchful eye, or hearing the rest of it. I stand absolutely still, trying to block it out.

"Fuck it, Ryan. This was important!"

"You read the CVs. If you didn't make it to the interviews, that's up to you."

"I made my feelings clear about them even *getting* another intern down here. It's a project, not an office. I'm not a fucking university tutor."

"Well, Peter McLeod wanted another intern, and so did Dad. And they wanted her here. So she's all yours."

"Thanks. That's great. Really great."

"Sean. Cut the crap, please. Take away your big head and your fancy awards, and you're barely five years out of internship yourself. You're only doing any of this because of *who* you are. Give her a chance to prove herself. Peter liked her — thought she had flair. Our father liked her enough to convince Graham and me. She's top of her class from Nottingham. I'd have been stupid to disagree."

"Bullshit. There were two dozen good applicants. I read the CVs, remember? We both know who convinced who, and why."

"I'm a happily married man, Sean. It's you with the track record."

"That's shit and you know it."

"It didn't used to be."

"Things change. Maybe I'm the only one around here who does, but *I* want to keep things professional."

"Is that what you told your last intern?"

"Don't fucking go there."

"I'm sorry. I didn't mean—"

"I *said* don't go there."

"Fine. Okay. But like I said, Sean, cut the crap—"

The door-handle plunges suddenly, depressed from the other side. With barely a second's warning, it opens. Ryan's feet thunder on the stairs. I stand, trapped, rooted to the spot, ice-cold water soaking into my shirt cuff. He reaches the bottom and stops. For a fraction of a second, a look of uncertainty crosses his face. I gaze back at him, cheeks aflame.

"Alright, Livs?" With admirable smoothness, Ryan recovers his cool. He flashes me a comradely smile and then disappears, the cabin door banging closed behind him.

I drain the water from the cup, and sit back down at my desk with a painful bump. The laptop screen is blank. I flick the mouse, and nothing happens. Perfect. It's crashed again. Apparently it's as keen to work with me as everyone else. I glare at it.

"Livs?" Katie's voice is soft. I turn.

"Are you . . ." She pauses. "Do you need a hand with anything?"

I shake my head. "No, thanks." I start to gather together the notes from my desk. I'm probably not going to need them in Oxford.

"You made quite an impression earlier."

"Huh?" I glance up.

"With Fin. I knew it." Katie slips her phone into her pocket. "Claire's just texted me to see what happened. Ryan couldn't believe it."

"Oh." I lower the papers slowly. "I don't know why. He didn't actually *speak* to me."

Katie looks at me for a moment.

"He doesn't," she says at last.

"What?"

"Speak. Fin doesn't speak." She pulls a folder from her bag and lays it down on her desk. "That's what his appointments are about. They don't know whether it's that he can't, or he just won't. But he doesn't."

"Oh." I frown.

"He's . . . I don't know." She shakes her head. "Not quite like other four-year-olds. Troubled."

Troubled? I think of the dreams in his clear, dark eyes. Four years old. Different, yes. But troubled?

"They only moved back from Dubai with him six months ago. I guess it's been a lot for him. He was just a baby when they moved over there." She shrugs. "I didn't know Claire that well, then. I hadn't seen her since we were at school. But it must have been a lot of upheaval."

"Mm." I'm not sure why I can't make myself agree.

"I'd better get this finished." For a moment, Katie's eyes rest on my face. "I have a couple more calls to make, and I need to get back to Truro this evening."

"Sure."

I listen to the sound of her dial tone, my desk moving in a haze beneath my eyes. *We need talent on this, someone who can pull their weight. Not—*

Not me. He hadn't needed to say it.

The truth is, I have no idea. I have no idea what I'm supposed to be doing. Whether I'm meant to be carrying on, or going home and packing. Short of bursting into the back room and asking for clarification, I'm at a loss. And I'm not in a hurry to voluntarily present myself to Sean Lorchann.

I turn off the laptop. After a second's deliberation, I mount the steps onto the mezzanine. I turn on the lamp over the drawing boards and take out the tray of drafting pencils.

By five, the worst of my misery has subsided. Engrossed, I barely notice Ryan come and go, and it's not until Katie's light touch startles me out of my rapt sketching-induced reverie that I realise it's got dark.

"You should go home, Livia." Her smile is sympathetic. Her eyes fall, fleetingly, on what I've been doing. She glances back at me. "Don't let the Lorchanns get under your skin. Either of them."

Either of them? Only one of them is an issue.

"Oh, I won't." I smile back bravely. "Thanks."

"Really." She touches my shoulder. "If Sean can't see how much you've got to offer, that's *his* loss. Don't let it be yours."

I nod, not quite sure what to say. Her touch on my shoulder transitions from friendly to awkward. Katie lowers her hand.

"See you tomorrow, Livia."

"Night," I murmur.

My head aches. I blink and pick up the pencil again as she disappears into the winter darkness. The sensation of the strokes is soothing. Two different ways of getting around every problem. Three different ways of making it work to the development restrictions. Four different elevations, sketched, cross-hatched, shaded . . . The receding noise of Katie's car fades distantly in the drive. I listen to the silence. It sounds like the rain might have stopped. I rub my cheek, and then realise that the side of my hand is covered in shiny graphite.

She was right. I should go home. I unclip the sketches. Maybe now that they're out of my head I'll find it easier to draw a line under the whole sorry episode. Maybe Oxford is what I need. Sensible. Nearer home.

Average.

There's pencil on my face. I rub at it again, distracted, and roll my sketches into a cylinder, pulling the elastic tie from my hair to fasten them so that I can carry them home. A curtain of unruly curls falls over my eyes. I flick it back, and start.

How long he's been there, I just can't tell. Suit jacket and Levi's, framed in the doorway. I hadn't even realised he was still in the building. Sean closes the door with a soft click.

"I expect you in for eight tomorrow," he says.

I open my mouth, and then close it again.

"To go through the brief. With Gordon-Heyers." His eyes alight darkly on mine. I tighten my hands around the paper tube. Stare at him in disbelief.

"We're meeting at the Hall, not here. Don't be late."

A thousand thoughts race through my head. Questions. But before I can formulate a reply, he's gone, shrugging on his coat and dematerialising into the darkness.

I wait a long time before I venture out after him. It's a relief to discover that my car is the only one left in the driveway. I drive back at a snail's pace, my eyes poorly adjusted to the pitch black of the rural landscape; in Nottingham it had never been dark.

Late is exactly what it is by the time I turn on the lampshade-less light of number thirty-one and toss my drawings onto the unmade bed. The unfinished impressions of the clifftop at Trethallyan are nothing more than a green-blue colour chart on my easel. I move to inhale the smell of the drying oils. *Passion.*

On sudden, breathless impulse I open the fridge and swipe the bottle of white that Jen, my housemate, gave me when I left Nottingham. I fling open the flat door and descend the stairs, Kris-style. The door to 29a opens before I've even knocked.

"You are falling, or visiting?" Niklavs appears vaguely alarmed. I blush.

"Visiting," I clarify.

He stands back with a smile.

"Then perhaps purpose of your visit is that you do not have glass?" He's looking at the bottle.

I bite my lip. "I do." I look at it too. "I'll fetch them, if you like."

"No, no." Niklavs' lips twitch. "I have glass also. You are welcome to use."

"It's to share." I hold up the wine. "I'm celebrating. I hoped you might join me. And I wanted to thank you for the help, and the kettle."

"So this is party?" He's amused. "Although I think it is in fact *you* are joining *me*?"

"Oh." I glance around his flat. It's not very warm inside. The fire isn't lit today. There's an open window high in the wall at the other end of the kitchen letting in an eddy of cold air, and a cat curled up on one of the fireside chairs. "I guess I am. Do you want to come to mine instead?"

Niklavs shakes his head. "No, I think not. We can celebrate here. We are celebrating what, exactly?"

"Stubborn pig-headedness."

"Job is going well?" He raises his eyebrows.

"Brilliant." I pull a face.

"You have met Graham Gordon-Heyers?"

I shake my head. "Only his daughter and son-in-law. And the architect."

A fleeting frown creases Niklavs' forehead. I look at him in surprise.

"Do you know them?"

He shakes his head. "Rumour only. From what I have heard, apart from hospital, Gordon-Heyers leaves estate very little, these days. Must be much neglect there, now. Even twenty years ago things starting to fall into disrepair. Very sad."

"Yeah." I glance at him, uncertain. An awful lot seems to get shared by rumour in this place.

Niklavs shrugs. "You want to drink wine, or not?"

"Oh." I turn my attention to the bottle. It's corked. Great. Now he's going to think I've only turned up for a corkscrew.

"Here." Niklavs holds out his hand. "Let me."

I pass it to him without protest. He moves through to the kitchen.

"You went for jog early today."

I smile. "I don't jog," I retort softly as he sets to work on the bottle. "I run."

"I see." Niklavs smiles too, extracting the cork with a gentle pop. "I get up at five. And already you are returning."

"Do you ever *sleep*?" I accept a glass of wine from him, and perch on the edge of his table.

Niklavs grins. "Do you? I, no, not much. I have less life left than you; I must make best of it, not sleep time away."

"You're not that old," I tell him. "And I'm not that young."

"You are baby." Niklavs smirks. "My daughter's daughter soon be your age."

"How long have you lived here?" I sip my wine, curious. Niklavs peers into his glass.

"Here, at Sunnyside, three years almost."

"Did you say you moved to Porthtrevelen forty years ago?" Thinking about it, perhaps that does make him older than I'd thought. "What made you leave Latvia?"

A cloud crosses Niklavs' face. "Mm. Good reason, bad reason." He shrugs, but I can't help noticing that he doesn't quite look back at me. "Long time has passed now. Everything much changed there since then."

"Yeah." I nod. Don't I know how quickly things change?

"You run cliff path?" Niklavs diverts back to our original subject. He's drained his glass with startling speed.

I nod. "Mmhm."

"How far?"

"Five miles."

"You cut five minutes off time, this morning," he observes. I glance up at him, surprised.

"Forty-one twenty-six." I agree, embarrassed.

"Impressive run. Path is steep." He nods. "You run in Nottingham?"

"I grew up in Cumbria." I look back at my half-empty glass. "I did a lot of fell running there with my father. Hills, crags . . ." I shrug, suddenly keen to change the subject too. "You know."

"Not ballet dancer, then." Niklavs puts down his glass with a smile. "Runner. That explains it . . . You know, if you extend route half-mile past rocks at Witch's Cat, there is path on right that cuts back directly through woods to bottom of next road. I walk it in past." He stands up and moves to root in the back of one of the sitting-room shelves. "I show you on map."

"Witch's Cat?" I frown.

"Formation of rocks, mile or two northeast of where promenade ends. Quite distinctive shape. Like angry cat."

He shoots a glance at the mound of tabby fur sleeping in his chair, and unfolds a tattered OS map onto the table. I slide to my feet to look at it with him. Niklavs points to a W-shaped cluster of grey blobs jutting out from the shoreline.

"Well-known place. Very beautiful. Good for painting, from clifftop. But not from rocks." He shakes his head. "Dangerous tides. Much like Trethallyan." He frowns. "Rips at Trethallyan have claimed more life than one since I live here. Anyway. Here. There is car park here, and track goes inland this way. If you pick up footpath here." He traces one brown finger over the dotted line.

"I see." I measure it with my eyes, following the route back down its contour into the edge of the town. "This is Sunnyside?"

Niklavs shakes his head. "The Slipway, here. Sunnyside from here."

"Ah, okay." I pause. I'm not quite sure where the question has come from, or why it matters. But suddenly I can't help myself.

"Niklavs." I look up, oddly hesitant. "Who lived in my flat before?"

The silence is tangible. In an instant, the cloud has fallen back over Niklavs' weathered face, a deep frown creasing between his brows. He withdraws his hand from the map and folds it without looking at me.

"Girl, your age." He shrugs stiffly. "I did not know her well." He moves quickly to replace the map in the bookcase, and for the first time since I've met him, I have the unsettling feeling that he's hiding something. "She was writer, I think. Kept herself to herself."

Life's all about the stories. The good ones, the bad ones. The ones that wake you, sobbing, sweating, praying for them to end . . .

Niklavs turns back, and for a split second his expression chills me: a strange, strained blankness. I swallow. In an instant, it's gone. He picks up the wine.

"Another drink, Livia?" He gestures to my glass, as if nothing's happened.

"Thanks," I whisper.

"You invite me to my own house," he jests lightly. "And I offer you your own wine. Good party."

"Yeah," I murmur.

Niklavs smiles.

"Now. Tell me about — how you call? Stubborn pig-headedness."

I don't. I don't tell him about Trethallyan Edge, or Sean Lorchann, or two different ways around every problem. I tell him about lines on paper. About vanishing points and curvilinear perspectives. And he tells me about mackerel fishing, and teaches me blackjack, and we evade each other's more probing questions, until the clouds outside the window break to reveal faltering stars and Niklavs gently points out that I need to sleep if I'm planning on getting up at five to run again.

I climb the stairs slowly, and deadlock my door. The uneasy feeling hasn't faded, despite Niklavs' general cheer and half a bottle of wine. My flat is freezing. I can't bring myself to undress. Instead, I climb under the covers fully clothed, pull the duvet up to my chin, and open Swift's book on my knees.

When I first came here, I was afraid.

I toy with the edge of the page. A girl, my age. Somehow I'd already known that. Somehow, I know more about her than either she or I would care to realise.

The paper is flimsy and creases easily, lined in faint blue with no margin. Her handwriting is effortless and stylish; I can imagine her writing it, engrossed in thought and lost in the flow of words. Not so different from my own sketched flow of ideas, and the smooth, soothing sensation of pencil-strokes. I frown.

Afraid of what I'd come looking for, of not finding it — my something to live for. Or even worse, of what would happen if I did find it. Afraid of the job, the empty flat, the streets after dark. Of the people, the place, of myself. I came for all the wrong reasons. I came because I couldn't forget. I came in search. I told you about the missing piece.

But every morning, I put on my face. The one that contained things. Until I started to forget to take it off again. Until the piece that was missing was a different shape, and I wasn't even sure it would fit.

Somehow, things slip past your guard. Things you never expected. A single word. An outstretched hand . . .

The image is vivid in front of me. A soundless step, a held-out hand small enough to fit completely inside my palm. Finbar's clear, otherworldly scrutiny, the ringing smack of skin on skin; *high five.* My lips half-form the words. I look down at the book.

It's hard, being unwanted. Isn't it? Unwelcome. It's impossible to escape when the only place for the fear to go is inward.

I suddenly realise I'm holding my breath, and let it out in a rush. No. Who wrote this? And how could they know? *Girl, your age.* How can she know about me? How can she know any of this? As if she's here . . . as if she's watching?

Ridiculous. I grit my teeth and blink away the blurred edges from my vision. I'm tired. It's late. I've drunk too much, again. There are dates on this. I flick back a page, to remind myself. *01/06/2021, 11/06/2021.* Months ago. Long before I came here. Long before I had ever even heard of Lorchann McLeod.

Is it my secret, or someone else's? I'm not sure. But there's a darkness here that I can't get away from. No matter how hard I try.

Darkness? I smooth the page and inhale sharply. Instead of Swift's handwriting, suddenly all I can see is a picture: a memory, vivid and impossible to blink back. And it isn't Finbar's dreamlike gaze that's staring into mine. It's someone else's completely, intense and forbidding. *I will push you. Hard.*

I grit my teeth and will it away, glance up into the mirror instead. For a fleeting second, she's there. Featureless, a form only, slim and pale, like me, her knees hugged to her chest beneath the covers, her indiscernible eyes locked back on me from the other side of the glass.

Maybe I brought my own shadows with me. Maybe I made that decision when I came here. Some things can't be undone. They can't be forgotten, only buried deeper. You have to choose. Choose to close the door. Choose not to let it out, the fear. To move forwards. There are different kinds of freedom. Freedom to, and freedom from. I haven't read that book in a long, long time, but the point stands. Never underestimate the power of freedom from.

She's still there, if you look hard enough. She's still there, in your memory, the girl in the grass and the dandelion stems. Can you see her? I never realised, but I think I can. If I close my eyes, I'm there . . . I can still run barefoot. I can still dance.

I can still hear birdsong.

CHAPTER 7

Birdsong. It spills from the trees, a dawn chorus. I slam the car door and run across the gravel. After the wine and the late night, I slept well. Too well — this is cutting it finer than I intended. For a change it isn't raining; there's actually sunshine, an amber-red warning light that burns between the pillars of the porch as I tiptoe up the steps and press the bell.

Silence. I shift on the spot. I can hear my watch ticking and my slightly too-fast breathing. A blackbird flies low across the drive behind me and alights on the bushes at the corner of the house, its bright eye fixed on me. I shiver.

"Livs!" Claire opens the door. From the gloom behind her, a pale, pointed face watches me like a ghost. Finbar tightens his arms around his chest and stumbles backwards, melting into the shadows.

"Come on in!" Claire plants a kiss in the air beside my cheek. "Daddy and Sean are already upstairs. They're in the reading room — first door on your left."

"Thanks." I gulp. Another flight of stairs. I'm breathless as I reach the top. I glance at my watch. Ten to eight. I'm okay. I run the last few paces to the wide oak door, and falter. There are voices coming from inside, muted and serious. I can't make out what they're saying.

Nine minutes to. I don't have time to lose my nerve. I make myself breathe out slowly, and grasp the brass doorknob.

It's somewhere between a conference room and a Victorian library. The rising sun streams in columns through the vertical blinds, and the walls are lined with books. A long table of polished dark wood stretches a good proportion of the floor, with a chess-board out of place at its far end. I close the door with a bump. Sean looks up.

"Frost." He inclines his head.

He's turned in his chair to face me, barely more than a silhouette. At the end of the table the man beside him has looked up too, an old man — no, a gentleman — his hair silk-silver and his tweed blazer too loose for his frame. Sean's eyebrows lift and I blush furiously.

Eight. He said eight. I glower at the clock on the angled screen of his laptop, and slip into the empty seat beside him. 07:52.

"It's good to meet you, Livia." Graham Gordon-Heyers rises to his feet. He's taller than I expected and broader in the shoulder — it's the rest of him that seems to have dwindled; his sleeves hang limply around his bony wrists and I can see all the sinews in his neck as he holds out a buckled hand. His fingers are crooked and spotted with age. I stumble to my feet and take them hesitantly. His grasp is surprisingly firm.

"I'm Graham." There's something shrewd in his calm blue eyes. He sits down again, and I do too, pulling my chair in close to the table.

"Hi." I have to clear my throat. "It's nice to meet you."

Sean closes the laptop with a snap and turns back to Graham, dark gaze level and serious. "You've given me a lot to work with."

Graham smiles wryly. "Not too much, I hope."

"Not at all."

"You haven't changed, Sean." The old man folds his hands on the table, and I catch myself looking at them again, gnarled, weakened — like the limbs of a tree that's borne the brunt of too much weather. I frown. There's a drafting pencil on the table. Familiar. *0.7 mm.* I let my fingertips stray to it as I listen, and roll it closer.

"And that's exactly why I asked your father to send you here. Trethallyan is in your blood. You grew up here as much as Claire did. *You* understand. I married Clarissa in that chapel. I want it to be the shrine it should have been. I want to stand there — where I stood with her forty years ago — and worship the view again. And if we—" He pauses. Every sinew in his neck and jaw has tensed, suddenly. He gets to his feet. "If we get her home again, I want to be able to take her there. To keep her there, where she can see it — our view — every day for as long as she lives. That's what I want."

Slowly, Sean nods. I see his eyes travel from Graham's clenched jaw to the colours of the new day outside the window. For a split second, something in his expression shifts. I can see it: the same gleam of excitement that replaced his frown on the clifftop at Trethallyan Edge.

"I'll do what I can," he murmurs.

There's silence. In front of the laptop, there's a pad of paper that I hadn't noticed before, a few words scrawled on it in black pen: numbers, thoughts. Sean drums his fingers on it lightly.

"It's going to be more complicated than the other work Peter and I have already done here. We're working within more restrictions, because of the site. But they passed the outline. Over the last few days, Livvy and I have gone back over everything." His eyes rest briefly on me. I twist the pencil in my fingers. *One wrong step away from a fuck-up.* I swallow, nervous.

"The potential—" Sean's gaze is still on me. My heart rate accelerates. Sweat has broken on my upper lip. "—even within those boundaries, is huge."

I let out my breath. A rectangle of dazzling sunshine is penetrating the slats of the vertical blind. I stare at the expectant air between them, trying not to frown. Sean is sitting very still, waiting. Graham hasn't spoken. I toy with the end of the pencil, engaging and retracting the graphite, remembering what Ryan said on my first day about Trethallyan Edge, and the way that Claire had shut off at the suggestion. We aren't on safe ground. And I can't help feeling like Sean knows it.

"Did you have any specific ideas . . ." Sean pauses. Our eyes meet. I put down the pencil. Then, very deliberately, he reaches past me and takes it. He retracts the tip, and lowers it to the page in front of him. ". . . of how you want it to look?"

"I'd like it if you could preserve something of the chapel." Graham is looking away, out of the far window where the plaintive keening of the seagulls has drowned out the chorus from the trees. "It holds . . . memories. Apart from that . . ." He shrugs. "We've discussed the budget. I know what Claire thinks, but I don't want it to be an issue."

A hint of a smile plays at the corner of Sean's mouth.

"Okay." He nods.

Silence again. My whole face is burning. The relentless attack of the sunlight is making my eyes water with a vengeance.

"Ryan wanted me to check with you," Sean rises smoothly to his feet and closes the blind, "that you've given full consideration to the work you might want to do on the Hall, and any financial implications, once building on the chapel site is finished."

He releases the blind cord. The table plunges into shadow, and I dash a hand across my eyes in relief.

"Of course I have." Graham turns back sharply. "You're an intelligent man, Sean. So's your brother. I've discussed this with him before. I'm not making any decisions now."

Another pause.

"No." Sean's nods. He moves, catlike, to sit back down at the table beside me. "I understand."

It's a good thing *he* does. I don't. I squint at the pad of paper, trying to make out his scribbled writing in the semi-darkness. I don't understand any of it: the sense of foreboding, the unsaid words. I sink backwards into my chair, wishing I could vanish into the shadows like Finbar. What had Sean meant, one step away from a fuck-up? A point of contention? And more to the point, why didn't I take the one piece of advice he offered me, and accept the job in Oxford?

I could have been out of here by now. I could have been packing my bags, and salvaging what little remained of my self-respect before he obliterates it with another well-aimed, biting remark.

". . . to show you. Livvy had started some sketches."

What? I glance up in alarm. My attention must have wandered. I haven't been listening. Sean pushes the drafting pencil into the inside pocket of his jacket. Waiting. He's waiting. I stare at him in horror. "I . . . uh—"

"Hadn't you?" His gaze meets mine squarely. And I realise. Four different elevations, outlined, cross-hatched, shaded. Suit jacket and Levi's silhouetted in the doorway.

"Yes — No—" I'm a rabbit in headlights, trapped between the two of them. "I mean, I . . . I don't have them here . . . They weren't accurate. I . . ."

Sean's eyebrows flicker upwards. He doesn't speak. I realise I'm biting my lip, and release it quickly.

"But I can . . . I mean, I'll—"

Sean turns back to Graham. "You'll know as soon as we have something to show you."

"I appreciate it, Sean." Graham holds out his hand. "I can't tell you how glad I am your father's released you to be down here to work on this. Please thank him for me."

"Of course." In a heartbeat, Sean's on his feet too, and they grasp hands, firm and uncompromising and so strikingly reminiscent of the boardroom handshake in the glossy Lorchann McLeod brochure that I have to suppress an unprecedented urge to roll my eyes.

"I'll be at the hospital." Graham is buttoning his blazer. I jump up hastily as he tucks his chair back under the end of the polished table. "Thank you, Sean. Livia." He inclines his head in my direction. The door creaks as he pushes it open and disappears. After a beat, Sean follows him out, and very suddenly I'm alone.

I don't quite dare to sit down again. I glance around at the half-dark silence, the tiny, almost illegible shapes of Sean's handwriting staring up at me from the notepad.

Everything in this room feels old. There must be thousands of books. Maybe it's their weight that lays so heavily in the muted air, I'm not sure. I drift away from the table to run one hand over the faded spines, looking at the other oddities balanced on the shelves: an old clay pipe, a dusty fossil, a few black-and-white pictures in heavy frames.

I stop dead.

At the end of the shelf, something has caught my eye. I reach out to pick it up with the same uneasy feeling that I couldn't shake last night. A polaroid photo, its colours dulled with age, fitted poorly in a wooden frame. Beside a much sturdier and smiling-eyed Graham Gordon-Heyers, the chiselled, weather-beaten face is disconcertingly familiar.

Niklavs was good-looking, as a younger man.

"You'd really be better off working with Peter."

Shit. I drop the photo back on the shelf with a crash. I didn't even hear the door open. How does he keep doing that? My nerves are shot. I try to gather them and fail miserably. Sean Lorchann strides across the floor towards me, then stops, as if he's changed his mind.

"I'm okay. Thanks." I draw myself upright.

Sean regards me in silence. The vertical shadows of the blind fall across his face.

"I'm not sure what I've got to offer you," he says at last.

I step back to the safety of the table.

"I'll take what's going," I tell him.

The stare becomes a frown. I watch him lay his hand on the table. What is it about the way he looks at me that puts my pulse into double time? I draw a deep breath.

"I've been honest with you." His teeth are gritted. "You'd be better off with Peter. He's very used to mentoring interns. And I don't know that I'm the most . . . appropriate person for you to work with." His fingers are on the edge of the notepad. "I usually work alone."

"Right." I narrow my eyes.

"This . . . this estate," he traces his handwriting with one fingertip, "it's not an easy place to work."

And why's that? I bite back the words. Stand absolutely still and try to ignore the rush of blood in my ears.

"I never got anywhere by taking the easy option before." My words are even, measured, and I don't have any idea where they're coming from. I feel like I'm listening to myself from a distance. Sean has paused, unsmiling. It's hard to say if he's ever really smiled in his life.

"Bring the sketches back," he says suddenly.

"What?" It slips out unchecked.

Sean raises his eyebrows. "I can't mentor you without seeing your work."

Oh. I look up at him, wordless.

"They . . . They were only rough," I whisper.

"I can do rough." His gaze is locked on mine, totally unreadable. "If I have to."

A shiver runs down my spine.

"Okay." The oddest sensation has taken hold in my chest. An unsettling, electrifying feeling that we might not be talking about the same thing.

Sean shakes his head. Flips open the laptop and swings himself back into the chair without another word, crossing his long legs under the table. The laptop hums decisively into life. I start for the door, almost falling over my own feet.

"Frost . . ."

I spin.

"Don't forget what I said. About the dream." There's something disturbingly perceptive in his glance. "Getting screwed over is reality."

"Yeah," I breathe. "I'm starting to see that."

"The point is, if you're good, it doesn't matter." He reaches up and plucks the pencil from his jacket pocket. I watch him lay it back down beside the pad, where it started.

"No, I guess not." My throat is unreasonably tight.

I hesitate at the door.

"My name's Livi*a*," I tell him with as much acidity as I can muster.

Sean Lorchann's eyebrows flicker.

"I know," he says.

* * *

01/07/2021

I'm still here. I'm sorry it's been so long. I'm sorry I haven't written. I haven't forgotten. A lot has happened. That's why I thought I'd bring you with me, tonight, here. The ocean is incredibly beautiful. I'd like to say that's why I've come. But it isn't. I'd like to say I'd come for inspiration, for work. For anything, other than the truth.

"Livs?"

I look up quickly.

"I'm popping out." Katie is beside my desk. "I told Claire I'd bring back fish and chips from town. Do you want anything?"

"Um." I glance around at the empty cabin. The sky outside has clouded over, blotting out the invasive Friday morning sunshine, and a few not-quite-committed raindrops are blowing in a flurry across the windows. "No, thanks. I brought lunch with me."

"She's really pissed. Ryan's had to go and fetch Fin from school because his teacher thinks he has chickenpox. How was your meeting?"

As if on cue, the door opens. I look up, uncomfortable. Claire's on the phone, face tense.

"Uhm." My stomach tightens into a knot. I shift. "It was fine."

"How was Sean?"

I glare at my hands. "For someone so taciturn, he's *incredibly* arrogant." I can't quite repress the outburst. Katie snorts. From the other side of the room, even Claire smiles. I suddenly remember the back room, and glance nervously at the closed door, as if there's a way he might have heard.

"Oh, I don't bloody know." I pick crossly at the corner of my keyboard's burnished *s* key. There's something reassuring in the tiny, amused shake of Katie's head. Maybe it's not just me.

"Are you sure you don't want anything, Livs?" She roots in her bag for her purse.

"No," I shake my head. "I'm good, thanks."

Katie shoots a look over her shoulder, to where Claire is still muttering into her phone. She lowers her voice.

"Livia, we should talk about stuff." Her gaze is meaningful. "Later on. If you want to."

Stuff? I shiver. Then it occurs to me that she probably overheard the cut-the-crap conversation too, and that she might be able to fill in the gaps. The last intern. *Don't fucking go there.*

"I'd better go." She stands up quickly. "What's your number? I'll call you from town if I get held up. Here, write it on here." She pushes a diary into my hands, open to the back page. I scribble at the bottom of the scrawled list of other numbers and pass it back. It's only as she takes it that I catch sight of something out of context. Handwriting. A name? I freeze, unease reclaiming a momentary stranglehold around my throat.

"Awesome." Katie closes the diary with a snap and pushes it into her bag. "I'll see you in a bit."

"See you." I'm imagining things. I spent too much time reading the journal last night in the dark, with the covers over my head.

Claire is still talking. The melodious rise and fall of her voice washes over me as I sit and stare at my laptop. No blackbirds today. No swifts. Nothing unexpected. Not even an unread email.

I can't stop myself from wondering. Who she was, what she did . . . why she lived in my flat. How she knew what it was like, how she could spell out the words from my head when she'd never even met me. A writer, Niklavs said. A journalist, perhaps? Or an author? I wonder what happened to her. Where she is now. Whether she's still here, in Porthtrevelen.

I open the web browser on impulse, hit Google and type in her name, then realise instantaneously what a ridiculous idea it is as a page of birds, caravans and financial telecommunications companies takes over my screen. I backtrack. *Swift, Porthtrevelen.*

Nothing. Car adverts. A boat for sale. What did I think I was going to get? I close the browser quickly. Stupid.

"Livs?"

Claire's standing behind me. She looks as effortlessly perfect as ever, demurely dressed in a figure-hugging dress and designer cardigan, a warm wrist-to-below-knee flow of fashionable prints and cashmere. It occurs to me, as I look at her, that I'll probably never stop feeling inadequate in comparison, so I should stop comparing. *No more comparing.* That's not even a clinic rule. That's just common sense.

"Thanks for being so nice to Fin yesterday." She steals the chair from the desk that Katie's been using and wheels it over to sit down beside me. "He didn't stop talking about you all day!"

I frown, confused. I thought he didn't, couldn't . . . ? I glance at her, uncertain.

"He signs," she explains without me needing to ask. "Makaton. All he'd do last night was brown hair—" She shows me. "Over and over again." Her cheeks dimple with a smile. "We had to keep telling him your name."

Keep telling him my name? I snort inwardly at the irony. He isn't the only one. Claire must catch sight of my expression.

"He can be difficult, can't he?"

"Hm?" I'm taken off guard. I hesitate, unsure how to reply. Claire shakes her head, and her scarf slips undone, falling over her shoulders. She reaches to fix it, and as she does I can't help noticing the marks on her neck. Jesus Christ, that's more information than I needed. I avert my eyes, embarrassed. Thank God Ryan isn't here.

"Sean, I mean," she adds. "When you don't know him."

"Oh." I look back at the laptop. "Um . . ."

"Try not to take it personally." Claire's gaze rests on my slightly too flushed cheeks. "Once you've worked with him for a bit, you'll understand, I think. If you give him a chance."

"I'm not sure that I'm getting any chances from him," I point out.

Claire's smile broadens, crinkling around her eyes. "You will. With Sean everybody tends to get *one*."

One? Great. I regard her dubiously.

"Oh, Livs. Honestly. It'll get easier. I've known Sean since we were kids. I know he's difficult — he's got himself a bit of a reputation, it's true. But behind it all, he's amazing; he's got such vision, such drive . . . And he's really *not* a bad guy. Not as bad as Katie would have you believe, certainly." She laughs. "You'll learn a lot from him. He took the mentor thing very seriously before. With the last intern."

The last intern. I sit very still in my seat. I knew it. I've known it since Ryan's elusive reply when I asked him on my first day.

"That's probably part of the problem," Claire carries on, oblivious. "He ended up feeling responsible for what happened, I think."

What happened? I look back sharply at her face. What *did* happen?

"What do you mean?" I prompt cautiously.

"Well, they were friends."

Oh, great. I stare at the keyboard. Even better. That's it? I'm stepping into shoes I can't fill.

"For a time, anyway. Don't get me wrong. It wasn't straightforward. She was very immature. Vindictive, even — she almost ruined Sean. Started saying things . . ." Claire breaks off, voice lowered. "Awful things. He had to step back. In hindsight, it's best that he did, the way that things ended. So, if he's not befriending anyone this time, that's probably why."

"Oh." I have to fight the urge to cross my arms around my chest, Finbar-style. I'm not sure if I want him to have an excuse. It isn't an excuse, surely? To be so bloody—

"Hi. Dad?" Claire's on the phone again. I didn't even hear it ring. She scoots the computer chair back from my desk, and slips hurriedly out into the rain, mobile tucked under her chin. I watch her through the window for a moment, talking, her smooth forehead creasing intermittently, drizzle clinging to her flaxen hair. So things ended badly with the last intern. Why doesn't that really surprise me? Suddenly, Katie's offer of a chat has taken on a whole new meaning.

I swallow. I'm still none the wiser as to what Sean actually wants from me. But whether or not he approves, he's right — I have boxes to tick and exams to pass — and I'm not going to waste my time sitting around and waiting for him. I tug the bundle of old university notes out of my satchel and spread them on the desk. Outside, the sun is struggling to penetrate the clouds. I've been clenching my teeth so hard that my head's starting to ache.

What colour? I focus my mind on my old distraction trick. What colour for the hazy sun in the glass? For the crisp edges of the fibreglass desks? Burnt Ochre, Payne's Grey, Ivory Black: every colour of dark. I turn my attention to my reading.

Katie's the first back, before Claire's even off the phone, with a carrier bag of grease-stained paper and polystyrene cartons. She sits cross-legged on the computer chair, balancing a tray of chips on her lap, and picks up the pen from my desk.

"This is beautiful." She turns it to examine it.

"Oh. Mmm." I nod. "It was my father's. It doesn't write properly anymore."

"A R Frost." She runs a finger over the engraved lettering. "Why have I heard of that before?"

"Heard of what?" Claire has slipped back in, unnoticed. She perches on the corner of my desk and roots in the bag for her food.

I stare at the desk, my eyes suddenly smarting. How many times? How many times do I have to have this conversation? How many years before it stops happening?

"My father. Andrew Frost. There's still a few posters around." I shrug.

"Posters?" Claire sits up, eyes bright with interest.

I smile faintly. "His last book."

It's back. The blockage in my throat. The one that happens every time I try to talk about it. I screw my fingers into my palms under the table, willing it away.

"He's an author? Really?"

Katie puts down her chips on the edge of the desk. "Not as in *the* Andrew R Frost?"

"Mmhm." I duck under the table to get my salad out of my bag.

"Oh my goodness. Livia, that's amazing! *He's* your dad? He wrote *Fellrunner*, didn't he? And *Mercy's Child* — that's literally my favourite book of all time! I cried so much! They're doing a film adaptation, aren't they? Didn't he recently win some kind of pri . . . oh." Katie tails off abruptly. I feel the realisation in her silence, even though I can't quite bring myself to look at her.

I finish for her. "Posthumously. Yeah."

"Oh, Livs, I'm so sorry. He . . ."

"It's okay. It's been two years." I shake my head, not quite able to meet her gaze.

"It's the most amazing book." Katie's voice is soft. "You must be really proud."

"I've never read it." I examine a cherry tomato before returning it to its Tupperware prison.

"Oh." Katie pauses, taken aback.

"Some of it's a little too close to home." I scuff the toe of my boot on the floor, and put the salad to one side, closing the lid. There's an uncomfortable silence.

"Have *you* read it?" Katie turns to Claire. "*Mercy's Child*?"

But Claire isn't looking. She's not looking at either of us. Her gaze is fixed somewhere else entirely, vacuous and unmoving.

"Claire?" Katie nudges her arm gently.

"No, I—" Claire jerks abruptly back to life. "No," she admits. "No, I haven't." She fumbles to pull her phone from her pocket, suddenly all fingers and thumbs, but the door opens before she has the chance to dial.

"Hi, team." Ryan gives a mock salute as the small, fair figure trundles in under his arm and halts on the doormat. I watch as Claire hurries to them, fussing over the child's unfastened coat and the grazed grey knees of his trousers. She pushes the mop of pale blond hair back from his white forehead. At her murmured direction, Fin obligingly holds up each of his arms in turn, so that she can roll back his sleeves to examine them.

"There's only three spots." Claire sounds perplexed. "Are they definitely chickenpox?"

I glance up to see Ryan shrug. He flashes a guilty grin. "No idea," he mouths at me. His smile is so disarming that I can't help but grin back.

"They *look* like chickenpox." Claire kneels down. "This one on his chin really does. They won't have him back if it's chickenpox. Not for at least a week . . . maybe two."

Fin looks up. His round, dark eyes fix on mine. He doesn't smile. I don't, either. I keep absolutely still, as if moving might startle him away. Slowly, his arms drift back to his sides.

"I don't know what we're going to do . . ." Claire shakes her head, despairing. "He's only just gone full time, and now . . . Oh, Fin. What are we going to do with you?" She gets to her feet, one hand caressing his silky hair. Fin shrugs his shoulders. His gaze follows her as she turns to Ryan.

"I have an appointment this afternoon. Two thirty. Who's going to have him while I go? I can't let Dad have him. He's never had chickenpox — not ever — imagine what would happen, at his age . . ."

"What appointment?" Ryan frowns.

"The doctor . . . dentist." Claire is suddenly flushed, not her usual smiling self at all. "Like I told you this morning."

"Right . . ." Ryan plunges his hands into his pockets. "Oh, it'll be fine. There's no reason he can't stay with me. I just have a few bits that I need to do here, but then everything else is calls, which I can make from home. I'm sure you can entertain yourself here for half an hour, can't you, buddy?"

Fin blinks. Claire pulls a face. "What about the others?"

"I've had chickenpox." Katie slides to her feet with a shrug. "And I've got to head back to Truro now anyway." She rewraps her tray and throws it in the bin. I suddenly realise everyone's eyes are on me.

"It doesn't bother me." I shrug.

"If you're sure." Claire looks disproportionately relieved. I glance from her to Ryan, not quite sure whether to point out that no one has considered if it'll bother Sean.

Claire leaves not far behind Katie. Ryan re-embarks on his filing cabinet mission and pulls out a ring-binder of official-looking documents and invoices. He frowns at them for a moment, then picks up the phone. Only the tick of the clock and the tinny overspill of the receiver break the silence. I shift in my seat. Ryan lounges across the spare desk, pulling faces to the hold-music, apparently oblivious to his son dissembling the contents of the desk drawers underneath him.

I doodle on the page in front of me, trying not to look like I'm watching. Fin has salvaged a pot of brightly lacquered paper clips and is sorting them into perfectly aligned colour-order on the carpet.

"Oh, *shi—*" Ryan censors himself mid-word. "—gar!" He hangs up the phone and lurches to his feet, scattering paper clips in ten different directions. Fin and I both glance up, alarmed.

"Livs." Ryan turns to me, wide-eyed and guilty. "I've just realised I was supposed to make the bank for Graham before closing. I'd completely forgotten. You couldn't . . ."

I follow his gaze in slow motion to the small figure on the floor.

"Could you?"

Dread lands like a leaden weight in the pit of my stomach. I gape at him.

Livia, be a darling . . . check on Toby . . .

I open my mouth, but Ryan speaks before I have the chance.

"You're a legend, Livs." He throws me a beguiling smile and grabs his coat from the back of his chair. His voice lowers. "Don't tell Claire. Or Sean."

I nod, speechless.

"I'll be twenty minutes." He's backing out the door. "Half an hour, max."

I stumble to my feet. "Sure," I croak.

Then he's gone.

I look down. Fin has mounted a rescue operation. Blue, green and yellow clips are already restored to their ranks. He scoots past my feet to retrieve the last red as I stand, rooted to the spot in horror. I have no idea what to do. Something? Anything? I watch apprehensively as Fin finishes laying out the final row in his paper clip army. He sits back on his heels and we regard each other in silence.

"High five?" I offer.

Fin hesitates. Then he stands up and lands a glancing blow on my palm. He grins, and the impishness of it downgrades my terror to anxiety.

Breathe in, lengthen, out. Twenty minutes. We only have to survive twenty minutes. Twenty minutes would be barely beyond the end of the promenade, two miles. He literally won't leave my sight. I attempt a smile back.

"What do you want to do?" I ask him.

Fin raises mystified eyes to my face.

"Um," I flounder. "We could um . . ." My gaze falls on the drawing boards at the same moment as his does.

"You like to draw?" I breathe.

He nods.

I ride the wave of relief almost as far as the boards. Fin runs ahead of me, clambering up onto the stool and kneeling tall to reach the paper. It's only as I stretch a hand into the drawer in search of a pencil that the thought hits me — 0.7 mm resting motionless on the page — and I stop mid-breath. *Don't tell Sean.*

Crap. I don't even know where he is. I never saw him come out of the back room. What if he's still there? I chew my lip. But even if he is, there's no reason he should need to open the door for the next twenty minutes. I release my lip, ears burning.

If he is, how much has he heard?

I shove the thought from my mind, seek out an HB for Fin, and watch him touch it tentatively to the page, making the tiniest mark on the white paper. He pauses, pencil poised and upright, dark eyes intent. I frown. I was expecting scribbling, a thick black line, a wild scrawl — a bold attempt at a shape, or a person, or a name. Part of me wants to voice my encouragement. But I can't find the words.

Fin crouches closer to the paper, his grip so tight on the pencil that his knuckles are white. Painfully slowly, he traces the pencil down the page and back up again. His face is scrunched tight in concentration as he finishes the wobbly outline of his square, and draws an irregular rectangle inside it, a second, a third: a narrower one — a door with a handle. He adds a roof, and with meticulous care, he starts a feather-light zig-zag over the top.

I pull up a stool and kneel beside him.

"A house?" I whisper.

Fin turns. I'm not sure if he nods.

I try again. "Is this grass?" I touch the zig-zag. Never mind that it's on the roof. I sigh. "I wish we had some colours."

This time I do get a nod. I hesitate, something occurring to me. I slide from the stool to my feet, hopping as pins and needles claim my right leg. There's a four-way biro in my satchel. I fetch it.

"Here." I show him. "It's not very good. But if you push the button—" I press the end. "Red . . . green."

Fin's lips part in the ghost of a smile. He reaches out and takes the pen, turning it over to examine it. Clicks through each colour and back to green. I watch him trace the pen carefully over the lines he's already drawn. Green grass.

"It's a house?" I touch the picture again. Fin looks at me warily.

"Okay." I nod my understanding, and withdraw. He curls his fingers around the biro, and I listen to the sound of the pen on the paper as his colouring gains confidence.

"It's a brilliant house," I tell him.

Up, down. He's still drawing, one spiky blade at a time.

"I like to draw houses, too." I move around the desk to fiddle with one of the scales, the metal cool under my fingertips. "If I could draw any house I wanted, it would be a bit like yours." I remember not to touch, and point to the oversized windows instead. "There'd be big windows, like yours, that all looked out at the sea. Lots of light, so that when it was sunny, the whole house would be lit up inside. And it would have lots of grass like your house, too. A garden, so that when the weather was nice, I could go there to paint. Do you like painting?"

Fin doesn't answer. He puts down the pen and runs his finger over the shiny indentations of the green ink. *Green like the dandelion stems.* For a moment, I watch him. I watch him live his daydream on the page: the most important thing in the world. And for a split second I forget everything else, everything that went wrong — Dad, the Solent, the clinic, *don't let the Lorchanns get under your skin.* I forget about Sean Lorchann's indifference and Niklavs' untruth, and I think instead about the girl dancing barefoot on the grass, and wonder what happened to her.

* * *

The truth is, I couldn't stay in the flat.

I haven't told anyone that, apart from you. But sometimes, I can't be there. I have to get out. I have to get away from the mirror. Because, sometimes, I see reflections in that mirror. And they're not mine.

Writing that makes me sound like I'm crazy. I'm not crazy. Or at least, I don't think I am. I know people who are — or were. My mum was crazy; but at the time, when you're sucked in, you don't always realise. She's not crazy anymore — which is a relief — although sometimes her sanity is more wearing than the lack of it. She spent a long time trying to persuade me not to come here.

I imagined in a thousand ways what things would be like when I got here. He was never in my imaginings. He was barely more than a name to me, he was never factored in. I don't know when or how that changed. It shouldn't have changed. I was so sure I knew what I needed. But he sat on the harbour front with me tonight, and he talked to me. Like he understood everything, all of it, even though that's impossible. And just for a split second, I could see a different destination, like the clouds had parted — just for a moment. He told me to lose the self-doubt. That it's dangerous to doubt yourself. Perhaps he's right. Perhaps it is dangerous to doubt yourself.

It's not always about what you did, or what you do. Sometimes it's about what you didn't do. What you gave up. Those are the mistakes you can never rectify, the wounds you can't heal, the lies you can't un-tell.

But sometimes I think it's more dangerous to doubt your self-doubt. Perhaps self-doubt is self-preservation.

My father lied to a lot of people, for a long time. It caught up with him eventually. The funny thing was, when he went to prison, I couldn't filter out which bit had been the lie — that he loved us to start with, or that he didn't by the end. How is it that the lies of the people closest to you are the ones you never see through? He had another family, another wife and two sons. He embezzled money for fifteen years, longer than I'd even been alive. And that whole time, people trusted him. People believed in him. People loved him.

That's why I brought you here. I'm still not sure which part of all of this is the lie. Nothing is like I imagined.

If there's anywhere I can make sense of it, it's here. This place is the most beautiful place on Earth. I wish I could capture it in the pages for you; if I could paint or take a photo that would do it justice, I would. Tonight the sea sounds hungry, like it would swallow the rocks if it could, but it can't quite reach. I like it best when it's already taken the sand, when I can sit here and feel the danger rolling towards me. It's like a dance, sea and land, until the lust gets so strong that they swirl together instead, so passionate that they throw up pieces of themselves into the sky. More often, it looks calm. But even on those days the rips here are deadly. You wouldn't think it for looking — it looks like a postcard or a Turner painting. Except in postcards, the sun is always shining, and in postcards you don't see the death under the water: the sailors, the boats, the lost souls. There are skeletons, just off these rocks.

Deadly. That's what this place is to me. Not just the cove. Not just the cliffs. The whole of it. Porthtrevelen. I can feel myself being sucked closer to the rocks, closer and closer. I promised I wouldn't be sucked in again. That I wouldn't be so naive this time.

I shouldn't have come here. But it's too late to change that now.

If I could paint . . .

Sunlight is dripping over the edges of the easel. Saturday. I'm cold, aching, motionless. Since dawn I've been sat here, staring, the shades and shapes of Trethallyan Edge burning themselves into my consciousness, beautiful but deadly. And I can't. I can't paint.

I listen to the sound of my breath. Watch it mist on the windowpane as I stand up and look from a different angle instead. I can't paint. Every colour I mix is dark, the colour of Finbar's and Sean Lorchann's eyes, and no matter how hard I try, I can't see past the fall of shadows on the canvas.

I sit down again. My father died on a Saturday. Winter, like now. It had started to snow as I sat there with his hand in mine; I'd looked at the snow falling, through the window and the tears, and marvelled at how silent it was, until the doctor arrived, and my mother, and the peace was irretrievably broken, never to be recaptured. February 2nd, 2020. Two years ago on Monday.

I get up. The kitchen floorboards creak languidly as I cross them in my socks and check my phone. No messages. I texted Kris at nine, and knew at the time that it was optimistic. After I came out of Verity House, we met at one every Saturday in a café in the old Lace Market. He was never up before midday. He'd order breakfast while I ate lunch, and we'd watch the ebb and flow of the Nottingham shopping rush blur past the single-glazed windows.

Breakfast. I consider the point guiltily, and then pour half a bowl of muesli, my eyes glued to my phone as if he might catch me erring. If I eat it before he calls back, I won't have to lie. 385 kcal. I move to write it down on the pad beside the fridge as I chew and swallow, then make myself stop and stand still. *It's dangerous to doubt your self-doubt.* I really have to try harder.

I put down the bowl on the side, and go back to my canvas, touching a finger to the drying oils. To the shadow, every shade of dark. I frown. Despite me, it's made it from my colour chart onto the page, where it has no place, shapeless and formless, someone or something that I can't name waiting beyond the periphery of the picture. A reflection. A girl in the mirror.

As if to reassure myself, I walk to the dressing table. Look into my own face a hundred times over in the old glass. *Livia . . . Frost . . . Intern . . .*

Sean. Lorchann. Architect.

I open the drawer and feel to the bottom, scrabbling underneath the discarded book-jacket and the picture frame with my nails. The chain is right at the back, where I left it, cold and glinting as I pull it out, its delicate pendant the only part that doesn't catch the light. Whitby jet. My father bought it for me when I was twelve years old. There was a time when I wore it every day. A time when everything was different. The last time I wore it was to his funeral.

I reach to fasten the chain behind my neck. Screw forgetting. I never promised to forget.

I sit down on the edge of the bed. The journal is still open. A prickle creeps along the back of my neck. Coincidence, if that's what put her scribbled memories in my hands, is a strange and terrifying thing. In place, in person, I should have known her. She would know me. It's only the dimension of time that means we've passed instead of colliding in the empty gloom of number 31 Sunnyside.

I trace one finger over the contour of the tiny bird, my thoughts dwelling briefly on pencil drawings and paperclips, and on Finbar Lorchann's silence. Perhaps I'm not the only one who's lonely.

And, perhaps, I'm not the only one who's afraid.

CHAPTER 8

"*Labrīt*, Livia. Good morning."

I turn, blinded by the glare of artificial light from Niklavs' doorway.

"You make late start today." He waves me out first as he opens the front door to retrieve the milk from the step. "Is almost seven."

"Oh." I hop on the doorstep to adjust my trainer. "I overslept."

"Did you have pleasant weekend?"

"It was . . . good. Thanks," I lie. Good, apart from my utter inability to sleep. Apart from the all-pervading coldness, the impending death-anniversary, and the Trethallyan darkness that penetrated everything I tried to paint. Apart from the fact that there's a picture of him, Niklavs, in Graham Gordon-Heyers' reading room, when he told me he's never met him.

"I am glad." Niklavs' smile is so genuine that it throws me. "How is painting?"

"It's good." I shrug, lost for words. What can I say? *Come up and see if it looks familiar? Maybe tell me a bit about your buddy Graham Gordon-Heyers while we're on the subject?* I scrape the toe of my trainer on the step. "I finished it. It's drying . . . You can come see it, if you like."

"I would like." Niklavs nods. "Very much. I come tonight, if you are in."

"I'll be in." I make myself meet his eyes. They're steady blue, like my father's. No hint of guilt or deceit. "After six. Come whenever."

"Thank you, Livia." Niklavs picks up the milk bottles and tucks one under his arm. Condensation is starting to run down the glass. "I will. Now, though, you must start run, or you will be late for job."

"Oh," I mumble. "Yeah."

"Go." He grins as I falter on the step. "I will see you later."

"See you," I whisper.

The door crashes shut. I rack the volume on my phone up to full, and ram my headphones into my ears. What isn't he telling me? And how am I going to ask him? Salt air hits my face as I take a few skipping warm-up steps. More to the point, *why* isn't he telling me? The two men in the picture aren't strangers. Or enemies. So what is there to hide?

The residual taste of betrayal is faintly bitter in my mouth. I brace myself against the cold clifftop wind, draw in a deep breath, and dive out into the first chilly suggestions of dawn.

* * *

Kris is never up this early, but there's a message by seven fifty when I make the last corner into Sunnyside. I'm going to be late for work. I wipe my sweating fingers on my leggings and pull out my phone.

U ok? I meant to call.

Am I okay? How am I supposed to answer that? February 2nd. I promised, a few long months ago, not to lie to him anymore.

Betrayal. I remember that betrayal, too. The terror rising in my chest when my own brother refused to leave the house until he'd seen me eat. When he turned his back on me in the hospital bed as they tried to sell me stories of dangerously low heart rates and persuade me to have my bloods taken. Did they think anything they could tell me was scarier than an empty bunk bed and a muslin blanket in the sea?

It was the only means I had left of protecting myself from the abyss, and he sided with them. I remember thinking that. It didn't feel like he was saving my life. It felt like he was ending it. Replacing it with a new kind of alone. The kind you don't come back from.

Seven fifty-one.

Except I did come back. My legs shake on the stairs. I forget the broken slow-close, and the flat door slams as I deposit my keys on the dressing table. At least Niklavs is already awake.

I turn on the shower and hop into the kitchen, tugging off my leggings. I pause at the notepad beside the fridge and tear off the week-old shopping list. Pick up the pen and twirl it in my fingers. Forty-five minutes. Speed equals distance over time. 5.2 miles according to my phone. 7mph. 400 calories.

Am I okay?

I put down the pen.

The bathroom is full of steam. I shower and dress in barely the time it takes the kettle to boil. I finger-comb and half blow-dry my hair, gulp my scalding coffee and pull on my coat, throwing one last glance at the mirror on my way out. *Sometimes, I see reflections . . . and they're not mine.*

There's already a coffee on my desk when I arrive at work. I glance from Katie to Ryan, unsure who to thank, but Katie's on the phone, and I'm not quite brave enough to ask. I open the laptop instead and watch the screen like a hawk. Katie hangs up.

"Hey, Livs." She sweeps up her coat and pulls an apologetic face. "Sorry, I've got to dash. I'm not even meant to be here this morning." She swipes a mains plug from the socket and shoves the cable into her handbag. "Truro. Total disaster. Craig's going to kill me!"

"Oh." I blink. "No worries. See you . . ."

"Friday," she smiles, and bolts for the door. "I'm at Mum's for the weekend, so I'll drop in on my way there. Otherwise, next week, if you're around."

I nod. "I'm not going anywhere," I add dryly, but she doesn't hear.

"See you, Katie." Ryan glances up too as the door shuts. I hear her car pull away.

I reach out to pick up my mug. The contents are cooling rapidly. I stare into the murky depths. *February 2nd* . . .

"Frost."

The cup is at my lips. I gulp a much bigger lukewarm mouthful than I intended, and teeter for a moment on the boundary between choking and swallowing. Sean regards me in eyebrow-lifted silence as I recover.

"Yes?" I stand up, eyes watering. He's holding something out to me. I take it without a word. Fuck him and his superciliousness.

"These are some sketches for the chapel." His dark eyes meet mine squarely. I haven't brought my drawings back, and we both know it.

"This is the outline planning permission. And this is the consent from English Heritage. You . . ." He doesn't look away. Neither do I. "Are going to make these . . ." He jerks his head at the papers in my hand. "Into a full set of drawings for Gordon-Heyers — floorplans, elevations and sections."

Oh, I am? I let my fingers close around the edges of the pages, not sure whether to be outraged or triumphant as I look down at his pencil lines. 0.7 mm. So he's trusting me with something. Or, maybe, he's going to let me get halfway through then revoke the privilege and finish it himself. I glower at the sketches. They're good — even though he can't have spent as much as half a day on them. And accurate. More accurate than the rough, furiously drawn idea explosion on the roll of paper under my bed.

"Okay." I put them down on my desk. "Thanks."

Something in Sean's expression shifts subtly. I see his gaze flicker to my two-thirds-full mug.

"The coffee here's shit," he observes softly.

"Yeah." There's a pause. He lays a hand on the desk, finger and thumb toying with the corner of his drawing.

"We meet Gordon-Heyers again next Monday." His voice is low, inscrutable. "You can show me beforehand."

I make an effort not to frown. There's something overly personal in his critical dark stare.

"Sure." I keep my voice smooth. Sean withdraws his hand.

"You know where I am if you run into problems." He shoots a glance at the back room. I nod. He takes the steps in two graceful strides, and I hear his footsteps recede hollowly across the mezzanine. Problems? I glare at his microscopically messy handwriting. I only have *one* problem. I glance at his empty desk.

Half an hour passes alarmingly quickly, given the impossible deadline I've just acquired. Ryan finishes with whatever it is he's allegedly been here to do, and comes to lounge against my desk instead, the fibreglass flexing under his weight. He reminds me so much of Kris that it's unreal.

"Nice wellies, Livs." He's looking at my site-bag, and his voice is teasing. "Can't wait to see you in these."

"Ugh. Right." I put down Sean's drawings to look at him. *So* much like Kris. Kris in ten years' time. Except I can't even fathom the idea of Kris having a child. The very idea fills me with dread; he's accident-prone enough himself. It would be a disaster.

"Claire says you should come over for dinner. Maybe one night this week, if you don't have plans." He picks up the mug and examines the film that's formed on top of the coffee. "You've got a place in Porthtrevelen, haven't you?"

"A flat," I affirm. "Sunnyside. The other side of town."

"Nice."

"Nice might be pushing it." I pull a face. Ryan grins. "How's Fin?" I venture.

"Itchy." It's his turn to pull a face. "Not sleeping well. We're all feeling the pain. What're you doing today?" He glances at Sean's sketches. I hesitate.

"Improving on these," I tell him wryly. He raises his eyebrows at me. I raise mine back. Ryan laughs.

"Good luck." He shakes his head. "Look, if you're bored later, come up to the house. It'll just be me and Fin — Claire's taking Graham to the hospital. You know." He shrugs. "If you get lonely."

Is it my imagination, or does his gaze travel in the direction of the back room too? I bite my lip.

"Maybe." My cheeks are still a little too pink. "Thanks."

"Any time." He pushes his hands into his pockets. There's something meaningful in his glance. Insightful. "I mean it." He withdraws one hand, keys dangling, and gives a noisy parting salute. "Later, Livs."

"Later," I murmur. I watch him go. Figures, that he'd have married Claire. A perfect-world romance, with sunset beaches and childhood sweethearts, all dimpled smiles and boisterous masculine charm. I stare into Sean's pencil lines. If only everyone's life turned out to be that perfect. I trace a finger over the light indentation of the graphite. Perhaps this is my own fault. I've missed my chance; if I'd brought my drawings back like he'd told me to, I could have been working on my own ideas, not his.

Except he'd already started these, an unwelcome corner of my mind reminds me. *Even before you didn't bring the drawings back*. I scowl at the paper. What was it Swift said? That it's worse to give things up. That those are the mistakes you can never rectify . . .

I stand up abruptly. She's right. I'm not that person. I don't give up. I sweep up the sketches and my case of drafting pencils in one hand, stalk to the mezzanine and carefully acquire three or four sheets of expectantly clean A2 with the other. Then I push open the door to the back room.

Sean looks up. The room is so still that walking to the table feels like parting the Dead Sea. The laptop in front of him has gone to sleep. He's been writing instead; the side of his hand is smudged with ink on a page dark with tiny figures and notes. The air crackles with static.

I smooth my paper across the opposite end of the table. Put down my pencil case and pull out a chair. There's a paper windmill standing, off balance, in the pen-holder on the windowsill, all the colours of the rainbow. I sit down.

"Is there something you need?" Sean lays down his pen with a click.

I shake my head.

"No." I fight the urge to whisper. My voice sounds somehow too loud. "I'm good."

"You've got a problem with the sketches?" His eyebrows lift.

"No." I flatten the corners of my paper and very deliberately unload two or three pencils beside it. A glorious stream of February sunshine illuminates my empty page, a glow of determination. I sink my teeth into my lower lip in concentration as I extend the lead of my pencil and lay out his sketches at an angle beside me. He's still watching. I take out the site map and scale.

"We have drawing boards," he says at last.

I nod.

"I know." I start to mark out a series of faint construction lines for my elevations, and turn my head to study his sketch again. There's a loaded pause. I line up the scale.

Sean folds his arms.

"You have a desk," he points out dryly.

"Uh-huh." I nod again. "So do you."

Another aching silence. He regards me across the table. For an uncertain fraction of a moment the hint of a smirk plays at the corner of his mouth. He folds his hands to rest two fingers against his lips, a languid gesture that's more contemplative than angry. I don't look up from my drawing. There's no way I'm going to let him shake my resolve. I release my own lip from my teeth, and start to draw.

Time has never passed so slowly. Sean stirs the laptop back into life, and for some reason the soft tap of the trackpad won't fade to background noise. Every time I glance up he's focussed on the screen, one finger still resting idly against his lips or toying with the redundant pen. I'm acutely aware of every movement of his hand on the keyboard and every languorous shift of his long legs under the table. I try to blur him out.

I hear the clock chime eleven, and then midday. Sean gets up suddenly and closes the lid of the laptop. He disappears without a word. I carry on working. My determination to outperform his expectations is growing more stubborn by the minute. There's more than a week's work here, if he wants it finished to any kind of standard. He knows that as well as I do. But if he's anticipating that I'll have nothing to show him, he's wrong. I'll have what he says he wants, even if I have to work every hour between now and Monday to do it. Shit, I'll make sure I have something to show today, by the time he comes back from wherever it is he's gone.

If he comes back.

I narrow my eyes at my drawing, remembering what Claire said about him. Would he have imposed the same ridiculous deadline on himself? Looking at his sketches, I have the sudden uncomfortable feeling that perhaps he might. He wants perfection — he's never made any secret of that. And he doesn't think I can do it.

The fingers of my left hand close briefly around the jet necklace. What does *he* know? What does he know about perfection?

I eat at my desk, more out of a feeling of obligation than hunger: two cereal bars, not lunch but an almost forgivable proxy. I hope Kris doesn't call. I really don't want to lie.

I've finished one elevation in graphite by the time he gets back, and set it aside to start a second. His designs are crisp, clear and to the point. Where my own rushed plans held a dreamlike quality, the genius of his is in their apparent simplicity; a simplicity so complex that it makes my head ache — every idea fits so neatly together that I can't fathom how he came up with it. I can't help feeling like the drawings lack something. But the more I think about it, the more I start to realise that maybe what's missing is the starry-eyed excitement I felt that first day on the cliffside — how did he put it? The unrealistic enthusiasm. I pull my knees up to sit cross-legged on my chair. Sean double-clicks something on the laptop's trackpad. His voice startles me.

"You're still here."

Nothing like stating the obvious. I don't even glance up.

"Mmhm."

"Have you eaten?"

His question surprises me. I nod the half-truth, and stuff the cereal-bar wrappers deeper into the pocket of my chinos.

"No one'll thank you for not taking breaks," he informs me under his breath.

"I guess not." I go back to my drawing, dry-mouthed. I fidget with the necklace, running it back and forth along its chain. My back's starting to ache. I'd have been so much better off at the drawing board.

Sean sits back in his chair, ankles crossed in front of him. His dark eyes fix on my face.

"You never stop fiddling, do you?"

I let my gaze flick up.

"Nervous habit," I say, deadpan.

Sean regards me for a moment.

"Do I make you nervous?"

His voice is very soft. I freeze. What kind of a question is that? Carefully, I lower my pencil.

"I don't know," I reply.

He shakes his head. It's there again. The fleeting, sardonic suggestion of a smile. I scowl at my drawing, perplexed. For a while, neither of us speaks. He turns his attention back on his work, and I finish marking out my next set of construction lines with wrist-aching care. Three. The daylight is losing its edge. I remember Niklavs, and grit my teeth. I'm going to have to ask about the photo. What other choice do I have? He's my only friend in this place; I don't want to stop trusting him.

Rain is battering the windows. It always seems to be raining. I consider getting up to turn on the light, but Sean beats me to it, rising silently to flick on the brilliant-white desk lamp. I blink a couple of times. He doesn't sit down again. He walks to the window to look outside, then strides back, pausing beside the table to pick up my finished elevation.

"You work fast," he comments.

I set down my pencil. "Is that a bad thing?"

The stillness buzzes around us. Sean straightens the page to look it over.

"No." He shrugs. "It's technically flawless."

Technically? I link my hands on my lap, out of sight. He's standing very still, one palm resting on the empty table-top.

"But?" I query.

"But there's nothing else to say for it, Frost." He shakes his head. "There's nothing original here."

I fight to keep my face impassive. My lips tighten. Nothing else to say? Nothing original? They're *his* fucking designs. I turn my gaze back on the paper, glowering at my own nanometre-precise lines.

"It's like I said." He lays the drawing down without a sound. "Average doesn't cut it. Everyone keeps telling me you're supposed to have flair. Where's the flair in this? Where's the passion?"

Passion? I feel my eyes narrow as he sits down at the end of the table and picks up his pen. I look up, straight into his level stare.

"I wasn't aware that was what you wanted," I tell him archly. "And I wasn't sure that 'passion' was something you'd relate to."

For a moment, he's completely silent. Blood rushes into my cheeks. *Shit.* I actually said it. I keep my lips pressed tightly together. My pulse is beating loudly in my ears.

Agonisingly slowly, Sean Lorchann leans forward to rest his arms on the table. His gaze doesn't leave my face. For a torturously long second his eyes lock with mine, unreadable. Amused? Suddenly I can't tell.

"Try me," he says.

* * *

06/07/2021

There's a girl in the mirror, and I don't recognise her face. I don't know when I stopped knowing her, or whether I ever really knew her at all. There's something in her eyes that frightens me: a light, a spark that I haven't felt for almost as long as I can remember.

It's the strangest thing. The way you can believe you have something, until you truly have it . . . and then what you thought you had turns out to be nothing more than a shadow, an empty husk. But it was impossible to know — at the time — that what I clutched so tightly in my hand was fool's gold.

Perhaps I was a fool then. Perhaps I am now. This is foolishness. I know that. But I've never felt this before, not about anyone. Not just a desire, but a need. With him, I feel whole. The last person I ever expected might complete me. I almost feel like I might be worth something. I feel alive, for the first time.

I'm so glad I have you to tell. I'd be terrified if I didn't. I'm terrified anyway. Have you ever been afraid? I wonder if — and when — your heart has been broken? How many times? You can tell me, if you want to. I won't tell a soul. I promise.

I said I'd tell you everything, and I haven't. I will, one day. One day, I'll be brave enough to tell you what I did . . .

What she did? I trace the words with one finger, uneasy. What was she so afraid of? I glance at the mirror. Here, in my flat. A girl, my age, who wrote for hours to nobody, who 'kept herself to herself'. Who was she?

On sudden impulse, I get up from the bed and pull the door open. Downstairs, the hall is in darkness. I flick on the light and cross the floor to the dusty pigeon-holes full of accumulating junk mail. The dried flowers smell musty and stale. Even a first name would do. Some clue as to why she left or where she went—

"Now is good time?"

I spin, cracking my hip against the table. The door to number 29A must have opened almost as I passed it. Was he listening to me in the hall? I back away from the mailbox without quite managing to see inside, as if I've been caught in the middle of some heinous crime.

"Sure." I find a smile. "Come on up."

Niklavs drops his key into his pocket, and pulls his door to.

"You have good day at work?" He gestures me first and follows me up the stairs.

"Better than ever," I mutter as I let us in. Niklavs pauses in the doorway. A broad grin splits his weathered face.

"*Ak Dievs.* Livia!" Finally he crosses the threshold, and the door crashes shut behind him. He strides to the easel and stops again, a foot away from it, beaming from ear to ear. "It is . . . *apbrīnojams* — amazing. This is in estate! The cove, at Trethallyan Edge. There is old chapel—" He takes another step forward, then pulls up short, as if noticing his own slip. I've noticed it too. I stare, eyes narrowed, at the tufts of grey hair poking out under the back of his hat.

"It is," I reply stiffly.

For a moment neither of us speaks. Niklavs slides his hands into his pockets, and walks a concertedly casual arc around the easel to examine the painting from every direction.

"You always do the painting with oils?" he asks at last.

"Mm-hm." I nod. There's a strained silence.

"My daughter used to paint — how you call? — watercolour." Niklavs thrusts his hands deeper into his pockets. Is it my imagination or is he not quite making eye contact? I draw in a deep breath.

"There's a picture of you in Gordon-Heyers' library," I say.

Niklavs pauses. He's very still.

"Yes," he sighs at last. He's still facing the other way. I look at the way his hands have tightened into fists in his pockets, where he thinks I won't see.

"I thought you said you didn't know him?" Part of me wants to loose the questions at him like a quiver of arrows. The rest of me wants to take it back and pretend I never saw. He still hasn't moved.

"No. I do not." It's tight, constrained, nothing like his normal voice. "Not anymore."

"You did once?" I can't stop myself. I regret my interrogation the moment it's out of my mouth. Niklavs turns.

"I did once." His face is dark with clouds. Storm clouds, navy-grey and forbidding. "I worked for him, once. We were both younger men. Different men. I wish not to talk about it. I wish, now, not to remember it. You can respect this?"

I feel the colour flood my cheeks. I hesitate, overcome with guilt. What right did I think I had to ask? I bite my lip.

"Yes." I look back up at his face and his creased blue eyes. Suddenly I feel like a child. "I'm sorry," I whisper.

His expression softens. "Do not waste life being sorry, Livia." He shakes his head. "It is far too short. Painting is beautiful. Spend time on painting, not on regretting."

I swallow. "My father taught me always to apologise when I'd been unfair to someone."

Niklavs shakes his head again. He smiles, faintly, and reaches to rest one weathered hand on my shoulder.

"Then I am sorry, too," he says.

* * *

I never called Kris. He never called me. Morning has dawned, and there are three hundred and sixty-four days before we have to broach the subject again.

I blow out, watching the steam of my breath disperse on the bitterly cold air. I pull my sleeves further over my stinging hands and screw the Lycra between my fingers.

Fool's gold.

The perfect job, the perfect opportunity, the idyllic seaside setting. None of it looks so sparkly up close. The sea is grey, thrashing onto the abandoned dawn beach. And the job? Frankly, I never want to go back to work again. The thought of what happened makes me cringe. I even looked him in the face when I said it, like some kind of bratty child. All I can remember is the look he gave me, the long, penetrating look. I can't forget the glimmer of amusement, barely hidden. He was laughing at me. Sean fucking Lorchann. *Do I make you nervous?*

I slam through the kissing gate, teeth clenched. No. Not nervous. Fucking mad.

What am I going to do? I speed up inadvertently. I've almost reached the limit of my normal run. I consider what Niklavs said about extending the route, the path back into Porthtrevelen — what did he call it? The Witch's Cat. With deadly rips, like Trethallyan Cove.

A mile or so further. The path grows narrow and takes a sudden dive before it ascends steeply heavenward. The salt spray thrashes my face; the narrow trail is dizzyingly close to the edge and the gradient is pleasingly punishing. A hundred yards more, and the rickety wooden fence gives up its struggle altogether, leaving me terrifyingly exposed. The clifftop towers high, a thousand wild white horses galloping full pelt at its foot, the tide turned unlikely shades of pink and navy-black by the brooding dawn. It's beautiful. But something about it makes me shudder. What was it she wrote? *The death under the water.* Skeletons, boats, lost souls.

A muslin blanket . . .

No. I grit my teeth, and deliberately block out the view with my phone. Seven twenty-five. I need to find the path back to Sunnyside. I try to picture Niklavs' finger on the map. *A car park, here.* Yes. I can see it, deserted bar a single parked four-by-four and a dilapidated ticket machine. Half a mile further. A track going inland. A footpath. I ease myself back to a run. The descent is satisfyingly sharp; I relish the stretch through my hips as I adjust my stride to absorb it. Beside me, the fence briefly re-establishes itself, an uncertain army of wire and wood battling the tangle of leafless bushes, until the ground drops away, scattering wooden casualties over the rocks below. There's a sign blocking my way. I slow, defeated. *Unstable Cliffs. Following winter storms and recent heavy rain . . .*

A diversion. Great. Plastic orange fence hangs between temporary steel posts a metre or two from the brink, rippling in the wind. I'm going to be late to work again. On top of everything else. I dash the sweat from my upper lip and move to look over the edge. I've never been afraid of heights, but for some reason a shiver runs along my spine. For the tiniest fraction of a second, I can't help imagining what it might be like to step off.

I turn quickly back to the path. So, I'm bearing right. I accelerate to a cautious run, a slow curve inland between coalescing gorse bushes; I have to keep my elbows tucked uncomfortably close to my sides or risk lacerations. The cliff cuts inwards and the curve of the path tightens sharply, my running shoes pounding the damp sandy soil at the apex of the corner as I slow to check my step. I look up again, and almost trip.

There's a figure ahead, another person on the path, not quite discernible in the dawn light. It hadn't even occurred to me that I might meet anyone else crazy — or dedicated — enough to be out this early at this time of year. I watch the newcomer's silhouette enlarge gradually, until the curve of the path throws him out of shadow and into sharp relief.

Shit. I swerve sideways, and dive behind an outcrop of rock before I've considered my course of action. Gorse snags at my hair and my clothes. No. No way. Sean Lorchann. Before seven in the morning, in the middle of nowhere, after everything that happened yesterday. I drop to one knee, damp and sweaty, and concentrate fixedly on tying my shoelace as I hear his footsteps draw closer, keeping my face out of sight behind the low shrubs. Maybe he hasn't seen me. Maybe he wasn't close enough to recognise me. Maybe—

I gasp. Without warning, a wet black nose is pressed against my leggings. The dog lifts its silky head and scrabbles around the bracken to investigate me more thoroughly, a border collie with glossy brown and white fur. It sniffs both of my already-tied shoes, flicks its eyebrows in further assessment, and then turns tail, disappearing back out onto the path after Sean Lorchann's boots.

I exhale. The footfalls have passed and faded. I'm safe. I give it a couple of seconds more, stand up, and nearly drop my phone.

He's standing absolutely still, a few steps along from where I made my unplanned departure from the path, his breath misting in a cloud in front of his face. A leather dog lead hangs from one of his hands, his thumb hooked loosely through the belt-loop of his jeans.

His voice is quiet. "Sit, Max."

He doesn't look at the dog. He's looking at me. The collie trots obediently back at the almost imperceptible gesture of his hand to sit at his feet. I fumble to pull out my earphones.

"You dropped something." His eyes are still on mine, breathtakingly dark. He holds out his hand, and I realise there's something dangling from his fingers. His brows lift as I step forward to take it from him, and he lowers the jet necklace into my palm. It's warm from his grip. My heart's hammering: I must have run harder than I thought. I focus desperately on making my breathing return to normal.

"Thanks," I murmur. If my cheeks are red, at least it's attributable to the wind. I realise I'm biting my lip and make myself release it. Sean rolls the dog lead between his finger and thumb, turning the soft leather so slowly that I can almost feel it, supple and smooth, almost smell its faint distinctive scent. For a split second, his gaze travels over my dishevelled hair and the flush of colour spreading downwards from my cheeks. I fasten the chain around my neck, overly conscious of him watching.

"Don't bother going to the cabin." His quiet voice surprises me. I let go of the necklace quickly.

"What?"

"We should meet at the chapel." He loops his thumb back through the dog lead, and jerks his head. The collie rises lithely to its feet and stands, waiting.

"Okay . . ." I breathe.

I can feel the pulse bounding in my wrists as I link my hands behind me. How can he stare so unabashedly, and for so long? And why does it still affect me like this? I stare back. His hair has grown longer since the first day I met him, black-brown and windswept. He's wearing a high-end waterproof instead of his suit jacket, and hiking boots under his Levi's. I try to remind myself about *nothing original*, that he laughed at me; that he despises me, and that the feeling's mutual. But for some reason the dawn light and the teasing rush of the sea are making everything less clear-cut.

"Why?" I add.

Sean doesn't miss a beat. "There's some stuff we need to go over. I'll see you there." He clicks his fingers, and the dog dashes back onto the path, dancing circles around his legs as he begins to walk.

"Enjoy your jog, Frost." His voice, as ever, is impossible to read. It carries on the wind as he turns away. "The views are spectacular this time of day."

I hesitate. Part of me wants to watch him go. To make sure this time. The rest of me won't give in. So I don't. I listen instead to the receding rhythm of his boots on the sandy earth, until they're drowned out completely by the sea. Until he's gone, leaving me utterly alone, and shivering, with my mind overrun by thoughts of fool's gold, and the smell of leather.

CHAPTER 9

2015

"Sophia, have you got a moment?"

No. *No.* She ground her fingernails into the battered cover of her French book. Not now. She turned around.

"I was wondering if I might have a word?" Miss Grégoire had stood up. The classroom was emptying. *Not now.* He was waiting for her. She'd been able to see his car from the window for the last half an hour, tucked almost out of sight behind the X2 stop.

"How the mighty have fallen." Michaela Allen bumped her deliberately on the way past, almost knocking the books from her hand. "Stanley's in detention again."

Sophia didn't reply. She stood absolutely still until the others were gone.

"Yes, Miss Grégoire." She was careful to keep her face smooth, her voice impassive.

"Come and sit down." Her teacher cleared a second chair at the front. "If you can spare me five minutes?"

No. She couldn't spare five minutes. But she walked to the front compliantly and sat down, keeping her hands folded around her textbooks.

"Is everything okay, Sophia?" Miss Grégoire sat down too. There was a pregnant pause.

"Everything's fine," she replied lightly. She fought the urge to fiddle with the edge of her folder, and raised her eyes just enough that she wouldn't look like she was being rude.

"I couldn't help noticing it's the third time in as many weeks you've been late with your prep, or not handed anything in at all." The teacher folded her manicured hands in her lap. There was an engagement ring on her finger. A diamond. Sophia stared at it assiduously.

"I'm sorry."

"I wasn't asking for an apology, Sophia. I was just concerned. It's not like you. I wanted to make sure everything was all right."

"Yeah, it's fine." She was all at once very conscious of how much she was blinking. She checked the sleeves of her school jumper. They were still pulled safely over her hands. "Thanks. Everything's . . . good."

"Okay." Miss Grégoire paused again. Outside, the school turn-out had gained volume and raucousness. The teacher stood up and closed the window. Cleared her throat.

"A few people have mentioned they've seen you meeting someone, Sophia."

"What?" Her head snapped up.

"After school." Her teacher's voice was quiet. "There've been a few questions—"

"What kind of questions?" Her face was suddenly on fire. She clenched her hands around the textbooks.

"That perhaps he's . . . older . . . Someone—"

"Who said that?"

"Do your parents know, Sophia?"

"Of course they do," she snapped. It wasn't even exactly a lie. Her mum did know him. Just not *about* him.

"Okay." Miss Grégoire nodded slowly. "I didn't mean to pry, Sophia. I just need to know that you're . . . safe."

"I'm perfectly safe."

"Mmm. Okay. But if you ever need to talk to someone in confidence — an adult — someone outside of home . . ."

"Can I go now?"

"If you need to." The French teacher got to her feet. "If you're sure there's nothing—"

Sophia stood up too, quickly. The textbooks were heavy. They were starting to make her arm ache.

"No." She shrugged. "There's nothing. Thanks. Sorry about the prep."

"Do you have a lift?"

What? Fuck. She thought on her feet.

"No, I'm getting the X2."

"Okay." Miss Grégoire glanced at her watch. Something in her voice had softened, relieved. "You'd better go then. Don't miss it."

She wouldn't. She ran down the two flights of stairs, the books and ring binders slipping under her arm, and seized her bag from the form room. She wouldn't miss it.

She burst out into the sunshine behind a group of other people heading for the stop, and blended into their midst, trying not to glance over her shoulder. She loitered, anonymous in a crowd of third-formers, itching to make a dash for it but not quite brave enough, until the bus finally rounded into sight and came to a squealing halt at the kerb. Then she ran.

The car door clunked. The seat was hot against the backs of her legs from being in the sun. Hotter, with his eyes on her. Sometimes, she wondered if he enjoyed watching her squirm; he stared until she was breathless and uncomfortable, and then grinned at her, making her lose her battle with the seatbelt so that it slid from her hand and reeled back in. Not seeing him only strengthened it. The days he was away, or that Leon and Mum had prohibitive plans, left her aching and hungry. School was becoming an unnecessary obstacle. She suddenly remembered Miss Grégoire, and froze.

"What's up?" His hand slid over her leg to her thigh. But the tension had established itself. She glanced stiffly over her shoulder.

"We should go," she mumbled.

"You should put your seatbelt on, then." He leaned over to kiss her, his teeth grazing her earlobe. She shivered, thinking of the French-room windows.

"Please," she said.

What business was it of theirs, anyway? It was *her* private life. It had nothing to do with any of them. She shouldn't have to be looking over her shoulder. They had no idea what this was, and they'd make assumptions about him without ever even meeting him. Without any idea of the way he cared for her. How he'd changed her life. That he loved her. That she could tell him anything.

He started the engine, and they jolted over the first of the speed-bumps as he accelerated away. She let out a sigh of relief. Within seconds they were out of sight of school, and joining the main road. He turned to her suddenly.

"I *said* wear your fucking seatbelt," he snapped, with such force that she jumped. She fumbled for it, frightened by the look on his face.

"You don't have to shout," she said petulantly. She plugged the seatbelt in, slightly shaky.

"Sorry," she added. He didn't reply. She sat, motionless, trapped in a turmoil of remorse and unbearably intensifying lust. The muscles in her belly were clenched tight. She squeezed her legs together.

He sighed, exasperated. "Sophia," he muttered. His hand found its way back to her thigh, and she felt her whole body loosen under his touch.

"Aren't we going back to yours?" She glanced out of the window. It didn't look like it. She'd been holding out all weekend to go back to his. The wait was getting painful. She tried desperately not to shift under the heat of his hand, wanting. She hadn't seen him since Thursday. He'd been away on a course; she hadn't even been able to call him because there was no signal at his hotel. He had to go to a lot of courses and conferences. He hated them.

"Not yet," his voice was low, sexy. "What's the hurry? Why so desperate to get away, anyway?"

She fidgeted, nervous.

"People at school have noticed."

"Noticed what?"

"You."

He shot her a sideways glance. "And?"

The car slowed. He spun the wheel with one hand, and they bumped over the uneven surface of a gravelled car park.

"And they're asking questions." She checked the sleeves of her jumper again. Suddenly she was flushed. "I don't know what to tell them."

He looked amused. "Tell them . . . I don't know." He killed the engine. His arm slid behind her back, bulky and warm. "Tell them I'm your tennis coach or something."

She stiffened. This was much too much of a joke to him. She glared at the dashboard.

"I hate PE."

"Then tell them I'm a family friend. An uncle."

"What?!" She twisted free of his arm. "No fucking way. That's creepy."

"Then . . ." He leaned closer. "Don't tell them anything . . ." He kissed the corner of her lips, and his other hand found her school tie and tugged at it. She took the hint and slipped it off.

"Get changed," he said.

She hesitated. She hadn't reckoned on this.

"Here?"

"Uh-huh." He folded his arms across his chest.

"I can't."

He glanced around at the empty car park. "There's no one here," he pointed out.

She rolled the cuff of her jumper in her hand, trying to look like she was assessing the car park too. Fuck. In his room, in the dark, he wouldn't have seen. She could have passed it off. Here—

"What's the matter?" His voice had hardened. She didn't miss the edge to it.

"Nothing," she told him tersely.

It had been Thursday night. A spiralling moment, after he dropped her off, desolate and not completely sober. The house was empty and she'd gone to her room, dizzy, and sick with shame. Six hours. Six hours, they'd spent in his flat alone, touching, whispering, teasing. Six hours of his hands on her body, of her mouth on his, of every kind of temptation. And then, after all of it, she'd let him down. She hadn't been able to do it, what he wanted — she'd been too afraid. *If you loved me you'd try.* That was what he'd said. She did love him. So she did try. But she couldn't do it. She couldn't handle the pain, and he'd stopped, and she'd heard the disillusionment in his silence as he'd found his release elsewhere.

So she'd let him drive her home. And she'd opened the drawer beside her bed, and she'd locked her bedroom door. The razors were easier to take apart than she'd realised, held over a candle so the plastic softened and the blades came loose. It didn't even hurt her fingers.

She'd lost her nerve the first time, and barely made a scratch. It wasn't like the saying at all; the first cut definitely wasn't the deepest. The second was deep enough though, deep enough to hurt. The bite of the blade had been somehow liberating, enough to teach her not to be afraid of the pain. She'd been so sure that the scar would bear testimony. That the next time, she wouldn't let him down.

It was scabbed now. Healing. If she'd thought about it, she'd have worn a long-sleeved blouse. She could have kept it on with her jeans.

"Come on." He was getting impatient. She could tell from the way his hand drifted to the phone in his pocket, the way he crunched the car keys into his palm. She twisted sideways, fixed her eyes on the dash, not his face, and fumbled in her bag for her clothes. Pulled off her jumper and shirt together, in the hope that distraction would be the better part of valour, and scrambled quickly to get into her clean top. She could feel his eyes on her from behind. A hundred hurried explanations and excuses bottlenecked in her throat. She froze.

One second. Five seconds. Ten. The tight fabric clung to her arms and her midriff. He hadn't spoken. High with relief, she unfolded her jeans and arched upwards from the seat to wriggle into them. One of his arms snaked around her to cup her behind.

He hadn't noticed. He couldn't have noticed. Her breath escaped in a rush.

"Are you buying me dinner?" She was emboldened by her own success.

He smirked and released his hand. "If you want."

* * *

She did want. It turned out she was ravenous. She'd skipped lunch again and concealed herself at the back of the library with *Madame Bovary*, eating granola from a tub as she interspersed Flaubert's debut with snippets of tantalising daydream — somewhere between anticipant fantasy and inappropriate flashback — until the bell sounded her out and she had to rejoin the masses. She'd fidgeted and clock-watched all afternoon, barely able to sit still for the thought of him touching her—

"What're you thinking?" He was regarding her over the table, amused. He flipped a beer mat with one finger and caught it without looking.

"Nothing."

"You're thinking something." He grinned and flipped the mat again. Sophia looked down at her own mat.

"I'm hungry." She looked back up, under her lashes. He laughed.

"We're fixing that, aren't we?"

"I hope so," she muttered. As if on cue, a girl had arrived with their plates of food; Sophia eyed her tight black skirt and platinum hair with distrust.

He leaned forward, and his hand found her knee under the table, moving possessively over her thigh.

"Oh, we will be," he murmured.

She ate fast. The incentive was almost more than she could bear. He picked disinterestedly at his own plate of chips, watching her eat. After a few minutes he pushed himself to his feet, nodding towards the bar.

"Want anything?"

She shook her head. He disappeared. She finished her food and sat back in the uncomfortable wooden chair. The single-glazed window beside her was transmitting a wash of cool air over their table. She shivered. He'd left his jacket on the back of his seat, and she reached over to take it and put it on, the pockets hanging weightily past the tops of her thighs. Jesus, what did he keep in them? She plunged her hands into their depths, jangling through the melee of keys and loose change. A phone. She felt the edges with her fingers. No. Two phones.

She paused, uneasy. Two phones? She pulled them out to look. His normal, scratched Samsung, the time winking up at her from its broken screen. And another phone, one she'd never seen before; an iPhone, brand new. She put one finger to the screen so that it lit up, and stopped.

The photo was in vivid colour. A woman, standing against a blue sky, blithe and laughing, her natural glossy hair aglow in the bright sunshine. Like some kind of a model from a country living catalogue, all healthy curves and rosy, dimpled cheeks.

Suddenly her arm felt weak. She lowered the phone to the table, sick.

"Hey." His voice made her jump. He put down a full pint on the table, lager slopping over the edges. She wasn't sure that she could speak at all.

"You . . ." The word almost choked her. "You got a new phone."

"What?" he snapped.

She saw his eyes fall on it, on her own shaking hand beside it on the table-top.

"That? Fuck no." He slid his hand across the table to pick it up. "I fucking wish." He examined the cover. "It's my brother's. He left it in my car. Twat." He shook his head fondly. She was still staring.

"Your . . . brother . . ." She tried to process it.

"Yeah." He shrugged.

"Oh." All of the air had left her lungs. How could she even have thought it? She slumped in the chair, limp. He sipped his drink and pushed it across the table to offer her some. She shook her head.

"I want a smoke. Fancy going outside for a bit?" He reclaimed the pint and stood up. She followed suit, a turmoil of relief and want. His arm slipped around her, pulling her close to feel in the pockets of his jacket for his lighter, his breath warm and dizzyingly close against her ear.

"Come on," he murmured, drawing her with him. She didn't resist. The wooden decking outside was deserted, a couple of bent parasols flapping in the wind. She pulled the jacket tight around her. He lit a cigarette, and then remembered himself and held them out to her, just like always, except this time she took one and held it in her lips and let him light it. She took a deep drag and her throat constricted. The headrush was dizzying. He watched her exhale the cloud of smoke.

"I'm teaching you bad habits," he commented.

A cough forced its way from the back of her throat. She struggled to hold it in, eyes watering, as his hand slipped into her back pocket. He took another sip of his drink, and she breathed another lungful of smoke. It wasn't as bad the second time around, and the third was an improvement on bearable. She could feel it starting to take effect in her brain, like a spell, darkly compulsive. He'd finished his pint. His other hand found its way into her other pocket, drawing her close against him.

"Still hungry?" he whispered. She nodded.

She waited in the car while he went back to pay the tab. His real phone was still in the pocket of the jacket, battered and familiar. Something occurred to her, and she flipped down the vanity mirror to look at herself. It took her three, four attempts before she got a picture she was happy with. She quickly set it as his wallpaper, and dropped the phone back into his pocket as he climbed into the car.

"Ready?" His smile set her on fire, from her cheeks to deep in her belly. She pressed her thighs together and fumbled to put on her seatbelt, remembering her earlier chastisement. The speakers were whispering Radio 1; she turned the volume up, suddenly overtaken by unbidden thoughts of Emma Bovary and Rodolphe.

It was dark in his flat, and he flicked on two of the low-watt wall-lights as she shrugged off the jacket and threw it over the end of the black, fake leather sofa. He picked it up to empty the pockets. Sophia drifted to the window, looking at the photo-frames on the sill. His brother. She was still dazed with relief. With anger, at herself, for even contemplating—

"What the fuck is this?"

She spun. He was holding up the Samsung, furious. The thunder in his face stopped her dead.

"I—"

"What the fuck do you think you're doing?!" He clicked rapidly through the menu. She watched as the picture disappeared from the screen. "What were you *thinking*? What if someone saw it, at work?"

For a moment there was silence. She was holding her breath. Still looking at the backdrop of the phone, returned now to factory settings.

He breathed out slowly, exasperated. "Sophia." His voice was low, pissed off. "Your date of birth is on your bus pass. You think I don't know? You're fucking jailbait. Do you have any idea what I'm risking for you? Anyone finds out about this, and I'd go to prison or something."

For her? He was risking it for *her*. Shit. She hadn't thought of it that way. She swallowed. His expression softened, and he put his arms around her.

"Besides," he murmured into her hair, "I don't want my friends looking at you. You're mine." His hands were on her, skimming the close-fitting silhouette of her top, gripping the hem to pull it off, inverting it over her head. His fingertips traced patterns over her skin to the waistband of her jeans; she revelled in the relief as he slid them down, and reached to take off his shirt. She pressed herself into him, trying to rein back the acceleration in her breathing. *His.* She was his.

He kissed her, hard, and pulled her with him to the sofa. She felt the faux-leather against her knees. The legs of his jeans were pressed against the cushions, either side of hers, his hands roaming over her behind. *His.*

He thrust his tongue deeper into her mouth. Then he broke off and let go of her, sitting down so that she was left standing between his knees, paralysed with anticipation.

"Kneel down, Sophia." His voice was rough, impatient. His hands travelled over her as she did what he said, upwards over her sides to her bra. He unzipped his fly. Her body was singing, her throat thick with anxiety as she leaned forwards uncertainly at his bidding. A tiny groan eased itself between his lips. She tried to remember what he'd told her, tried desperately not to gag, although the tears hit her eyes with a vengeance. Finally he caught hold of her chin and pushed her off, and she steadied herself, dizzy. She heard the rip of foil as he moved around behind her. He planted one hand on the back of her shoulders and pressed, ramming her face into the black PVC cushions. His other hand travelled over her thigh, reigniting the need that had been gnawing at her all day in a sudden, engulfing burst.

It was over quickly, crudely. He disposed of the foil packet and sank back in the sofa, searching out another cigarette from his discarded jacket. Sophia climbed in beside him as he lit it, and watched the smoke curl from his lips. She hesitated.

"Do you love me?" she whispered.

He turned, lowering the cigarette to look at her through his lashes. Her heart almost stopped altogether. Then he gave her a lopsided smile that melted her nerves completely.

"Of course I do." He blew out a perfect smoke ring between his lips. She took the cigarette and inhaled a little breath, not too much this time, letting the buzz of euphoria fill her. He picked up his shirt and draped it over her shoulders. They sat in silence for a while, and Sophia finished the cigarette. She leaned back against his arm and turned her face away from the clock, trying to eke out the seconds.

"When can I see you again?"

"Wednesday?"

"Not tomorrow?"

His jeans creaked against the fake leather as he turned to face her. "Not tomorrow. I'm working late."

"Wednesday." She reached to touch his arm, tracing an imaginary line over his biceps. "What about the weekend? Can I come at the weekend?"

He turned the rest of the way and caught her hand. For a fleeting second, his fingers touched the scab on her arm. "I'm sorry, Soph. You know weekends are bad for me." He leaned down to kiss her mouth, silencing her disappointment. "I can't. I've got people staying, and I don't really want you to meet them."

"Why not?" Her eyes were stinging. The nicotine had given her a headache.

"They wouldn't understand." He let go of her hand.

"Understand what?"

"*What you do to me* . . ." he whispered. His mouth was against hers.

"Ohh," she inhaled.

"Anyway, come on." He sat back abruptly, and in an instant she had crashed back to earth. The clock read five to ten. If the drive took more than half an hour, Leon would ground her. "I need to get you home."

How the mighty had fallen. For an unwelcome moment, Michaela Allen's smug face drifted at the periphery of her vision. Sophia picked up her clothes and resigned herself to the inevitable. The achingly wordless car journey. His departure. Her airless bedroom in St George's Road, French homework. She pulled her sleeves down over her hands. A door that locked. She tried not to focus on the idea, to blot it out.

But it was too late to turn back. And as they descended the stairs to his car in the dark parking lot, all she could console herself with was the thought of a clean cut, and of a pain that she could get her head around.

CHAPTER 10

2022

1921. I gaze up at the hard-edged inscription above the chapel door. The lettering doesn't look that old. It's not resplendent, or especially godly. The grey render is falling off the walls and the boards in the arched windows are rotten.

I can't fathom why Graham Gordon-Heyers wants to save this place. I circle back to look at the only remaining stained-glass window in the end of the chancel. It's difficult to make out; it doesn't depict anything traditional — no crucifixion or nativity. It's an abstract of coloured fragments, a Blessed Virgin in blue, weeping crimson tears over a sleeping child. The expression on her Picassian face makes me shudder. There's something grotesque about it. I've never seen a picture like it — why would she have grieved when he had only just been born, when she didn't know how it was all going to end?

There are still icy puddles on the concrete by the chapel door; the surrounding brambles and bracken are wet with thawing frost. I push through them. I'm glad of my wellies over my work clothes; the thick vulcanised rubber does a good job of repelling the thorns, even at the risk of attracting further faintly misogynistic compliments from Ryan.

"Frost."

I turn. Sean is approaching over the crest of the cliff, hands thrust into the pockets of his Levi's. He barely looks any different than he did an hour ago. Except he's lost the dog. And gained a sharp white shirt collar under his waterproof.

"Sean." I incline my head and make a passable attempt at sounding polite. Aloof is what I'm aiming for, but his name feels strangely natural on my tongue, easier than I'd expected, and it puts me off guard. He springs up the last few metres of gradient to join me.

"Did you enjoy your jog?" he asks. I pause.

"I don't jog," I tell him. "I run."

Sean raises one eyebrow. "Your *run*," he amends.

"Yes, thank you. It was good, on the whole."

"On the whole?" He folds his arms across his chest, and unfathomably I catch myself staring at the profile of his lean, muscled shoulders. I look away quickly.

"I'm not used to interruptions. It definitely wasn't a personal best."

Sean doesn't unfold his arms. "I'll remember that the next time I'm walking that way." His tone is opaque. Mocking? He drums his fingers against his sleeve.

"Now." He jerks his head at the chapel. "Tell me what you see."

I falter. What I see? I see the Virgin Mary crying blood, a chapel on the verge of collapse, and a seascape worthy of a Turner painting. What does he want me to see?

"Go ahead."

"What?"

"Tell me what you're looking at." He starts to walk, thorns plucking at the legs of his jeans.

"Um." I take a deep breath. "Well the footprint runs from here." I hop elegantly over the brambles to the corner of the chapel. "The wall of the barn that was here before they built the chapel lies here." I take a pace. "And from *here*, there's still not even line of sight to the embankment and ditch that English Heritage were worried about. There's potential ac—"

"No," Sean cuts me short. "None of that. I'm not interested in practicalities, Frost. We've already spent two weeks establishing that you know what you're talking about. Tell me what you *see.*"

Oh. I come to a dead stop, teetering on the ruin of the overgrown stonework. I know what I'm talking about? My painting is vivid in front of my eyes. Niklavs' broad grin. *Ak Dievs;* my God.

"Windows." I exhale. "A picture window. In a gable end to the north. Looking over the sea." I close my eyes for a moment, conjuring the memory, *the dream*, the one we aren't supposed to be living. I open them again. The historic remnants of the barn wall stick up from the ground like a puckered, uneven scar; I balance a few steps along it, heel-to-toe like a child, and leap down into the bracken with more grace than I really deserve.

"A pitched roof, slate, local stone. Two storey — to the height of the original barn — three, if you want to use the roof space. The whole structure's brought forward on the footprint, with a spur back from it at ninety degrees to incorporate the chapel. The altar faces east, so you could retain the stained glass — it'll need restoring — if Gordon-Heyers wanted to, I mean. Then the front of the house faces west, so you'll see the sunset from every window . . ." I trail off, abruptly recalling his drawings and the elevations I've started work on that look nothing like what I'm describing.

Sean is watching me, unspeaking. He mounts the one concrete step and tries the locked chapel door. Then he jumps down and moves around the side to look at the chancel, pacing the distance. I see him take mental note.

"You want to keep the window?" He's looking at the crying Virgin. I look up at her, too.

"Not really," I mutter.

"No?" He raises his eyebrows. "She's probably the only thing of any value here."

"She's creepy." I drop my gaze to the carpet of ivy that swarms around the foot of the wall.

"You've spent too much time listening to Claire." His voice changes on the name, making me glance back at him in surprise. I remember the way she leapt to his defence when she came for lunch at the cabin.

"All her crap about it being haunted." He shakes his head, derisory again in an instant.

"I don't believe in ghosts." I say it with more emphasis than I'd intended. "But I don't know why anyone ever commissioned something so horrible."

His eyes flick to my face. Surprised? I can't quite tell.

"Nice to hear you can feel so strongly about something," he comments.

I frown as he picks his way through the brambles and strides downhill towards the cove, pausing on the treacherous barrier of the rocks that separate sand from cliffside, and assessing the waves as they crash towards his feet.

"I need to go and make some notes." He turns suddenly and starts back up in the direction of the track. "I'll be at the cabin. Once you've reconciled your differences with Mother Mary."

I pause. There's something in his voice I can't work out. Some kind of taunt. Some kind of dare. I take a single step after him, then stop.

"What was this about?" I stand very still. "What do you want from me?"

Sean turns back. His expression is smooth, unreadable, his eyes perilously dark.

"I want what you're not giving me, Livia," he says softly. His gaze is intent. Inescapable. "Until you do, we're not going anywhere."

I can't think of a reply. I stare after him, winded and oddly invigorated, as he resumes his path on the loose granite, his long strides athletically easy. What does he mean, what I'm not giving him? I'm making up *his* drawings. I've worked myself into the ground researching. I've fulfilled every letter of the job description. What else does he want?

Passion.

Try me.

There's a nervous feeling in the pit of my stomach.

I look back up at the weeping Virgin and the broken render. What's with this place, anyway? What's the deal with a church locked up and left to rot? What's here that Graham is so desperate not to lose? The place is the epitome of desertion. I scramble around the side to the boarded windows, at head height, and stand on tiptoe to try and see in, but I'm not tall enough. I scrabble at the render with my fingernails, and find enough purchase with the toe of one boot to haul myself up. The boards are giving way almost enough to see through. Overwhelmed by curiosity, I grip the window ledge with both hands and pull myself higher, gaining a toehold in the knots of ivy, until I have both arms and then both knees on the window ledge.

I pause, breathless. A strange thrill runs along the back of my neck. The boards really are rotten. With a little bit of persuasion—

I never meant for the whole board to come away. My intention wasn't to do anything more than look. But as the damp wood splinters and bows inwards, the gap at the side of the window is more than big enough to see through. It's big enough to fit an arm through, a shoulder, a head, a hip . . .

I land inside with a thud so forceful that for a second I'm scared I'm going to fall through the wooden floor. The mist of my breath curls in front of my face as I recover my balance and test a cautious step. The dust must be a quarter of an inch thick. The filtered light is somehow unsettling, seeping around the boards in the windows with a few pallid tendrils of misplaced ivy. I feel in my pocket for my phone and flick on the torch.

I'm not sure what I was expecting — aside from dereliction — but whatever it was, I'm disappointed. There's nothing much here. The room is empty, not especially big, and littered with broken wood and the carcasses of four or five chairs. The plaster on the walls is damp and cracked, coming away to reveal uninspiring pre-war brickwork; the only surviving clues as to the room's intended use are a granite baptismal font, tipped on its side beneath a sorry-looking timber cross nailed to the far wall.

I tiptoe nearer to look. There's no altar. If there ever was one, there's no sign of it now, not even an impression of where it might have stood. The floor of the chancel is raised by a good few inches and I remember, with a sudden shudder, reading about the vault underneath. What if there are people buried there? Dead bodies right under my feet? The red-tinged tears of the Virgin Mary look somehow sinister in the torchlight. I take a hasty step back.

But no. There wouldn't have been burials here. I wet my lips nervously. Would there? Graham wants to build his house here. It doesn't seem likely that he'd want the corpses of his not-so-distant predecessors buried in the foundations.

No bodies. Nonetheless, I suddenly don't feel inclined to hang around. I've seen what I need to. There's very little inside these walls besides the lingering smell of unfulfilled potential and decay. I glance uneasily back at the window. The sound of the sea is muted, distant. But for a fleeting moment, I almost think I've heard something else. Something closer at hand. Some—

Without as much as a flash of warning, the phone dies. The torch goes out, plunging me into darkness. I take another step backwards in alarm and something hard strikes me in the backs of the knees; I trip and buckle, landing sprawled in the skeleton of one of the chairs. Blind, I'm choking on dust, tasting it; all I can hear is the accelerating drumroll of my heartbeat.

I fumble for my phone. Someone's there. Someone—

I seize the phone and stumble to my feet. Something cracks as I trample through the remnants of the chair, the sound ricocheting loudly off the crumbling plaster. Wet wood forces its way under my nails as I scale the wall to the windowsill and explode unceremoniously out into the wan daylight.

My gasps of relief are short-lived. I exhale my second slightly dizzy lungful in a rush.

"Livia." Graham Gordon-Heyers inclines his head. He hasn't missed a beat at my sudden theatrical appearance; he's standing still and pensive, half facing the sea.

"Sorry," I burst out.

Sorry what? Sorry I'm not at work? Sorry I broke into your chapel? Holy crap. I stand, gaping, not quite able to put together the rest of the sentence.

Graham shakes his head. "Don't be." He turns the rest of the way to face me, and I can't help but suddenly notice just how much like my father he looks in his oversized chequered shirt and loosely hanging chinos. I swallow. "There's no other way in." There's something desperately sad in his smile. "The key was one of the things that went missing during the burglary two years ago, while we were in Montreal. Clarissa always said she kept a spare, but only she knows where it is now." He glances back out over the ocean, thoughtful. "I ought probably to employ a locksmith," he adds. "But there doesn't seem much point."

I follow his gaze, speechless.

"I remember before it was shut up." He's watching a seagull hovering, off balance, on an eddy of wind. "I used to come here, as a child. There's quite a large vault underneath, you see; we used it for air-raids, during the war — it's been filled in now. Later, we held recitals here. My father loved baroque music — Vivaldi, Albinoni. He tutored a string quartet, which was how I met Clarissa. She plays — played — the cello."

The seagull dips and wavers, wing tips trembling. I draw a deep breath, but I can't think of a reply.

"It got difficult to maintain." He shrugs. "I had it boarded up twenty years ago. Claire and the boys used to play down here. We had a couple of cricket balls through windows, then the escapade with a broken wrist — it all became a bit too dangerous."

The boys. Ryan and Sean? Really? So Sean already knows this place. No matter what his facade, it must be more than just any old job to him. I squint back at the stained Virgin Mary. If Graham decided to board the windows, why didn't he cover her too? The only thing — as Sean had pointed out — of any value? But perhaps value isn't just monetary.

"I'm sorry about your wife," I say at last.

Graham turns to me.

"Yes." He nods. "So am I. And I'm sorry about your father, Livia. Claire told me. By account of the literature, he was a great man."

"Oh." My throat has constricted. "Yeah." I look at my hands. "I mean, yes. He was."

"Do you have a place that reminds you of him?"

I look up, frowning. A place? A summit, the compact snow glistening, frozen and re-frozen, a dazzling spectrum of white and blue with only crampon scars to mar its perfection. Boxing Day. Ice axes, three sets of boots, steaming breath and pounding hearts.

A bedroom with closed curtains and ink stains in the carpet, the tick of a syringe-driver. *Dad, it's okay. It's okay to go. Think about Helvellyn. Think about Boxing Day. Think about Striding Edge in the snow . . .*

Graham meets my gaze levelly. And for a moment, he's not an old man. He's not rich and influential, or the employer of my employer. He's a second lost soul, with dimples in his cheeks, like his daughter, and an incalculable sadness in his eyes. I bite my lip.

"Helvellyn," I whisper. "In the ice."

He nods. We watch the seagull swoop and plummet, and disappear from view.

"This is Helvellyn, Livia," he says.

* * *

There's no light in this room. No speck, no single photon. Not from the gap under the door. Not even from outside, in the road, where only the silence is bigger than the darkness. Could it be that it's all gone? Every last glimmer of it? Imagine, if the sun didn't rise again tomorrow. Imagine if this was it. The beginning of darkness . . .

Darkness. I can't get rid of it. On my canvas, in every corner of the flat. Between the shrubs and tree branches. Under my skin.

The cabin door is ajar. My boots scrunch on the neglected gravel path as I walk to it slowly, concentrating on my steps. The sky is Manganese, the sun Ochre with Iridescent White, and the dust on my shoes is Burnt Sienna. The gravel is Pewter, shot through with glimmers of Indigo. There's still frost in the shadows and there are still shadows everywhere.

I walked from the chapel. Left my car overlooking the view and trampled blindly through the bracken until the wild gorse and bloomless heather transitioned to lawns and rhododendrons, until the wind obliterated any trace of tears from my cheeks. But it can't obliterate the thought. The word Helvellyn has lodged firmly in my throat, and I can't do anything to shift it.

I push the door. It seems it's been left open on purpose; it's hot in the cabin. I slip inside, and stop. So does the tap of fingers on keys.

Sean looks up from his desk. I waver. His eyes are darker than ever, smouldering with challenge.

I pause in the doorway, momentarily speechless.

"You have a desk," he reminds me under his breath.

I move to sit down, trying not to stare. His desk. He's working at his desk. I shoot a glance at the closed door to the back room. So does he.

"You've made your point, Frost," he remarks dryly.

He picks up his pen from beside the keyboard. His shirt-sleeves are rolled; I can see the ripple of tendons in his wrist as he flexes his fingers. I swallow and slip off my coat, the elbows of my own blouse suddenly uncomfortably tight.

I want what you're not giving me.

I sit down, resisting the urge to scrub at my cheeks. I unpack my satchel onto the table-top and falter, a wave of hot and cold flashing in my gut. I don't have Dad's pen. It's nowhere on the desk. I tip out my case of drafting pencils to check, and shake the satchel onto the floor, fighting panic.

It's not there either. As if today could get any worse. I can't have lost it. Dropped it? It was here. Right here.

I clench and unclench my jaw.

I'm not going to cry again. Not over a pen. I can't even imagine what Dad would say. I gather the pencils quickly and stand up, my roll of drawings grasped tightly in one hand.

Sean glances back up. For a split second, his gaze lingers on my cheeks, and he frowns. I move away quickly to the drawing boards, not daring to look back at him. As if I cried today, when I didn't summon a single tear at the funeral. Today, when Sean Lorchann is here, waiting for me to pull myself up to his exacting standards.

Helvellyn. I spread out my paper on the board, every muscle in my core clenched tight. *This is Helvellyn.* Technically flawless will be enough over my dead body.

Minutes blur to hours. I shut out the tick of the clock and work without intermission, even though I can feel him behind me, even though I can sense, every so often, his fleeting sharp scrutiny across the empty room. Even though every tiny shift of movement reminds me acutely of his presence, the sinuous stretch of his long legs as he straightens them under the desk, the brush of his thumb and finger against the lightly stubbled angle of his jaw. I clamp my teeth until my head aches. Toss my hair back from my eyes for the hundredth time, and sweep it into a messy knot without looking, pausing to scan over my drawings as I do.

The vibration of my phone across the room is so loud and unexpected that I stand up in alarm. I must have left it at my desk. I didn't even realise it was working again.

Sean has looked up too. But his eyes aren't on the backlit screen of the newly resurrected phone. They're on me. I drop my gaze and descend the steps hastily to answer it.

"Hello?" I breathe.

"Livs!" Claire sounds relieved. I blink, surprised, and start back towards the drawing board. "Are you at the cabin?" She sounds like she's on the move, outside somewhere, walking. I can hear the wind blustering across the mouthpiece.

"Yeah." I mount the steps, careful not to look back.

"Oh, brill. I'll be there in a second." She doesn't say goodbye. She hangs up. Moments later, the cabin door creaks on its hinges.

"Hi, Sean." Claire flashes her dimpled smile in his direction.

"Claire." He inclines his head.

"I've come to borrow Livs." She springs up the steps to join me. "Wow!" Her gaze falls on the sketches. "Is this the old chapel?"

"Oh . . ." I quickly reposition the top sheet to hide the drawing underneath. "Yeah." I pause, slightly at a loss.

"That's amazing!" Claire moves around me to look from a different angle. "What do you think to it? The chapel? I told you it's haunted . . ."

Behind us, Sean's chair scrapes quietly on the wooden floor. He pushes himself to his feet. I look round in time to see one of his eyebrows flicker tellingly. Then he picks up his wallet and keys from beside his laptop, and disappears.

"Dad says he bumped into you there this morning." Claire picks up a scale to examine it, then lays it down again. She turns to me suddenly. "He's just left for the hospital. Actually, that's what I needed to talk to you about." She's not exactly smiling anymore. Her dimples have faded. She looks anxious.

"He'll need to stay there this evening, too. There's a specialist coming to see Mother. And Ryan and I are supposed to be at a do in Plymouth — tonight — with some of his old work colleagues, from Rivent. We have to set off by four if we're going to make it, but we're totally stuck for a babysitter. Sean can't b . . ."

I don't hear what Sean can't do. The sound of my own blood rushing in my ears drowns out the rest of her discourse. I stand absolutely still. All I have to say is no. Not this time. I'm not doing this again.

Be a darling . . .

"Ryan said not to bother you, but I just thought . . . knowing how he took to you . . . Fin might be okay with you . . ."

Helvellyn. I close my eyes for a fraction of a moment. Make myself breathe out. Paperclips. Dandelion stems. Daydreams.

No. The word seems to catch in my throat. Like I can't quite part with it.

"Yeah," I whisper. "Okay."

CHAPTER 11

Could it be possible that it's my fault? That it always was? Could it be possible, after everything, that it's worse to wrongly begin a life than it is to end one? To condemn someone, right from the start?

I can't sleep. Maybe it's this room. Look around. There's something here, something hiding in the shadows. Something wrong about it. Don't you think? Like it isn't what it was supposed to be.

I can't sleep. Even the image of his face isn't enough. Faces become ghosts when you sleep. Ghosts that you can't run from.

I told you I love him. Well, maybe I didn't tell you that, but it's what I meant. I thought I was in love, once before, but I wasn't. I know that now. Then, I was a stamp pressed onto an envelope. This is different. This is worse. Pieces of me have been opened up, parts I didn't know I had, opened up to feelings I didn't know existed. And now I do know, their emptiness is destroying me. The problem is if he knew the truth . . . if you knew the truth — about me — you'd despise me. The way I despise myself, at night, when the only thing bigger than the darkness is the silence.

Close your eyes. You can't block it out. You can't fill it, can you? You can't escape it. All you can do is wait. Wait for the morning. Wait for the sunrise, and just keep believing that it's going to come . . .

Wait for the morning. That's all I have to do. Wait for the morning. Not even the sunrise. Just the early hours, one or two o'clock. They won't be later than that. Claire promised. Probably no later than midnight. Eight hours. Only eight hours; four-hundred and eighty minutes; not quite twenty-nine thousand seconds. I perch on the edge of the leather sofa at the far end of the sizeable slate-and-oak kitchen. Strange, to think of Sean and Peter McLeod designing this house, when now here I am, rattling around inside it. The Old Gatehouse. From what I can surmise, Claire and Ryan are living here for free. It's huge; it could envelop my parents' old house twice over. The kitchen alone is bigger than my flat in Sunnyside, the conservatory an octagon of gleaming glass expanding beside it. The lounge and snug are cosily finished, with tasteful simplicity that speaks more of Sean's input than anyone else's. Upstairs, the three vast bedrooms are furnished with oak and designer fabrics that I can almost picture Claire wearing. Well, two of them are. The third is more of a mystery; I've done little more than poke my head around the panelled door to make out the Spider-Man bedspread, discarded iPad and an abnormally tidy pine chest filled with toys.

Claire left me instructions, and a chart of images that were meant to resemble signs — a crash course in Makaton. I didn't even have time to try them out before she left: thank you, please, Mummy, Daddy, drink, toilet, hungry, hurt. But she told me about the thing with boundaries. Some days, it's the bedroom doorway. Other days it's okay, as long as you're careful and don't touch.

I slide to my feet from the warm, slightly worn leather cushions. I have no idea how I'm supposed to know which kind of day it is. Fin is at the kitchen table, where he's been since we got in, a dog-eared book laid flat in front of him on the splash-resistant tablecloth. When I picked him up from the pebble-dashed primary school at three his teaching assistant came with him. Even without her explanation, it was fairly obvious he wasn't going to relinquish the book. She'd read it to him five times over the course of the morning, and the trainee teacher who came in after lunch had been coerced into another three. So they let him take it — possibly they were happy never to have to read it again — thus *Thomas the Tank Engine and Friends* was clutched tightly in his hands as he trundled his way out through the walking gate and clambered into my car.

I look over at him, not sure how long I should leave him to it before I intervene. He's knelt up on his chair, tracing one finger thoughtfully back and forth across the page. His half-eaten plate of fish fingers and pasta has gone cold. Seeing it reminds me that Claire left the rest of her shopping in the hall. I leave Fin looking at the book, and go to fetch it. He isn't actually turning any pages.

Ten to seven. It's completely dark. I can't find the light switch, and have to half-feel my way past the stairs to the chaos of shoes and shopping bags beside the front door. I squint out through the glass into the driveway. I can't remember if I locked my car, not that it really matters; the small gravel turning circle and narrow track from the Hall are deserted and shadowy, framed by the silhouettes of the trees. I pick up the bags of food and take them back through to the kitchen.

My stomach lurches.

Fin is gone. My eyes scour the kitchen. My hands tremble as I lower the shopping to the floor. Vanished. There's just an empty chair, abandoned in the glow of the wall-lamp. Vacant shadows . . .

"Fin?" I rasp. "Fin?!"

Nothing. I let go of the bag handles. On the table, the book cover lays prostrate amongst the carnage of its own dismembered pages. He's torn them out. Every one. The air is suddenly chill as I tiptoe closer, the edges of the ripped paper lift slightly with the unfelt stir of my movement. How hadn't I realised how dark it is? I reach to turn on the rest of the lights, and two of the pages blow from the table to crease on the floor at my feet. I crouch to pick them up.

"*Fin*," I exhale.

He's there. Huddled in a ball underneath the furthest dining chair, his skinny arms wrapped tightly around his knees, a smudge of blond hair against the charcoal tiles. His whole body fits in the footprint of the chair, crammed between its wooden legs.

"What happened?" I whisper.

He turns his lucent liquid eyes on me.

"What happened to your book?" I pick up the pages. Fin's lips purse tightly together. For a moment there's utter silence. We face each other, deadlocked. It occurs to me that I should probably be angry, at least reproachful. But my heart's beating much too hard.

"Will you come out?"

Fin shakes his head.

"We can mend it." I try my best to sound reassuring. "If you come out, we can mend it."

He regards me, statue still.

"I'll help you Sellotape it. We can explain to school." My legs are starting to ache. "I'm not cross. I promise. Come on."

Painfully slowly, he shuffles forwards. I hold out a hand to help him up but he doesn't take it; he pushes himself to his feet and moves without me to the eviscerated cover, touching the glossy front picture mournfully with his forefinger.

I eventually manage to find Sellotape in a drawer in the snug, and I hold the pages in place one at a time while Fin puts the tape on. The middle two or three are almost completely destroyed — we have to piece them together like a jigsaw — and I'm not sure once we finish that the story even makes sense anymore; one page appears to be gone altogether. But our repair job seems to make Fin feel better, even if Claire or I will end up quietly replacing it, and after half an hour of worried staring at the Sellotape, I manage to persuade him to let me put it away. I slot it into his book bag; *St Anthony's C of E Primary*. There's a printed rainbow on the polyester. St Anthony — the patron saint of the lost. Out of nowhere, I remember Dad's pen, and turn away. There's no point in dwelling on losses.

It's half past seven. I blink hard at the dull face of the kitchen clock. Babysitting was an appalling idea. How did I let Claire lure me here? As if high-fives and biro houses could ever have been enough. Fin has gone upstairs. I hear the soft tread of his socks on the creaking landing floorboards, and follow him up.

He's turned his bedroom light on, and I stop in the doorway. In quiet acquiescence, he's already got changed; his school uniform is a pile of crumpled blue and grey on the cream rug, the over-sized arms and legs of his Spider-Man pyjamas almost drown him as he climbs onto the matching bedclothes and sits down, watching me.

Warm milk. Claire had said something about warm milk.

"Do you want a drink?" I ask.

Fin shakes his head.

"Some milk?" I start through the doorway, then remember not to. I step back again. "Do you need any help to brush your teeth?"

Another shake of the head. But he gets up obediently, and moves past me to the bathroom. I stand at a distance as he clambers onto the plastic step in front of the sink and picks up a bright red toothbrush. He squashes the almost-empty toothpaste tube against the back with two fingers, and pauses. There's a momentary silence.

"Oh." It takes me a second to realise. "Do you need help?"

He raises dark eyes to my face. I see his lips press together. Then he holds out the tube. I take it and persuade a blob of toothpaste onto the brush, and he starts to clean his teeth with assiduous care. For such a small, silent four-year-old, he's incredibly self-sufficient. I stand back, useless, and let him take himself back to his room. He peels back the Spider-Man covers and climbs in. Then he lays down, his eyes still on my face. I falter, not quite catching on, then realise the bedroom light's still on.

"Off?" I whisper.

He nods. I reach to turn down the dimmer switch. Fin regards me, mute, his brown eyes huge in the almost-darkness. I pause.

"All the way off?"

He shakes his head. I withdraw my hand, leaving the light burning low.

"Mum and Dad will be back soon," I whisper. I'm toeing the line between doorway and bedroom carpet. "Really soon."

Something catches my eye. There, on the shelf beside the bed. A paper windmill, all the colours of the rainbow.

"Goodnight, Fin," I breathe.

Not a sound. Not even a movement. I hesitate, suddenly reluctant to turn my back. What do I think's going to happen? I grasp the doorframe, rigid with fear. Then I make myself let it go. Nothing. Nothing's going to happen. Not here, in the isolated safety of Claire and Ryan's house, hidden away amongst the pine trees, rhododendrons and protective shadows of Trethallyan Hall. Here, where there are locked doors and security lights, and gates with keycodes.

Livia, be a darling . . .

No, no, *no*. I tiptoe across the landing, resolute. Time to forget, remember? I descend the stairs into the hall and stop, listening.

Nothing.

Exactly as it's meant to be. I wrap my arms around myself, and walk back to the kitchen, still on tiptoe. He's sleeping. A paradigm of too-good-to-be-true child behaviour. This is it. For four hours. All I have to do is survive.

I pick up Fin's empty glass from the table. The beginning threat of rain is pattering lightly against the windows. I curl my toes inside my socks, standing as still as I can on the tiles. This isn't the Solent.

The crash comes out of nowhere, and it's almost as if I'm expecting it. Almost as if my anticipation has brought it into being. The rush of wind. The slam of a double-glazed sash window against its frame—

The glass falls through my fingers and hits the tiles with a deafening smash, shards of shattered glass spraying the floor. I take off through it, oblivious to the pain, mounting the stairs two at a time.

Silence. I come to a dead stop, berating myself. I've imagined it.

No. A howl . . . A clatter. My blood has turned to ice.

Fin—

I look around the door.

The Spider-Man bedroom is absolutely still. His small shape under the bedclothes is a slow-breathing mound of sleeping silence. The window is closed, the curtains two-thirds drawn. I sag backwards.

I'm insane.

I limp across the landing, suddenly dully aware of the pain in my foot. The bathroom window is open a crack; all the bottles and lotions on the windowsill have fallen over. The blind is swinging in the draught, its bottom bar striking the glass. I bang the window shut and draw the blind all the way down.

There are Elastoplast in the bathroom cabinet. I peel off my sock to inspect the damage. The cut on my heel is small but deep. I cover it with shaking fingers and replace the box in the untidy shelves of the cabinet. The action is enough to unbalance everything: tubes of mascara, shaving cream, deodorant. A green paper prescription falls out and lands in the sink. I snatch it to safety, but I can't help catching sight of the details on the script. Temazepam 20mg. Fluoxetine. The second name's familiar. An antidepressant. They kept trying to prescribe it for me, for months. They wanted me to take it while I was in hospital. I refused. I'd been allowed to refuse things, by then.

I slide it back into the end of the cabinet and close the door. I should never have agreed to this. I hobble to the other two bedrooms, check the windows and draw the curtains. Everything sounds so loud. Every normal house sound. The central heating. A ticking clock. I'm almost sure I can hear the creak of feet on the stairs—

But I can't, can I? I grip the headboard of the spare bed and stand very still, making myself concentrate on my breathing. *In. Lengthen. Out.* What was it all for, the clinic, Verity House? All those hours of counselling? I'm being ridiculous.

I make myself go back downstairs. The hall is cold. Colder than I remember. With a seeping feeling of dread, I tiptoe to the front door. The keys Claire left me are still hanging in the lock, swaying gently. A cold breeze is squeezing past the door; it's on its chain, rattling. I freeze, immobilised. It wasn't on the chain before, was it? It was closed.

Wasn't it?

Who's to say? I breathe out, hard. It was dark before. I couldn't even see my way to the light switch. Would I really have noticed?

I close it and lock it. Fight the urge to look out through the diamond pane of glass at the drive. I put the keys on the sideboard. Enough. Crazy or not, I'm not doing this anymore. I scramble back upstairs and touch Fin's bedroom door. It creeps an inch wider open. Still nothing. Silence. I'm holding my breath.

I lower myself to sit, upright and exhausted, against the wooden doorframe. How can I stop myself from listening? For anything? A whisper, a sigh, a movement?

I count the seconds, paranoia growing. Can I even hear his breathing? I strain my ears, but all I can hear is my own pulse. I stretch forwards to look around the end of the door. His shape is small and motionless beneath the shadowy covers. I watch until I see him heave a sigh, then duck quickly back out of sight to resume my vigil.

Time elongates. Minutes, a quarter of an hour. My legs are numb and my back's aching. He still hasn't even shifted under the covers. Surely that's not normal? The adrenaline swells again in my bloodstream. I push myself to my feet.

He's lying absolutely still, tousled blond hair sticking out in every direction from his head, and his eyes are open. He doesn't move an inch at the indolent moan of the door. Doesn't make a sound. I falter. Soundless tears are sliding over his porcelain cheeks, accumulating in rivulets and dripping onto the pillow to soak dark holes in Spider-Man's mask.

"Fin?" I exhale. "Fin?"

How long? Oh, God. How long has he been like this? Helpless — wretched — I push open the door and start toward him, then stop, almost tripping over my own feet as I remember about boundaries.

Fin's eyes widen, alarmed. He still doesn't move. His knees are tucked up to his chest, the shuddering rise and fall of his stifled breathing almost imperceptible.

"Oh, Fin!" I can't help it — what else can I do? I blunder to the bed and kneel down beside him, remembering at the last moment not to touch. "What's the matter?"

No response. The tears stream silently. I wrack my brains for the Makaton signs, hoping I can encourage him to tell me, but I can't remember them.

"Hurt?" I attempt. He doesn't even blink.

Mum? Dad? I have no idea. I give up on the gestures and sit back on my heels, somewhere between despair and panic. I have no idea. What am I going to do?

"Fin." I swallow. "It's okay. Mum and Dad'll be home soon. Everything's okay. It's okay. I promise."

His eyes are on me, pools of bewildered darkness. His heart might be breaking, and I'm utterly powerless to stop it.

"What can I do? You need to sleep. How can I help?"

Nothing. I can do nothing.

"*Fin*," I breathe.

Darkness. Absolute, lapping, beckoning darkness. I squeeze my eyes shut. Think of something else, anything else. A colour. Any colour . . .

"Red . . . and yellow . . ." My voice is husky, practically tuneless. "And pink . . . and green . . ."

I'm five years old. Standing in the garden, in the twilight. Turning on the spot, turning round and round, a bright blur of meadow flowers, the whisper of a breeze.

"Orange. And purple. And blue . . ." The only song I can think of. The only lullaby I know. My jaw is aching. Every night, every night, my father's hand on the bedcovers . . .

"I can sing a rainbow, sing a rainbow—"

I look down. Fin has turned his face upwards, the tears gathering gradually in one huge glistening droplet on his pointed chin. I unfold my legs from beneath me. Somewhere between inspiration and desperation, I reach for the paper windmill.

"Sing a rainbow too." I touch a finger to the delicate blades, so that they turn. A slow half-revolution to the right. *And straight on 'til morning.*

"Red and yellow," I'm gaining confidence, "and pink and green. Orange . . . and purple . . ."

Very slowly, Fin's hand creeps out from underneath the covers. He reaches for the windmill, taking me by surprise. I almost stop singing.

". . . and blue." It's a croak. The ache in my throat has become unbearable. His finger has stopped on the blue blade. He isn't crying anymore. He's gazing at me with his strange, soul-shattering eyes, lids dropping even as I watch. His breathing is growing heavy.

"I can sing a rainbow . . ." It's all I can do not to yawn. He's still holding the windmill between his finger and thumb. The blades won't turn. "Sing a rainbow . . ." I lay it down gently on the pillow beside him without breaking it from his grip. His small back is rising and falling, the knot of his body uncurled at last under the duvet, like a half-opened flower turning to the light.

I let go of the stem of the windmill. I don't want to get up, or whisper goodnight and shatter the silence: the only thing bigger than the darkness. I lower my hand.

* * *

It starts with coffee. Coffee in a paper cup. The way dreams start, in the middle, never at the beginning. The cabin is flooded with daylight, but I have the lamp on anyway, bent close against the angle of the drawing board. I have my headphones in, like I used to in the workshop at uni; maybe that's why I don't hear him arrive. Then again, I never hear him arrive. He possesses a stealth that isn't human, a singular ability to wrong-foot me with just a glance.

I'm drawing, absorbed, focussed on the tiny, perfectly-to-scale details. Details of the house at Helvellyn — well, as close as you could get: on the road out of Glenridding where my father used to park the car and we'd change our boots in the rain.

The strap of his watch catches the end of the desk. I start upright. Sean puts down the coffee. His arm is inches from mine, the paper cup laid down like a challenge between us. Steam curls softly from beneath the plastic lid as he runs one finger around its circumference to press it more firmly into place. He doesn't speak. Neither do I. Instead, he reaches out and takes the drafting pencil, *0.7 mm*, from my hand, and I watch, wordless, as he sets it down with a firm click on the fibreglass table-top.

"Where's the flair, Frost?" he whispers. "*Where's the passion?*"

I don't have a voice to reply. It's caught in my throat, arrested by the proximity of his fingertips to mine. He lets go of the pencil. His eyes fix mine. His index finger traces the back of my hand. I gasp.

Then his hand closes around my forearm, strong and surprisingly warm, and he's leaned over Helvellyn to murmur against my ear.

"I want . . . what you're not giving me, Livia."

* * *

I jolt upright, disorientated.

"Livia." The whisper is close at hand, familiar. I blink, trying to get my bearings.

"Livia." Ryan's hand rests fleetingly on my shoulder. I sit up quickly. The low hum of the dimmed electric light pervades my senses as I try to piece together where I am. I stumble to my feet.

"You look shattered." Ryan's voice is low. He stands back to let me out of the room first, then kills the light, plunging the shadowy Spider-Man shapes into conclusive darkness. "Sorry it's so late."

Late? I glance around groggily, trying to make out a clock.

"Thanks so much for stepping in." He leads the way downstairs. There's a lamp burning on the sideboard in the hallway. Quarter past three. I rub my eyes, bemused. "You're an absolute saviour. I don't know how we'll ever make it up to you."

"Not at all," I gulp. "It's not a problem."

"Was he okay? He didn't give you any trouble?"

"No." I shake my head. "No trouble." Now doesn't seem like the time to go into details. I'll explain to Claire about the book tomorrow.

"Good." Ryan sounds relieved. "I feel bad for letting Claire ask you. Are you going to be okay getting home?"

"I'll be fine." I look at the lamp, and the confusion of keys underneath it. I suddenly remember locking the door, and shiver. My foot's aching.

"You're sure?" He finds my coat. "Claire's gone straight to bed. I don't mind running you home. I can pick you up in the morning so you can get your car."

"Honestly," I mumble, embarrassed. "It's fine."

"Okay, Livs." His hand brushes my arm again, and gives my shoulder a brief, friendly squeeze. "Thanks so much. Anything we can ever do to reciprocate . . ." He pauses. I nod.

"The invitation's open," he reiterates. I glance up at his easy smile and the wide shoulders of his now slightly crumpled suit, and blush.

"Thanks," I whisper.

Ryan raises a hand to his forehead in his customary, boyish salute. "See you later this morning, Livs." He holds open the door for me, and I descend the one stone step and push open the wrought iron gate onto the drive.

"See you," I murmur. I don't wait for the door to close. Overly aware of him watching, and inexplicably tremulous, I run to my car.

* * *

It's very cold in Sunnyside. I park right beside the door, and don't let myself look over my shoulder. I don't let myself run, either, swamped with relief as the outer door closes behind me, leaving me in the thick, muted silence of the hallway. Niklavs' lights are all out — or not on yet, depending how you look at it. The familiar stuffy air is welcoming, secure somehow, as I hurry up the stairs and let myself into my flat.

Swift's flat. I'm not sure why the thought of her company makes me feel safe.

I undress, clean my chattering teeth, and cocoon myself under the duvet. This faceless girl who doesn't even know I know her, who no one else will *ever* know the way I do.

I pick up the journal, and press my thumb to the tiny washable-ink bird. It's too late to read. I know that. In three and a half hours, I have to get up for work, and suddenly all I can think about is paper coffee cups and drafting pencils. I flip through a few journal pages, the muscles in my abdomen clenched tight.

> *I try to keep believing. But there's a profound loneliness to being unrequited. To being secret. To having secrets . . . such terrible secrets.*
>
> *He was innocent. And now he's dead, because of me.*
>
> *There it is. I've said it. Written it. A signed confession.*
>
> *I killed him.*

Holy shit. My eyes come to a dead stop. The bedside lamp seems to have dimmed; the tick of the World War Two clock is deafeningly loud. I gaze at the words.

I killed him.

I lower the book, head spinning. Safe, in her company. Alone, in her flat . . .

> *I made a choice. I condemned him to his death. I was responsible, and no one will ever know. No one except me. There can be no justice, when I'm my own defence and prosecution. My own judge, jury and executioner. I got so good at lying to myself.*
>
> *Don't abandon me. Please, please don't. I know it would be no more than I deserve. I thought it would feel better, to have told you. But it doesn't. All I am now, is afraid. I'm afraid of being found out . . . I'm afraid of being alone . . .*

I screw my eyes tightly closed. She couldn't have killed someone. Someone would know something.

Except she said no one knew. I pull the pillows to me and hug them against my chest. She couldn't have. Not deliberately . . . But something must have happened. Something had happened, and she blamed herself. And she was afraid, so afraid, that someone would find out . . .

I don't open my eyes. I let the book slide onto the floor, and reach to click off the light. It's so easy. So easy to blame yourself.

"I won't abandon you." The ache in my throat has returned with a vengeance. "I won't abandon you. I promise."

CHAPTER 12

2015

Never in her life had Sophia been interested in cleaning. For a while she had been forced into it, when the kitchen overflowed with dirty dishes and Mum still didn't come out of her room. She'd managed the bare minimum, hoovering the carpets when the grey dust got too visible, sticking bleach down the toilet every now and then. Since Leon had moved in, nothing was ever dirty. Dishes, carpets, bathroom — Leon was like a machine, and he had a tight schedule. Chores got divided out because cleanliness is next to godliness, or something like that. Sophia had baulked at it. Until today.

Today, there was no Leon in his rubber gloves. No Mum. They were in Walsingham, on retreat, whatever that meant. What it really meant was that she was home alone for four days. Four whole days of the Christmas holiday. When Mum had asked if she'd be okay, Sophia had waved her in the direction of the stacks of revision on her desk, which seemed to satisfy everybody.

But she hadn't revised. She had tidied. Cleaned. For the first time in her life. She had woken up in a panic at nine to his messages. *Infinity Lounge. Tonight? I'll come to you.*

Infinity Lounge was the coolest club in town. A few of the sixth-formers were old enough, and loaded enough, to go. She wasn't either. There was no way she'd get in . . . ?

Except she'd be with him. And he could get into anywhere.

And he was coming. *Here.*

She hauled the Hoover into her room. She'd already done the hall, the sitting room, the stairs. Hidden all the notes and pictures from the fridge in a kitchen drawer. The sight of her bedroom filled her with fresh panic. She stripped off the bedding and stuck it in the washer, then stole the guest bedding out of Mum's ottoman and the velvet cushions from Mum's bed. Dumped all her schoolwork in a Tesco crate and dragged it into the bottom of the wardrobe, stuffed all the loose clothes on top. The mementos, trinkets and porcelain figures from her bookcase — a whole collection of Beatrix Potter — went unceremoniously into a box and under the bed. She screened through the posters and took most of them down. There was nowhere for the teddy bears or Barney the purple dinosaur, her remaining childhood friends. She bagged them up in bin liners and hauled them up Leon's precarious step-ladder into the loft, only sparing Rosie, the threadbare rabbit who had been her faithful companion from birth to secondary school, with her cotton tail and big blue eyes. She moved the bed through ninety degrees, made it up and draped it with the living-room throw and the velvet cushions.

By the time she had finished, the room was so bare it echoed. She arranged *Anna*, *Madame Bovary* and her newly acquired (okay, borrowed from the library) *Notes from Underground* on her bookcase, above the acceptable paperback classics. She put Rosie on the picture shelf behind the desk; she didn't quite have the heart to banish her to the darkness and cobwebs.

By the time she was done it was getting dark, and dust was sticking to her sweat, and she had to put all her clothes in the washer with the bedding. She showered and washed her hair, and spent nearly an hour straightening it, the excitement and apprehension bubbling in her abdomen. She was still putting on her make-up when the doorbell rang. With one last glance around at her new and unfamiliar room, she lurched down the stairs and unlocked the door.

Here. She couldn't even process it. Here, inside the cramped papered walls of her childhood.

"Hi," she breathed.

"Hi." He smiled his knee-weakening smile and stepped in, shutting the door behind him.

She didn't know what to do next. Here, everything seemed different. Seeing his reflection in the overly ornate mirror was wrong, somehow. He was too handsome, too unbelievable, too sharp, in the jaded, dull-carpeted 1980s semi with its dated veneer doors and heavy pelmets.

"Hot." He traced a thumb under her smoky eyes and grazed a smoky kiss against her cheek. "Am I too early?"

"N . . ." She inhaled the word, nearly choked on it. "No. Never too early."

"Good," he purred. "Are you going to change?"

Change? She glanced down, wrongfooted, at her ripped jeans and cami.

"Um . . ."

"Here." He produced something from behind his back, making childish excitement flutter in her chest. "I thought you could wear this."

"Ohh." She unfolded it from the bag, stomach tightening, pulse racing. She would never in her life have contemplated buying something like it. A bodycon minidress, completely black, with a price tag that made her eyes widen.

"I hope it fits." His eyes travelled down over her cleavage, without any effort to pretend otherwise. Sophia sucked in an unsteady breath. There were no fresh cuts, and he'd never mentioned the old ones. She let him take her by the hand, and led him upstairs. He slouched carelessly amongst the cushions and watched her change. She fiddled with her hair, suddenly anxious.

"You know I'm not old enough to get into Infinity Lounge," she blurted.

He smirked. "I know. But I know someone. Besides . . ." He pushed himself to his feet and ran an appreciative hand over her backside, lowering his voice to a gravelly whisper. "You look twenty-one and fucking awesome, Sophia."

Fucking awesome. She was smiling helplessly. She looked up at him through her lashes.

"Really?" she whispered back.

"Really." He ran a finger through her hair, making her shiver. "So let's make you feel it."

"Feel what?"

"As fucking hot as you look." His mouth was against her ear. "What do you think?"

She didn't know what she thought. She had no idea what he was talking about. He unfolded something from his pocket and laid it on the dressing table.

"I brought you something else." He steered her to sit. Tipped it out onto the table-top, and she felt herself freeze as he started dividing it out into two lines.

"You know what to do?"

For a moment all she could do was stare at it, shock claiming a stranglehold around her throat. He laughed out loud.

"What's the matter?"

"I—"

"It's only a tiny bit. A buzz. Everyone will be doing it. It's no worse for you than a smoke. You want me to show you?"

"I . . ." Panic was threatening in her gut. "I'm not su—"

"C'mon, Soph." He was smiling, seductive. Impossible to say no to. "It's only once. I want you to have a good time . . . you have no idea." His hands came to rest on her hips. "Try it. For me."

No worse than a smoke. Only once. For him. She closed her eyes and focussed on the words. On the feeling of his hands on her hips. *Do you love me? Of course I do.*

Even as she acquiesced, she didn't believe she was doing it. She was watching someone else, someone she didn't know. Hesitation, then certainty. A copycat deep sniff in, a tang of chemicals in her nose and mouth that somehow wasn't as bad as the fear. Hyperventilating, she could see her own white knuckles on the edge of the dressing table, over-analysing every near-death sensation. And yet, moments later, she didn't feel any different. The world still looked the same. Felt the same.

The drive into town was fast and clear, and at last the fear waned. As they parked in the multistorey, Sophia realised the anxiety was gone, and the churning in her gut was excitement. *Fucking hot.* He was right. The dress was perfect; it hugged her body, made her legs long. *Twenty-one and fucking awesome.* She realised in an instant that there wouldn't be a problem getting into the club. On his arm, she was *meant* to be there. She was vibrant, stunning; she could feel the jealous glances from the other girls. Feel the pulsing of desire that ran in currents through both of them. She couldn't remember the last time she'd felt so alive. So free. So comfortable in her own skin.

She'd never been in a club before. She gazed around in sharp focus at the darkness, the light, the movement. He brought her a sticky sweet drink in a plastic cup, which she drank too fast, and put his hands on her hips and danced indecently close, the pulse growing stronger in time with the heady beat of the music. They stopped only for another drink, or maybe two. The beat surrounded her, sucked her in; she'd never even realised she could dance until tonight, and tonight it was in her bloodstream, her body moving against his in a way she could never have imagined, every sensation in high definition.

When he pulled her off the dancefloor, she thought that something was wrong. He laughed and told her that it was nearly three and the place was closing. For a moment she thought he was joking, until she realised the room was almost empty, and the panic returned in a little stab. Three?

The echoes and dispersing drunken shouts in the dark street put her on edge. For some reason, every little sound seemed to make her jump. By the time they got back to his car, she was feeling distinctly sick, and uncomfortably hot. She wished he wouldn't drive so fast. About a mile into the journey, she noticed the headlights behind them. By two miles in, it was obvious they were being followed. She gripped the sides of her seat.

"Is that a police car?" She didn't dare turn her head to look. Sweat had broken on her upper lip.

He grinned. "Relax, Soph."

"But is it?" There was a shrill note in her voice. They were going to get pulled over. He was doing nearly seventy in a fifty. There was no way he'd pass a breathalyser and they both knew it. And Mum and Leon would find out where she'd been. And what she'd done—

"What do *you* think?" His voice dripped with sarcasm as he accelerated out onto the main road.

"I . . ." She turned to look. There was nothing there. No car. Just the intermittent flash of the streetlamps as they flicked by. "Oh."

"Fucking lightweight," he muttered.

He parked right outside the house for the first time ever and she could sense his impatience as she opened the door. They went straight to her room. His hands were on her dress, *the* dress. Her feet were throbbing in her five-inch heels; she stooped to undo the first one, wobbling against him.

"*What are you doing?*" His snarl took her utterly by surprise. She grabbed at his shirt to save herself, and the next second something hit her face and redness exploded across her left eye. She staggered. He lowered his hand.

"*Leave them on.*" She could barely recognise his voice. He pushed her roughly up against her desk. A sob of pain and shock slipped out unchecked. And before she could comprehend the switch, he was kissing her.

"I'm sorry." His mouth was on her hair, her ear, her neck, tender and warm. His fingers were around her wrist. "I'm so sorry. I . . . I don't know what came over me."

"Please—" she choked out. Please what? She didn't even know. *Please get out and never come back.*

"Soph . . ." He stroked her hair, pulled her hand backwards to wind his fingers through hers. Even though she was still pressed against the desk. Even though she could feel the mark of those same fingers throbbing on her cheek.

"I'm so sorry. Oh, Jesus." He pulled her face around to kiss her. She could feel herself giving way, giving in. He rested his forehead against hers, and for a disconcerting moment she thought she saw the glint of tears in his eyes.

"It's okay." She heard the words leave her against her will. "I know." She wanted to reach around and stroke his hair. To forgive him. To take the blame. She'd pissed him off. She felt him sigh. He let go of her hair, and took hold of her hip instead, hitching up the dress, his other hand still holding hers fast.

"You're so fucking hot, Sophia," he breathed. "So fucking hot."

He tightened his fingers through hers, twisting her arm behind her, bending her over the desk. She tried to remember. Tried to remember that all week, all week she'd been wanting, waiting for this. Desperate for this. That she needed this, more than anything. Her feet were hurting. Her head was hurting.

Maybe he was gentler than usual. Although she could barely balance in her shoes, and the desk was unsteady. It seemed to go on forever. When he'd finished he zipped up his jeans and left her to clean herself up as he fished the cigarette packet out of his back pocket.

"Smoke?" he offered at last.

Sophia pulled down her dress. Managed to shake her head. Her throat was almost too tight to get the words out.

"Not in the house . . . They . . ." She couldn't bring herself to say the rest.

He nodded. "Sure. I'll wait 'til I'm outside."

"You're . . . you're *going*?"

He didn't reply. Just drew out a cigarette, and pushed the pack back into his pocket. Mum's cushions were squashed and sagging on the bed. The electric buzz of the lightbulb seemed to fill her ears, deafening.

"I . . ." she tailed off. His eyes were hard. With tiredness? Just tiredness. It was so late. Or early. Early morning. Gone four.

"Awesome night, Soph." He folded the cigarette between his fingers. "Now get some sleep."

And with that he was gone. He let himself out onto the landing, and she didn't follow. She heard the front door close on its Yale lock. She didn't move. Didn't breathe. Just stood, motionless, staring at her reflection in the mirror. At the red marks on her arm that would be a bruise by tomorrow. At the weal on her cheek, the faint outline of finger-marks on flesh. *Do you love me?*

Rosie was still on the shelf. Watching her with sad blue eyes, eyes that had seen everything. A dry sob rose in Sophia's throat. She ripped the rabbit down from the shelf and hurled her into the wastepaper basket. Then she flung herself onto the bed face down, and let the tempest break.

CHAPTER 13

2022

I'm late. The driveway at the Hall is deserted, the house a silent and decrepit monument to the dawn. The sky has cleared; there's sunshine illuminating my bleary-eyed arrival as I slink between the rhododendrons.

I'm relieved to see that Sean's car isn't in the drive. After three hours' sleep I feel hungover with tiredness, faintly nauseated. Or perhaps it's the lingering smell of day-old coffee from the Thermos mug in my car. I let myself in through the cabin door without really looking, and then do a double-take as I notice him at his desk. Crap. How?

"Good morning." It's quieter, breathier than I intended. There's a paper cup on the desk beside him encased in a cardboard sleeve, its upturned plastic lid beaded with condensation.

"Frost," he murmurs.

For some unfathomable reason, I turn red. I sit down quickly at my laptop and punch the on button. Sean rises to his feet and I glance up, unable to stop my eyes from following him. His eyebrows flicker. He walks to the door and jerks it open. There's a brooding seduction in his silence:

an undisguised warning to keep my distance. I swallow. He pauses in the doorway as if he's going to say something, but he doesn't. The door closes behind him and I hear his feet crunch on the path.

I look down. There, on my desk, is Dad's pen. I pick it up, frowning. Click the end in and out, recover a discarded envelope from the bin, and press the ballpoint to the paper, drawing a deep blue line. My frown deepens. I draw on my fingertips just to make sure, then lower it, uneasy. It hasn't written properly for weeks.

I blink. I'm dazed with tiredness. I need to make headway with the sketches; I've only got until Monday. I've almost finished the designs he gave me to make up. But that's not flair. I check the door and relocate to the drawing boards. Graham Gordon-Heyers wants Helvellyn, and I'm going to bring it to him if I have to stay awake every hour between now and Monday to do it. I arrange my sections of Sean's sketches on top, then flip the paper over to resume work on the detail of my own drawings underneath.

It's an hour before I look up again at the click of the door. I expect it to be him, and replace the top sheet quickly, but it isn't. Katie gives me a tiny wave and deposits her bag and coat. Her tread's light as she climbs the steps to join me.

"Nice work, Livs." Her voice is hushed with awe. "God, I wish I could draw. Is that Sean's design?"

I nod.

"He's infuriatingly good."

"Yeah," I concede. It sounds a little too much like a sigh. Katie sits down on one of the stools.

"How's it going with him?" She scrutinises my face.

"Okay." I shrug. "I think."

"Sean is what he is." Her gaze is level. "You shouldn't let it bother you."

"How long have you known him?"

"A few years. I met him through Claire a couple of times when we were kids. Once, after that, just after we finished uni — he'd gained himself a reputation even by then. Then at the start of last year he came back down to Porthtrevelen with Peter McLeod, when Graham decided to start selling off the estate — I guess, with Covid, the weddings and open gardens just weren't paying the bills."

"A reputation?" I don't really absorb the end of her sentence. She isn't the first person to have said that. "What kind of a reputation?"

Katie raises her eyebrows. For a moment there's silence.

"Oh, come on, Livia." She must see my expression. "It's hardly surprising, is it?"

No. I let out my breath slowly, unable to stop myself from picturing penetrating dark eyes and rolled shirt-sleeves. I suppose it isn't.

"Did you know the last intern?" I change the subject.

Katie pauses. "Yes," she concedes finally. "We . . . spent some time together."

"Claire mentioned that they were friends. Her and Sean. She said that something hap—"

"It's probably better not to ask, Livia." Katie slides to her feet. "I don't know what Claire's said, but I don't think you can lay the blame entirely one way. If anyone's going to tell you about it, it should really be Sean."

Oh. I tuck my hair behind my ear, uncomfortable. Some change of tune from *we should talk*. Katie descends the steps to unpack her laptop.

"Has Graham seen your designs yet?"

I shake my head. "No, Monday."

"Oh." There's something perceptive in her smile. "You look like you've been at it all night. I thought maybe you were showing him today."

"Oh, no. Not today." It's good to know that I look as exhausted as I feel. "I babysat Fin last night. Claire and Ryan got held up."

"Christ, Livia." She rolls her eyes. "Don't let them start calling you in for favours. There'll be no end to it." She taps a password into her laptop. "Claire's never had to solve her own problems in her life. She had a nanny herself until she was about thirteen. She's used to other people picking up the slack for her. I'm not sure how Ryan puts up with it."

"I'm not sure that Ryan picks up any slack," I point out. "He seems pretty horizontal."

Katie snorts.

I start to draw again. "Did you say they did weddings and open gardens here? At Trethallyan?" I focus back in on my cross-hatching.

"Mm. Before I really knew them properly." Katie's typing without looking at the keys. "Claire and I weren't close, but we went to the same school. The gardens here were open a lot, like three or four days a week, for quite a while. Claire's mother used to spend a lot of time on them . . . even until quite recently. Until 2019, I think it was, when there was the burglary and they sacked the groundskeeper. Graham and Clarissa were abroad when it happened. They never really got back to it after that. Covid sort of did for it."

"There was a burglary?" I remember my conversation with Graham Gordon-Heyers. "Was a lot of stuff taken?"

"Yeah, it was pretty bad. It was round about the time that Claire and Ryan moved to Dubai, and the place was all locked up. Quite a lot of valuables and antiques from the house went — all insured, but irreplaceable really. The feeling was that someone with inside knowledge must have been in on it."

"The groundsman," I nod slowly.

"Mm. He'd been left acting as caretaker while it was empty. I don't think they could ever prove anything, though."

"That's awful." I finish the cross-hatching and sit back to examine it from a distance.

"Isn't it?"

"Isn't what?"

I start. Claire's head is poking around the edge of the door.

"Oh, you're both here!" A broad smile dimples her cheeks. "Do you mind if I come in?"

She doesn't wait for an answer. She swings around the door and starts to take off her coat.

"I was telling Livia how your parents used to have the gardens open." Katie glances up from her screen.

"Yes! Didn't you know?" Claire comes to peer over my shoulder at the drawing board. "Would you like to see them? They're nothing compared to what they were then, because there's no one to look after them except Dad and the man who comes in to mow the lawns. But you can get a feel for how beautiful they used to be. All the bushes and roses have gone wild, now. We still get ducks on the pond though — they nested in the boathouse last year."

"O . . . okay." I glance uncertainly from her to Katie. But Katie's attention is turned fixedly back on the laptop. I hide my new drawing under Sean's design. "Why not?"

"I'll stay here." Katie doesn't look at Claire, but her eye catches mine fleetingly. I shrug. She gives me a told-you-so smile, and I follow Claire obligingly out into the crisp sunshine.

"This way." She gestures me right, through an almost overgrown wooden archway between the shrubs. She seems unreasonably bubbly, given that she can't have had a great deal more sleep than me. "We used to have an Indian garden down here, with statues that Granddaddy Heyers brought back with him after his posting there." Claire gestures at two empty stone pedestals, grown over with ivy. "And through here . . ." She squeezes through a barely existent gap between two no-longer-trimmed box hedges. "Was Mother's rose garden. Not that there's anything to see of it now."

There isn't. I take in the centuries-old low edging stones. There's nothing growing except a tangle of last year's grass.

"It must have been stunning," I offer, unconvinced.

"My favourite bit's through here, though." Claire shows me out through another imaginary gap in the bushes, twigs and leaves snagging at my hair. I run a few steps to catch her up. The once gravel path has been overrun by mud and leaf litter, with converging rhododendrons and vigilante nettles that make it almost impassable. After a minute or two, the shrubs open out into lawns of unkempt green. Strangely shaped trees that were once pruned to perfection now erupt like accidental sculptures from the roughly mown grass, with clumps of snowdrops clustering determinedly around their bases. Ahead of us, the ground slopes down to an elliptical pond, surprisingly devoid of algae given its otherwise general level of neglect. A tiny boathouse with a pitched roof is collapsing on the opposite bank, tangled in creepers and reeds. At the far end the box hedge resumes, with a narrow stone bower nestled in its overgrown depths. Claire picks her way along the bank towards it.

"There must be dozens of cricket balls in this pond." She smiles. "My father always promised to get them out, but he never did."

I envisage the three of them playing on the lawns: her, Ryan and Sean. Sean can't be older than her. Maybe even younger. I imagine him following the pair of them along, fighting to hold his own. Or maybe, from what Claire said, it was him and her that were friends, and Ryan was the bigger, braver ringleader, responsible for cricket balls through windows and the escapade with the broken wrist.

"How much older is Ryan than Sean?" I ask, without really thinking.

"Five years." Claire slows. "Ryan was ten when their mother died. Sean was only five. It was terribly sad. Aisling was driving Ryan back from a friend's house, when a lorry crashed into their car. She died at the scene. They had to cut Ryan out. Neither he nor Sean ever got over it. Not really." She ascends the bank to the hedge, and stops at the bower. "Sean's never spoken about it at all. He was at home with his father when it happened."

"That's . . ." I stop too, staring at the black-mirrored surface of the water. "That's horrible."

"I know." Claire nods. "Unimaginable. Here." She gestures me to the stone bench in the bower. "Sit here. This is where I'd always come, when I was little. I still come here now, sometimes, if things get too much."

I don't really want to sit down, but I do. There isn't quite space for both of us on the bench. Claire perches on the other end.

"Thanks so much for last night, Livs." She sighs. "You have no idea how grateful I am. And Fin . . . I've never known anything like it. He's so different with you . . ."

"Oh." I think of the book. "Actually—"

"The Thomas book?" Claire smiles. "Don't worry about it. Fin showed me. Ryan's ordered a replacement. They were okay about it."

"Oh, good." I exhale slowly. For some reason, I can't help feeling on edge. Is it the memory? Or something else? I glance around at the dark water and the dense wall of bushes and shrubs. Is there someone there? A chill creeps down the back of my neck.

"You wouldn't think about watching him again, would you?" Claire's voice has softened. She turns beseeching eyes on me. "Aside from Sean, we do struggle to find anyone who'll have him. And you were so good with him. If you ever—"

"No," I cut in huskily. "I'm sorry, I . . . really . . . couldn't. I'm no . . . no good with kids."

On the surface of the water a shadow flicks across the sun. I glance up. So does Claire.

"Sean!" She jumps to her feet. He's stopped at the other end of the pool.

"I was just showing Livs the gardens." Claire takes a few skipping steps back down the bank. I rise too, and follow at a distance. His eyes are on me, not her.

"How was your meeting?"

"It was fine," Sean says. His gaze still rests inscrutably on my face. "There was nothing new to add, really. We're going to meet properly on Monday to go through the drawings."

"That's exciting." Claire's cheeks dimple. There's a momentary pause. "I should probably let you have Livia back." She glances from him to me, unusually perceptive. I swallow. The reflections of the rippling water play with the shadows across his face.

"See you later, Livs." Claire makes a graceful exit onto the lawn, leaving us alone. We regard each other in silence. I move toward the path at the same second as he does, and we both stop. Sean gestures for me to go first.

"Did you have a good run this morning?" he asks. I almost halt in surprise.

"Um, no. Actually." I clear my throat. "I . . . didn't go. I had a late night."

"You were at Ryan's." His sideways glance is impossible to read. I blush. How does he know that?

"Yeah," I admit.

"Graham says he saw you at the chapel yesterday." The path widens, and he catches up to walk beside me, his strides lithe and long on the gravel. "*In* the chapel," he adds dryly.

"Uh. Yeah," I mutter.

Something glimmers at the corner of Sean's lips. A smile? I hesitate. His dark eyes are very astute.

"You like to do your research."

"I like to get things right." I fold my hands carefully into my coat pockets.

"Uh-huh." It's deadpan. Impenetrable. We walk for a while without speaking.

"You know," he half turns, and for a split second his gaze fixes mine, "there's a level of persistence that's only liable to lead you into trouble, Frost."

"Who with?" I retort lightly. But my heart's in my throat. One of Sean's eyebrows lifts a fraction. He doesn't reply.

"What kind of trouble?" I press. It's supposed to sound like a challenge, but it comes out as a whisper.

"The kind you'd be far better off avoiding." His voice is very soft. "After you." We've reached the cabin, and he holds open the door. I step inside. Katie looks up from her laptop. I move quickly to the drawing board, and Sean sits down at his desk without another word, snapping the lid back onto the paper cup and throwing it, in one well-aimed shot, into the bin.

I pick up the 0.7 mm drafting pencil from the table.

* * *

"Last card." I smack three twos onto the top of the pile. Niklavs regards me coolly over his empty glass.

"Pride comes before a trip, I think."

"A fall."

"A fall," he corrects himself as he lays a jack of clubs on top of my last two. I glare at him.

"Where did *that* come from?"

"Top of pack." His face is utterly straight.

"Ugh!" I reach for the deck and count out thirteen new cards. "As if!"

The phone on the mantelpiece behind us starts to ring, making me jump. Niklavs stands up to answer it.

"*Sveiki.*" His face creases, puzzled. "Hello?"

I pause. There's an expectant silence.

"Is for you." Niklavs hands me the phone. I stare at it, perplexed.

"Is customary to speak, no?" he suggests.

"Er . . ." I hold the handset to my ear. "Hi, it's Livia?"

"Livs! Where the hell have you been?"

"Kris?" I tuck the phone under my chin and go to lay down the rest of my cards. "What . . . ?"

"I've called your phone like twenty times! Last night you didn't answer, *and* this morning, and now it's just going through to voicemail!"

"Oh. Crap." I glance down at my work clothes, remembering. "I think I left it somewhere."

"Serious, Livs?" His exasperation is undisguised. "I just spent an hour going through the phone book online to see if you have any neighbours who could make sure you're still alive."

"Oh." I chew my lip. At the other end of the room, the tabby cat squeezes its way through the open window and jumps down onto the floor.

"What's up, anyway?" I try to claw back my good humour, aware of Niklavs behind me trying not to overhear.

"Where *is* your phone?"

"In my flat, maybe?" I glance up at the ceiling, as if the answer might reveal itself there. "I'm not sure. I haven't had it today . . ."

All day. I haven't had it all day. The thought occurs to me suddenly. In fact, I haven't set eyes on it since I was cooking Fin's tea yesterday evening.

"Can you fetch it?" He's speaking very patiently now. Like he's trying to get sense out of a small child.

"No. Look, I think I left it at a friend's house. What's the matter, anyway?" I move towards the open window, the micro-climate of cold air whisking around me, and the cat darts past my feet.

"I was thinking of coming down. Next weekend."

"Oh!" A broad grin spreads across my face.

"Yeah. Friday night or Saturday. What d'you reckon?"

"That would be amazing!" I whirl on the spot, all at once bubbling over with excitement. Kris, visiting Porthtrevelen. Meeting Niklavs. Coming to the beach . . .

I look out of the window at an empty carrier bag being blasted along the road by the bitter wind. Well, perhaps not the beach.

"Definitely! Come as soon as you want! I'll get an airbed or something, there's loads of room in the flat. Are you sure? It's a long way, just for the weekend . . ."

"Yeah, uh, *totally*." I can hear him grinning too. "You think there's any surf schools this time of year?"

"Um . . ." I fight to suppress a smile at the idea of my bulky, uncoordinated brother trying to balance upright on a surfboard. "Maybe not."

"I'm glad you're okay, Livs." His voice grows serious again. "I've got to head off. Extra practice. It's the Trent match tomorrow. Friday, though. Or Saturday. I'll be there. I'll text you when I've booked a train."

I hear muffled voices in the background and the sound of thundering feet. Kris has never had a knack for descending stairs quietly.

"Okay."

"Text me when you get your phone back, right?"

"Right." I roll my eyes.

"Livia!"

"Okay, okay," I mutter, placating him. "I will. I'll go see if I can find it now. All right?"

"Right."

"See you, Kris."

"Talk later, Livs."

"Bye!"

I hang up and falter, not sure where to put the phone. Niklavs holds out his hand, and I pass it to him.

"He is brother, or grandmother?" he teases.

"Oh. I know." I pull a face. "It's only because he cares. We've got each other through a lot."

"He plans to pay visit?"

"Next weekend."

Niklavs smiles. "In that case, I look forward to meeting brother who is able to lift ridiculous heavy case." There's a wicked glint of humour in his eyes. "Perhaps he may discover new calling to take up fishing."

"Hah. We'd be lucky." I pick up my blackjack hand, apologetic. "I'm really sorry, but I'm going to have to leave this. I need to go and find my phone. I've left it somewhere."

Niklavs examines my cards. "You have lost, anyway," he tells me, unconcerned.

"Oh. Good." I seek out my keys from the pocket of my coat. "Thanks."

Niklavs grins. "See you light and early, Livia. I hope foot is better for your run in morning."

"Thanks. Me too." I can't help smiling as I pull open the door. "Goodnight!"

Niklavs raises his hand in a wave. I start across the hallway, then waver, my eyes falling on the pigeon-holes, and the collection of unsorted mail on the table.

Mail. I stop in my tracks. I still haven't checked.

I count through the numbers to my own compartment. I've never told anyone my address except Kris, my mother, and the LMLA application forms. I feel right to the back of the wooden hole, and there's something inside. A stack, two or three items. Triumphant, I seize them. If they're for her, they might help me trace her. The rest of a name. A previous address . . .

Miss Livia Frost. The top one's a card, my mother's handwriting. *Good Luck In Your New Home.* The next is *To The Occupier.* I breathe out, disappointed. The third.

Mss Swift.

Oh. I stare at the title, and the typo, exhaling the rest of my breath in a sigh. No first name. Nothing. I hold the envelope up to the light, but there's nothing to see. I'm no further forwards. Disillusioned, but not quite ready to give up, I slip my mother's card and the letter into my coat pocket.

* * *

It's pitch dark at Trethallyan, away from the glow of the streetlights. Neither Ryan nor Claire's cars are in the Gatehouse drive, but there's a light burning at the back of the house. I cross the gravel and tap on the door. The wind gusts, buffeting the back of my waterproof; I wait until my legs start to ache and tap again. No answer.

There's definitely a light on. I step back, straining to make out the crisp edges of the small front lawn and the path. I tiptoe to the side gate, and try it cautiously. It's open. It creaks indolently closed behind me as I squint my way along the path past the wall of the kitchen. The garden is newly landscaped and smells of topsoil and creosote; the light from the conservatory spills out in a warm pool over the grass. I knock gingerly at the kitchen door. The lights are on; I can see my phone on the end of the worktop. Still nothing. I take a tentative step sideways.

The conservatory lights are all on too, the blinds open. I can see right in: Fin is lying on the rug, pressing Lego bricks with rapt attention onto the top of a half-finished house. And there, beside him . . .

I hesitate. Sean is lying on his front on the wooden floor, absorbed in fixing something. I watch as he finishes it and holds it out, and Fin reaches up to take it from him. My hand drifts back to my side. I'm not sure how long I stand there, unnoticed. The silent intensity of their interaction is mesmerising. Sean moves his hands, and after a second I realise that he's signing. Fin smiles.

I remember myself abruptly. What if one of them looks up and sees me? I mount the kitchen step and knock again, more boldly.

Fin turns, his pointed face pale and serious. I see Sean look up too, and pause. He stands slowly, with a gentle, reassuring touch on Fin's head. *I'll be back in a minute.* I see his lips move. Then he disappears.

The door opens. Suddenly I'm rooted to the spot.

"Livia?"

His body is silhouetted by the light from inside, a bright rectangle escaping past him to fall at my feet. He looks different out of context, without the lanyard and designer shirt. Casual . . . younger, effortlessly good. He hasn't managed to hide his surprise.

"Hi," I whisper. Jesus Christ, have I lost my voice? What's the matter with me?

"I left my phone," I blurt out quickly. "Here. Last night. I thought I'd . . . I just came to . . ."

"Do you want to come in?" He hasn't moved. It's a replay of the first day; his gaze travels over me as I stand immobilised, staring back.

"No," I manage at last. "I mean, thanks. It's just there. On the side."

He steps back, turns.

"This one?" He picks it up. I watch his fingers close around the edges. He's looking at the photo on the back of the plastic case. The one that Kris took: me and my father. Helvellyn in the ice.

"Quite a view," he observes. He passes it to me. I withdraw quickly and slip it into my pocket.

"Thanks."

"No problem." He pushes his hands into his pockets too. For a few agonising seconds, neither of us moves. There's a crash from the other room. His head half turns.

"You need to go," I say.

He nods. "Have a good weekend, Frost."

I turn away. I hear the click and latch of the door, sense the balanced retreat of his footsteps, the change of shadows in the conservatory, a flicker of movement. I tighten my fingers around my phone, and remember what Claire said about the last intern. *He ended up feeling responsible.* I know what it's like to feel responsible. After dark. When you're alone.

Livia, be a darling . . .

* * *

I never went back to Helvellyn.

I lay down my brush, and look at the painting. It's small, barely bigger than a postcard. I select a brush with a finer tip, and hover over the mixes of green. It isn't Coniston, or Trethallyan, or anywhere I've ever been. It's a house from a picture. I flick the last few texturing touches, and smile wryly at the painting. A little house with grass on the roof: a tiny iron-age-looking dugout fortress with over-sized windows that all look out at the misty effervescent sea. Lots of light, even though the sky is grey. A garden, for painting, where accidental sheep stray over the rugged grass. Fin's house, brought to life with snatches of stone and a few stolen ideas from a magazine article stuck in the back of my scrapbook.

Despite everything, when Claire called me to ask if I could babysit tonight, I didn't manage to refuse. I could hear Katie's voice in my head, even as I gave my reluctant assent, but Claire has to go to the hospital, and Ryan's playing rugby, which brought such strong images of Kris to mind that I just couldn't turn them down.

I worked all weekend. On Saturday, I pulled the folding-leaf table into the window in place of my easel and drew until I fell asleep. Yesterday, I walked to Trethallyan instead, with my sketches rolled in a poster tube inside my coat. Happily, I didn't encounter anyone in the foggy grounds, and nobody noticed or thought to question the light on in the cabin. I finished at midday, and walked to the chapel, although I didn't linger there long. I had the uncomfortable feeling that I was being watched as I looked up into the baleful luminance of the Virgin Mary's eyes.

I glance at the clock. Ten to eight. After the first proper sleep I've had in days, I got back from my run with time to spare this morning. I stand up to wash my brushes. We're meeting with Gordon-Heyers at half eight. The moment of truth. Time to find out whether or not my persistence really is going to lead me into trouble. Trouble that I'd be better off avoiding . . . My heart's beating fast as I lock my door behind me and descend the stairs.

There's a clear winter sky over Porthtrevelen. A freshness to the air that there hasn't been for days. The sun has already melted the frost on the driveway at the Hall; even the reading room is light, in its encasement of heavy books and disowned photographs.

I sit in silence as Sean and Graham talk. I haven't planned my course of action. There's a definite possibility that, after everything, I'll bottle it and the second set of drawings will never make it out of my bag. Sean's presence beside me has thrown me off balance, the memory of Makaton and the Gatehouse tying knots in the threads of my thoughts.

I watch Graham flick from elevation to cross-section and back again. I'm holding my breath. And I know Sean Lorchann isn't. He's sitting back in his chair, long legs folded calmly in front of him. He's already got contractors lined up, a gamble on the full permission that we haven't even applied for yet.

"They're very good." Graham speaks at last, his voice level. Is there a note of disappointment in it? Or do I just hope so? “Very good.” He’s nodding business-like approval. “Nothing short of what I expected, Sean. And the level of detail . . . This is *your* work, Livia?”

“Yes,” Sean answers before I can. “It’s Livvy’s work.”

I glance up sharply. Liv-I-A. *Livia.* I glare at him. He knows, and he said it anyway. But he’s not looking.

“I especially like the use of the roof space. And the windows. It’s north facing?”

“Yes.” Sean sits upright to orientate the page. “The gardens here face south, and include the chapel.”

“I see.” Graham scrutinises it again. Turns back to the floor plan, then forwards. Adrenaline is pooling in my gut; my limbs are weak with realisation. It’s now. I have to speak now.

“Um.” The hot adrenaline surges into my bloodstream. “The alternative is to face it west.”

Silence. They both turn to me. I’ve done it. I feel my cheeks ignite in the disbelieving blaze of Sean’s stare. My hands are shaking under the table as I take out my drawings.

“With a picture window in the gable end, to the north, so the lounge and master bedroom look at the sea.” I’m talking fast, too fast. “They’d both have a dual aspect, north and west. The body of the house could be brought forwards on the footprint of the original barn. Like this.” I spread the paper on the table. “Then, from the front, every window sees the sunset . . .”

I swallow. Neither of them has said a word. Graham is staring at the sketched elevation, his jaw clenched tight. Panic washes over me. I want to take it back. Swallow my words and sink through the floor. But it’s too late not to carry on. My eyes are smarting.

“It’s an oak frame,” I whisper. “Stone faced. The chapel’s here.” I have to clear my throat. “With the altar facing east, the stained glass is . . . I mean, it could be . . .” I trail off. From the bookcase behind Sean’s shoulder, the Niklavs of times past is watching me crumble. Graham sits back heavily in his chair.

"Clarissa loves the sunset," he remarks quietly.

Sean draws himself upright beside me. There's no pencil to confiscate from me this time. No distraction. I don't dare look at his face to see his reaction. I try to remind myself that the only reaction that matters is Graham's, but I can't quite banish his voice from my head. *I want what you're not giving me, Livia. Until you do, we're not going anywhere.*

Graham touches a crooked finger to the outline of the picture window. The seconds tick loudly into a minute. He looks up.

"This is it," he says simply. "This one." He gets to his feet. "I'm sorry. Excuse me."

He's gone. The reading-room door bangs closed. I stare at the upside down sketches, stunned into silence.

"You should have run that past me." Sean's low voice makes me jump. I turn.

"You *really* should have run that past me." His eyes burn with challenge. Something else. Something I can't put a name to. I swallow.

"Sure." I nod, scratching a fingernail against the polished table-top. "I'll make sure I do next time."

Sean pushes his chair back from the table.

"You've been holding out on me." His arms are folded across his chest. "All this time." His gaze has fixed darkly on my face. An inexplicable shiver runs through me. I take a deep breath.

"No." I spin to face him fully. Without warning, the weeks of bitten-back anger erupt. "You know what? *No.* I haven't been holding out! I've been doing exactly what you've asked! But I won't. I won't . . . do it anymore! You were supposed to . . . to inspire me! To—"

"I was *supposed* to teach you about the reality of the job." He's on his feet, a spark of danger alight in his eyes. I stand up too.

"Well, maybe the reality is that I'm *not* average." I face him, unflinching. "I'm good. And you're not going to scare me away."

Sunlight is streaming through the blinds. Outside, even the birds have stopped singing. I swallow.

Very slowly, a smile spreads across Sean Lorchann's lips.

"Don't walk into this lightly, Frost." He unfolds his arms, and it suddenly occurs to me just how close we're standing. "You don't know what you're getting yourself into."

"Well, then tell me." I don't step back. Even though every muscle and nerve ending in my body is trembling with tension. "Teach me. I want to learn."

Silence. His smile fades. There's something calculating in his pause; his gaze is inescapable.

"What is it you want to learn?"

And suddenly, somehow, we're not talking about designs on drafting paper, or heritage officers, or promontory forts. The adrenaline rush hasn't faded. It's intensified. I'm breathing in double time.

"Everything," I whisper.

CHAPTER 14

Everything. Everything's changed. I thought I'd seen a path through this, the break in the clouds, but suddenly I can't, not tonight. I can't see. The missing pieces. I can't see forward or back with any clarity. The way's forked. I'm lost.

I wish I could ask you for directions but you have no idea who I am. Neither do I. I'm looking into the mirror again, and I don't know who I am. I don't know.

Scars shouldn't be able to scar again, right? But what if the wound never closed? I've looked over my shoulder, and now I wish I hadn't. I wish so much that I hadn't.

I've loved him, so hard. I'd like to lie. I'd like to pretend it isn't true. That it's never even crossed my mind. But it has. More than a thought, more than a dream. An infatuation. Because that's what it is, isn't it?

I hid the rosary beads under my mattress. They were my mother's. She wanted me to pray. She told me God would forgive me. That it didn't have to matter. That it didn't have to change everything. But it did change everything. And maybe God did forgive me. But what's the point, if you can't forgive yourself? It turns out I can forgive anyone, except myself . . .

I'm lost.

But I'm not, am I? I know exactly where I am. I'm back in the Gatehouse, trying to remember how to breathe. Trying not to notice how much Finbar Lorchann's dark eyes look like Sean's. He's standing on the sofa, high out of harm's way, arms hugging his chest as he assesses me from his vantage point.

"Hey, Fin. I brought you something. Look," I hold out the package to show him his name on the brown paper. "For you."

Fin regards me for a moment more, then unwraps his arms from around himself. The sofa cushions crease under his feet as he climbs down.

"Here." I hold it further out. "You can open it."

He strokes a hand over the thick paper. I let him take it. For a while he just looks at it. His fingers work their way over the Sellotape, and I watch, perplexed, as he picks off a piece at a time, folding each one into a tiny rectangle. I'm not sure what I expected. Any other four-year-old would just have ripped the paper. But Fin isn't any four-year-old. I stand back a little way as he slips the painting out of its wrappings.

I bought the frame on my way home at an antique store in a back alley of Porthtrevelen. It doesn't have any glass, but it doesn't need any. I cut the canvas to fit, and although it's lost half an inch of sky and a sliver of cliff in the process, the faded wood complements the misty greys and greens to perfection. Fin lifts the picture in his hands, owl-eyed.

"It's your house." I'm not sure why I'm whispering. "The one you drew."

He lowers the painting to look at me, a shock of wispy blond hair and round midnight eyes gazing over the frame. He pads to me and pushes one side of it back into my hand for me to hold. I take it, puzzled. Then he points to the bottom corner of the canvas.

"Oh." I bite my lip. "It's a blackbird." He raises his eyes to my face. *Blackbird.* For a moment, I could swear that his lips shape the letters. "I put her on all my paintings."

Fin regards me for a moment, thoughtful. Then he takes his picture back, folding both hands carefully around the frame.

"It's what my dad used to call me," I add, to no one in particular. It doesn't really seem like Fin's listening. He's on the move again, disappearing out into the hall and up the stairs. I pause. The house is very quiet. I try not to remember last time. Would it be weird to lock the doors again? Shadows from the trees outside dance in patterns across the floor. The oak bookcases seem to swallow every sound. I move to look at them. My eyes drift over the spines of the books — a disorganised collection of paperbacks and children's stories that contrast starkly to the heavy non-fiction volumes in Graham Gordon-Heyers' reading room — and come to a sudden halt. There's a blackbird on the bookcase, too.

I ease it out. The same limited-edition cover looked down from all the station poster-boards last summer. *Andrew R Frost, winner of the Banks-Hewitt Novel Award 2021*. The paperback cover is dog-eared, the spine creased in so many places that it could be fifty years old. I slide it back in carefully. Nice to know someone appreciates it.

The tug at my sleeve makes me jump. Fin's back, picture still tucked under one arm. I hadn't even noticed. I look down, startled out of my thoughts. He pulls my sleeve again, and points towards the stairs.

"Oh. You want me to come?"

He nods. I follow him cautiously to his room. He takes out the painting and props it on the bedside table next to the paper windmill, then turns back, an impish smile spreading across his pointed face.

"You like it?" There's a glow of gratification in my cheeks. Fin nods. He glances from the picture to me, and lifts his arms from his sides. Wings, like a bird. He points at me again. I smile.

"Yeah, that's right." The warmth has spread inwards, an unbidden bubble of happiness that makes it almost impossible to swallow. What's happening to me? Sing a rainbow. Blackbirds. Everything I've never told a soul . . .

Fin flaps his wings. He flaps all the way to the low wooden windowsill and clambers up to perch on it, looking outside. I step further into the room. The bed's made, smooth and untouched. The toybox is overflowing.

"What do you want to do?" I ask.

Fin jumps down from the windowsill, landing on both feet. I watch, surprised, as he kneels beside the toybox and roots through it. I didn't really expect an answer. He pulls something out and holds it up for me to see. A bucket and spade.

Right. I glance from the slightly grubby plastic to the cold February afternoon sunshine. Then something in me relents. Why the hell not? Ryan won't have finished his rugby game for at least another hour. The tide will be out. And the cove at Trethallyan Edge is perfect for sandcastles.

"Okay." I grin despite myself. "Come on."

We drive the length of the track. Fin runs ahead over the stone chips as I lock the car, the bucket swinging from his hand. He's still ahead of me on the descent, until the rocks, where he stops and waits for me to help him over. For some reason, the deceptively gentle wash of the waves makes me nervous as he launches himself across the sand. I don't take my eyes off him, texting Ryan without looking, and walk a semi-circle that keeps me between him and the sea.

"What are you going to build?" I crouch as Fin plops down on the damp sand in his swathes of woollens and waterproofs. There's no getting around it. It's freezing. I only have my work blouse on under my suddenly inadequate raincoat. My hands are already aching with cold.

"A house?"

He shakes his head.

"A castle?" I test the sand with my fingers. "Here? It's a good place. The sand's just right."

Fin crunches the spade decisively into it, so that clumps flick up and shower us both.

"What kind of castle?" I help him fill the bucket, scooping mounds up with my numb hands. The wind whips my hair across my face, but I'm too sandy to contemplate pushing it back. Fin kneels up tall, and reaches an arm-span forwards. He drags his finger through the sand, marking out an outline.

"A big one?" I sit back. "*That* big?"

He nods.

"Am I allowed to help?"

Another nod. I smile, breathless. Fin thinks for a moment, then passes me the spade.

"You want me to dig?"

He nods.

"Okay." I set to work on the moat as Fin inverts his bucket and hits the top, turning out a square keep, which he sets about decorating with pebbles and shells. I'm already shivering hard; it's bitter, but Fin doesn't seem to be feeling it. We work in silence: wordless understanding that shifts gradually from content to uneasy. As I stop to zip my coat up over my neck, I can't quite shake the feeling that we're being watched.

I take my phone out. No word from Ryan. I scan the rocks under the pretence of looking at the sandy touchscreen. Nothing. I'm getting paranoid. What's wrong with me? I slip the phone back into my pocket, rigid with shivering. The sun's sinking. Water is seeping into our moat; Fin has sat back on his heels to regard it with glee, the king of his small fortress. We're both damp and filthy. I don't want to have to tell him that our time's almost up, that soon we'll have to abandon our palace to the sea.

Maybe I won't. I hear rather than see the movement. The soft scuff of approaching trainers. Ryan.

I look up.

My gaze falls on loose-fitting sweatpants. A red and black hoody with a crest: *Porthtrevelen RFC*. A heavy kit bag slung over one shoulder. Damp, dark tousled hair. I drop the spade.

Sean strides across the sand without a word. His shadow falls long over the keep. Fin looks up too, and a huge smile breaks across his face. He leaps to his feet, and in a single bound he's over the moat, and his arms are wrapped around Sean's legs, hugging tight. Sean's hands shape a symbol, and after a beat Fin's move in reply. I rise to my feet, suddenly surplus to requirements as Sean lifts his nephew onto his shoulders.

"Ryan and Claire are on their way." He turns to me. Fin is clutching onto the neck of his hoody with both hands, at risk of strangling him. "Ryan had to go and pick Claire up from the services at St Erth."

"Oh," I manage through my chattering teeth. "I hope everything's okay?"

"Her car broke down, coming back from the hospital." His voice gives nothing away. Fin tugs at his collar to get down, and he lowers him easily to the sand.

"They asked me to come and meet you, in case you needed to go." Sean's gaze flickers momentarily downwards. My shivering must be visible.

Fin grasps his hand and pulls him towards the sand fortress; I stand at a distance and watch as he shows him the bridge over the moat and the disintegrating turrets. Watch, as Sean kneels beside him and takes up my spade. An architect building sandcastles. I can't help but smile at the irony. He's mending the turrets. I hesitate. Then I step over the moat and crouch down to attend to the opposite one, moulding the wet sand with my fingers. Fin jumps up in delight and hugs the bucket to his chest. My gaze follows him anxiously as he skips to the sea and stoops to fill it, meticulously avoiding the water with his feet. *Lapping, beckoning—*

A shudder runs through me. I wrap my arms around myself and straighten, convulsed with shivers.

"When are you going to start looking after yourself?"

I turn back, startled. Sean's on his feet too. His teeth are gritted.

"What?" I have no idea what he's thinking. How, this far in, can I still not read him?

He shakes his head. Without a word of explanation, he pulls off his hoody, exposing the black skin-tight jersey underneath, and pushes it into my hands. For a split second, I've stopped breathing altogether. I raise my eyes from the red piping on his tight-fitting sleeves to his face. Our gazes lock.

"For fuck's sake, get warm," he mutters.

Jesus Christ. He's watching me, waiting. The sun is sliding out of view. I'm so cold. The folds of the hoody fall invitingly over me as I grip it in my hands. It smells of bodywash, aftershave, faintly of sweat. He doesn't look away. I unzip my jacket, and the wind hits me in a blast. I peel it off slowly, shivering harder than ever in his scrutiny, and pull the hoody on over my shirt. *Porthtrevelen RFC*. I try to divert the direction of my thoughts. He must play, too.

"Hey, buddy!"

The shout rings out across the empty sand. I start. Fin turns back, eyes narrowed against the sunset. Claire and Ryan. Already. They're picking their way over the rocks to join us, the model couple more than ever, even in windswept waterproofs and jeans. I wasn't expecting them so soon. I fasten my jacket quickly back over the hoody.

"Livs, thank you so much!" Claire clambers elegantly down and encloses me in a brief hug. "I'm so sorry we're late for you *again*. Oh . . ." She releases me and holds me at arm's length. "Look, we have the same coat."

"Oh." I blush and pale in rapid succession, painfully conscious of the over-sized hoody underneath. It must reach almost to my knees, a lot lower than the hem of my coat. But she doesn't seem to have noticed.

"Did you drive? Come on, Fin." Claire moves past me in an ineffectual effort to attract the rest of her small family from the water's edge. "It's time to go home."

"Come on, buddy." Ryan takes charge of Fin's bucket and starts back up the beach. I hesitate a moment, letting them draw ahead. Fin isn't coming. He's standing very still, looking at the reflection of his bright blue wellies in the water. The seconds lengthen. Everyone else traverses the rocks, voices fading. I frown. Fin's face is pale, wisps of flyaway golden hair blowing around it in every direction. He's still staring at the waves.

"Fin," I murmur.

He doesn't turn.

"Fin?" I move tentatively to stand beside him. He doesn't move.

"Are you coming?" I look at the sea too. Fin raises one hand to point at the distorted image of our faces under the water. Another wave rolls in, breaking the reflection into pieces.

"It's just a reflection," I reassure him.

He raises his eyes to my face.

"Come on," I say. I hold out a hand before I remember about not touching, but Fin takes it anyway. We start up the beach together, and I slow my strides to match his as he struggles over the incline.

". . . you're just encouraging it."

"As far as I'm concerned, if he's happy, then it's all okay."

I falter. Fin stumbles, putting out his hand to save himself. Halfway up, almost level with the chapel, I can see Sean, his arms folded across his chest.

"I'm not sure it *is* okay, Sean." Ryan's voice is hard. "It's not normal."

"Fin's fine." There's a stubborn note to Sean's voice that takes me by surprise. "Some kids just don't speak as much as others. *I* didn't speak much."

"I worry about him letting people in." Claire's there too, just out of sight in the bracken. "He's four, and sometimes he doesn't let anyone go in his room. Not even me . . ."

"Oh, and I don't know anyone *else* who wouldn't let people in his room as a kid." Ryan cuts across the end of her sentence pointedly. There's an icy pause. "In fact, not much changes, does it?"

Fin's back on his feet. I help him over the last rise, oddly uncomfortable. I'm suddenly not keen to burst into view.

"Some of us just need our privacy." Sean's voice is cool. I swallow and let go of Fin's hand.

We emerge only a few paces behind them. Ryan unlocks his car with a clunk and a flash of lights.

"There you are." Claire smiles, and gathers Fin up in a hug. "Have you had a good time with Livs?" She kisses the top of his head. "Say thank you to her for looking after you."

Fin twists to look up at me. He touches his hand to his mouth.

"You're welcome," I whisper.

A tiny smile creeps over his lips. He breaks free of Claire to raise his arms at his sides. A bird. My heart swells.

"See you later, Fin." I blow him a kiss. He grins, and climbs into the car as Ryan holds open the door.

"Thanks, Livs." Claire kisses the air beside my cheek and gets in too. Ryan flashes me a parting salute and starts the engine. I watch as they reverse and pull away, leaving a sudden aching silence in their wake. I turn back towards my car.

"Frost."

The sun is threatening to set. Sean is standing beside the Defender. There's a look on his face that I can't name. Indescribable. Achingly dark.

"I spoke to Peter about the chapel." He's leaning against the front wing, keys in hand, his eyes fixed on mine. "He liked your idea, too."

My idea? I come to a halt. He means it. I don't really know what to say. Sean pushes himself to his feet. He unfolds his arms and buries his hands in his pockets.

"Tomorrow," he says finally.

Tomorrow? A storm of apprehension and triumph rises in my chest. Tomorrow what?

"There're one or two minor changes. That's all." He's read the question from my face. He opens his car door and swings himself into the driver's seat. "Nice work, Livvy."

I open my mouth in wordless protest, somewhere between elation and disbelief.

"Livia," I say to the car door as it closes behind him. "*Liv-ee-uh.*"

An elusive smile curves his lips. Then he turns the key in the ignition and pulls away.

I step back, watching him go, leaving me alone in the twilight. Alone, with just the gleaming gravel and the advancing tide. There's a piece of paper at my feet, fluttering like a stranded butterfly amongst the stones. I stoop to pick it up. A receipt. *Arrow Writing Supplies. Ballpoint refill.* I frown at it.

It's cold in my car. I turn up the heater and watch the mist dissolve from the windows. Take off my coat and roll the over-long sleeves of the hoody between my hands, breathing its smell. Breathing it in: the inconceivable truth.

It's the same. Worse. More than a thought, more than a dream. An infatuation. Because that's what it is, isn't it?

No. I close my eyes, and think of jet, fool's gold, Makaton. The blaze of unsmiling excitement in his eyes.

Isn't it?

CHAPTER 15

2017

Two years. The X2 stop was empty. She stood, looking at the puddles. A Friday night. *Tell me how old you are.*

There was a lump in her throat. A sick feeling in her stomach. After two years, how could this be happening? It had never been like this, not ever, not even when he was away on all his stupid conferences and courses. He always replied. Always.

It had been forty-eight hours, and there was nothing. She'd rung her own phone from the house phone, to make sure it was working. Tried the SIM in an old handset. Tried everything. His car wasn't at the flats, or at the office. His mobile just went to voicemail. At first she'd thought he was planning something. A two-year anniversary surprise. The day they'd met. Strawberry cider. She'd held out, in a buzz of anticipation all night. But it had come and gone; she'd fallen asleep with reruns of *Breaking Bad* flickering across her bed and the phone in her hand and woken to daylight at 10 a.m. when Mum and Leon got back from church.

Panic had set in by midday. She'd thought of calling the police and reporting him missing, then realised how stupid it would sound. She'd tried to console herself. He'd been called away. A family crisis. A last-minute work commitment. His phone was out of range. He hadn't been able to let her know.

But the truth was she couldn't see the family crisis. Or the short-notice call from work — what would they need him for on a Sunday, anyway? The truth was that for two days, she had been imagining the worst. A hotel room somewhere, or someone else's flat. That his patience had worn thin, like she'd always been so afraid it would, and even as the steel blade sketched its new blood-beaded line into her skin, he was waking up with somebody else.

The sudden certainty had almost made her vomit. She'd had to leave the house, before she attracted unwelcome attention from Mum or Leon. There were barely any buses on a Sunday, and she'd ridden the protracted journey in a nauseated daze.

Sophia felt in her pocket. The X2 had pulled away, splattering the back of her jeans with dirty water. She lurched forwards into the bus stop and lit two Marlboro Silvers one after the other in quick succession, drinking the smoke like vaporised Valium until the sickness subsided.

That wasn't it. It wasn't. She knew it wasn't. It was an irrational thought and she was immediately guilty for thinking it. She pulled out the phone again, tearful, and redialled. One ring, two, four, eight—

"Soph."

She crushed the phone in her hand. The line was terrible; his voice was cut up into static. For a moment, she was too shocked to respond.

"Soph, can you hear me? Hold on—"

Ridiculously the tears spilled over. She swiped them from her cheeks. Her voice came out choked, pathetic.

"Where are you?"

"Soph, are you okay? Wait a minute, let me move."

"Where are you?!" Suddenly she was shouting. "Where—"

"Hey." His voice was warm, liquid. "Don't cry. Why are you crying? What's up? It's okay . . ."

"It's . . . n-not." She sat down with a bump on the plastic seats. "It's not okay! Tell me where you are."

"I'm in Newquay. I told you I was—"

"No!" She stood up again, fists clenched, her stomach knotted with outrage. "What do you mean you told me? You never told me. You never even called — I had no idea where you . . . if you—"

"I'm sorry." It was soft, soothing, but not sorry. She could hear voices in the background. Laughter. "There's fuck all signal here. I tried to text you when we got here."

"Got *where*?" She dashed another wave of tears from her face, cold. "With who?"

"With my brother. Like I—"

"Your brother?"

"And some friends. Why?"

"Not with anyone else?"

"Anyone el . . . Fuck, *Sophia*. That's what you thought?"

"No," she lied. Her nose was streaming. Tears were running over her mouth and dripping from her chin. She scrubbed her face with her sleeve. "No . . ." Her voice sounded thick. "I just . . . I . . ." She had to get herself together. For fuck's sake. She kicked angrily at a piece of chewing gum on the kerb. "I had no idea where you were . . . I was scared—"

"Hey." He sounded somewhere between appalled and repentant. "Soph. Come on. There's a sevens tournament. I'm sure I told you."

"You . . ." she sniffed. Her throat tightened with anger and misery. "You didn't even . . . I could have come. You knew that! So you didn't want me to? You didn't want me—"

"Of course I did. But you had exams. I couldn't take you a—"

"They finished a week ago!"

"Look, Sophia." His voice softened, appeasing. "You really wouldn't have wanted to be here. My brother can be a bit of a prick. And you hate sports. Don't you?" She heard the hiss and rustle of him shifting the phone. "Don't worry about it. We'll have plenty of time to make up for it when

I get back, now that your exams are over, right? We can maybe even do next weekend, go away or something, just for a night."

Away for a night? A thrill ran through her. She swallowed back the tears and pressed her sleeve to her nose.

"What kind of away?" she whispered.

"I don't know. London? Whatever you fancy. You can choose."

She drank in a jagged breath. London. Images of hotel rooms and West End shows flashed through her head. White Egyptian cotton, high-rise views. He wanted to take her away. She exhaled slowly. How could she ever even have thought . . .

"I've got to go, Soph. I'm sorry." The words were rich and warm. She could picture them leaving his lips, regretful, quiet, and it made her want to wrap her arms around him. She tightened them around herself instead.

"Okay." There was a lump in her throat again, but it was for a different reason now. He was there without her. With his brother who didn't understand him — she still hadn't met him and wasn't sure she wanted to — but nonetheless alone, on the other end of a crackly phone line. She would have given anything to dematerialise and reappear beside him. Anything.

"I love you," she breathed.

"See you soon, Sophia," he said. Then the line went dead.

* * *

I love you.

She gripped the bathroom door-handle. Tried to remind herself. Her shirt felt rough and abrasive against her skin, bruised from the persistent assault of his hand.

I love you.

She unlocked the door. Went back through to the living room. The curtains were drawn and the TV was on, the volume turned down. Misery had uncurled in her chest, reaching cold hands upwards to grip her throat. She hadn't been able to eat anything all evening. Monday. It was half term. Mum and Leon were in France. Half eleven. Later than she'd ever been here. London seemed like a lifetime ago. The high rise hadn't been that high, and he'd humoured her through *The Taming of the Shrew,* but she could tell he hadn't enjoyed it.

She paused in the doorway. He was lounged across the sofa, hands buried in his pockets. All evening, she'd been scraping together her courage. She steeled herself.

"I want to stay," she said.

He looked up. "What?"

"I want to stay tonight."

"You can't." He flicked the remote and the TV screen went black. She stared at it.

"Why not? Leon and Mum are on a prayer course; I won't even have to make an excuse about where I am." She padded across the floor and put her arms around him as he rose to his feet. He stiffened.

"We don't do that, Soph."

"Why?" The misery unclenched its hand then closed it again, grinding its fingers into her windpipe.

"You don't need to stay over. I can take you home after." He didn't really answer the question. His lips grazed her neck. One of his hands reached inside her shirt. She shivered.

"But what if I want to?" she persisted.

"Sophia." He stepped back abruptly, the annoyance undisguised in his face. "Why do we have to go into this again?"

"Because you always fob me off with excuses!" It burst from her before she'd censored it. "Because I'm not a kid anymore!"

Something flickered across his expression. She took a step back, frightened.

"For fuck's sake, Sophia," he snapped.

"It's not fair—" she began.

"Not fair?!" It was a snarl. In an instant he had hold of her arm, paralysing her with shock. His grip was painfully hard. "You know what's not fair? You making fucking threats like that!"

"*What*?" she choked. For a second she didn't understand. "I didn't . . ." It suddenly occurred to her. Not a kid. "No . . ." Her limbs felt weak with terror. "No, it wasn't a threat! I didn't mean—"

"Then what did you mean?" His voice was dangerously quiet.

"Just that I'm . . . I'm old enough to decide. And I want to—"

"You want to stay over?" He spat it. "Fine. *Stay* over. Come on." He hauled her with him to the bedroom doorway. "You know where to go."

She stumbled away from him. The bedroom was untidy from earlier, the bed stale and unmade. She faltered. Suddenly she wasn't sure that she *did* want to. The realisation was like ice in her insides. He looked so unlike himself, rage twisting his handsome face, that suddenly all she wanted was not to have said anything at all.

"You normally get undressed to go to bed?" His voice dripped with sarcasm. She looked up at him, dazed and hurt.

"I . . ." She started to peel off her tights, tremulous. He stood watching her.

"Do you want to stay over or not?" His voice was hard.

"Yes," she whispered.

"Then get into bed."

She undid her skirt and stepped out of it. Somehow, she didn't want to take off her shirt, so she didn't. She left it on and took another uncertain step towards the bed.

"What are you doing?"

"I thought I—"

"What?" He grabbed her arm again. "You thought you'd *what*? Fuck with my head and then refuse? Do you think I'm fucking stupid?" He dragged her around in front of him, fingers cutting into the flesh of her upper arm. "Get on the fucking bed."

She gasped. He flung her down with such force that her head slammed into the headboard. Then he was kneeling over her.

"You don't get to manipulate me!" His arm was across her throat, almost suffocating her. He was so angry that flecks of saliva flew with the words from his trembling lips. With his other hand he pulled out a foil packet and unzipped his jeans. "Do you understand?"

She was starting to feel light-headed.

"Yes," she choked out. "Sorry."

He released his arm suddenly. She lay beneath him, gasping. Without another word, he dealt with the packet and lowered himself onto her.

I love you. She said it in her head over and over. *I love you. I love you.* A single sob escaped from her lips as he finished and rolled away. It was her fault. She closed her eyes. She knew it was.

"Please." She wasn't sure who she was whispering to. She kept her eyes closed, so that the tears couldn't get out. So he couldn't see them. "Please . . ."

"Oh, Soph," he exhaled. She breathed slowly, barely daring to listen. She couldn't help flinching as his arm snaked out to her under the covers. His voice had gone back to normal.

"Sophia, I'm sorry." He pulled her close, face buried in his chest. "I didn't mean to hurt you."

She couldn't reply. Her whole body throbbed with pain. Her fault. She hadn't listened. She'd pushed him too far. Hurt him, by not thinking about the stupid words before they came out of her mouth. *Not a kid.* He thought she was threatening him. He thought she'd tell.

"You know what you mean to me." His hand stroked her hair. "Just . . . when you said *that.* You made me lose my temper. I didn't know what I was doing . . ."

"I'm sorry." She didn't try to move. She kept her face pressed to his chest, where she could hear his heart. "I wouldn't . . ." Her voice was thick. "I would *never* threaten you. I would never tell about us. Not *ever.*"

"Not ever?" He stilled. The vibration of his voice was barely even audible. His hand had stopped stroking, holding her head immobile. She breathed out.

"Not ever," she whispered.

CHAPTER 16

2022

I can't draw. Can't think. The clock is ticking with agonising slowness, the hands edging their way millimetre by millimetre closer to midday. Katie's in the cabin, typing up a long and comprehensive-looking report. I started the morning at my desk. But I couldn't hack it. At five to eight, I lost my nerve, and bolted for the back room when she wasn't looking.

Desperate for a distraction, I've got out my uni notes and my portfolio, photocopied the Trethallyan Edge sketches, scanned them and filed them. I busy myself organising, underlining the curriculum. *Boxes to tick.* I can't quite banish his comment. The memory of our first conversation still chafes, a stinging counterpoint to the surge of adrenaline every time I hear the cabin door open.

What was it he said? *If you're good, it doesn't matter.* Doesn't it? And am I? As good as I said?

As good as him?

I take out Dad's pen and rub the engraved metal to a shine with my sleeve. Since Friday, it's worked perfectly. There's no denying it, just as there's no denying the paper windmill on

Fin's bedside table, Swift's journal in my satchel or the dust-jacket in my dressing-table drawer.

I stand up and walk to the window. The receipt's still in my pocket. The first few daffodils are starting to bud, taut with anticipation and promise. The door opens silently. I turn.

"Frost." Sean's gaze is astute. He lets go of the handle, leaving the door ajar.

"Lorchann." I quickly slide the pen into my back pocket.

"You've been in here all morning." He folds his arms across his chest.

"Yes." I cross my arms too. We regard each other in silence. His brows lower.

"You're avoiding me," he says at last.

"No." I unfold my arms.

"Right." His lips are unsmiling but there's a note in his voice that defies them. "So you're in here because . . ."

"Because I feel like a change." I keep my face impassive. "Why? Is this the place to go when you're avoiding someone?"

"You tell me." A tiny smirk plays on Sean's lips. "Is it? I just need to know where to look when I need an intern to outperform me."

I fight to suppress my smile. "I didn't realise you'd need to look. I was pretty sure you said you worked alone. That you didn't want an intern."

He strides to the table to look at my portfolio, scanning the sketches and pages. An undisguised taunt smoulders in his dark eyes. "Do you fancy doing any actual work today, Frost?"

I scowl. A smile teases at his mouth.

"The chapel. In half an hour. You can use your breaking and entering skills." He turns away. "Before you finish the details on the oak frame design, Katelyn's going to enlighten us as to whether your idea is feasible, or whether you'd be liable for making the whole place fall down."

"You'd be liable, too," I remind him.

"Trust me," he says over his shoulder. "I know." He's across the mezzanine in a couple of strides, down the steps.

I stand absolutely still as he disappears outside into the sunshine, focussing on making my breathing return to normal.

I'm not the first. I try to remind myself that. I'm not the first person to stand here. They were friends — Claire said so — him and the last intern. They worked together for months. I start to gather together my portfolio abruptly. For some reason, I don't want to think about that. I slip back through into the main room. Katie stops typing and closes her laptop. She's watching me.

"You okay, Livs?"

"Fine, thanks." I didn't know she was a Katelyn. I stow the portfolio under my desk and turn, suddenly very conscious of the appraisal in her stare. "Why?"

"How are things with Sean?" she asks pointedly.

I pause, frowning. Again. She's asking about Sean again. Why? Why is she so interested?

"They're fine." I fiddle with a thread on my sleeve, uneasy. "Why?"

"He liked your designs?"

"I think so." My cheeks are hot. "He told—"

"He's given me a copy to look at." Of course he has. She's coming to talk us through the survey. She knows all about it. Katie stands up, pushing the laptop into her bag.

"Can't you see there's something risky about it, Livia?" she says softly.

"What?" I look up sharply. The plans? Her gaze levels on my face.

"What's wrong with it?" I bite my lip. "Is there—"

"Not your design." She comes round the desk to join me, worry creasing between her brows. "Him. The way he looks at you. The way he talks to you—"

"I don't know what you're talking about." I reach quickly to tie back my hair. It's not just my cheeks that are hot now.

"Really . . . ?"

"Really." I try to change the subject. "We should go. Are you going to walk to the chapel, or drive?"

"Maybe you should have taken him up on his offer." Katie's voice is quiet. I freeze. "Of going to work with Peter in Oxford." She carries on quickly, before I can argue. "I know it wouldn't have been Trethallyan. But Peter's very good. And it might have been safer."

"What . . . do you mean?" I breathe.

"Sean has a reputation for being pretty good at getting what he wants from people." She's not meeting my eye. She reaches down to pick up her diary from the desk, folding it carefully closed. "I think you should know that. That's all."

"It's about the project," I assert stubbornly. "Not about him."

"Be sure of that, Livia." She shakes her head. "I'm not convinced that that's the way *he* sees it." She pauses, and the silence rings around us. "You haven't asked him. Have you?" Her voice is low. "About what happened with S— oh . . ."

The door swings open.

"Ryan!" I've never seen Katie look flustered before. She snatches up her coat from the back of her chair, her lips pressing tightly together like a child who's been caught whispering in class.

"Hi, Katie. Livs." He glances from one to the other of us, mystified. My eyes are watering with self-consciousness. Katie's cheeks are pink. "Is Sean around?"

"I . . . uh . . . don't think so," I manage. "I think he's headed up to the chapel. Is there something I can help with?"

"It's okay. I'll ring him. Thanks, Livs." He swings the door open, then stops. "Although, while you're both here . . ." He glances furtively over his shoulder and pushes the door to again. "It's Claire's birthday on Sunday. I'm trying to organise a bit of a get-together — a few drinks at ours, Sunday evening. It would be great if you can make it. Craig too, of course." He flashes Katie a tension-melting smile. "How's the wedding planning?"

Sunday. *Kris.* I almost forgot. My spirits lift. Kris will be here in three days. Niklavs has even dug out a serious-looking airbed for him to use that appears to owe its existence to some kind of historic military.

"Are you going up to the chapel now?" Ryan turns back to me. I start out of my daydream.

"Oh." I nod. "Yeah."

"Could you ask Sean to give Peter McLeod a call back when he gets a chance?"

"Sure. No problem."

"Oh, and, Livs . . ." He pauses in the doorway, suddenly serious. "The picture's amazing. You made the little guy's week. You painted it?"

"Yeah." I swallow. For a moment Ryan's eyes are on me, ascertaining.

"It's somewhere you know?"

"No." I shake my head, embarrassed. "It's a picture he drew . . . Fin, I mean."

"Right." He nods. There's an odd silence.

"Come on, Livia." Katie touches my arm. "We need to go. Do you have keys?"

"I can lock up." Ryan roots in his pocket for his lanyard. "Sunday. Both of you. Right?"

"My brother'll be here," I mumble, not sure if it's an excuse or not. "I'll let you know."

"You have a brother?" Ryan dangles the lanyard from his fingers as we step outside. Katie has already drawn ahead, apparently out of patience. "I never realised. Bring him! It would be great to meet him."

"Maybe." I nod and turn away. I hear the key in the lock as I start after Katie along the gravelled path. She doesn't speak. Neither do I. I scan the driveway for Sean's car as we pass, but it's gone.

We cut through the gardens under the shadow of the Hall, through the overgrown archways and between the tangled sculptures of dark ivy that line the box hedges. The sky is starting to cloud over. I shiver. Maybe the leafy paths and borders were beautiful once. But now they seem home to something uncomfortable, a never-quite-banished presence. The inescapable feeling of unseen, watching eyes. It's a relief to step back out into the sunlight. The wind roars past my ears, whipping a fresh surge of colour into my cheeks.

Pretty good at getting what he wants from people. I focus on my footsteps, trying not to complete Katie's penultimate sentence in my head. I haven't asked him what happened with his last intern. She's right. I haven't. And I'm not going to. Because I'm not sure I want to know. I don't want there to have been another intern; I don't want anyone else to have worked with him, argued with him, seen themselves reflected back in the silence of his dark eyes.

I glance up. Katie is still some way ahead. I lengthen my strides to catch her up.

"Graham chose your drawings over Sean's?" She turns to me with a smile, at last. I bite my lip.

"Mm." I can't help smiling too. "He did."

"What did Sean mean about breaking and entering?" she asks, curious.

"Oh." I fight back a guilty grin. "I um . . . was . . . researching. And I . . ."

I trail off. Beside us in the trees, something's moving. A chill runs along my spine. I make myself breathe out. Nothing. It's nothing. A bird. The wind in the branches . . .

A face.

I gasp. Katie stops so suddenly that I almost trip over her.

"Did you see that?"

"What?" I whisper. It's not just me. She saw it too. I want to say no. No, there's nothing there. There couldn't be anyone there. Just like there wasn't anyone in Trethallyan Cove. Or in Ryan and Claire's house . . .

Katie glances at me sideways.

"Livs?" she breathes. The bottom suddenly seems to have dropped out of my stomach.

"You saw him, right?" Katie's voice is shaky. I can't quite drag my gaze away from the pine trees. *Ghosts that you can't run from . . .*

"Bloody ramblers." She lets out a tremulous breath. "He really made me jump, Livia. What a creep."

"Yeah." I'm still breathing too fast.

"Another one. We ought to tell Ryan, really. It's private land." She's quietly indignant. "People just don't seem to get it. There was some guy a few weeks before you came, poking around the stables. Totally out of order. Graham still lives here, for goodness' sake — how would they feel if someone was in *their* garden? Just because it's a stately home, doesn't mean it's open for people to come nosing around. It's trespassing."

She's started walking again and I have to run a few paces to catch her up.

"Yes," I whisper. "You're right."

"Is that Sean's car?"

It is. He's there, waiting. Just like I knew he would be, lounging against the wall with his arms crossed over his chest and his long legs folded in front of him as he watches us on the incline. I try not to look. Try to focus, instead, on Katie beside me, and the drawings that are etched in their every detail onto my mind. Try to shut out the soft, mocking murmur of his greeting, the serious set of his lips, and the receipt in my trouser pocket.

Because she's right. Because, after everything, there's something risky about it. I know there is.

* * *

Oh, if only you knew. If only I could forewarn you. The truth is, you always want what you can't have. And it hurts. It hurts so much, doesn't it? But you can't stop. You just can't stop . . .

I can't take this path again. I can't. Because I know the price from last time. I know how it ends. I've felt this all before. The hate. The love, in equal measure. The way the illusion shatters, smashed into a thousand pieces that he's driving deeper under my skin. But the truth is, I don't want him to stop. I'd give him anything. I'm not afraid of the pain. I want him to touch me, even if he can't love me.

There's a word for this, I'm sure there is, but it eludes me. I can think of a lot of other words. Words I don't like as much. Words that frighten me. Captivated. Consumed. Under the thumb. Things change, and they don't change. I was so desperate for this. So sure . . .

The interior light dims. I reach above my head, eyes not leaving the page, to switch it back on. It's cold in the car. My breath is misting the windows. Ten past eight. The train's late, and the station car park is deserted. I pull my coat from the passenger seat over my legs, overcome with shivers.

I'm not sure, now. There are so many possibilities that I don't want to consider. Have you ever been here? Teetering, on the edge? So afraid that in a single breath you'll be lost, banished to a place you don't want to go back to . . . Afraid because you know you can't do it again. That you might not make it this time?

Tell me about you. I want to know. I want you to tell me that you have. That you've been here, that you understand. Tell me about the worst thing you've ever done. What is it— the secret you bury? Is it something terrible? Something you know you shouldn't ever have done? Something you started that you should never, ever have started? Something you finished in a way it should never have come to an end?

Have you ever slipped so deep you might drown?

"The train shortly arriving at platform two will be the delayed 19.15 service to Penzance."

I start. The pages crease.

"The delayed 19.15 service to Penzance, next train to arrive at platform two."

Kris. I glance at my phone. He hasn't texted yet, even though he must be seconds away. I grip the journal with both hands. For some reason, my heart is racing. I'm almost at the back. There's hardly anything left — a page or two — yet I'm not sure it's reaching any kind of conclusion. For all her promises, the only thing Swift has left me with so far is a mind full of questions.

I check the clock. There's time. I have to know, now. It might be stupid, but I have to know how it ended, however sad or sordid. She's said all along that she'll tell me when she's brave enough. All these pages, she's been building up her courage. Perhaps, once she put it into words, there was nothing else to write . . . ?

> *I need to tell you. I keep trying to write it, but I'm afraid it won't be enough. How will this ever be enough, these paper confessions and penances? How can they be, when the second I let them go, I start along the same path again in ever shrinking spirals?*
>
> *Tell me it's a mistake. That it's not too late to turn back. Tell me. And I'll tell you. The reason you're wrong. The rest of the story.*
>
> *I remember the word, now. The word I was looking for was damned. Because here it is. What I'm truly guilty of . . .*
>
> *My name is Sophia Swift. And when I was seventeen years old, I killed my*

I turn the page so quickly it almost rips.

What? My fingers are trembling. My what?

It's the end. I flip it over and back again. Nothing. It finishes mid-sentence.

No. *No.* I stare in disbelief. Ragged remnants of paper are stuck in the binding. Ripped out — the rest is ripped out, like the pages of Finbar's schoolbook. There isn't a single word more. Just a thin leaf of printed paper, folded over and ironed flat against the cover, the way you'd press a flower for safekeeping. I draw it out and unfold it with not-quite-steady fingers. The typeface is small and familiar.

A R Frost. 431

"That's it," she concludes, and her gaze drops to her hands and her ballet-dancer arms. "I'm sorry. You don't have to ask any more questions."

But he does. He does have to ask.

"What did you hope I—"

His voice fades in his throat.

She has risen to her feet, light as a bird, dark hair dropping out of its braid as she turns away. A daughter of night time. She's whispering.

No. Singing.

Red and yellow and pink and green . . .

He's about to blink. He's about to blink. And when he opens his eyes again—

"What?" I whisper. "What?"

"The train now arriving at platform two is the delayed 19.15 service to Penzance. This train is for Penzance only. First-class accommodation is situated towards the rear of the train. Platform two for the delayed 19.15 . . ."

Reality hits me in a jolt. There are lights on the horizon, the warning chick-and-hum of wheels on tracks. With an explosive clatter and a judder that exorcises the rain from my car windows, the train screeches into view. He's here.

I lurch upright in my seat. The page of *Mercy's Child* trembles in my fingers. I fold it hastily and shove it back inside the journal, snapping the cover shut. Then I bury the book deep in my satchel and push it under my seat.

It's dark on the platform. There's only one light over the signboard. Empty hanging baskets, cradling the corpses of last year's flowers, swing in wild abandon from either end. I walk in sped-up-slow motion alongside the protesting carriages as they decelerate, doors and dark windows groaning past me until the abrupt, inevitable stop. Momentary silence. Then a hiss of air, the bang of locks and opening windows. One or two hands reach outside for aged latches. The door beside me swings open and a man falls out, clutching his umbrella to his chest as the wind catches him. He stumbles a few steps along the platform and disappears into the gloom. I shiver.

"Platform two for the delayed 19.15 service to Penzance. Calling at Penzance only. Would passengers intending to travel on this service please board the train now, as it is ready to leave. Platform t—"

"Livs!"

"Oh—"

He hits like a hurricane. Kris Frost, his father's son, larger than life and not in the slightest bit subdued by the seven-hour journey. His arms crush my shoulders, and in an instant my feet have left the floor. He's a chaos of backpacks, hoody and headphones, and he smells of hair gel — and home. For the briefest of moments, I close my eyes. He lowers me to the floor. I hug him hard.

"Kris." Finally, I extricate myself. The darkness suddenly doesn't seem as dark. The wind has dropped and the train is pulling away, wheels groaning.

"Livs." He pushes me to arm's length to study me. "You look . . . different."

"Different?" I hold out a hand for one of his backpacks, but he shakes his head and slings one over each of his shoulders.

"Yeah." He pauses. There's an uncharacteristic softness to his voice. "Yeah. You look . . . amazing."

"Really?" I raise a cynical eyebrow at him. "I came straight from work and I haven't showered. Your eyes need testing."

He pulls a face at me. "You look health . . . happy, Livs. That's what I meant. Aren't you pleased to see me? Or have you forgotten me, with all those fishermen?"

I roll my eyes. "My very own resident fisherman is dying to meet you. Come on." I start along the platform. He follows me, one long stride to two of mine, headphones dangling from his back pocket. He looks every part the student. Glancing down at my own shirt and chinos, my Lorchann McLeod lanyard and car keys, I'm suddenly not sure when things shifted. Can I really have changed that much, in just a few weeks?

We eat Latvian food in the comfortable simplicity of Niklavs' flat; he has cooked in honour of the occasion and efficiently sets about plying us with sailor stories and *Melnais balzams* — a herbal liqueur that could knock me out in a single shot. By midnight, he and Kris are trading rugby songs for sea-shanties, and by one Kris has developed a new vocabulary of Latvian expletives while Niklavs giggles at his pronunciation. At two, after several near-misses on the stairs, I steer my brother onto the airbed with a bin and a pint glass of water, and crawl into my own bed, trying my hardest to keep the rest of my thoughts at bay beyond the slowly revolving alcoholic haze.

Here it is. What I'm really guilty of . . .

My sleep is fitful. I dream of pounding feet and watching eyes. When I wake at seven, the bed is damp with sweat.

I tiptoe around Kris's prostrate blanket-covered form to get my running stuff. The wind hasn't dropped; it's brutal as I complete my clifftop loop, focussing on my steps and not on the hungry dark waves sucking at the foot of the cliffs.

Kris isn't up when I get back, and I sit at the easel for hours, lulled into timelessness by the peaceful rhythm of his breathing. I don't paint anything. Just colours, a series of Umber, Charcoal and Black. I can't stop thinking. *I just can't stop.*

Kris wakes at eleven. It's midday by the time we walk into town. We get fish and chips on open trays and spend the first half of the afternoon digesting, skimming pebbles over the high tide and reminiscing about family holidays in Whitby and afternoons at the Abbey, where our father spent hours penning notes in his Moleskine books. Once the fried-food stupor relents, we walk. I find my feet taking us in what my senses know to be the direction of Trethallyan; we skirt around the headland away from town. I don't know the way from here, although it can't be far. I find my eyes scanning the horizon for the dark silhouette of the chapel in the outline of the cliffs, but I can't make it out. Kris hires belly-boards, and I shiver on the sand in a wetsuit as he wades determinedly into the sea. He doesn't last long. According to the blackboard, the water's only eight degrees.

As we ascend the beach back towards the harbour front, I can't help thinking that it's strange. Before the Solent, before Dad, before Nottingham and the eating problem, we were never close. We didn't even go to school together; my scholarship was to an all-girls boarding school, the one the Rainworths paid thirty grand a year to send Hannah to. But as the darkness closed in, so did the net of responsibility, until things would never be the same again and the future was spelled out in frank austerity — you have each other and that's it. With the exception of sport, we aren't even that much alike, for all the comments. Kris externalises what I keep inside, parties when I'd rather paint, and seems to have no burning desire to bring home a girl for more than a night or two. In many ways, I've been glad of that. Our monopoly of confidences made me feel safe in the long, brick-walled hours of inpatient units and exam revision. I got out of hospital three months before finals, and struggled in every way to haul myself back up to speed. Some days, only his exuberance dragged me out of my room at all.

Porthtrevelen is deserted as we pick out a pub, and Kris orders his second thousand-calorie meal of the day, while I agonise over the menu. There's a plasma TV behind the bar playing rugby highlights without sound. I take off my coat.

"Livs." Kris is leaning on the pub's wooden table.

"Mmm?"

"I don't know." He regards me through slightly narrowed eyes. "I've been trying to figure it out."

"Figure what out?"

"How you're different."

"Huh?" I lay down the menu.

"Not in a bad way . . ." He toys with his pint, thoughtful. "You seem . . . good. Confident. But kind of quiet. And you haven't told me anything about your job."

"No." I chew my lip. "I guess I haven't."

"You're working on some stately home?"

"Mm-hmm." I take a sip of my drink, wary of his direction of questioning.

"Dad would have killed for that." He grins. "Whereabouts is it?"

"Just outside town. Right on the coast. It's pretty amazing. Actually . . ." I pause, thinking about Ryan. "We could go up there. Tomorrow. If—"

"Go to your work?" Kris pulls a comical face that reminds me painfully of my father. "On your day off?"

"Not exactly." I fiddle with my napkin. "There's a birthday party. One of the people I work for. You're invited."

"In the stately home?" Kris gives a low whistle.

"The Gatehouse, actually. But yeah." I shrug. "If you're up for it."

"Totally." Kris grins. Then something occurs to him. "Will the architect be there?" He folds his arms.

I hesitate. Somehow, the thought hadn't even crossed my mind. I realise I'm biting my lip and release it quickly.

"Probably," I mutter. Kris frowns.

"Is he treating you any better? Or is he still a bastard? You know, you should tell him where to go, Livs. You shouldn't put up with it."

Somehow, I've paled. *Nice work, Livvy.* I screw my hands into fists under the table, where he can't see them.

"Um." I shrug. As if it doesn't matter. As if he can't see straight through me.

An infatuation. I make myself breathe out. *Can't you see there's something risky about it?*

"No." I whisper at last. "I know."

CHAPTER 17

My name is Sophia Swift. And when I was seventeen years old, I killed my

"Livs, are you ready?"

"Yes." I slide the book back under my pillow like a thief. Kris has re-emerged from the bathroom without me noticing, catching me mid-transgression.

Sophia Swift. *Ms S Swift.* It wasn't a typo. The letter is still in the top drawer of my dressing table, unopened.

"Then let's go. Come on." Kris examines his reflection in the tri-fold mirror, popping the collar of his polo and smoothing the front of his hair. "How long does it take to get there?"

"Ten, fifteen minutes?"

"I thought you said it started at eight."

"It did."

"It's already quarter past. I'm only going to get an hour before I have to get on a train."

"Oh." I'd forgotten about the train. My heart sinks. Sunday night, and he's leaving. We've pre-emptively booked a taxi from the Gatehouse for nine thirty. He'll travel back as far as London tonight and on to Nottingham in the morning. I glance at my own reflection in the mirror beside him with a twinge of regret. It's so far. If I'd taken Oxford, he'd only have been two hours away, not seven. The weekend has gone so fast.

He misreads my sigh. "Livs, you look awesome. Stop worrying about it." I glance down at my dress. It hadn't even occurred to me to worry about it. It's too late now, anyway. "Can you even drive in those shoes, or do you want me to?"

"You're not driving my car." I scowl at him. He grins. "Worth a shot."

I pick up my keys from the dressing table and wave them at him tauntingly. "Shall we?"

Kris rolls his eyes. We descend the stairs and I let us out into the road and unlock the car as he checks his reflection again in Niklavs' front window. Seriously? I shake my head.

There's a car stopped on double yellows across the road. Dark red, with misted-up windows, and I feel like I've seen it before.

"Alright, Livs?" Kris turns to look at me.

"Uh-huh. Fine." I shake it off. I'm being ridiculous.

"These people are loaded then?" He strains to look out of the windscreen, as if Trethallyan will appear instantly on the horizon. I shake my head.

"You could say that."

As if in affirmation, the Gatehouse is resplendent. A swinging trail of white fairy-lights adorns the garden path and arches over the porch. I lead us through the side gate instead, in the hope of going unnoticed, and into the crowded conservatory. It doesn't work.

"Livs!" Ryan's arm encompasses both of my shoulders, and before I know what's happening, there's a glass in my hand. "White?" He must catch sight of Kris's suspicious look as he fills my glass. "Is this your brother?" He releases me abruptly to offer his hand as Kris deposits his bags in the doorway. "Ryan Lorchann. Livia's been working on my father-in-law's estate. It's great to meet you."

"Kris Frost." His scowl has faded slightly at the words father-in-law. *Not the architect*, I mouth at him. But he doesn't see.

"Have you travelled far, Kris?" Ryan shakes his hand firmly.

"Nottingham."

"Nottingham? No way!"

Oh, here we go. I fight the urge to roll my eyes. I take a gulp of my wine and go in search of a place to leave my coat and my present for Claire. By the time I re-emerge from the hallway with my drink, they're deep in conversation.

"Cripps . . ."

"Hugh Stu . . ."

"Trent match last week . . ."

"Totally!"

"Hi, Livia!"

Claire kisses me on both cheeks. "You look beautiful! Thanks so much for coming! Hasn't Ryan done a good job?"

"Oh . . ." I hug her back. "Yes. Happy birthday!" I withdraw. She smiles. I take another sip of wine.

"I'm just popping across to the Hall to check on Fin. I'll be back in a bit."

I nod. "Sure."

"Livs." Kris's voice filters over the noise. "Come and get another drink!"

With no opportunity for protest, Ryan tops up my glass. There's another new face beside him, tall and blond with a wicked smile and a ski-goggle tan.

"Livia?" He holds out a hand. "James Holdsworth." After a second's hesitation, we shake. "I've been hearing all about you from Ryan."

"You have?" I blush, taken aback.

"Absolutely." He smiles. "Only good things, of course."

"Right." I bite back my own smile. Trust Ryan.

"Ryan, Sean and I go way back. Their old man used to coach the Junior Fifteens at home when we were kids. So, you're working with Sean?" He flashes me a knowing smile. "Fuck, I have so many stories you should hear. We were roommates for a while, at UCL."

Stories? What kind of stories? I blink up at him.

Life's all about the stories. The good ones, the bad ones. The ones that wake you, sobbing, sweating . . .

"Food?" He gestures to the kitchen table which is completely covered in sandwiches and canapés. Claire's right. Ryan has certainly put in a good effort. I shake my head.

"Shall we find a seat somewhere? I think there's a few of Claire's friends in the other room, if you know any of them."

I don't, but I follow him anyway. The lights are low, and a Bluetoothed iPad is pumping music through well-concealed speakers in every room. I glance over my shoulder, relieved to see that Kris and Ryan aren't far behind us.

"Livia!"

I turn quickly to look behind me. A couple are approaching from the border of the group of friends. I almost do a double-take; Katie looks completely different with make-up on and her hair loose.

"Livia, this is Craig, my fiancé. Craig, this is Livia, the new Lorchann McLeod intern."

"Nice to meet you." Craig's quiet voice is unassuming. It doesn't take much scrutiny to see who does the talking in their relationship.

"You look lovely, Livia." Katie gives me a brief hug.

"So do you," I say, and mean it. Her cheeks are pink, her hair falling like a silk-smooth waterfall to the scooped neckline of her black dress. It's little wonder that Craig's eyes haven't left her.

"These are some of the girls from school." She nods back at the group as the volume of chatter rises another notch or two. "I'll have to try and introduce you. Did you say your brother's here?"

"Yeah." I have to clear my throat, not quite sure why I'm suddenly uncomfortable in her presence. Something to do with infatuation. *What you can't have*. I excuse myself: "Kris. I should probably find him. He doesn't know anyone."

It doesn't take long to locate Kris. In fact, I don't really have to look. He's standing with Ryan by the iPad dock, and James is showing them something on his phone that has them cracking up with laughter. So much for not knowing anyone. I'm much more alone than he is.

I slip in beside him and look down at the iPad. There's a logo on the back of the case that's oddly familiar. A tiny golden boat in an arc of writing: *Rivent Master Yacht Builders*. I stare at it, trying to work out where I've seen it before.

". . . Livs went once, didn't you?"

"What?"

"Girls' rugby." Kris's lips twitch. "Dad vetoed it. Said you'd end up being the ball."

"Shut up." I grin, despite myself.

"I bet you'd be fast." Ryan looks me over. "You run, don't you? Here, let me top you up."

"Yeah." I shrug, embarrassed, and relinquish my glass. "Sort of."

"Sort of?" Kris pokes my ribs and I wince. "Never, *ever* run with her. It's like . . . bloody murder."

"Where do you run?" Ryan passes me my drink and balances his plastic pint glass to pour the rest of his bottle of Guinness into it.

"Just a loop from my flat." I'm blushing.

"Just a loop." Kris rolls his eyes and slings a heavy arm around my shoulders, taking a swig from his own bottle. "Yeah, right. Livs can run up mountains; she's won all kinds of crazy-ass races. I bet she didn't tell you that. She's a fucking legend."

But I've stopped hearing. A thrill has crept along the back of my neck. The unmistakable feeling that I'm being watched.

I look round. My gaze falls on tousled hair and raw-umber eyes. Sean Lorchann's arms are folded across his chest. I feel the laughter fade instantly from my face.

"I . . . uh. I'll be back in a moment," I murmur.

He has moved into the far corner, and is examining something on the bookcase. I don't join him. I slip away to one of the coffee tables instead, where someone has arranged chairs that no one's sitting on, and sit down with my wine.

There's a glass bowl in the middle of the table, holding a candle that has almost gone out. I reach in to right it, wary of burning my hand.

"Frost."

I don't jump. Somehow, I already knew he was there. I withdraw my hand from the candle carefully.

"Lorchann." I look up, and wish I hadn't. The moody conflict of his expression makes my heart lurch.

"You seem to have lost the varsity jock." His eyebrows are raised a fraction as he glances over at Kris. I glare at him.

"Be careful what you say. He's my brother."

Sean sits too, and sets down his glass and a bottle of designer mineral water on the table. I take a nervous sip of my wine.

"Well, that's a relief." He pours the water into the glass without looking. "I thought he seemed very immature for you."

"What's that supposed to mean?"

He shrugs.

"You seemed to be spending an alarming amount of time in his company."

I hesitate.

"*You* don't seem to be spending much time in *your* brother's company," I point out.

"No," he agrees. "Mostly because I don't need to spend any more time with Holdsworth." There's a distinct edge to the way he says the name. "I think you and he have met."

"James?" I look up, surprised. "You don't want to spend time with him? Why?"

Sean shrugs. "I don't have anything to say." His voice is quiet, opaque. He folds his hands. "Obviously, for someone so arrogant, I'm incredibly taciturn."

Shit.

I clutch my wineglass. Sean rests his index fingers against his lips, disguising the faintest hint of a smile.

"I . . . think it was the other way round," I murmur.

His brows flicker, dark eyes alight with amusement. "Right."

"I . . ." I study the coffee table. "I didn't actually mean . . . I . . ."

Jesus Christ. What else has he overheard? My eyes are stinging with a vengeance.

"So, he's your brother."

"Yes."

"Try not to break your glass," Sean advises me softly. I put it down.

"How much more did you hear?" I look up at him, every muscle in my abdomen clenched. Sean raises his eyebrows.

"How much more *shouldn't* I have heard?"

"Tell me."

"Why?" His eyes don't leave mine. "Does it really matter?"

"Yes."

"A few things. But I don't believe everything I hear, Livia. I like to make my own judgements." He picks up his own glass. Bubbles rise indolently in the sparkling water as he replaces it on the coffee table. "You told Claire you were no good with kids."

"I'm not."

"I saw the picture you gave to Fin." He sits back, arms folded. "You never mentioned that you paint."

"I didn't think it was important."

The reprove in his voice takes me off guard. "Of course it's important."

The most important thing in the world. Something constricts in my throat. I screw my hands into fists and try to think of a safe reply.

"You were unhappy," he observes.

I look up sharply. "I—"

"Are you unhappy now?"

"I . . . don't know." I make myself release my hands. "No. I don't think so."

"Good."

There's a pause. I look down and catch myself staring at the profile of his folded arms, at the way his fingers drum against his shirtsleeve. I swallow. For someone who doesn't have anything to say, he's doing an awful lot of the talking. I glance over the room. I can't see Kris anywhere. Ryan's showing Katie and Craig something on the iPad, though Katie doesn't really seem to be paying attention. Her eyes travel from the back of Sean's head to my face, and I pick up my drink and drain it, trying to look like I haven't noticed.

"What did Peter McLeod say?" I ask, without looking at him.

"He wanted to know if you were still interested in the Oxford opening. I told him you weren't."

"It's still available?"

Momentarily, something in his expression wavers.

"Yes," he says. "Why? Should I have told him you've changed your mind?"

It might have been safer.

"No." I shake my head. Silence again. The music has progressed from relaxed ambience to vaguely familiar noughties pop that transports me back to school halls and prom dances. I draw in a deep breath.

"You would have, wouldn't you?"

"Would have what?"

"Sent me there."

"If you'd wanted to go, I couldn't have stopped you."

"But you don't want me to?"

"No." His lips curve. "I don't."

Oh. I let out my breath slowly. Well, that's a revelation. I chew my lip.

"That's a change of tune."

"Your work's something else, Frost. Sending you to Oxford would have been the second-worst mistake I ever made."

I pick up my glass again, and toy absently with the stem. "The second. What's the worst?"

A wry smile plays on his lips. He doesn't answer.

"What's the worst?" I repeat, a whisper.

"Livs!" Out of nowhere, Kris is hanging on the back of my chair. "What are you doing sat down? C'mon . . ." He grabs me by the arm with a disarmingly boyish grin, and prises me from my seat.

"Kris . . ." My protest falls on deaf ears. He drags me with him to the iPad and changes tracks. I feel Sean's inscrutable gaze on us.

"Kris, you're drunk," I mumble. "You're going to miss your train."

"I won't." He has to raise his voice over the music. "Come on!" He takes both my hands to pull me along. I laugh. But the burning hasn't receded from my cheeks.

"Where?"

"Nowhere . . . Here . . ." Kris gestures at the abandoned glasses and the cluster of vaguely swaying ex-school-friends. "Dance with me, Livia!" He scoops me up in a crushing, bouncing hug, and I stumble, overwhelmed by his exuberance, into the middle of the floor.

Dance with me, Livia.

I close my eyes and suck in a deep breath, winded.

Livia, be a darling. Pop and get Hannah, and ask her just to check on Toby, will you . . .

I can feel the memory tightening my throat, ringing in my ears. I force my eyes open in time to see Claire slip back in. *Just to check . . .*

A tremor runs through me. Kris pauses, suddenly sober.

"Are you okay?" His voice is low enough that only I can hear it. I look up quickly.

"Fine," I breathe.

"Livs?" His eyes narrow.

"I'm fine." I flash him an artificially teasing smile. "You're a crap dancer. You always stand on my feet."

"You're a crap liar."

"Touché. And you're not even drunk." I let him twirl me around. "So what are you doing?"

"I wanted to see you before I go. And . . ." He pauses as the music changes, the lively beat throwing us completely out of time.

"And?"

"And I wanted to get you away from the architect." His lips tighten stubbornly, in a way that reminds me too much of myself. "You were right not to like him. Something about him . . . seems like bad news."

For fuck's sake. Him, too? I grit my teeth and try not to look over at Katie, cocooned unaware in Craig's arms.

"He's my boss," I mutter. "What do you want me to do about it?"

"Just be careful, Livs." He takes both my hands again. But this time he isn't laughing. "Promise me, right?"

"I promise to be careful." I slip my hands free of his hold.

"Livs—" The ring of his phone cuts off whatever he's about to say. He swipes it up. "Hi." He pauses. "Sure. Two minutes. Thanks." He ends the call without so much as a goodbye.

He turns back to me. "I have to go."

"I know." I nod.

"Come back to Nottingham." His arm slides around my shoulders. "I know you're all besotted with the scenery or whatever. But when this is done, come back."

For a moment, his grip is tighter than it really needs to be. Then he lets go. I follow him to collect his bags and watch as he tugs his headphones from his pocket, pops the collar of his polo and pulls on his coat. Very suddenly, I can't help noticing how young he is. How different everything used to be in my own days of budget train fares and canvas shoes, before the cancer phone call, before the Solent.

"Miss you, Livs." He gives me one last hug for good measure. I hug him back tightly.

"I miss you too." My voice is husky. "See you, Kris."

He releases me slowly. "Better do. Hockley Hub's gonna go out of business if you don't come back for breakfast soon."

"Lunch," I tease.

"Bye, Livs." He grins. I raise my hand in a semi-wave. And then he's jogging across the drive, and the taxi door closes, and he's gone, the tyres crunching on the gravel.

I turn and make my way back into the buzz of voices and music. Kris has set a trend; as I edge in through the sitting-room door everyone seems to be dancing: the school friends, a scattering of couples, even Katie and Craig, their arms still locked around each other. I stand for a moment, lost.

"Here."

I jump. James pushes a wine glass into my hand.

"Drink up. I can dance better than your brother anyway." He steers me with him, and I acquiesce, glass in hand.

"I'm not sure if *I* can," I inform him. He laughs. I tighten my fingers around the glass and drink the wine faster than I mean to.

"You're an architect, then?" James leans closer, raising his voice over the music. "Like Sean?"

"Almost." The glass is at my lips.

"You went to Nottingham?"

"Yeah." I nod, frowning. "How—"

"I told you, I've heard all about you." James touches my waist, moving me aside to let one of the school friends squeeze past. I raise my eyebrows.

"Exactly what have you heard?"

"I've heard you're an artist?"

"Not exactly." I look back at the empty coffee table. I wonder how long ago he left. *The second-worst mistake . . .*

James's hands are still on my waist and his shirt smells faintly of cigarette smoke. "I've always wanted to paint. If you ever visit Oxford you'll have to come and give me a lesson."

I suddenly don't feel entirely sober.

"You live in Oxford?" I murmur. The bottom half of the glass of wine is making it easier to move in time with the music, and to take his undisguised attention at face value.

"Mm-hm." He nods. I feel him move, the slightest shift of his hands. "I have a flat there. Why, do you know it?"

I shake my head. James relieves me of the empty wine glass.

"What can I get you?"

"Oh . . ." I glance down at the stem in his fingers. "I don't think I . . . Just an orange juice. Thanks."

"Sure thing." He smiles. "I'll be right back."

"Okay." I wrap my arms around myself as he disappears. My face is flaming, but the rest of me is cold.

I know before I see. Before I raise my eyes to look, uncomfortably aware of being watched.

He's there, in the bay window. Sean Lorchann, statue still, arms folded across his chest, face grim. He hasn't left, after all. Pain stabs in my gut. His eyes alight on mine. For a split second I look back at him, mute. Then I turn and flee.

The kitchen is full of people. It's a relief not to come across James as I navigate my way through the guests to the conservatory and lean my aching head just for a moment against the cold windowpane.

"There you are."

I jump. James hands me the drink. The juice is so cold that condensation is starting to bead on the glass.

"I'm going to have a walk and a smoke." He gestures at the conservatory doors. "Do you want to come?"

I hesitate.

"No. Thanks."

"In that case," he leans close to my ear as he moves past me, "I'll cut out the walk. I'll be two minutes. Don't go anywhere."

Where would I go? I hover by the window. In the hallway I can hear someone saying their goodbyes, a burst of Ryan's laughter, Claire's gush of thanks and well wishes. Home? Tipsy and miserable, to the disarray of the empty flat, the journal with no more pages? Even the crap music and James's unsubtle advances have to be better than that. I raise the glass to my lips, and freeze.

Sean Lorchann is in the kitchen doorway, his expression so black that I take a pace backwards. My pulse bounds in my throat, adrenaline washing out every thought except the answer he didn't give. *What's the worst?* I open my mouth. But before I can voice whatever it is I think I might say, he strides forward and sweeps the glass of juice from my hand. I stare, stunned as he retraces his steps and pours it into the sink.

"What do you think you're *doing*?" I hiss. I watch as he replaces the glass on the glossy countertop with a click.

"You a favour," he speaks through his teeth.

"What?" For some reason, I'm seething. "It was juice. Not that it's any of your business."

"You want a new one?" There's an undisguised challenge in his dark glare.

"No." My hands are shaking. I face him, incredulous. "No, I don't. Actually . . . actually, I think I'm going to go home."

"Good idea," he snaps.

"What is your *problem*?" The rest of me is shaking, too. I clench my hands into fists. Sean doesn't reply. I stalk past him towards the door, and he stands back to let me go.

The hallway is mercifully empty. I search through the stack of coats on the pegs, cursing under my breath as half of them fall in a heap at my feet.

"What are you doing?"

I jump. He's followed me. I glower at the fabric landslide.

"Getting my coat. What does it look like?"

"Have you called a taxi?"

"No." I seize my coat and struggle into the sleeves. "I'm going to walk." I grab my bag and turn to leave, but he's faster. He steps into my path, blocking the door. The look on his face is so forbidding that it stops me in my tracks.

"No you're not," he growls. "Don't be ridiculous."

"It's not ridiculous." I try to dodge past him, heart racing. "I'm going to walk. I don't want to wait for a taxi. I need some air."

"You've been drinking." There's accusation in his voice. His arm bars my way, tense and muscular. My breath sticks in my throat.

"Not enough to impair my judgement."

"Then I don't think much to your judgement."

"Well I don't think much to yours," I retort, with slightly less conviction than I hoped for. He lowers his arm.

"You're not walking." His voice is dangerously quiet.

"I'm over the limit."

"But your judgement's intact?"

"You're angry," I whisper.

"Yes, Livia," he speaks between his teeth. "I am."

"Why?"

"Livs!" Claire has appeared suddenly from the sitting-room doorway. "What's . . ." Her gaze travels from my coat to Sean's terrifying frown. "Oh, are you going?"

"Yeah." I zip up my coat.

"Oh, that's a shame!" She moves to hug me, and Sean steps back in silence. "Thanks for coming! You know, if you can wait two minutes, James already has a taxi on its way. I'm sure he'd be happy to get the driver to drop you off on the way back to his hotel."

"Of course he'd be fucking happy," Sean mutters under his breath.

The silence is stony. I let go of my zip.

"Um." I avoid both of their gazes assiduously. "That's really kind—"

"But I've already told Livia that I'll take her back." Sean cuts across me. I freeze.

"Er. Okay . . ." Claire glances from one to the other of us, surprised. "Are you sure?" I can't tell whether the question's aimed at Sean, or at me. I push my phone further into my pocket.

"Are you ready, Livia?" Sean's voice is impossible to read. I don't move.

"Honestly, don't go out of your way." I voice the challenge despite my better judgement. "I'm happy to wait for the taxi."

Sean's teeth clamp together. "Let's go."

I don't even dare to shoot a parting glance at Claire as he jerks the door open and stands back to let me out.

"Happy birthday," I mumble from the doorway.

"Thanks, Livs."

"Will you say bye to James for me?"

"Sure."

"Night—"

The door crashes closed. My breath is misting in the sudden assault of cold March air. Sean pulls a car key from his pocket and gestures me to go first, and I cross the gravel to the Defender as he unlocks it. We both climb in without a word. The leather dog lead is coiled around a pile of loose change on the dashboard tray. I concentrate on the glint of the coins as we pull away and bump onto the uneven contours of the track. It seems to take a lifetime to reach the road. His knuckles on the gearstick are disconcertingly close.

"Which way?"

"Left." I don't look up from the dashboard. The collection of coins slides as we corner. We drive for a few moments in silence.

"Do you make a habit of getting yourself into trouble?" His gaze flickers sideways. I feel the blood rush into my cheeks.

"What?"

Sean shakes his head. "Never mind."

"Self-sabotage didn't used to be my specialty," I mutter. He turns his head. I shrug, staring at a twenty-pence piece that has fallen into the footwell. "Not that you'd have any experience of that."

"Oh, I don't know, Livia." Sean's voice is enigmatically soft. "It turns out that on occasion I can be quite proficient at self-sabotage."

I look up sharply, but his face gives nothing away. Intermittent moonlight flickers between the houses, lighting the inside of the car with an eerie pale glow.

"Left here," I whisper.

Two or three more coins gather momentum and plummet between my feet. I pick them up.

"You weren't drinking," I observe.

"No."

"Any particular reason?" I tip the coins into the tray on the dash. Sean doesn't look round. He tightens both hands on the wheel.

"I like to be in control, Livvy," he says quietly.

"Oh." My throat is suddenly dry. I watch the seconds tick past on the clock, then realise I'm holding my breath and let it out in a rush.

"Next right." I feel in my bag for my keys. The Land Rover makes short work of the cobbles. We draw to a halt. The one streetlight seems to have stopped working; Sunnyside is very dark. Sean releases his seatbelt and climbs out to hold open the car door, his fingers gripping the metal firmly against the wind. His shirt-sleeves are still rolled, rain landing on the skin of his forearms and running in rivulets over the tendons of his wrists. I undo my seatbelt, try not to look. But I can't stop looking. He catches my elbow to help me down, and for a fraction of a moment, his face is against my hair.

"How are you so infuriating?" he breathes.

I freeze. His hand around my elbow is warm and strong, and sends a paralysing bolt of electricity through me. I step away quickly and pull out my keys.

"Which one's yours?" He glances around at the empty terraces.

"This one." I mount the step. There are no lights on. Even Niklavs' apartment is in darkness. The outer door is barely discernible. Sean has stopped.

"You live *here*?"

I glance back at him, unnerved by the tone of his voice. "Yes."

For a painfully long moment, he doesn't reply.

"You'd better go in." I hear the soft fall of his feet on the cobbles and turn my key in the lock. The blood is rushing in my ears. I draw in a deep breath. The hallway is a pool of shadows, and I step inside, letting them wash over me. I wrap the key into the palm of my hand and hold it hard.

"Goodnight, Frost."

I spin back. He's stopped in the open doorway. Neither of us moves.

"Thanks." My voice is husky. "For the lift."

"Any time." He still doesn't move. I see him glance over his shoulder, out into the street, and sense returns to me in a rush.

"Goodnight." I almost trip up the first stair. The banister is cold under my fingers. I don't look back. One second. Two seconds. Five.

I stop, and lean against the wall. Let out a few shuddering breaths. Try to pull myself together.

Are you unhappy now?

I grip the banister. He's gone. Gone, with his stark dark-eyed anger and his smouldering smile and all the words that I can't make sense of. The worst mistake. Self-sabotage. I start to climb again slowly. For fuck's sake, Livia. I screw my hands into fists. Outside, the wind has resumed its mournful wailing, howling along the old walls, and a prickle runs down the back of my neck. Something slams.

A door.

I stop dead.

The broken slow-close. *My* door.

For long seconds I can't move. I stare at the darkness, sweat breaking on my upper lip. I can't even turn on a light; the nearest switch is in the hall. Logic tells me I should go back down, but I can't do that either.

Ridiculous. I uncurl my fists. I'm being ridiculous. I've drunk too much. Take hold of the banister. One step. Two. There's nobody in my flat. I scour the shadows nonetheless. *Except Sophia Swift.* A chill runs over my skin as I mount the last step.

Something erupts in front of me, warm and alive. I trip before I can save myself, the scream of fright half-strangled in my throat. My hands contact warm flesh. Fur—

Niklavs' cat. I curse out loud and feel my way upright, deafened by the sound of my own heartbeat. The cat scarpers. I'm almost at my door. The landing window has been left half open; the net curtain is fluttering in the breeze. No wonder something banged. Moonlight is falling through it in a square onto the floor, like a spotlight that all at once I'm too afraid to step into.

Suddenly, all I can think about is the face in the pine trees. The red car with the misted-up windows. Ryan and Claire's swinging front door . . .

The low creak of the stairs behind me almost isn't a surprise. The lurch of motion. The stab of adrenaline, fight or flight, except there's nowhere to run—

Sean Lorchann's hand closes around my arm, arresting my blow mid-air, his fingers encircling my wrist entirely. For the briefest moment, I struggle. And then we're both motionless, looking at his hand around my wrist, at my slowly uncurling fist. He lowers my arm. His eyes lock mine.

"Are you okay?" It's softly dark, like black velvet, a cloudy midnight sky. He hasn't let go.

"I thought . . ." My voice is jagged, uneven. "Thought there was . . ."

His gaze holds mine, and suddenly the presence in the shadows and the open window are nothing compared to the danger in his eyes. He still has hold of my arm. We both notice at the same second. He releases me.

"*Livia*," he says.

Then his hand cups my cheek. All I can focus on is his mouth, the way his lips shape my name, how close they are to touching mine. His thumb on my cheek, his fingers in my hair . . . My keys slip through my grasp; a cloud has covered the moon, and in the split second as it drifts away its light reflects in the numbers on my door.

31.

The key hits the floor with a crack that echoes around the empty stairwell like a gunshot. Sean withdraws his hand as if he's been burned.

"This . . ." The colour has drained from his cheeks. "*This* is your flat?"

"Yes."

"Shit," he exhales. "*Shit.*"

I stare, mute, at his white face in the sliver of cold moonlight. He pushes his hands back through his hair.

"I have to go." He takes a sudden step backwards and I stumble away.

"I don't . . ." My voice won't emerge at all. It's a ghost. An empty breath. "*What?*"

"Jesus." He's pacing, still gripping his hair with both hands. "*Jesus Christ . . .*"

I stoop to pick up the key.

"Sean?" I whisper.

He stops dead. I push the key into the lock and he flinches visibly. As if it isn't a key at all, but a knife, and I've plunged it into one of us.

"Don't." The raw note in his voice makes my blood run cold. There's something in his eyes that chills me to the core. "Don't stay here."

"*What?*"

He lets go of his hair. The look in his eyes hasn't gone. It's shifted, intensified.

"Just . . . don't." He speaks through his teeth. "Find somewhere else. Anywhere . . ."

"What are you talking about?" I let go of the key, cold. Inexplicably, my eyes are prickling with tears. "*Why?*"

He's at the top of the stairs.

"It's . . ." He pauses. I see his jaw clench, unclench. His voice is a whisper, evasively low, as the first stair creaks under his weight.

"It's thirteen, backwards," he says. And then he's gone.

CHAPTER 18

Speed equals distance over time. I wrap my arms around my knees. If only I wasn't so good at maths. I let the shower run over me, huddled under its scalding flow, staring at the bath taps. Thirteen backwards. I dash a hand angrily across my cheeks. As if I can cry about this.

The milk was still on the doorstep when I set out to run. But even five miles of pounding feet and much-too-loud music weren't enough to exorcise his words. Thirteen backwards. What? I screw my fingers into my wet hair and picture him doing the same.

I pull the plug and rise slowly, turn off the shower and stand, shivering. I didn't run the cliff path. I couldn't risk the possibility that he'd be there. And now what? I have to go to work. It's already eight. I've been sitting here so long that my skin is wrinkled and my legs are seized with cramps that hurt a lot less than the idea of opening the cabin door and facing the truth of my Armageddon.

My work clothes are still wet. The radiators don't seem to be working. Last night I slept — or tried to — with the spare duvet I bought for Kris layered over my own. I drag on black jeans and an old blue blouse. It's much too late for first impressions, anyway.

The landing is quiet. I deliberately don't look back at my door as I pull it closed behind me; I take the stairs two at a time, cross the hall and pause on the front step. The milk's still there. Niklavs didn't say he was going anywhere. He's always up by now. I pick up the bottles, uneasy.

"Niklavs?" I tap on his door. I'm shaken out of my preoccupation. "Niklavs?"

Nothing. I stand on tiptoe to look through the peephole. The door opens.

"Oh—" I nearly drop the milk.

"Livia." He manoeuvres to one side. The crutches in his hands creak under his weight. I stare, horrified.

"What *happened*?" For a moment, it doesn't even occur to me to go in. His right leg is in a cast to just below his knee; a gash across his bushy eyebrow is glued closed and Steri-stripped. I remember the milk and follow him in.

"It is good, I think, that you were out at party." There's a grim set to his mouth as he struggles with the fridge. I open the door for him, troubled.

"What?"

"There was intruder, last night. I hear noise, and go to check, and there he is in hallway." He wheels around to face me. "Complete stranger. At mailbox of number thirty-one." His sharp gaze meets mine. I freeze.

"*What*?"

"I confront him. He try to run." Niklavs shook his head. "I catch him up on step. I think he does not escape unscathed, but I am not such young man these days. I must trip, fall." He looks down at the cast. Suddenly I feel sick.

"*Niklavs*," I whisper, appalled. "You should have called me! You—"

"Small scratch." He shakes his head again, dismissive. "Ankle will mend. Four hours in emergency room worse than this." He uses a crutch to gesture at the cast. "Half past three I get home."

"Ouch," I murmur. My heart is beating too fast.

"Thank you for milk, Livia." He moves to sit down in one of the fireside chairs, leaning the crutches against the arm.

I follow him. "Is there anything I can do? Anything you need?"

He glowers at the crutches. "I need to have these with me last night," he says darkly. "Then I do better job of stopping bastard."

"How did he get in?" I'm shivering. "Did you see his face? What did he want?"

Silence. Niklavs grits his teeth.

"You think he was stealing the mail?" I press.

"I do not know, Livia," he snaps at last. I hesitate, startled by the tone of his voice.

"I don't *get* mail." I can't quite let it drop. "There's only ever been letters for her."

Niklavs' lips press tightly together. I swallow. He knows something. I know he does. I grind my fingers into my palms.

"I have one upstairs, actually. I need a forwarding address. Did she leave the details with you? Her name was Sophia, wasn't it? Sophia Swift?"

"I tell you already. I not know!"

The crutches fall over with a crash, making me jump. Niklavs is on his feet, face dark with anger. "If letter come for her now, it is junk. Rubbish! You should destroy it. Throw it away." He bends to retrieve the crutches. "It is of no matter."

"Well, it *might* matter." My heart's pounding. I've never imagined Niklavs angry. "You don't *know* that it's not important. She must have left a forwarding add—"

"Not with me." He sweeps up the crutches. "Do you not have job to go to?"

"Yes. But—"

"Stop asking questions you do not need to know answer to."

"But I *do* need to know." I can't stop myself from arguing with him, injured or not. His stubbornness is only spurring me on. "And if *you* won't tell me, then I'll call the landlord."

"I wish you will not do that, Livia." His voice falls ominously. I pause.

"Well, do you know where she is, or not?"

Niklavs' mouth twists.

"Yes." He turns away. His shoulders hunch. "Yes. I know where she is."

"You . . . you *do*?" My mind's racing. All this time he's held the key. After everything . . . I can find her. I can return the journal; I can find out what happened, to the rest, to the missing pages . . .

"Yes." Niklavs turns back suddenly. "I do." His knuckles are white on the crutches. "She is in graveyard, just outside Oxford. She is not needing mail."

My sudden intake of breath almost chokes me. I open my mouth, speechless.

"Now you understand? Dead. You are so desperate to have answer from me, well there it is." He limps with ferocious skill to the door and balances the crutches in one hand to open it. "You are late for job, I think."

"How . . . ?" It's a croak. "When . . ."

"I will talk no more of it. Dead is dead. I want no more thinking on it. You, or me. It is past. What is she to you? You never even have met her. Enough questions. Go."

I stumble to the door.

"Niklavs," I breathe. "Who was she?"

"Nobody." He ushers me into the descending shadows. "Go to work. Before you lose job."

"But—" I start. The door crashes closed.

Dead.

Sometimes I see reflections in that mirror. And they're not mine . . .

I blunder down the step into the road, and come to an abrupt stop. My car is at Trethallyan. How could I have forgotten? I flounder for a moment.

Swift's dead. The girl in the mirror. The voice that echoes my darkest thoughts. Dead, and I have no idea why.

My hands are trembling. *You never even have met her*. No. Maybe I haven't. I haven't met her. I've done more than just meet her. I know her, like no one else knows her. I've felt what she's felt; I promised her I wouldn't abandon her. How can I, now?

I clench my fists in my raincoat pockets. What choice do I have? She's gone. I'll never know how the journal ended. I have to focus on reality, like Sean said. The reality where I have no car, and I'm going to have to walk to Trethallyan, and it's already nine o' clock. Niklavs is right. I need to go.

* * *

There must be a shorter route onto the estate across the cliffs, but I don't know it. I go through town instead and out onto the coast road, feet aching in my thin-soled pumps. The sky is heavy and brooding with clouds. It's a miracle that they don't empty their wrath onto me before I reach Trethallyan, the way that everything else is turning out.

I feel sick with dread as I punch in the keycode and let myself into the drive. The hall seems darker and more forbidding than ever. I move between the rhododendrons, clutching at every strategy I have to banish the image of his face. *Thirteen, backwards. It's thirteen, backwards . . .*

I plunge my hand down on the cabin door-handle, and nearly break my wrist. It's locked. I squint through the windows. The inside is in darkness, the roof-blinds still drawn. Ten o'clock, and it's deserted. For some reason, that doesn't make me feel any better. I crouch down to rifle through my bag for the key.

"Livia. Thank goodness!"

I leap almost out of my skin. Katie materialises out of the bushes, her cheeks red with cold.

"I've been here for *ages.* Did you walk here? Tell me you have a key?" Her teeth are chattering. "I came without mine. I've been to the Hall and the Gatehouse and I can't find *anyone.*"

"Um, yeah. I have one." I let us in and halt just inside, contemplating the silence. Sean's never late. For anything.

"I wondered where on earth you were. I think Claire and Ryan must have taken Fin out somewhere. It's half term." Katie peels off her coat and makes a beeline for the heater, flicking it onto full whirring power. "Graham's out too. Goodness, it's freezing. Where's Sean?"

"Uhm." I sit down at my desk and fiddle with the laptop. "I don't know. I thought he was here."

"Right."

There's a loaded pause.

"You *have* heard what happened last night?" she says at last.

"Last . . . night?" I swallow. Try not to frown.

"After you left?" She crosses the floor to perch on my desk. I look up at her, not quite comprehending.

"What happened after I left?"

"There was a fight." She regards me levelly across the desk. I can see she's waiting for an answer, but I still can't quite process what this has to do with me.

"A fight?"

"Mm." Her gaze is unnervingly direct. "Craig and I were about to leave. It was all wrapping up — people were saying their goodbyes, and then . . ." She hesitates.

"Then?" Something in her expression has turned my insides to lead.

"Then Sean stalked back in with murder in his eyes, in front of everyone, and accused one of Ryan's friends of spiking your drink."

I feel the blood drain from my cheeks.

"Shit," I whisper. Oh, shit. I draw in a deep breath and hold it.

"I don't know who threw the first punch." Katie's shaking her head. "It could have been either of them. It was awful, Livs. They were brawling like a pair of thugs. Ryan and one of his rugby lot had to step in to separate them."

Brawling. I open my laptop with trembling fingers. Sean. It doesn't sound likely. It doesn't sound *possible.* Why would he have gone back, after he left Sunnyside? *I like to be in control, Livvy.*

"Livia, are you alright?"

"Fine," I mumble.

"You *weren't* spiked, were you?" Her forehead is creased with concern. "Do you feel okay?"

"I'm fine." I jab my password into my keyboard.

Katie moves to the spare desk and starts to unpack her laptop.

"You can talk to me," she says quietly.

Can I? Really? I stare at my hands. Can I ask her why she dislikes him so much? What it is that everyone — her, Sean, even Niklavs — is trying to hide?

There are so many questions, and none of them have answers. Why did Sean Lorchann freak out at the sight of my front door? Why did someone break into Sunnyside?

How did Sophia Swift die?

I shiver.

"Livia." Katie's gaze has shifted to the window. I turn to look over my shoulder. "Graham," she points out, like I might not have seen.

The knock comes seconds later. I catch myself glancing in the direction of the back room, as if Sean might materialise from behind locked doors to save the day. Quarter to eleven. Where is he?

"Katelyn. Livia." Graham Gordon-Heyers steps inside and pauses on the mat. The uncertainty in his entrance is somehow endearing, given that it's his summerhouse we're sitting in.

"Is Sean here? I had a question for him." He surveys the empty desks. I shake my head, strangely tongue-tied.

"No," I whisper. "Do you want me to call him?" Even as I say it, my stomach sinks. *Please don't. Please don't make me call him.* I'm not sure if I can handle the sound of his voice.

"No, don't worry." Graham shakes his head. "I can call him myself. Actually." He pauses. "Actually, while I'm here, I was wondering if I might look at the drawings again."

"Of course." I almost fall over myself in my haste. "They're just here." I gesture him into the back room, ears burning. "In here. I need to finish putting them into the

CAD software, and add the details. But, I mean, take as long . . . as long as you want. I was going to photocopy—"

"Livia." His voice is calm, firm: frighteningly like my father's. I stop in my tracks. "Please." His gaze meets mine squarely. "Stop worrying. This . . ." He lays a crooked hand on the corner of my drawing. "This will mean the world to Clarissa and me."

"Oh." My eyes are watering. "I'm glad. I—"

"Claire mentioned that she'd overheard you talking about leaving."

What?

"She . . . she did?"

"Something about an opening in Oxford, and changing your mind." Graham withdraws his hand and turns to face me. "I hope not."

"Oh." I exhale in a rush. "No." I shake my head. "No, I'm not going to leave."

"Good. I'd be sad to lose you. You and Sean . . . you've brought a future to this place that I didn't think it had."

There's a momentary silence. I don't know what to say.

"I should let you get back to work." He touches a finger to the paper. A single tentative ray of sunshine is breaking through the blind.

"Thank you." I hesitate, open the door. Look at him looking, for just a second more, before I tiptoe back to my desk. My head's aching. I take out my phone and stare at Sean's name in my contacts list.

"Livia, are you sure you're okay?"

I jump. Katie's frowning at me.

"I'm fine." I rub my forehead. "I just have a bit of a headache. I might go get some pills . . ."

Katie's eyes follow me across the cabin as I make for the door. I take a few steps along the gravelled path, out of sight, then stop. The bushes are flailing their branches wildly in the wind, and the air smells like rain. I duck into their shelter, trying to regain my composure. Somewhere ahead of me, a car door slams, feet and voices tumbling out onto the gravel. I shrink further into the bushes. Through the turbulent dance of the leaves, I can make out the shape of Ryan's BMW on the drive.

"I don't like it."

"He was a baby. He won't remember."

"I don't know. I'm not sure it's—"

The chime of the phone in my pocket makes me start. I fumble to silence it. An email: *seanlorchann@lmla.co.uk*. The surge of adrenaline is paralysing.

Assuming you're at work. Can you get to the chapel please?

I swipe down. Nothing. No explanation. No instructions. Not a word more. Suddenly I'm cold. He's found a problem. There's something wrong. The planning permission . . . Shit, maybe that was where he's been this morning, while I've been wallowing in uncertainty and self-pity. The shadows around me are Courbet Green and Ivory Black, the phone a giveaway bright glow in my hand. I shove it back into my pocket. The footsteps are coming closer.

". . . that's the last time!" Ryan's voice is uncharacteristically short. "I've had enough."

Claire's face is strained. "Can't we just—"

"No," he snaps.

They're walking fast. I stay absolutely still as they pass, try to melt into the gloom, praying they haven't seen me. Fin's trailing a few steps behind them, arms hugged around his chest, his ethereal gaze scanning the bushes. He stops.

"Come on, Fin." Ryan sounds impatient.

Fin hesitates. He's looking right at me. He releases his arms. Very slowly, he raises them at his sides. A blackbird. My heart is pounding. He takes a little hopping step. I put a finger to my lips. Fin pauses. A broad, impish grin spreads across his face.

"Fin. Come *on*."

He flaps his wings. I smile back, just for a second. Then he's gone, fluttering along the path after his parents, and I'm left to catch my breath and think about sandcastles, and a house with grass on the roof.

I wait until I hear the cabin door close, then jog to my car to fetch my boots. The sun's out, yet somehow it's starting to spit with rain, surly droplets speckling my jeans as I begin to walk. Davy's Grey. Idanthrene. Ochre. I fill my mind with colours. Cerulean Blue. Raw Umber.

It hurts so much, doesn't it?

The clifftop's deserted. There are no cars parked on the stone chips. Not even tyre tracks in the mud. I stand for a moment, buffeted by the wind and starting to shiver. This place. This view. There aren't enough names for the colours; even if I mixed every shade of every combination, I'd never do it justice.

I take a deep breath and start to scramble downwards, my boots skidding on the loose stones until the brambles grab at my legs to break my fall, and I come to a conclusive halt.

There's no one here. Only the wind, lamenting my mistakes. The sun and rain are at odds over the water, a battle of rainbow and threatening storm. I pick my way between the gorse-flowers, and put out a hand to steady myself against the broken render.

"Frost."

I spin.

Nothing. I can't see anything. Rain is blowing into my eyes.

"You got my message."

"Yes." I exhale. I still can't see him. I turn on the spot, searching the cliffside, contours, clouds. The breaking sun is blinding.

"Good."

He's there. Little more than an outline, his features indistinguishable in shadow. He isn't dressed for work. His jeans are surprisingly worn, the denim soft and frayed, and spattered with mud. Rain is beading on the sleeves of his unfastened waterproof and soaking the front of his shirt. I take a bitingly cold breath.

"I don't . . ." I trail off. He's stepped forward, shading us from the glare. A vivid, angry bruise is turning purple on his cheekbone, a split in its centre dark with dried blood.

"Here." He's holding something out. A roll of glossy A4 paper, flecked with rain. I can't help noticing the grazes on his knuckles as I take it. He stands back and I unroll it slowly, looking at the colours and dotted lines. Empty text boxes and tick boxes. Sean's fists are clenched.

Lorchann McLeod. I stare at the paper, wounded.

"What's this?"

"Application forms." There's something stubborn in the set of his mouth. "For the internship with Peter. He says they'll only be a formality. They just need signatures."

I glance back up at his face, pain contracting in my chest.

"No," I breathe.

"The deadline's tonight." His lips have tightened. "You can scan them and email them."

"No." Colour floods my cheeks. "I don't want them." I thrust them back at him. "Keep them."

There's silence. Storm, ocean, gritted teeth.

"Is that what you brought me here for?" My eyes are stinging. "To try and get rid of me? Is that what you do? When things g—"

"I thought you might have changed your mind."

"What?"

Sean shakes his head.

"You want to walk?" He gestures towards the path between the wet bracken.

"Okay."

He motions for me to go first, and I take a few hesitant strides, leaping over the crags and contours in the path. I hear his boots crunch on the trail behind me. The rainbow has faded, leaving just a glimmering mist over the sea. The tide's coming in. I look down at the diminishing white sand and broken rocks, making myself concentrate on imagining the brush strokes as the incline of the cliff grows steeper. We walk for a long time in silence. Sean pauses as I venture off the path to look over the edge. The drop beneath us is sheer, and I have an absurd impulse to raise my arms, Finbar-style, and trust my weight to the wind.

"Are you afraid, Livia?" He's much closer behind me than I realised, and I'm shaking from head to foot.

"I'm not afraid of heights," I say carefully.

"No," he says under his breath. "I didn't think so."

I step back from the edge. For the first time in my life, I'm not quite sure of my own footing.

There's a fork in the path, one limb leading inland, away from the sea, the other winding dangerously downwards, barely visible between the banks of bracken. We take that one. Water is accumulating in its rocky crevices; it plunges with the line of the cliff and corners out of sight. Sean motions me first, and I descend ahead of him until the path evens out, until there's room to walk side by side, and we make our way, unspeaking, between neck-high gorse into a copse of thickly-woven shadows.

The sudden hush in the trees is unsettling. I glance up at the dark patterns of the young leaves across his face, and wish I hadn't. A bramble snags in my hair.

"Shouldn't . . ." I stop and reach to disentangle myself. "Shouldn't we be talking?"

Sean catches the bramble with one hand.

"What do you want to talk about?" His voice is very soft, disconcertingly close. I extract myself quickly.

"Last . . ." I can't make myself say it. "This morning. You weren't at work."

"No."

"Why?" How I manage to get the word out, I'll never know. I feel myself pale. Hear him take a step behind me, the rustle of his coat sleeves as we resume our descent.

"Why do you think?" It's so bitter, so forceful, that I look back in surprise. Sean's voice drops, painfully quiet. "Why do you think?"

"Graham came to the cabin."

"I know."

"You weren't there. I didn't know what to tell him."

"You managed just fine, from what he said on the phone."

"Where were you?"

"Does it matter?"

"Yes."

"I was here." The words hang heavily in the silence between us. "I needed time to think."

"About what?"

The trees have petered out. We're out in the open, stood at the edge of a desolate cove, half the size of the beach at Trethallyan Edge; tiny and windswept, hidden from the world by the cliffs. A strip of sand a few metres wide, studded with pebbles like stars in the night sky. The conflict of the sun and the storm on the sea is breathtaking, a contrast of shimmering colours. The tide's almost in.

"About what?" I persist.

"You really don't know, Livia?" His voice is bitter, hard. "You really don't see? I can't work. I can't sleep. I've tried. Fuck, I've been trying for weeks. Trying everything I can think of not to—"

"Not to like me," I finish it for him. He doesn't have to say it. My throat is aching. I avoid his gaze.

"No."

Without warning, his fingers curl into my hair, making me face him.

"No. Trying not to love you. But I haven't done a very good job, have I?"

A tiny sound utters from my lips. And then his mouth is on mine, a fierce, unrestrained kiss that leaves us both gasping.

What you can't have. You know you can't . . .

He steps back abruptly.

"You should go," he mutters. His fingers are still in my hair, loosely ensnaring. "You shouldn't have come."

I take a shuddering breath.

"You shouldn't have left," I counter, a whisper.

Silence. The enormity rushes over us, swamping us like the sea. I look down.

"Livvy." His voice is hushed. His thumb moves against my lips, and fear spikes through me. Anticipation. Need. I raise my eyes to his.

"Fuck," he exhales. "What am I doing?"

Then his arms close around me, his hands meeting in the small of my back to pull me against him. His kiss is slow, illicit in every way; the tide has claimed us, the water lapping at our entangled feet. There's no way back.

We scramble our retreat onto the rocks. There's a path upwards at the other end of the beach. My boots struggle for purchase on the wet granite; Sean leaps the last crevice and turns back, his hands closing around my elbows to help me over, and suddenly I'm held tight against him on the uneven path, and we're both breathing harder than the exertion really merits. The wind catches us, whipping rain against my cheek and tearing at his unfastened coat, scattering glossy paper like winter blossom on the tide.

I'm light-headed, out of focus. Still dreaming, maybe, of coffee cups and 0.7 mm pencils. But his hands around my arms are real.

"Where are we going?" I breathe.

A tiny smile lights his raw-umber gaze.

The ascent is steep, the rocks sharp and abrasive under my hands. We emerge into heather, wind-beaten and wild, and I stop. We're at the end of a track, gleaming fresh wet granite chips, a sharp curve cutting off the view of whatever road or village lies beyond. Judging by the silence, whatever it is, is a long way away. We're utterly alone.

Beyond the stones, gorse becomes grass and then drops away into oblivion. A thousand white stallions pound the wave tops, rearing and tussling; the rainbow is gone, and so is the sun. The clouds are gathering for a final assault, heavy droplets of rain flying at our faces like loosed arrows.

And beside us, there's a house. Perhaps not even a house: a fortification of pebbles and rocks, dry-stone walls contrasting with crisp wood and gleaming glass. It's built into the cliff, roofed over with grass and granite. Vast windows stare out at the view. A house with grass on the roof . . .

There's a date, in the stone lintel above the door that comes into view as we ascend the gravel. A name beside it. *The Lookout.* A magazine: a photo stuck in the back of my scrapbook . . . an oil painting. I frown, comprehension dawning. Turn to look back at him. Sean's eyebrows flicker.

"Trethallyan wasn't the first project I worked on down here," he concedes.

The house that Fin drew . . . I'm lost for words. And the view — Graham Gordon-Heyers might think he owns the best view in the South West, but he's wrong.

There's a pair of boots and a dog lead beside the crisply weatherproof wooden door. A car parked on the wet granite chips, a Defender. Sean stands at a cautious two-pace distance, watching. Watching me realise. The darkness in his face is perilous, consuming. For a split second, our eyes meet.

I'm not even sure which one of us moves first. But suddenly his hands have closed around my wrists, and in a few short steps we're at the door; suddenly he's kissing me, his hands and his hips pinning me against the warm wood. *An infatuation. Because that's what it is, isn't it?*

"This . . ." His voice is against my cheek. "Is a really . . ." He lets go of my wrist to search his pocket for a key. "Bad . . . idea . . ."

"I don't care," I whisper.

He reaches past me for the lock and the door gives suddenly, sending us stumbling into a tiny rectangular hall, aglow with ocean light and beachcombers' treasures. His mouth is on mine as I struggle to kick off my boots and we lurch through the next door, colliding with two wooden chairs at a table set with slate. There must be a view, from the vast canvas of the seascape windows, but I don't see it. Don't see the details of the light-soaked open-plan room: the wood-stove, the drawing board beside the window. Because all I can see is him, his sodden shirt clinging to his chest, his damp tousled hair. I reach to touch him and he inhales. Then his fingers clamp around mine.

"Stop," he rasps.

You can't stop. You just can't . . .

"What . . ." I'm incoherent. "Why?"

"Because we can't do this." His voice is terrifyingly soft. He defies his own instruction. His lips brush my cheekbone, my neck, sending an agonising bolt of desire along my spine. The epitome of darkness. Bittersweet bliss.

"No . . ." I exhale. "We can—"

He pulls me with him, away from the table, a flicker of shadow and light, into the muted stillness of another room: a room of blues and greys like the sea. And then he's kicking the door closed behind us, and I hear my breathing accelerate, shallow, rapid, as he pushes his hands back through my hair. His voice is against my ear.

"I'm a bad choice, Livvy. Everyone must have told you that . . . And they're right." It's a whisper, a conflict of seduction and warning. "They're right."

His hands aren't in my hair anymore, they're on the buttons of my damp shirt, paralysing me with shivers. He traces my lips with one finger, a torment of intent. *I wasn't sure that passion was something you'd relate to.* My knees collide with the side of the bed. And then I'm lying on the covers, clutching at his hair, and our kisses are gaining in urgency. He drags down my jeans; I struggle to unfasten his shirt, and he pulls it off, half-buttoned, over his head.

"You still don't understand. Do you?" His voice is achingly dark.

"What?"

"*This* is the worst mistake."

His eyes are on mine, and the look in them takes my breath completely, a sultry darkness like summer nights and unquenched embers that no amount of blue-grey seascape can ever put out.

"Maybe I want to choose badly," I whisper.

I lied, before. I *am* afraid. Afraid of his words and the hunger they provoke in me. Afraid of his touch, and his hold over me; afraid that I've never wanted anything so much.

"Livvy," he murmurs.

"Please . . ."

"Fuck," he growls. "*Livia* . . ."

His kiss is deep, insatiable, his lips parting mine as he lifts my hips to press me into him, the silk-hard heat of his skin. I run my hands across his shoulders, over the muscles of his back, curl my fingers through the tight, short hair at the nape of his neck until he grabs my wrists and forces them down into the pillows.

And I forget. I forget about thirteen backwards. Forget about Trethallyan, and reflections in the mirror, and that Swift is dead. All I can think about is the press of his body, the salty tang of his kisses, improbable and off-limits, his unrelenting grip on my wrists as he seizes them in one hand and pins them over my head.

I should want to fight. I should want to run a hundred miles. But I don't. I want his mouth on my mouth. I want his lips on my skin. I want his touch, deliberate, knowing; I want the hitch of his breath, ragged and harsh, and the answers to the mysteries in his raw-umber eyes. I want whatever he'll give — whatever he wants to take — so badly that I would sacrifice everything else in a heartbeat.

I hear his name on my lips. The colours of the shadows intensify, every shade of dark. And at last he takes me, slowly, relentlessly, until my body mutinies against the last shreds of my conscious thought and a stifled sound utters from my throat. I feel the muscles in his torso tighten; his hand clenches on my hip. Then he pulls me upwards, tipping my head back to capture my mouth with his, and we find our release together, voices merging in a garbled fusion of our names.

And then everything's still. So still that the world could have ended — that Armageddon could have struck — and neither of us would know, or care, if it had. Sean's eyes are on mine, infinitely dark. And for a moment we're frozen in time, jubilant and gasping, shamelessly illuminated in the remorseless spill of afternoon light across the sheets. He releases my hands, and I look down at the grazes on his knuckles. Back up, to the shadows in his face.

"Now do you understand?" he whispers. "I don't do this." His gaze is locked on mine. "I don't let people in."

"I . . ." I think of sandcastles. Running at dawn, graphite, leather.

"I know," I whisper back.

His fingers fold through mine, and I'm lost, utterly, to Raw Umber and an advancing tide. Sean smiles. A smouldering, fleeting smile that would break my heart if I looked for long enough.

"Self-sabotage, Livvy Frost," he breathes.

CHAPTER 19

It's dark. So dark, without the lights of Porthtrevelen, with just the sea beyond the glass. Always dark; the sun-swept sea-light was beautiful, but if I could keep a moment, it would be this one, the vast windows mirroring the flicker of the wood-stove, the floor tiles warm beneath my feet. Dark is his colour; I've already painted it in all its shades, a hundred times at least.

I can feel him watching me. I don't know how long he's been there. I have no idea of the time at all — I silenced my phone after the fifth missed call from Katie and I don't know where I left it. The day slipped by too fast, an ill-defined storyboard of images: bedcovers, sunlight, tousled hair and flushed skin. It's been a while since the sunset, but aside from that there's nothing palpable to grasp at, no way to ground myself, even if I wanted to.

I think of blackbirds. Of Fin fluttering away along the path. Of swifts. A grounded swift will die. The darkness is inside as well as out. I almost can't tease out which thoughts were my own, and which belonged to her. The worst thing you've ever done . . . the worst mistake. Something you started that you should never, ever have started, *and you just can't stop . . .*

I don't want to stop.

I half turn. Sean has stepped closer, out of the shadows.

"I wish I knew what you were thinking." His lips brush my cheek.

"Not much," I lie. I'm not a good liar. We both know it. He lifts my chin, so that our eyes meet.

"You're still infuriating," he whispers. "You know that?"

I close my eyes. His mouth on mine is intoxicating. Soon I won't be lying. Everything beyond him is out of focus. His chest is warm, his skin smooth. His hands meet in the small of my back, and I feel myself curl into him like we were made to fit, two halves. I can't remember the last time I felt whole. His kiss tastes of salt and unspoken words. He breaks off.

"Breathe," he murmurs.

Breathe. I try to process the instruction, but I'm not sure I can. If I do, what then? What does this become?

"Actually, I was thinking I should . . . go." I feel the shivers overtake me. Feel the wrench of my own words, even as I whisper them. "It's late."

"No." His arms tightens. "You shouldn't." Our lips are still touching. Neither of us makes the effort to disengage.

"We need . . . tomorrow . . . work . . ."

"It doesn't matter."

"You still don't want me to go back." Realisation begins to dawn on me. "To my flat. Do you? Is that it?"

"No." He doesn't release me. "It's not."

"Sean, I—"

But his mouth reclaims mine, darkly insistent, his teeth tugging gently at my lower lip. His hands move to my hips, drawing me into him, until I have no desire to do anything other than let him.

"Tell me the truth." My protest is losing its edge. "Tell me . . ."

"There's no solace in the truth, Livia." A wry smile lingers for a moment on his lips. "Only the things we try to deny ourselves."

"Then what . . . *what are you denying*?" I whisper.

"What are you?" His eyes lock with mine.

Breathe. I can't. Not anymore. I take his hands instead and twine my fingers through his, just for a moment, until his grip closes around mine and holds me fast.

"I don't want you to change your mind, Livia." He says quietly.

"About what?" I wet my lips. My voice won't come out. It's a silent question, an intake of breath. His thumb moves lightly against the inside of my wrist and I inhale sharply.

"About what?" I whisper. But I don't want him to answer. I can see it in his eyes, the drafting pencil, running at dawn, the flex of leather between his fingers, and I know it should terrify me. He doesn't move. His thumb continues its journey, back and forth, slow and careful, a seduction of Ivory Black and Indigo.

"I want to know." I meet Raw Umber with Prussian Blue. Hold the gaze. "I want to learn."

For a second, he's motionless. I see the memory flit over his face, the reading room. *Don't walk into this lightly . . .*

"What?" he whispers at last.

"Everything."

* * *

I'm not sure, anymore, that everything is enough. That it will ever be enough. The night doesn't last. People talk about longest nights, darkest hours, but I don't get to keep either. Daylight spills over me, forcing me awake. I'm disorientated by the sound of birdsong, not the crying gulls of Sunnyside: a peaceful flowing stream of notes enticing me to open my eyes.

A blackbird. It's perched just outside the recessed window, on the windowsill where a misplaced clump of snowdrops clutches at the dirt between the stones. *Trying not to love you.* The dawning reality is an ache, deep in my chest. I'm acutely aware of every sensation in my body, bare skin against smooth sheets. I wrap the duvet around myself. *Breathe* . . . in, lengthen out. I screw the cotton cover between my fingers.

It takes me a moment to realise that he's already awake. He's propped semi-upright against the pillows, expression guarded, gaze dark. How long has he been watching? An odd thrill runs through me.

"Katelyn's been calling you." His voice is difficult to read.

"Oh." I half roll: my phone is on the floor beside the bed. Nine fifteen. *Nine fifteen?* Shit. And eight missed calls. I feel myself flush and pale in quick succession.

"I'll have to call her." I hadn't realised how parched my throat is. I pull myself up to sit quickly. "Do you know what the time is?!"

"Mm. Let's hope she doesn't report you missing. I suggest you call in sick today." His intent gaze is impossible to second guess. I have no idea whether or not he's joking.

He swings his legs out of bed to pull on his jeans, the soft frayed denim hanging loosely from his hips. I watch him cross the floor to a wardrobe built of knotted, reclaimed wood. This is the strangest room I've ever seen: spacious, octagonal, the beams converging at one central point in the far wall, supported by steel and stone. The walls are white, the furniture sparse; besides the oak-framed bed and the wardrobe, the room is empty except for a vast abstract oil painting above the bed, every colour of the ocean. There's a book on the floor — in the absence of a bedside table — a weighty volume with a paperclip serving time as a bookmark near the back. I pick it up to look at it. *Notes from Underground.* I flip the cover open. *To Sean, Happy 22nd Birthday, Ryan.* I put it down again.

He's watching me. I slide from the covers and start to dress. His stare is inescapable.

"You really want to go back to your flat?"

I falter. Do I? Really? To the emptiness and the broken heating and the ripped-out pages of Swift's journal?

"Not really," I whisper.

The smile is back, fleeting, unreadable. He plucks a shirt from the cupboard, and his hand brushes my waist, gesturing me to go ahead of him. I screw up my eyes against the brightness. The house is full of light. The next room is an octagon too, a vast expanse of open-plan stone floors and oak beams, furnished in tweed, sheepskin and leather. The whole of the far wall is a vista of bay window; white gulls flecking a clear sky over the rolling expanse of sea. The wind is rippling through the heather.

The small kitchen is set back beside us against two of the angled walls, its stone worktops strewn with the pillaged remains of our late-night meal. Sean gathers up our plates from the glass coffee table in the living area and starts to organise the mess. I make a quick call to Katie to let her know I won't be in, and move hesitantly to the leather sofa, watching the churning luminance of the waves. The sun reflects off the empty drawing board.

There's a picture on the wall above it. I didn't notice last night. I sidestep to look at it, tracing a finger over the frame. A floorplan and section, details pulled out and arranged around it in pencil and ink; octagons, steel pillars and beams. It's initialled in the corner, *SCL*.

"My father had it built as a holiday home."

His voice at my shoulder makes me jump. I stare at the drawing.

"We finished it in spring 2018. His investment. My design. We site-managed together. In hindsight, it might have been a test." He rests an index finger against his lips, not quite concealing a faint smile. "He's a pretty hard master to his interns."

A test. I narrow my eyes.

"He's letting me live here until we finish work at Trethallyan. Graham wants me to project-manage the chapel build."

I nod, trying not to think about the original caveat. A year — or less.

"What happens after the chapel?" I try unsuccessfully to keep my voice light. Sean looks out of the window.

"Who knows?" He drums his fingers against the glass. "The original plan was to convert the stables, but the fact of the matter is the money's running out." He turns back. "Claire has this dream that they'll keep the Hall, she always has. But I don't see how they can. The upkeep's costing them almost everything. Ryan's been crunching numbers for months. They were offered the best part of five million for it last year, by a developer. If Graham were to invest in sub-dividing it and having it converted himself, he'd make a fortune, and we all know it."

"You'd stay involved?"

"If they wanted me to."

"And if not?" Two gulls are bickering high in the air at the cliff edge. I watch them swoop and dive. "You go back to Oxford?"

I'm not sure why I'm asking. I'm not really sure that I want to know. Sean doesn't reply. I look past him at the white wave tops.

"You've missed your run." He changes the subject. His voice is inscrutable.

"Mm."

"You didn't run yesterday, either."

"No. I . . ." I look up at him, something occurring to me. "I ran a different way. How . . ." I trail off. Sean's eyes hold mine.

"Oh." My mouth is dry. I remember the collie.

"Max has a run around the back." He's read my mind.

"He's yours?"

"Mm-hmm. I need to take him out." He moves around me, to the kitchen. "We should eat first. Are you hungry?"

I'm not. But the percolator of coffee simmering on the hob smells enticingly good. He pours two cups and passes me one, and the silence descends around us. I look at his rolled shirt-sleeves, the ripple of tendons in his muscular forearms.

"Why Porthtrevelen, Livvy?" His voice is very soft.

"Why not?" I wrap my hands around my cup. Sean shakes his head.

"Oh." He smiles, an enigmatic smile. "There're so many reasons why not."

So many reasons. He's right. But it's too late for reason.

We take the Defender. Sean drives, and we park in the empty beach car park and wander through the windswept low-season desertion of the open-air Minack Theatre, the only visitors lost among its Shakespearean echoes. I find myself wondering how many times he's been. He seems to know every turn and rock by heart, quietly narrating each nuance of its history for me without the need for me to ask.

We eat lunch in the theatre café and walk into Porthcurno, still strangely alone as we strike out across its white sands with Max capering around our feet. The clear sun lights the water like turquoise glass. We walk for hours, isolated from the world by the high-rise cliffs, into the next bay, to explore the tunnels and caves and the legends of loot-smuggling pirates, until we're damp and sandy, and my hair is stiff with salt. Our ascent back onto the coast path is a reluctant acceptance; Sean's fingers circle my wrist briefly before they fold through mine to lead us towards the car.

I stop at the rear bumper, turn to look back at the glittering sea. Sean unlocks the car.

"I need to take you home, Livvy Frost." He steps in to smooth away the hair from in front of my eyes. He's very warm. Very close. His hand lingers for a moment at the nape of my neck and his lips brush my ear, sending a swathe of goosebumps across my skin. "And I really don't want to."

"My car's at Trethallyan." Somehow, my eyes are smarting. "Maybe it's better if you drop me there. I—"

A pout tightens on his lips, forbidding and dark, and oddly reminiscent of Finbar. For a moment I think he's going to say something, but he doesn't. His silence unnerves me.

"I can . . . I'll drive myself back to Sunnyside," I whisper.

He doesn't argue. Part of me wants him to. He opens the door, his eyes not leaving me once as I climb into the car and fasten my seatbelt with trembling hands. The collie settles himself in the back without a word of instruction, flattening his lean body obediently under the folding seat.

We travel to Trethallyan in a silence laced with questions that neither of us is brave, or foolish, enough to ask. What happens tomorrow, the next day? What kind of act do we construct, around the plans on the drawing board in the locked cabin? Because it's fairly obvious that no one can know the truth.

Sean stops the car in the long shadows of the conifers before we reach the gates, the grey crenulated walls a flicker of shadow through the trees. I unclip my seatbelt and reach for the door, but he catches my hand.

"I warned you about trouble," he mutters. Then his mouth locks with mine.

Somewhere in the near distance, a door slams. I extricate myself, breathing fast. I can't formulate a single word as I unlatch the car door and leap down from the Defender. His eyes follow me across the track to the gate. I punch in the code. Don't look back as the engine revs and recedes back the way we came.

There's no one in the drive. I dart to my car and will it to start quietly, wincing at the loudness of the tyres on the grey granite. I drive home with the silence drumming in my ears.

Can't you see there's something risky about it?

"No," I exhale. "No."

The hallway at Sunnyside is awash with whispered echoes as I close the door behind me. I tiptoe to the mailbox, and touch a finger to the number, remembering with a chill what Niklavs had said about the intruder. There are no letters in the pigeon hole. I retrace my steps towards the stairs, and pause. Quarter to five. What am I going to do? Sit alone and contemplate the falling darkness, and the book without an ending?

I rap on Niklavs' door instead. Real life is returning with unwelcome clarity. There's a knot of guilt in the pit of my stomach.

"Livia." He limps back from the door. He's already ditched the crutches to hobble on his cast. I falter.

"Come in. Please." He doesn't seem angry. He moves to close the door behind me.

"About yest—" I start.

"Livia—" Niklavs says simultaneously.

We both stop.

"I'm sorry," I whisper. Niklavs shakes his head.

"No further mention of it." He moves back to the chair beside the fireplace, and gestures for me to sit down. "I apologise if I lose temper, but there are some things I will not speak of."

"Okay." I perch on the chair opposite him. "I . . . didn't mean to push my luck."

"You are early home from work." His shrewd gaze travels from my distinctly creased shirt to my unwashed, windswept hair. I fidget, uncomfortable.

"Erm, yeah." I look at the floor. The carpet looks like it was expensive once; it would almost be at home at Trethallyan, but the patch by the hearth is threadbare now, and showing its age.

"You did not come home at all, last night." His bushy eyebrows have lifted. I blush scarlet.

"No . . . I . . ."

"It is not my business, Livia." Niklavs shakes his head. "You are friend, not daughter."

Oh, God. I stare furiously at the carpet. Could this be more awkward?

"You would like drink? Cards?" He reaches for the side table to pull it nearer. "If you wish to put on kettle, you are more than welcome."

"I think I'm okay, thanks." I raise my eyes, scanning over the collection of oddities on the mantelpiece. A ship in a bottle. A barometer and clock. A brass plaque on a wooden mount: *Cornish Spirit Garden of the Year Award 2006*. I frown. Garden of the Year? He never mentioned anything about gardening.

"Actually." I stand up. "Maybe I'll make coffee. Do you want some?" I set inexpertly about brewing a pot, clattering the cups and making as much noise as I can to fill the uneasy silence. Weddings and open gardens. He'd worked for Graham Gordon-Heyers; he said so. And he's lived here, in Sunnyside, for three years. Three years — 2019. The year of the burglary.

I put the tray of coffee down on the side table with a jolt, slopping milk over my hand. Niklavs rescues the sugar bowl.

"As friend, not father, you know you can talk of trouble in confidence, Livia." His voice is quiet. "If you are needing."

Trouble? I swallow. *The kind I'd be far better off avoiding.*

"I . . . can't." I raise the coffee to my lips, but I can't drink it. The smell makes me think of rolled shirt-sleeves and sea-light. I lower the cup and watch Niklavs sip his instead.

"I should go." I get up quickly. My hands are unduly shaky. I probably don't need any more caffeine, anyway. "I . . . have to . . . have to shower."

"Mm." Niklavs puts down his coffee too. "And sleep also, I think." There's something stern in his appraisal as I make for the door. "You are not daughter. Which means I do not have place to meddle. Probably I am cynical old man." He manoeuvres himself carefully from the chair to face me, a frown furrowing between his heavy brows. "But remember. Offer is open."

"Me too." I can't quite meet his eye. "If you need anything . . ." I glance at the plaster-cast instead. "You know . . ." I shrug.

"I need bone to mend. That is all." His gaze is still on my face, uncomfortably perceptive. "Rest well, Livia."

"Thanks," I mumble. "You too."

It's dark in the hall. It occurs to me that Niklavs doesn't have my number. I scribble it on the back of the Arrow receipt and push it under his door. Just in case. I take the stairs two at a time and cross the landing, ears strained to listen for anything hiding in the shadows. A cat. A face . . .

Nothing. There's never been anything, except my imagination, and him — Sean Lorchann — with the moonlight reflected in his dark eyes. I let myself in and deadlock the door behind me. Turn on the bathroom light and the shower, and stand, immobilised, as the room fills gradually with steam.

Sophia Swift, the name without a face, the girl with the unfinished story. She lived here. She looked at her reflection in these misted tiles. Slept in my bed. Dreamed my dreams. Doubted my doubts.

What's the worst thing you've ever done? The thing you should never, ever have started . . .

I peel off my clothes. Duck under the water and wrap my arms around my chest. The images are a deluge, prohibited tantalising fragments of seduction and sedition. Flashes, like lightning strikes, out of time and context.

I needed time to think.

Time to think? To think about what? Rainbows over the rising tide, an architect building sandcastles. The little boy who wouldn't let people into his room. Armageddon.

I'm a bad choice. Everyone must have told you that. And they're right . . .

Are they?

I don't know. I squeeze shampoo into my open palm with force. The realisation of what we've done is only just starting to penetrate the defences I have raised around my mind. The realisation of what *I've* done . . . *Oh, come on, Livia. It's hardly surprising.* Even Niklavs can see it: the truth, written like guilt across my face.

I grind my fingers into the shampoo bottle until they hurt, scalding water running into my eyes. It's not like that. Is it?

Is it?

I don't want to think about it. The look in his eyes. Dark, consuming. The tiny, unreadable smile. *Self-sabotage, Livvy Frost.*

The water cascades over my body. I glance down at my skin, pale in the incandescent electric light. At the blush of red marks on the outside of my thigh. The imprint of his fingertips.

I withdraw my hand, terrified by the hunger that the memory stirs in some dark part of me. I turn off the shower.

The bathroom's cold. The rest of the flat is colder and the bed unmade, the curtains three-quarters closed. I rub myself dry and put on my pyjamas, even though it's only seven. Even though I know I won't sleep for hours and hours. Or maybe at all.

I sit on the edge of the bed, pull my knees up to my chest. What can I dream of, except the fractured dawn sunlight on his face, and the black, sultry certainty in his eyes?

It hurts so much, doesn't it? But you can't stop. You just can't stop . . .

I breathe out, lengthen, count. In again. What colour? What colour for the night sky beyond the glass? For the uneven wooden floor? For the fade of fingerprints in flesh? What colour for heartache? For the things we try to deny ourselves?

The journal's on the bedside table. I pick it up, run my fingernail over the tiny bird and turn the pages: one, two, ten at a time.

What is it, in a story? The fight? The passion? The pain? I hid the rosary beads under my mattress. They were my mother's. She wanted me to pray. She told me God would forgive me. That it didn't have to matter. That it didn't have to change everything. But it did change everything . . .

The rap of knuckles makes me start so violently that the journal slides from my lap, pages of notepaper creasing in dog-eared disarray on the floor. I stumble to my feet.

The second knock is louder. More urgent. Reality returns in a rush. What if it's Niklavs? Maybe something's wrong. What if—

I snatch it open.

"Livvy."

The light in the hallway silhouettes him against the stairwell. My gaze falls on the open collar of his shirt. Levi's. Unsmiling raw-umber eyes.

"Oh," I gasp.

"I needed to see you." His voice is low. "The door was open downstairs. I thought I . . ."

He trails off. For a split second, his gaze takes in the room: the desk lamp, the mirrors, the unmade bed. Then his arms are around me, his hands travelling possessively into the small of my back to pull me against him. I don't resist. Already, his presence is unravelling my self-will. Already, my breathing is heady and irregular. He's here, against all odds — despite thirteen backwards and the ghosts in the stairwell — and he smells of sea-spray and aftershave. His un-ironed shirt is creased and hot under my hands.

"Sean . . ." I inhale.

"You're right." His jaw clenches. "I don't want you here."

"What?" I whisper. But I already ache with longing.

"Come back." There's a determined set to his lips.

"I . . . I don't . . ." It emerges garbled, husky. "What about work? About the others? What if . . . I—"

Sean's hand closes tightly in my hair, tilting my face to his.

"Fuck work."

In a single stride he's inside, and his lips are pressed to mine. The door bangs closed, the Yale lock seals itself in his wake. *Pretty good at getting what he wants from people* . . . I should know. I should know better. But I don't — I can't — I don't care. It wouldn't make a difference anyway; I'm not strong enough to say no.

Whatever the truth, I'd only be lying to myself if I denied him. His biceps are warm and hard beneath my fingers and I feel him inhale as I reach for the open collar of his shirt and his hands move inside my clothes—

He pulls away sharply.

"I am not. Doing this. Here." His breathing is harsh and jagged against my hair. He steps back, and the flare of warning in his gaze immobilises me. I stand, frozen.

"Not here," he repeats, under his breath.

My heart's hammering. I put out a hand to pick up my phone from the kitchen side, my eyes not leaving his face. Speeds, times and distances look up at us from the pad beside the fridge, scribbled over with Kris's train times in glaring green ink.

"I need . . ." My voice is a croak. "I need to get some things."

He nods, unspeaking. I'm not thinking straight enough to pack a bag. I seize my running stuff and enough dry clothes from the radiator to see me through a day at work and ram them into my satchel. I change, in the bathroom, into jeans and a blouse, distracted by my distorted reflection in the tiles.

He's by the window when I emerge, his back to the room. The easel is still pushed to one side from Kris's visit, with my collection of started and finished canvases untidily stacked beside it, dust gathering on the half-dozen seascapes and landscapes and the paintings of the Solent that never quite leave me in peace. He's lifted the top one to look at it. I come to a halt.

He must sense me watching. He turns, suddenly, and the electricity in the lamp-lit air redoubles. He puts down the painting.

"Are you ready?" he asks.

I nod.

I take my car and he takes his. I park behind him on the granite chips and wait for him to unlock the door before I get out. We don't make it as far as the bedroom. My sharp intake of breath as he runs a finger through my hair is lust, a desperate ache for more; the graze of his teeth on my neck is a fleeting torture, withdrawing to reach for my lips instead as he bears me down onto the sheepskin rug.

We don't speak. Just feel, touch, explore, with shaking hands and hungry eyes, until it's impossible to bear. And then he pulls me on top of him, our shadows cast long by the glow of the embers in the fading wood-burner, and takes me slowly, watching me the whole time. Watching, as the sheen of sweat breaks over both our bodies. Watching, intent and inescapable, until at last I utter my surrender; and he draws my hands behind my back, and witnesses my undoing with triumph in his dark eyes.

CHAPTER 20

2017

She had never read Victor Hugo. Sure, she'd seen the musical once, three summers ago when Leon and Mum hadn't long been together — *I Dreamed a Dream* and all that. Mum had got all over-emotional in Leicester Square and they'd had to let three tube trains go by while she calmed down; only to find when they finally caught one that they'd missed the last train from Paddington.

The whole experience had put her off ever reading the book. There was a hardback copy in the library at school that no one had touched in so long that, when she did eventually take it out, half of the cover stayed behind.

She'd finished with *Fantine*, now, and finally made it to volume two — *Cosette*, where Jean Valjean had just plunged into the ocean; she'd read a chapter a day since her exams finished. There wasn't much else to do. With the conclusion of AS levels, and no momentum at school to start anything new in the summer weather, even lessons lacked substance. It was just as well, really; if she lasted more than an hour these days without needing to pee, it was a miracle. Soon, people would know whether she wanted them to or not.

She'd been ill all the way through her exams. Ever since April. She'd eaten something dodgy, one night when they went out in town, and she'd just never stopped being sick. With the start of the exams in May, she barely realised that she'd missed a period. It hadn't been until two weeks ago, with her head hung over the senior block toilets for the third morning in a row, that the reality had started to sink in.

The initial blind panic had given way to turmoil. Turmoil that lasted all the way to the antenatal clinic, and all the way to the room with the lady who showed her the ultrasound probe and explained what she could see on the pictures. The tiny, white, unfurling being, like a curled-up bud, the pulsing of an actual, undeniable life.

Mum didn't know. Sophia was seventeen. She didn't have to tell anyone. Not yet, anyway. Not until she stopped being able to hide it. Not until she'd figured out what she was going to do.

A thousand possibilities had burst in her head. None of them had stuck. The word *termination* had resounded like a starter-pistol, but the idea made her sick to the soul, and the printout of the scan pictures in her pocket only reinforced the knowledge that she couldn't do it.

A life. An actual life. A life that was as much his as hers, slowly taking form. With him, she'd attributed forgoing the coke and giving up smoking to a health epiphany — she was educated enough to know better — and he'd laughed and humoured her and teased her every time he lit a cigarette. Carrying off not drinking was harder; she didn't really have school as an excuse now, but he didn't seem to have noticed. Not yet. Even though her jeans were starting to feel tight, and for the first time in her life she had a modest cleavage to show off when they went out.

She'd spent hours alone, swinging between euphoria and despair as she tried to put together the pieces. How it would work. Pastel-coloured dreams of tiny clothes, a nursery, a house — their very own house — she wouldn't even have to go away; she could finish her A levels and apply to Oxford to study literature . . . Or, the other reality, where his flat was stale and stuffy, where there wasn't really room for the crib beside the bed, where she didn't have time to study and he had to leave his job, because they found out, at work—

Sophia lurched abruptly to her feet. Beelined for the bathroom with the book clutched against her churning abdomen, and barely made it past the cubicle door. She hung onto the sides of the bowl, trying not to think about the germs, as her stomach wrung itself out relentlessly, retch after retch until there was nothing left in her. She slumped back against the graffitied partition wall, gasping.

"Vomming again, Stanley?"

Fuck. A faint moan escaped from her throat. Sweat was trickling down the back of her neck. Not now, *not now*. Michaela Allen kicked the cubicle door, and it swung open, revealing her in every inch of her clammy vulnerability.

"What's the deal? Doesn't your paedo boyfriend like you if you get fat?"

"*Don't call hi . . .ughh . . .*." Sophia stumbled upright. She grabbed the grimy cistern, heaving. Michaela took a hasty step backwards.

"That's gross." Her expression screwed up in disgust. "How can you even *do* that?"

"*Go . . .*" Sophia gritted her teeth. Cold sweat was running down her face. "*Away.*"

All she wanted to do was rinse her mouth, get outside. Find somewhere to curl up and catch her breath. But Michaela was blocking the door.

"When you're finished hurling, Miss Phillips wants you in the art lab."

"Thanks." She leaned heavily on the cistern, trying to breathe. It was too hot. She felt faint. *Les Mis* was an immovable object at her feet. She wasn't even sure whether she could bend over to pick it up right now. She tried to twist her arms out of her blazer.

"Give up, Stanley." Michaela hadn't gone. She'd retreated to lounge against the sinks, the glossy tresses of her hair reflected in the mirror. "You should have left when you had the chance. You don't belong here. Your Daddy's dirty money's going to run out eventually. Can't make much in prison, can he?"

"Shut up."

"How many years has he got left? Five? Ten?"

"Go *away*. Please." She struggled out of the blazer and straightened, fighting back the dizziness.

"What's the matter? Aren't you counting down? Haven't you been to visit hi—"

"Leave me the fuck alone!" Sophia almost fell over the book as she started forwards. "Leave me alone!" She had never screamed like this in her life; she didn't even know where it was coming from. Her throat burned with bile. "Just get the fuck away from me!"

She abandoned *Les Mis*, and launched herself from the cubicle, leaving Michaela flattened against the sinks as she slammed out through the two sets of doors into the sixth-form corridor. Above her head, the bell screeched for third period. She almost ran the last few metres of corridor and burst through the double doors into the sunshine. Everyone else was going to class as she slowed to a cramping walk, out through the side gate and onto the road.

Oh God. She was gasping. Oh God. What was even happening to her? Her head was aching like crazy. She'd left her bag in school, her purse, bus pass, keys. Where did she think she was going? The phone chimed in her blazer pocket. From him? She came to a halt, taking shelter behind a parked van to get out of the sun. *Please let it be from him.*

It was. She exhaled, almost tearful with relief. Suddenly, all she wanted was to put her arms around him. She just needed to see him. She typed a message back quickly and sent it, trembling. God, she wanted a cigarette.

But she wanted this more. She felt the crumpled print-out. She'd never imagined that she would, but she did. How could she tell him? What if he was angry? What if he wouldn't let her go through with it?

No. Sophia blinked furiously. He would. He'd be a great father. She knew that. Sunny memories of her own childhood swarmed into her mind: riding on Dad's shoulders at the boat race, planting in the garden shed, Sunday cream sodas. Back when he *was* her dad, before it had all turned out to be an elaborate act.

She walked to the university parks with her phone in her hand. It was okay to be scared. Even the lady in the ultrasound clinic had said so. It was all down to what you decided to do about it.

Her finger was already on the button for the next chime; she cut it off on its first note to open his reply.

We need to talk. Are you free now?

Huh? She stared at it, light-headed. No. No way. The actual words that she'd been about to type. He'd typed them first.

He knew.

The realisation was like jumping into ice. Jean Valjean falling into the ocean. She pushed the phone numbly into her pocket, starting to shake despite the blazing June sunshine.

How could he already know? She pulled it out again.

I'm in the park.

She typed it, then deleted it. Typed it again. She heard the message go off the second that it sent.

"Sophia."

She jumped.

He'd stood up, right in front of her, from the bench facing the duck pond. He was already here, before she'd even sent the message. She hadn't been looking where she was going. Elation and fear went to war in her muscles; she started forwards then stopped. He hadn't come any closer. His hands were in his pockets; he was regarding her uncomfortably, an expression on his face that she had never seen before, not ever. Uncertainty. Almost trepidation. She faltered, unnerved.

He couldn't already know. He couldn't. It wasn't possible. No one knew except her.

"I got your text," she said.

"Yeah." He shifted on the spot. There was a painful pause.

She took a deep breath. "What did you—"

"Sophia, I can't see you anymore."

It hit like a bomb that didn't go off. She felt the impact, but no explosion, only the first jolt of collision ringing in her ears. The phone fell onto the gravelled path with a soft scuff.

"What?" she whispered.

"Sorry." He shrugged. He wasn't quite looking at her. More her feet. Her black school pumps were dusty from the gravel.

"I've been trying to think of how to do this." He kicked his own foot against the side of the bench, sending up a shower of tiny stones. "I wanted to wait until your exams were over."

"You . . ." Her voice didn't sound like her voice. It seemed to come from someone else, somewhere else. "Wh-what . . . what do you mean?"

Sunlight flashed off the face of his watch as he pushed his hands harder into his pockets.

"I mean we can't see each other anymore." He breathed out slowly between his teeth. "This is it. I didn't want to tell you like this, but I've met somebody else."

"Somebody . . . No. *No.* What are you talking about? No . . ."

She'd just needed to see him. To put her arms around him . . .

His face clouded. "Please don't make this harder than it needs to be."

"Somebody else. Somebody else." She was repeating it, half-witted; the blazer slipped through her hands and she almost dropped it. "Somebody else? Who? Why?"

“You wouldn’t understand, Sophia.”

“*What?*” Something snapped inside her. Suddenly she was shouting. “What? What do you mean *I wouldn’t understand?* What wouldn’t I understand?”

“It’s . . .” He paused. “It’s different with her. Look, sooner or later things were going to change. You knew that, right? This is . . . it’s time.”

“Time for what?” It was shrill, irrational. “*Time for what?*”

“I’m a grown man, Soph. I have a life to move forward with. And she loves me.”

“*I* love you! I—”

“Sophia . . . it’s not like that. She and I . . . we’re getting married.”

“You only just met her!”

He paused. The silence was excruciating.

“No,” he said at last.

She froze. Something was creeping downwards, from her scalp, numb, paralysing. She’d been breathing so hard that her lips were tingling. No sound would come out between them.

“No, I didn’t just meet her.” He withdrew his hands from his pockets to rest them on the back of the bench with strained patience. “Look, Sophia. I meant to tell you before. You just never gave me the chance.”

“No.” She was still shaking her head. Listening to him from a million miles away. “No. What do you mean? What . . .”

Newquay. The weekends away. The conferences and courses. The thoughts were hitting her mind like hailstones and bouncing off. Weeks? Months?

“How long?” It didn’t come out angry. It wasn’t a shout. It was a plea. She hated herself for how weak it was.

“A while.” He shrugged. There was another unpleasant pause.

“You don’t . . .” She inhaled, dazed. Stared at him, a sudden wave of hope flooding over her. Irrational conviction. He didn’t know what he was saying. That was all. He’d made a mistake; he didn't realise that he could go back on it, that she'd love him anyway . . .

"You don't have to choose her." She was light-headed with certainty. "You don't have to choose *her*. Just because she's older and she'll . . . you'll . . . I'm . . . I can be that too! I can be whatever she is. I can be more!"

So much more . . . if you let me . . .

"I can be better than her." The words were tumbling from her mouth, garbled. "I'm good for you. We can—"

"Sophia, stop." He let go of the bench. His voice had hardened. "Stop. I've told you. It's over. I can't see you anymore. I'm getting married in less than a month. She's pregnant. We're having a baby."

It was the shockwave that hit her, not the detonation: a soundless force that knocked the air from her lungs. A baby. A tiny white being shining into shape on the black glossy screen. Her hand shot to her pocket before she could stop it. She could feel the flimsy quality of the paper.

"No." She choked on the taste. Vomit. Folic acid. Everything that was secret. "No." She looked up suddenly, and for the first ever time in front of him, she failed to blink them back. The tears. Scalding hot. Forcing themselves out. Dripping sullenly down her nose. "No!" She dashed them away. "*I'm* pregnant. Not her! *Me*—"

Silence. He was staring at her, appalled.

"No you're not."

"I am!" Terror rose in her voice, high-pitched and unfamiliar.

"For fuck's sake, Sophia," he snapped. "Don't make stuff like that up."

"I . . . I . . ." A cloud had covered the sun. She fumbled with her blazer pocket. "I'm *not*! I'm not making it up. I can . . . I can prove it. I . . ."

The paper tore. Snot and tears were running over her lips. She scrubbed them with her sleeve. "I . . ." She pulled it out and held it up, triumphant, quaking. The truth. Now he knew, he'd stay. She'd been too afraid to tell him, but after everything he *wanted* a baby. He wanted one, and she'd do it, she'd do anything—

"*What?*" he hissed. He prised it from her fingers, ripped and trembling. Stopped dead.

"You little shit . . ." His eyes widened. "You little *shit!*"

He spun towards her. And for a brief, terrifying second, she thought he was going to hit her. She cowered. The printout fell onto the bench and slipped through the gaps in the wood.

"You did this on purpose!" he snarled. "You did it on purpose, didn't you—"

"No!" She was gasping, uncomprehending. "Why would I . . . How would I—"

He rounded on her. "Get rid of it."

"What?!"

"Get rid of it!"

"But . . . you . . . you want a baby. You just said so . . . I—"

"You're a kid, Sophia! A kid! You can't look after yourself, much less a baby!"

"*What?*" She took a step away. "No . . ."

"You and me, it was fun. But it was never going to be anything serious, was it?"

"U . . . uh." She pitched backwards. The sound had come from her own throat: a strange, guttural noise that she didn't even recognise. *Fun.* Her hand closed through the back of the bench, driving splinters under her fingernails. *Never anything serious.*

The ground was spinning under her. The printout had blown to her feet. The sky had darkened.

A sob rose in her chest, violent and irrepressible. The whole time. The whole time . . . The other phone, the brother she'd never met, the bright-eyed woman in the photo. Everything. Every lie . . .

She snatched the picture from the gravel and scrunched it in her hand.

And then she ran. Into the trees, stumbling on the gradient, her skirt rending as she half-fell forwards and the undergrowth shredded her tights. She didn't stop, didn't look back. Kept going, until her lungs were on fire and the tears squeezed themselves without mercy from her eyes; kept going until she hit the fence, slamming into the chain-links with both hands. She seized it, tore at it vainly, skirted its boundary for a way out. A way out . . .

Razor blades. Painkillers. She hadn't unlocked that drawer since the day of the scan. Her head was bursting.

There was a gap in the fence. She ducked down to crawl through it like a child, and the sleeve of her blazer caught in the sharp wire, tearing a hole the length of her forearm. The hill was steep and she didn't have enough breath left to run it; she crawled to the top instead and collapsed in the tree roots, gasping and filthy.

She opened her hand.

The printout was ruined. Screwed up in a ball. Weighty raindrops were blowing sideways onto the glossy paper and soaking through the ink. Sobs invaded her chest, deep and shocked; her whole body was racked with them.

"Please . . ." Her fingernails ground into the dirt. Panic had taken possession of her voice. "Please, please, please . . ."

Her knee was bleeding. She was sitting on broken glass, cast-off cigarette ends, Rizla packets. It was starting to rain: proper, torrential rain that gave a glancing warning to the leaves above her and then struck the earth with a roar, teeming over the loose soil and litter and plastering her hair to her head.

A termination. She was drenched and shivering. Sick to the soul. The paper was disintegrating in the rain. She tried to pick it up but it came apart in her fingers.

"Please," she sobbed. "Please. Please."

It was too late. Nobody knew where she was. Nobody would ever know.

You're a kid, Sophia. A kid.

If only she could be. She pulled her legs up to her chest, and buried her face in her knees.

If only. If only she was.

CHAPTER 21

2022

"All children, except one, grow up . . ."

The twilight outside has faded. Claire and Ryan's sitting-room lamps burn mood-lit low. *Mercy's Child* is gone from the bookcase — or perhaps I imagined it — there's not even a space where its ragged spine once belonged.

But there was another familiar cover on the bottom shelf, just as tattered, old-smelling and smudged with someone else's finger-marks. It feels at home in my hands, *Peter Pan*, the same edition as my father's. Fin's Spider-Man pyjamas stand out in skinny red and blue contrast against the cream sofa cushions. His arms are wrapped around his knees, his gaze turned to me, owl-wide, listening, and suddenly I have stage fright.

I'm not sure what time Claire will be back from the hospital. It's Wednesday evening; Sean's at rugby practice and Ryan is away up north on some kind of business. I was adrift when Claire called in the favour. Another favour. Perhaps Katie's right. And yet, lingering in the cabin alone seemed worse, somehow. The ache was excruciating five hours ago. Now, it's unbearable.

I turn the page. Shift around to face him, pulling up my own knees to sit cross-legged, the book cradled in my lap as I read to him. This book. Always this book. Always Neverland. Finbar has edged out of his sofa onto the leather footstool; closer, closer, a wispy, ethereal form, like a tiny bird that's not quite tame. He peers over my fingers at the pen-and-ink illustrations, and I flatten my hands so that he can see. Neverland. My neck is starting to ache, but my voice is gaining confidence. I'd forgotten how much I love this story. *The good ones, the bad ones. The ones that wake you—*

I glance over the pages at his tangle of twiggy limbs and his rapt expression. And I can't help thinking that if there's a way out of the silence, a way to reach him . . .

I clear my throat.

If I *could* help him . . . If I could help him, who would I be redeeming? The Lost Boy with the dreams in his uncanny eyes? Or the girl with the ruby balloons at the swing dance; the girl looking out through the rainy porthole, who would live the rest of her life knowing she didn't get there in time—

A page has become a chapter. I don't really know if I'm reading for Fin, or for me. But I've never seen him so absorbed; there's a brightness in his dark eyes that sends a shiver down my spine. A chapter turns to three. My eyes ache with focussing in the dim light. Fin's finger has crept onto the page, to trace the outline of the three children standing on the ends of their beds with their arms aloft, and the small boy dressed in leaves, blowing fairy dust.

"'Now, just wiggle your shoulders this way,' he said, 'and let go.' They were all on their beds, and gallant Michael let go first. He didn't quite mean to let go, but he did . . .'"

I trail off. Fin has stood up suddenly. He looks down at the illustration. Then he clambers with deliberation onto the end of the sofa, balancing precariously with his arms out at his sides. For a second, I'm too surprised to speak. I lay down the book.

"Did some fairy dust get on you?"

He nods. I can't help but smile.

"Can I have some, too?"

He nods again. Lifts up his hand like the boy in the book and blows on it. I feel the smile spread helplessly over my face. I stumble to my feet.

"Got it," I breathe.

Fin holds up his arms. Wings, like a bird. I climb onto the other sofa, the cushions giving under me, and test my weight on the arm, wary of falling through it.

"Are you going to let go first? Or am I?"

After a moment's hesitation, he points at me.

"Okay." I close my eyes. "Here goes."

I take a tiny tentative jump. Fin raises his arms even higher. Then he takes an almighty leap, and plunges into the depths of the cushions. I rise to my feet as he rolls over. His lips are clamped tightly together, his breath escaping in a noisy rush through his nose. I stare, startled. He's laughing, his whole body convulsed with silent giggles. I've never heard him make a sound before. I pick up the book. Draw a deep breath.

"'Oh lovely!'" My voice is oddly husky. "'Look at me! Look at me! Look at—' Ohh—"

A shadow has fallen across the page. I raise my eyes, speechless.

"I think you're supposed to jump on the wind's back." Sean's voice is achingly soft.

How long he's been there, I just can't tell. He's leaning against the doorframe, arms folded, and there's a look in his eyes that I can't begin to fathom. I lower the book.

"Right," I murmur. I put down the book on the sofa arm. My cheeks are on fire. Fin's mop of golden hair rights itself. He tumbles from the sofa to his feet, and runs over to take Sean's hand. I pause, thinking of boundaries and not touching. The little boy who won't let people into his room. I frown.

"Finbar." Sean signs something with his free hand. Fin smiles a lopsided smile. Then he slips free and disappears into the hall. Sean's voice is low.

"I've been looking everywhere for you." He moves closer, lifts a lock of hair from my flushed cheek to twist it around his fingers. "You need to stop caving to Claire's tales of woe. What've you been doing, anyway? Teaching him how to fly?"

I waver. For some reason, my throat feels strangely tight.

"The moment you doubt whether you can fly, you cease forever to be able to do it," I tell him, as my phone starts to ring.

Sean's smile is impossible to read. He shakes his head.

"Then you'd better not start doubting."

I answer the phone. "Hello? Livia Frost . . ." My voice sounds very unlike its usual self. I clamp the phone to my ear and take the opportunity to bolt from the room. Fin has gone.

"Hi . . . hi. Livia? Si-Simon here."

I stop by the front door.

"Oh . . ." Simon. *Simon?* "Hi . . . Sorry, who?"

"Simon. Your erm . . . your landlord. You're at number thirty-one?"

"Oh." Simon. I'm not sure I ever knew his name, although it must have been on the contract. "Yes. Yes, sorry."

"No . . . not at all, not at all. The apartment's in my wife's name, actually. I'm sorry to bother you. But we were wondering if you were available in the next few days for an inspection. Just a r-routine, you know, check."

"Oh. Sure." I switch the phone to my other hand. "Yeah. No problem. Actually, the heating's not really working. So . . ."

"Ah." He pauses. "Right. Yes. Yes, we can have a look. Hopefully nothing . . . erm . . . something simple. Yes."

"Great." I find myself giving the phone a reassuring smile. The poor guy sounds really nervous.

"Monday. Five p.m.?"

"Monday at five's great." Through the diamond pane of glass, Sean and Fin have appeared in the drive, hand in hand. Fin has the bucket, Sean the spade. They pause on the gravel, waiting. "Thanks."

I slide the phone into my back pocket and pull open the door. Something tugs in my chest, warm and aching. I jog across the gravel with the wind in my face and the sun in my eyes.

You'd better not start doubting.

* * *

It's cold. Too cold. Colder than it should be. I slam my car door. There's no movement, no sound, not even a breath of wind in the driveway at Trethallyan. The stillness is chilling. My jaw breaks into motion, as if in rebellion, my teeth chattering desperately as I fumble with my keys.

I'm not expecting company. The open door is a surprise. I push it tentatively. Katie?

No. Ryan.

I pause. Something's wrong. The door's open, and it's freezing. I pull it to behind me, and it's only as I do that I see the lock. I halt.

"Shit." My bag slips from my shoulder. I lower it, speechless. Ryan turns from the filing cabinet.

"Tell me about it." His voice is grim, his mouth a hard, set line. "Morning, Livs."

"What . . ." I gaze around at the room. The filing cabinet is open, its lock pried out of shape and all four drawers half out. A couple of folders have fallen on the floor, and cascades of paper lift slightly with the backdraught as Ryan steps away from them.

"What happened?"

There's surprisingly little mess. Apart from the paper, everything looks just like normal. The drawing boards, set squares, equipment; the designs are still laid out where we left them.

"They drilled the lock." Ryan moves past me to the door to push it closed. "Sometime last night, I don't know when." He looks exhausted. Perplexed. "Bastards were fucking tidy, that's for sure. It makes no sense. I can't even work out what they've taken."

"Shit." I don't quite dare to go any further in. I scan the room again. Sean's laptop is still on his desk, as is mine, in a sea of shading pencils and sticky notes. There's hundreds of pounds' worth of equipment stored tidily under the drawing boards, untouched.

"They didn't . . ." I frown. "Any . . ."

"No," he affirms. "None of it. I don't get it. Unless they were disturbed."

"What now? Does Graham know? Are the police—"

"No," Ryan cuts across me. He's shaking his head. "Graham's not keen. Nothing valuable's gone, if anything has at all. He doesn't want the intrusion. Replacing the lock'll be cheaper than the insurance excess would be, anyway. I guess we just have to clean up."

"Oh." I reach to pick up my bag, colder than ever. "Are you sure?"

"No." Ryan glances up. I've never seen him look so serious. "I'm not. But Graham is. I tried arguing it already, but he won't have it. He wants to carry on as usual. Said he's coming down to meet you and Sean at half past, as planned . . . Have you heard from Sean?"

"Huh?" I freeze. Somehow, his scrutiny brings a fierce blush to my cheeks. As if he can know. As if he can see inside my head — just from looking at me — the much-too-vivid thoughts of projected shadows in the firelight and the taste of sea salt on skin.

It was just daylight when we parted. We'd set out together, relived stories of oil paintings and dangerous rip currents, and swimmers lost to the tide. He left me at the kissing gate, walked with Max one way while I ran the other in the persistent grey drizzle of the Porthtrevelen dawn. I came to Trethallyan alone. It was an unspoken agreement, separate cars, different times, opposite directions.

"Oh. No. Not for a while." The lie drops surprisingly easily from my lips. "Have you?"

"Nope." Ryan kicks a brick behind the door to keep it closed, and stoops to pick up the paper from the floor. "I expected he'd already be here. I called, but he didn't pick up. I've left him a message. Gonna need some new drawers." He's turned his attention back to the filing cabinet. I look at it too, unable to suppress a shiver. Maybe Ryan's right, maybe they were disturbed. I think of Niklavs, and the intruder in the stairwell.

"Amazing to meet your brother, Sunday." Ryan shoves the folders back into the broken drawer and moves to fill the kettle. "You didn't tell me he's at Nottingham. Coffee?"

"No, thanks." I make my way to my desk, uncomfortable. I can't quite keep up with his change of pace.

"We're going to set up a reunion game." Ryan shovels a generous amount of sugar into his cup. "Alumni v Freshers. Sometime in April or May." He roots in his pocket for his phone. "He messaged me this morning — the twenty-first or the fourth. You should come and watch."

"Oh." I feel for my own phone, slightly unnerved. Kris messaged him, and not me? "Cool."

"Thanks for stepping in with the little guy again last night, Livs. You're an actual hero. You should come to dinner tonight. Claire's idea." Ryan sets down his mug on the spare desk and sits sideways to face me.

"Uhm." I glance at his face, and can't help thinking once again just how much he reminds me of Kristopher. "That would be great."

"Amazing. Say six, at ours, once I've got everything sorted here." His gaze lingers briefly on the ruined lock. "If that works for you. You're not vegetarian, are you?"

"Oh, no."

"Good. Well, I can't wait to hear about girls' rugby." Ryan's lips twitch. Suddenly the air has cleared. I grin too.

"I'm not sure I tell the story that well."

"I'm sure it's still worth hearing."

"Yeah, uhm—" I'm distracted by the sound of footfalls on the path outside. Sean? No, the gait is too slow, and uneven.

Graham Gordon-Heyers' beige trousers are flecked with weighty spots of rain. I check the time. Nine thirty already.

Sean's going to be late to our meeting. Where is he? Graham is already here. I spring out of my seat as the door opens.

"Hello?" Graham pokes his head around the door.

"Graham, hi." Ryan puts down his coffee and strides to greet him with a warm handshake-embrace that leaves me feeling utterly superfluous. In fact, if I think about it, I've never even noticed Claire seeming that close to her father. I hover at an awkward distance.

"We're okay, I think." Ryan lets go of his father-in-law's hand. "They don't seem to have got away with anything much. I was going to—"

"Whatever you need to do, Ryan. I'll leave it with you." Gordon-Heyers shakes his head. Weirdly, he doesn't seem at all perturbed. In fact, he's grinning broadly. I watch in bewilderment. Twenty years have fallen away from the creases in his face.

He turns to me suddenly. "Have you heard from Sean? The full planning's through. They've okayed everything!"

Everything. I stop abruptly beside the mezzanine, my grip tightening on the stair-rail. How does he know that before I do? My pulse has quickened. The full planning. *My* plans. A reality. I take a careful breath in.

"He's not here yet." I clear my throat, unduly nervous. What's wrong with my voice? I make myself let go of the stair-rail.

"Ah. He said he might be a few minutes late." Gordon-Heyers is buzzing, literally jittering with excitement. He nods to the steps. "May I?"

"Of course." I follow him up, hovering an anxious step behind him, then make myself take a pace back.

"I'm off for now, Livs," Ryan addresses me from the doorway. "I'd best go talk to a locksmith, and I need to get hold of Claire; she's taken Fin to the speech therapist."

"Okay." I glance up. Ryan gives his trademark salute. "Don't forget. Six. Tonight."

I smile. "I can't wait."

Graham Gordon-Heyers has made his way into the back room and hung his tweed jacket over the back of one of the chairs. He picks up the bundle of CAD printouts to flick through them. The silence transitions gradually to awkward.

"Can I get you a drink?" I ask at last.

"Oh." He glances at his watch. "Please, as Sean's been held up. If you have tea, that would be splendid. Thank you, Livia."

"Sugar?" My voice still isn't normal. I fight not to clear my throat again. "Milk?"

"Just milk."

"Sure."

I deliberately let the door swing closed behind me as I descend the steps to flick the switch on the kettle. The brushed steel handle finds its place with a gentle click. I slump against the work-surface and exhale a long, slow breath.

"Good run?"

Jesus Christ. I drop the coffee jar onto the side. Sean crosses the floor to join me, soft-footed as ever.

"Mm." Something in his expression makes me nervous.

"Good." An inscrutable smile plays on his lips. He takes a step closer. Dangerously close. I shoot a nervous glance at the closed door.

"The full planning's through. It looks like the first set goes to you, Frost." His mouth is against my ear. I extricate myself, heart hammering.

"I didn't realise it was a competition."

"Neither did I." The smile still lingers at the corner of his lips. "I'm used to winning. I'm going to have to up my game."

I raise my eyes to his. "What game?"

"The one I warned you not to play, I think." Sean's voice is very low. The top two buttons of his shirt are undone and I can't quite tear my gaze from them, overpowered by the faint enticing smell of aftershave and the memory of my lips in the hollow of his throat. I swallow.

"We start the footings next week." He's watching me looking. "Together; you and I are site managing."

"We are?" I look up sharply. "I mean . . . *I* am?"

"Uh-huh." It's a whisper. He catches hold of my braid and tugs gently, pulling my face to one side, and plants a less-than-chaste kiss on my lips, my jaw—

I gasp. Sean looks up: a guarded, vigilant glance in the direction of the rain-spattered windows and the abandoned garden.

"Sean—" I inhale.

"Fuck . . ." He stiffens. "Graham's already here, isn't he?"

"In the back room," I whisper. For the briefest second his thumb and finger linger at the nape of my neck. Then he steps smartly away. I study the worktop until I hear the door close and their exchange of greetings across the conference table.

Site managing. I focus on my breathing; *in, lengthen, out.* The game he warned me not to play. The kettle whines reluctantly towards the boil, and I snatch it up prematurely as steam billows from its spout, slopping more water than I pour. I pull the tie from my dishevelled hair and shake it out, the long tresses falling well below my shoulders. I pause. Then, very deliberately, I braid it again, before I fish the tea-bag out of Gordon-Heyers' mug and splash milk into what's quite probably the worst cup of tea I've ever made.

Sean's eyes follow me briefly across the floor as I push open the door and take Gordon-Heyers his drink. Then he looks back at Graham, and I sit down with a bump in one of the empty chairs.

Conversation moves rapidly from planning permission to practicalities. Footings, contractors, timescales. Money. I never imagined just how out of my depth I'd feel, swamped by the endless list of necessities and the sheer scale of what we're attempting. Sean isn't out of his depth. The smile hasn't quite faded from his lips, and the excitement in his eyes is thinly hidden. Looking at him has transitioned from risky to perilous, so I stare at my hands instead. We're suddenly a hundred miles from the Lookout.

A hundred miles. I look up, crashing back to reality. He's going to Oxford tonight. I forgot.

My drawings are spread out on the table: elevations, sections, floorplans. Sean has switched on the projector; he slices a finger across his tablet, flicking between the newly constructed computer-assisted details onscreen. Gordon-Heyers is nodding and I realise that, once again, I've managed not to listen to a word they've said.

I blink, and find myself face to face with a half-size digital reproduction of the stained-glass Mary, her eerie abstract eyes regarding me reproachfully across the table. Unnerved by her scrutiny, I pull out my pad and pen, and start to make notes.

It's eleven before the discussion wears itself out and Gordon-Heyers leaves for the hospital. Sean gets up to see him out, and I take my notes to my desk and sit down in front of my laptop. It's open. I don't remember leaving it open. I stir the mouse, and the screen lights up.

> *2 programs still need to close. To close the program that is preventing Windows from shutting down, click Cancel and then close the program.*

Force shut down. I click through quickly, and then stop. How was it logged on to start with? *Who* was logged on? I might have left it open, but I definitely didn't leave it logged on.

Something jolts in my abdomen. I click again, but I'm too late. It's already gone. The screen powers down, leaving me to stare at blankness. I press and hold the on button, and wait for the sign-in screen to appear, thinking inexplicably of the bird on the backdrop, and the girl in the brochure with the vacuous eyes.

"What are you frowning about, Frost?"

The door closes with a muted bang. My pulse accelerates.

"Nothing," I mutter.

Sean strides across the floor, catlike and predatory. He stops at my desk.

"Not very focussed today, are you?" he murmurs. I glare at him.

"Says who?" I punch in the password. In a swift, almost imperceptible movement his hand shoots out and catches my wrist.

"Me." His eyes lock mine. I rise to my feet, unable to disregard the danger in them.

"Are you arguing?" He toys with my wrist.

"No."

"Good." His grip closes around my arms, powerful and irresistible. "I've wanted to kiss that scowl off your face for quite a long time."

"Sean—" I start. But my murmur is incoherent; his lips take mine. I stumble, clutch at the front of his shirt, and we collide full-weight with the desk, pencils raining down, a cacophony of plunking wooden notes that scatter themselves in a greyscale rainbow across the floor.

If it's a warning, he doesn't heed it. His weight presses me backwards, his hips pinning mine against the side of the desk, until I have to put out a hand to save myself.

"Sean . . ." It's not a protest. His fingers penetrate the sections of my plait, holding me captive; I slide my hand between the buttons of his shirt to touch his smooth, forbidden skin. I've already forfeited every ounce of sense and reason, impervious to the risk, the crunch of tyres on gravel, the flicker of motion beyond the glass—

"We finish this later," his mouth brushes my ear. Then he's gone, retreated to the back room. I drop to my knees to pick up the pencils at the same instant that the door opens, the brick scraping across the floor.

"Hi, Katie." I don't quite look at her face.

"Oh!" Katie jumps violently. "Livia! I didn't see you. What's happened to the door? For a minute I thought—"

"Sorry." I bundle my pencils back into their dented tray. I count to five before I straighten, hoping that she won't notice the flush in my cheeks. "I didn't mean to scare you."

Scare? Is that the right word? Katie picks up an old Lorchann McLeod brochure from the floor by the filing cabinet. There's the oddest look on her face.

"Ryan didn't tell you about the break-in," I observe.

"No." She lowers the glossy leaflet. "A break-in? Here?"

"Mm." I swallow. "Last night. But nothing was taken."

Her eyebrows draw together. "That doesn't make sense."

"No," I agree. Isn't that exactly what Ryan said? I glance at the filing cabinet.

"Have you heard about the chapel?" I change the subject.

"The chapel? No? What about it?"

"The full permission's through. Since this morning. I thought that must be why you're here."

"Oh. No." Katie puts down the brochure. "Ryan asked me to come and finish the survey in the west side of the Hall while Graham and Claire are out, so I won't disturb anyone."

"Right." I nod, as if I understand. Which I'm not sure I do.

"Do you want to come?"

I hesitate. "No, um. I'd better not." I try to stop my gaze from straying towards the back room. "I have work to get on with."

"Sure." She nods. There's an uncomfortable pause. "Livia . . ."

"Mm?" I look up.

Katie takes a deep breath.

"Nothing," she says.

What?

"I'll catch you later." She scoops up a bundle of photocopies from the first drawer of the desk, and before I can challenge her, she's disappeared.

I sit down slowly. A survey for Ryan on the Hall? I can't help remembering the sharp reproach in Graham Gordon-Heyers' voice, and the tight edge in Claire's, at the only times that it's ever been mentioned. What does Katie know, that she's not telling me? A dark corner of my subconscious hasn't forgotten what she said back at the start. *We should talk about stuff*. Stuff. Stuff to do with Sean. It's not difficult to extrapolate; her every disapproving glance and worried frown in my direction screams it out loud. I wet my lips and pick up the notepad. Somehow, I can't quite bring myself to move. I'm not sure I can face another heart-racing encounter just at the moment.

I lay down the pad again with shaking hands. What am I doing? Am I crazy? Katie's right. He told me himself it's a bad idea. I stand up. Maybe it's a good thing he's going to Oxford. I need space. Release from his thrall. *Time to think*.

I don't go into the back room. I type him a text from the path outside the cabin, where it's too late for him to appear and beguile my better sense with his raw-umber stare. I walk to the chapel at half speed, and sit on the ridges of iron-age granite to sketch until the cold and the drizzle overwhelm me and my fingers are too numb to carry on. It occurs to me that I'm going to have to lie to him and tell him I've been for food. I can't imagine my skipping meals would meet with his approval.

To my relief, I don't have to lie. The cabin's empty when I reach it, the door held closed with a deftly-tied length of weathered-looking rope. I loop it free and go inside. My laptop's still open on the desk, and the silence is impenetrable. I flip through my notes from the meeting.

I've immersed myself in work by the time he gets back. He sits down at his desk, and it takes me every ounce of my willpower not to look at him. Not to see if he's looking back. A timely retort about focus lingers on my tongue, but I don't voice it. I keep my teeth clamped together, my back poker straight. I can't shut out the gentle creak of his chair, the brush of denim on denim as he folds his long legs languidly under the table. My mouth is mutinously dry.

At five, he gets up and stretches, and paces the distance to the drawing boards to look again at the plans, his tread light. My resolve has given way to conflicted longing, a heady, torturous blend of anticipation and confusion. Sean folds his arms across his chest.

"You need to go home."

"Mm." I close the laptop. There's silence.

"You could stay at the Lookout." His face gives nothing away. I swallow.

"I need . . . I need to go back to the flat."

"I thought you might say that."

"Why don't—"

"Take your laptop. I've put some files on it for you. Something I want you to read."

"Oh." I look down at it, surprised. It was him? The thought of his supple fingers on the keys makes me strangely breathless.

"Try and get it done tonight." Sean unfolds his arms, buries his hands in his pockets.

"Okay . . ." I narrow my eyes.

"You're going to have a lot to do tomorrow." A tiny smile lingers at the corner of his lips. "Have you made a list? I'd go for the council offices first. Then get in touch with George Sterman and send him these." He traces a finger over the plans. "You won't have time for casual reading."

Casual reading? I glance down at the laptop again, perturbed.

"Right," I murmur.

"I told Graham you'd update him in the afternoon. If you can get the last bit of CAD detailing done, then we should have everything tied up before the weekend."

"Mmm." I don't quite manage to keep the lack of conviction from my voice. Does he think I'm superhuman? The jobs I generated from this morning alone already constitute more than a day's work.

"I told you I'd push you," he points out softly.

"Yeah." I pull a face. "Remind me, what did your last intern die of?"

The sudden jolt of silence stops me in my tracks. Sean has frozen, every hint of a smile erased from his face. For a split second, a horrible certainty creeps through my veins, ice cold and unspeakable.

"Never mind," I gulp. "I . . . I mean, I should . . . I should go . . ."

"Livvy." His voice is terrifyingly quiet. "Please. Go back to the Lookout."

Suddenly I'm shivering.

"I have to go home." I say it with more conviction than I feel. Sean's shoulders are braced, tense. I can feel the measure in his breath out, the force of his gritted teeth.

"Okay," he concedes at last.

"I'll see you Saturday," I whisper.

Sean nods. The silence expands between us, all-consuming. I slide the laptop into my satchel. Walk towards the door. He doesn't stop me.

I falter, bewildered. That's it? He's just letting me go? I shoulder the satchel and push the door. Sean doesn't move.

"Have a safe drive north."

Shit. Rain hits my face, a deluge. I jog to my car and blunder in, slamming the door behind me. Unfathomably, tears are stinging my eyes. I give the key a sharp half turn in the ignition. It's raining so hard that the wipers can't keep up as I traverse town, glad of the reason to focus more intently on the road. I park in my usual spot outside Sunnyside. Fumble with my satchel, blinking hard.

In the driver's mirror, another car has pulled onto the cobbles. I pick up the keys and get out slowly. Close the door with not-quite-steady hands.

He's already standing beside the Defender. Rain's pelting his face, soaking his clothes; he pushes an agitated hand back through his hair and my heart almost stops.

"You . . ." I whisper. "You followed me."

Within seconds, my hair is plastered to my cheeks, the braid washed out by the downpour. I can feel the water trickling over my face and gathering on my chin.

"You left before I'd said goodbye." His gaze is endlessly dark. "I thought I'd say it now."

He steps forwards. His pull is stronger than gravity; I move without even realising, until we're both in the middle of the road, until his arms ensnare me, drawing me into him on the cobbles in the pouring rain. His cheeks are wet, his jaw, his lips as I run a finger over them. Raindrops are scattering on his breath, clinging to his lashes. And I want him, more than I've ever wanted anything on earth. Sean's hands grasp my hips, and at last he kisses me, tasting, teasing. I take a shuddering breath; he grips my hair either side of my head to rein back my hunger and prise me gently away.

"I have to leave." His murmur is soft, aching. "And I don't want to leave you here."

"It's only one night. Two," I correct myself. Only. Only, when all I want is to relinquish.

"Call me. Tomorrow." He winds his fingers into my hair. "I need to know you're okay."

"Why wouldn't I be?"

"Just promise you will."

"I promise."

"Oh, Livvy Frost," he breathes.

He doesn't say goodbye. Neither of us does. I brush the rain from his lips, and he catches my hand and keeps it there, warning aflame in his eyes. I watch from the doorstep as he drives away, watch until even the spray and the reflection of his taillights have faded. And as I turn to go inside, the empty summons of the rain on the window glass is louder and more inevitable than ever.

I move through the cold shadows of the hallway warily, like an explorer in some perilous half-known land. I'm afraid to misstep, afraid to breathe out. Two days, is that really all? It seems far longer.

"You are back, then."

I start. Turn. Niklavs' face is half obscured by the gloom. His crutches are leaned against the windowsill. I feel myself flush and then blanch in quick succession. His view of the road through the dusty glass is undeniably clear. He flicks the curtain across with one firm hand, apparently forgetting the crutches.

"How was job?" he asks opaquely.

"Um . . ." I falter, searching for a safe response. "Fine. It was fine. Thanks. How are—"

"Architect did not stay, then." His voice is sharp. I stop in my tracks.

"You . . . you mean . . ."

"Did not look like he was here to talk of building regulation."

"I . . ." My eyes are watering, the tops of my ears burning painfully. "I don't . . . He . . . Wait." My heart is hammering. "How do you even know who he is?"

"I know enough."

"What?"

Niklavs' lips purse.

"Young girls," he says tightly. "Always blinded by handsome man. But I am not sure he is good man. You ask yourself that. You may not like answer."

I stare at him, stung.

"*What?*"

He shakes his head. I follow him in through the door of 29A.

"No. How can you say that? You don' t even know him! You don't know anything about him. Do you?"

Does he?

It's thirteen, backwards.

I stop dead.

"He's . . ." I pause, the stomach-churning realisation finally dawning on me. "He's been here before, hasn't he?"

Niklavs' teeth are gritted. He doesn't say a word.

"Hasn't he?" I'm sick with certainty. "Why has he been here before?"

The ring of my phone makes us both jump. I fumble to silence it.

"Tell me." My voice shakes. "Tell me wh—"

The phone rings again. I waver, torn. Niklavs' eyes have narrowed. I pick it up.

"Hello?" I whisper.

"Livs! I'm so sorry," Ryan's voice, distorted with static. "About this evening. I'm going to have to postpone on you. Claire's not feeling well. She needs a bit of peace and quiet. I've said I'll take the little guy out instead."

"Oh." Dinner. Crap. I'd forgotten. I try to focus, to slow my racing pulse.

"We're going to the Fishbowl. You're welcome to join us, though."

"Uhm—"

"I'm sure Fin'd love you to come."

I take a deep breath. Fight to ground myself. I don't know what to do. Dinner with Ryan seems wrong somehow. But not with Fin there . . . and it's that or a night alone in number *thirteen backwards* . . . I glance at Niklavs. His mouth has clamped shut. He's not going to tell me anything.

And Ryan's the one person who always tells me everything . . .

I exhale, adrenaline pooling in my gut. Ryan's been here for seven months. He must know something. If Sean's going to have confided in anyone, who else would it be?

"It's on me." Ryan's voice is warm, persuasive. But suddenly I don't need persuading.

"What time?"

* * *

The restaurant's on the seafront, bigger than I imagined, and empty. Apart from a middle-aged couple in the far corner sitting with their empty plates, we're the only customers. Niklavs is right. Porthtrevelen has little to offer in winter.

Reflections of the dark tide lap on the ceiling over our heads as I read the menu, and Ryan hangs Fin's coat on the back of his chair. The entire length of the wall beside us is fronted with glass: the biggest fish-tank I've ever seen, filled with a multitude of fish, from tiny electric-blue flecks to large, dark, eyeless creatures that skirt the bottom corners, and hold Fin in fascination.

Considering there are no other customers, the service is unfeasibly slow. Ryan sits opposite me, hands buried in the pockets of his zip-through hoody, and we both hedge around any serious topics of conversation, and talk about the weather instead, and Kris, and matches at Grove Farm. Fin, never bored, wanders away to drift along the perimeter of the fish-tank, one careful finger pressed to the glass.

The food is almost worth the wait. The fish is very fresh, and the portions are Ryan-sized. Fin climbs onto his chair at his dad's direction, and uses his knife and fork adeptly to pick the fresh white flakes of cod out of the middle of his batter and nibble the ends off a third of his chips, before he returns to his post at the aquarium.

"He really loves those fish." Ryan shakes his head. "I'd get him some, but I have no idea how to look after them."

"No." I smile, slightly awkward, and glance over at the tank where an open-mouthed fish is following Fin's finger along the glass. For a moment, there's silence.

"Do you know anything ab—"

"Maybe for his birthday—"

We speak simultaneously. Ryan grins.

"You first. What were you saying?"

"Oh." I bite my lip. Suddenly I'm not brave enough to ask. Even though the question's consuming me. "Nothing. When's his birthday?"

"August." Ryan lounges back in his chair. "Can't believe he'll be five."

"No," I murmur. "I guess it goes pretty fast."

"Incredibly."

"Is Claire okay?" I push my knife and fork together.

"Yeah, she'll be fine." Ryan glances over my shoulder at Fin. "She gets migraines — the only thing that works is to sleep them off. She was going to go to bed. To be honest, I think she just needed me and the little guy out of the way."

"Right," I nod. There's silence again.

"How're you finding Porthtrevelen anyway? Where did you say you're living?"

My pulse spikes. Out of nowhere, he's thrown open the opportunity.

"The fishermen's cottages in Sunnyside." I keep my voice even. "The flats. Number thirty-one."

"Oh yeah." Ryan nods. There's no recognition in his expression. No spark of interest or jolt of memory. "I remember. You said you go running from there?"

"Mm." I try to fight away the anti-climax. "Yeah I do."

"Is your place nice?"

"It's okay." I think on my feet. "Except the heating's broken, and I haven't been able to get hold of the landlord." I pull a face. Only the second half is a lie. "You don't know anyone else who's rented there, do you?"

"Oh." Ryan frowns. "No. No idea, Livs." His brow furrows. "Surely that's not good? It's bloody freezing at the moment. Have you tried anyone in the other flats?"

"No." I shake my head. "Not yet." A slow trickle of disappointment is dispersing in my bloodstream. He doesn't know anything.

"Do you want me to come and look at it?" He sounds concerned. "I'm pretty useless with that sort of thing, but a second pair of eyes . . . I might be able to help, if it's something obvious . . ."

"Um, no. It's okay. Thanks." My cheeks burn with guilt. "I should probably keep trying the landlord."

"Sure. But the offer's there. Or come to ours. Seriously. Don't get cold."

"Thanks." Cold. I fight away the images of the Lookout, the log-burner, the heavy tumble of creased white bedcovers, flushed with shame. I glance at my watch. Sean should be halfway to Oxford by now. My hand darts to the phone in my pocket, as if I might feel any messages. Even the thought makes my pulse quicken. What would he say, in a message? If I can't read him in real life, how will I ever interpret him in text? Or perhaps he'll call. Shit. I hadn't thought of that. I shoot a furtive glance across the table at Ryan.

"It would be nothing, Livs. I mean it." Ryan leans his elbows on the table, uncharacteristically serious. "I'd like to help out." His gaze scours the aquarium briefly, locating Fin, out of earshot.

"You know, I've been talking to Kris a bit. He mentioned you both had some tough times, before you came here. About your dad, and stuff."

Oh, fuck. I grip the edge of the table and try to gulp back the obstruction in my throat. Why in heaven's name did Kris feel the need to tell him that? I clench my teeth together hard and try desperately to formulate a reply.

Ryan hesitates. "Look, I don't know if Claire mentioned it to you, but Sean and I lost our mother when we were kids. He was little, I don't know how much he remembers. But *I* remember. I was with her, when it happened. It's not something you understand, until you've been there — watching someone die. It changes you."

"Yeah," I croak. "Yeah, I guess it does."

The silence is painful. I stare at my plate. What is Kris's problem? How is it they're suddenly bosom pals after one drunken party and a couple of rugby-related phone calls? What else have they talked about? My eyes are stinging. The couple in the corner have got up and left. A waiter comes to gather their plates.

"So, yeah." At last, Ryan shrugs. "I'm pretty crap at the hugs and positive thoughts thing. But . . . well, if you ever need to talk, or whatever, just know you can, okay?"

"Thanks, Ryan." My whisper sounds hoarse. I look at Fin instead of at him, blinking ferociously as he stumbles back to us, signing something with two fingers. *Look*. He's gesturing at the fish.

"Hey, buddy." Ryan gets to his feet. "Do you want to come and say bye to Livs? I think she's ready to go home."

I glance back at him, surprised and grateful for the reprieve. His face gives nothing away. He touches Fin's fair hair gently.

"Didn't you have something you wanted to give her?"

Fin comes to an abrupt stop. He turns depthless eyes on me, and a tiny smile, much too old for his four and a half years, curls the edges of his lips. He looks so much like his uncle that I freeze, unnerved. He reaches into his pocket and pulls something out, slightly bedraggled from being sat on. A black feather. He pushes it between my fingers.

"Thank you." The lump in my throat hasn't quite gone. I touch a hand to my mouth. "Thanks, Fin."

He beams.

I push the feather into my buttonhole.

"See you."

"See you tomorrow, Livs." Ryan rests a hand on the top of Fin's untidy head. "Remember, anytime, okay?"

I nod. Anytime.

But not any time soon.

* * *

You have no idea who I am. Neither do I. I'm looking into the mirror again, and I don't know who I am. I don't know . . .

I pull the brush slowly downwards, watching the reflected tresses of my hair part and coalesce. Break off and start again, stroke after stroke. The journal is open on the dressing table. No matter how hard I try, I can't not look at it.

I hid the rosary beads under my mattress. They were my mother's. She wanted me to pray. She told me God would forgive me. That it didn't have to matter. That it didn't have to change everything. But it did change everything.

There's something mesmerising in the motion. The caress of the brush against my scalp, like fingers, gently tormenting; cradling, possessing . . . I breathe out, and my breath mists on the glass, obscuring my face, so that I could be any featureless, ageless girl, lost in her own shadow. I lay down the brush.

> *There's a word for this. I'm sure there is, but it eludes me. I can think of a lot of other words. Words I don't like as much. Words that frighten me. Captivated. Consumed.*

I close the book. The cloud fades from the glass. My reflection looks back at me with discerning blue eyes as I reach to fasten my necklace, then step away, out of the line of her sight.

There was no *casual reading* on my laptop. Just a note that made my heart race. My satchel and a bag of clothes are already in my car. I've been lingering for hours, a bird trapped in a cage. It's time to go.

* * *

He's waiting by the window as my car pulls to a halt on the stone chips. The door opens before I knock; his suit jacket and shoes are cast off on the floor.

"Frost." His eyes speak a hundred words that his lips don't. Words that leave me giddy. Breathless.

"Lorchann," I whisper.

"You did your reading."

"Yes."

"Good." He doesn't touch me, not quite, as he steps back to let me in. The hallway is cool and filled with low Saturday afternoon light. I slip off my coat.

"How was yesterday?" he asks opaquely.

"It was fine." I'm suddenly self-conscious as I follow him into the immaculate kitchen. He's still in his Levi's and crisp white designer shirt, but the tails are untucked and his feet are bare on the heated floor tiles. I catch myself biting my lip. He's watching.

"How was Oxford?"

"Dull." He pulls up short. "Noisy. Protracted." His dark eyes are ember-hot. "Would you like a drink?" He pours a half-inch of Scotch into the bottom of two glasses and fills them with ice. I take one uncertainly as he holds it out, remembering. *I like to be in control, Livvy.*

"I wasn't planning on going anywhere else today," he elucidates.

"Oh." I take a tentative sip. It's warm and ice cold all at once, sweet and pungent, scorching the back of my throat like fire. I swallow. He's still watching. I can feel the heat creeping through my veins, and I have no idea if it's the alcohol or just the way he affects me. Every muscle in my abdomen clenches.

"What is it about you, Livvy Frost?" It's a murmur, his lips against my hair. I catch my breath. About *me*? As if *he*'s the one bewitched.

"I can't work. I can't sleep." Sean's fingers are cool from the condensation on his glass. "I can't think. About anything except you."

The bedroom is soaked with faded sunshine. He follows me in, relieves me of my glass and sets it down with his beside the bed. I want to touch him, but I can't. I can't quite breathe out.

"Maybe we should go somewhere else." He makes no effort to move. Neither do I. I'm rooted to the spot.

"Why?" I whisper.

His gaze absorbs the details of my dress, the jet necklace. I feel like he must be able to see my pulse bounding.

"Because you don't look sure." His mouth is hot against my skin. "And I'm out of self-restraint."

Not sure? I take another jagged breath. I'm so sure that I'm light-headed. The heat has already washed out every reason that I should never have come here. His throat smells of aftershave and tastes of salt. I hear him inhale.

"I'm sure," I whisper.

It doesn't matter: whatever I thought I wanted, whatever we said we couldn't have. I never knew that I could feel so intensely. Need, so desperately. Right and wrong don't seem to have meaning here. There is no reality beyond the two of us. No boundaries that can't shift. No amount of restraint or surrender that could ever be too much. Nothing matters beyond the slaking of the hunger that threatens to consume us both.

* * *

As the daylight fades, I curl, spent, into the protective curve of his body, and I listen to him breathe. Raindrops spatter the windowpanes. And suddenly, and out of nowhere, I can't banish her voice.

Damned. The word I was looking for is damned.

"Peter still wants you to go and work for him." Sean's murmur startles me. I half turn. "Once we're done at Trethallyan."

"He does?" I look up, lost.

"If you pass your exam, there's a post for you in Oxford."

"Oh." My heart leaps. But something in his expression extinguishes my enthusiasm. I falter. "What . . . ?"

"I'm not planning on going back to Oxford, Livia." His voice is quiet. "I was hoping you wouldn't go there, either."

"I don't understand." I raise my eyes to his. "I—"

He reaches to brush back a strand of hair from my forehead.

"I'm not going back, when this is done. I told Peter yesterday. I'm going to stay here. Set up and work for myself . . . They were more supportive than I expected. Him and my father. Said they'd endorse it, if that's what I want. That I could use the company name."

"And you want me to stay here too?" Suddenly my chest's hurting. Sean twists my hair around his fingers.

"Like I said." The wry smile on his lips belies the aching intensity in his eyes. "Your work's something else, Frost."

Here. I gaze up at his shadowed face, trying to process it. He wants me to stay. To share his dream, work with him—

Sleep with him. The voice hasn't left the back of my mind. I don't even know whose voice it is. Swift's, Katie's, my own . . .

My muscles contract. No. That's not it. *Trying not to love you. But I haven't done a very good job, have I?*

Sean shifts beside me, the covers rustling. It's almost dark outside. The low light casts everything in strangely sharp relief: crisp-edged silhouettes and outlines, like the world is drawn in elevation. I lay my head on his chest and listen to his heartbeat. Close my eyes. Count.

But it doesn't work. The voice won't be vanquished. I turn my head against his chest, so that I'm not quite looking at him.

"There was another intern," I say at last. "Before me."

The silence is absolute. Neither of us moves, but I feel him stiffen: a tension that immobilises both of us from head to foot. Suddenly, I don't even want to breathe.

"Yes," he affirms.

"She left." Even as I say it, I realise I don't believe it. *Thirteen, backwards.* He doesn't reply.

"It's her, in the brochure? The red-haired girl?" I don't know how I'm so sure, but the certainty is an advancing storm, deadly and impossible to outrun. Sean nods.

"Yes."

I swallow.

"What was her name?"

Sean draws in a long breath. Holds it, for a moment, and then exhales. His voice is very quiet.

"She was called Sophia."

CHAPTER 22

My name is Sophia Swift.

My ears are ringing. The silence is like nothing ever before; it obliterates everything. The storm has broken. Lightning has struck, but not earthed.

Sometimes I see reflections in that mirror. And they're not mine.

I already knew. I must have known. Sophia. Sophia Swift. The last intern at Trethallyan.

"Livia . . . ?" Sean's voice is grim, dispersing the buzzing in my ears. I crash back to reality.

When I was seventeen years old, I—

"The flat." The words tumble out of my mouth before I can stop them. "Why don't you want me to go back there? It's not because of thirteen backwards. Is it?"

I look up at his clenched jaw, burning eyes. Burning with answers that I don't want to hear. He doesn't reply.

"Is it?" My breathing has accelerated. I'm light-headed. "It's to do with her, isn't it?"

Sean's expression is black, his mouth a hard, straight line. "Why would you think that?"

"It was her flat."

"Yes, Livia. It was her flat. And five months ago, I walked in through that door and I found her dead. With her dressing gown cord around her neck and a suicide note with my name on it."

Holy. Shit.

I'm staring. Disbelieving. Unable to look away from the flicker of pain in his face: the memory, the true horror of the reality that's expanding in the room between us. Thirteen, backwards.

"She . . . killed herself?"

"I'd imagined you'd already heard all this from Katie." There's an edge to his voice that I've only heard once before. Once, in the dark stairwell at Sunnyside.

"Katie knows?" I swallow. Of course she knows. The last intern. I feel sick.

"They were friends. Of sorts."

"She . . . she lived in my flat . . ."

Died in my flat. I'm shivering helplessly. Sean pulls himself upright and flicks his shirt from the foot of the bed to hand it to me. I pull it on, ice cold.

"Yes." His eyes are locked on mine.

"Claire said . . ." The fragments are fitting together, every last piece: words, places, the name and number in the back of Katie's diary. "Claire said you and she were . . . friends, too."

"Mm." Something falls over his expression. Flat, guarded. A barrier I can't see past. "Claire has a habit of seeing the best in things. Sophia was young. Twenty, twenty-one . . . A student, from Bath, doing a year's placement with us. I think she'd only done a year or two at uni. She was out of her depth, unhappy. I tried to support her."

To support her. *He ended up feeling responsible.* I'm not sure whether it's a wave of relief or dread that washes through me. *I've loved him, so hard . . .*

Fuck. I screw the over-long sleeves of his shirt in my fists, her handwriting etched vividly across my mind. It was him. She was writing about *him*. All along.

"I thought at first she was homesick." Sean's teeth are gritted. "But it turned out to be much more . . . complicated than that. Fucked up. I don't know." He shakes his head. I hesitate.

"What do you mean?" I whisper. "What do you mean, fucked up?"

Sean swings his legs out of bed abruptly. Starts pulling on his jeans.

"She had some kind of . . . problems." It's clipped, tense. "Something in her past. I think Katie knew more about it than I did."

"She . . ."

"She'd hurt herself before. Cutting, I don't know what else. Whatever it was, she didn't talk about it. Not to me. Not to anyone. I did my best." His lips have tightened into a Finbar pout, stubborn and strangely young. "I was meant to be her mentor. I tried talking to her, but it just made things worse."

"Worse how?" I wrap my arms around my knees, shivering harder.

"She got . . ." He halts suddenly, facing me. "Fixated . . . obsessed. Over that summer. She started saying things, doing things . . . She thought there was something between us that there just wasn't . . . I need you to understand, Livvy." He pushes a hand back through his hair, agitated. The shadows have converged in his face. "I tried to put a stop to it — fuck, the last couple of months I even started working from home. I was going to organise for her to go back to Oxford, where her mother lived. Work with Peter. But it was too late."

Tell me. That it's not too late to turn back. Tell me . . .

"It got out of control. I watched her lose her mind, Livia. I watched her turn into someone else. I watched her destroy herself — no, fuck, *I* destroyed her. She kept calling me, saying the same thing, over and over again. That she needed me to know the truth. I couldn't let it go any further. I'd spoken to Peter, he was going to take her on — it should have been finished. But she suddenly stopped turning up to work. Just like that. No one could get hold of her. No one had seen her, but her car was still on the road, outside the flats. I tried calling her, and it just rang and rang . . . I went to the flat. I think I knew. I had this sick feeling . . ."

Oh, God.

"She was in the bathroom. The shower rail . . ." He closes his eyes for the briefest moment, exhales slowly, a deep, shuddering breath. "Fuck. I knew she'd cut, she had scars, I'd seen them, but it never occurred to me . . . never . . ."

I let go of my arms, suddenly weak, limp. A dressing gown cord. Razor blades. *The pen is mightier than the blade.* Sean is stood, rigid, unmoving. I slide from the bed and go to him, too afraid, somehow, to touch him. To acknowledge it, the horror of the image reflected in his eyes.

"I'm sorry." For some reason, my eyes sting with tears. After everything, every hope and dream, she took her own life. She died alone, afraid, heartbroken. So much for the hope of redemption, the fight. So much for the girl in the dandelion stems. In the end there was no birdsong, no outstretched hands. Only fool's gold. Only silence. He's right. There's no solace in the truth.

"She left a note." He moves out of my hold to click on the light. His shoulders are tight. "On her dressing table. They gave it back to me, after the inquest. They found alcohol and cocaine, apparently, enough to have 'played a part in her state of mind'."

Her dressing table. *My* dressing table. Watched by an infinity of vacant-eyed reflections. I swallow. Sean reaches up and takes something from the top of the wardrobe: paper, covered with a film of dust. An envelope with his name on it, in agonisingly familiar handwriting. My hands shake as I take it from him, untuck the torn flap and pull out the page from inside. The paper's familiar, too. Notepaper. White notepaper, faintly lined in blue.

> *What's about to happen will hurt you. I hope you'll forgive me. I tried. I tried to think of a better way. But I wasn't strong enough. One day, you'll understand. One day, you'll understand everything.*

Thank you for believing in me. I know that was all it was. I know you could never have loved me. Not really. But —for a time, at least —you made my sun rise.

I'm sorry that it has to fall.

I'm sorry, for everything.

Goodbye, Sean.

Sophia

And there it is. The whole picture, every piece in place. Except one . . . *When I was seventeen years old, I killed my—*

He's watching me read. Watching my eyes scan over her writing time and time again. What can I say? That I already know? I already know more about Sophia Swift than she ever told anyone? That I know about *the hate, the love in equal measure,* the pain, the infatuation — *because that's what it is, isn't it?* That somehow we've lived and breathed the same moments, those dark moments before dawn. That maybe, just maybe, we've both made the same mistake in loving the same man.

Because I do. I raise my eyes to his face. I love him. And there's nothing that he can do, or say, to change it. Even if it will destroy both of us, like it destroyed her.

"Why . . . ?" My whisper sounds strangled, unfamiliar. "Why would she do that?"

"You think I haven't asked that?" His voice is painfully soft. "You think there's any answer I can give myself? Anything that can absolve me? Anything to console her family . . . her mother? Anything at all?"

"Sean . . ." I breathe. "No. It wasn't your fault—"

"Ask Katie." He turns away. Every muscle in his back and shoulders is taut. The bitterness in his voice makes me ache for him.

"No." I catch his hand. The grazes on his knuckles have healed. "It doesn't matter what Katie thinks. You weren't responsible."

"You don't know that, Livia." He turns back, and his expression is darkness manifest. "You can't."

"I can." My voice shakes. It *is* too late. "I do."

Sean pulls free of my hand.

"Then give up the flat." It's low, almost inaudible. "Give your notice, and don't go back." His gaze is raw, and locked on mine. I freeze, immobilised. What? He doesn't look away. His challenge lies heavily in the silence between us. I clench my hands into fists, and try not to think of Niklavs, or the blind cord rattling against the single glazing.

I suck in a deep breath.

"Okay," I whisper.

* * *

Everything. Everything's changed. I thought I could see a path through this, but suddenly I can't, not tonight. The way's not clear. It's forked. I'm lost.

I wish I could ask you for directions but you have no idea who I am. Neither do I. I'm looking into the mirror again, and I don't know who I am. I don't know.

I do. I do know. Her reflection in the mirror is growing clearer: red hair, empty eyes. Don't go back. I've had to come back; the work laptop is still on my kitchen side and I need a change of clothes.

I hid the rosary beads under my mattress. They were my mother's. She wanted me to pray. She told me God would forgive me. That it didn't have to matter. That it didn't have to change everything. But it did change everything. And maybe God did forgive me. But what's the point, if you can't forgive yourself? It turns out I can forgive anyone, except myself . . .

I strip back my duvet from the bed, and pause. Under the mattress? Tentatively, I lift a corner to look, but there's nothing there except cobwebs.

He's right; how can I stay here, now?

I drop the mattress. What am I doing? I've agreed to move in with him. After a week of subterfuge and illicit, passionate lies. The man everyone keeps trying to warn me about. The man Swift killed herself over. I sit heavily on the side of the bed.

> *What is it — the secret you bury? Is it something terrible? Tell me and I'll tell you. The reason you're wrong. The rest of the story.*
>
> *I remember the word, now. The word I was looking for was damned. Because here it is. What I'm truly guilty of.*
>
> *My name is Sophia Swift. And when I was seventeen years old, I killed my*

Something in her past. He has no idea. No idea what she was hiding. Killed *who*? My mouth is prickling with dread.

I pick up the loose page. *Mercy's Child.* My father's last book.

> *A R Frost. 431*
>
> *"That's it," she concludes, and her gaze drops to her hands and her ballet-dancer arms. "I'm sorry. You don't have to ask any more questions."*
>
> *But he does. He does have to ask.*
>
> *"What did you hope I—"*
>
> *His voice fades in his throat.*
>
> *She has risen to her feet, light as a bird, dark hair dropping out of its braid as she turns away. A daughter of night time. She's whispering.*
>
> *No. Singing.*
>
> *Red and yellow and pink and green . . .*
>
> *He's about to blink. He's about to blink. And when he opens his eyes again—*

. . . she'll be gone. I know the posters off by heart. Paper ones in the bus stops. Electronic ones flickering in the station foyer. *When he opens his eyes again, she'll be gone.*

Sophia Swift died in my flat. She ripped her suicide note from the back of her journal — the journal that she left for me to find. But the rest of the pages are gone. Where? And why? What did they say? My heart is pounding. What happened on those pages? What happened *to* them? Where did they go? Did she destroy them — her written confession? Or did she hide them, are they still here somewhere . . . ?

If I leave . . . if I leave now, I'll never know.

A month's notice. That's what I've told Sean. A month from tomorrow when the landlord visits and I make it official. It was a six month contract; I'll have to pay some kind of release fee. A month. I've got a month to work it out.

What am I going to tell Niklavs? I put the book down quickly, folding the note into the back and burying it in my suitcase. I'm not going to tell Niklavs anything. I can't. I fold my remaining pile of clothes in on top. Not yet.

I descend the stairs as quietly as I can, let myself out into the road and carry my possessions as far as the street corner, so that Niklavs won't hear the Defender, or the suitcase wheels on the cobbles. Sean's already waiting. He loads my case and my roll of canvases into the car, and we drive back to the Lookout in expectant silence.

I thought about telling him last night. About the journal. Just for a moment, enfolded safely in his arms in the flicker of the firelight, it seemed like the right thing to do. But when it came to it, I couldn't. Even though I didn't know whose confidence I'd be breaking.

"Are you okay, Livia?" There's something excruciating in his scrutiny. Intense and inescapable. Both his hands are on the wheel; I fight the urge to touch him, to reach out and trace my fingers over the residual pink hint of the bruises on his knuckles.

"Yeah." My voice is husky. I fight away the thought of the journal in my case. "I'm fine."

We stop. Beside us, the vista-window of the Lookout is a mass of reflections, like rippling black ink in the twilight. I climb out and stop. He's moved to meet me, a silent silhouette. His index finger curls under my chin.

"I need you to be honest with me." His stare is level, serious. So dark that my breath catches in my throat. His thumb covers my lips, cutting off my protest.

"*I* have been with you. And it would have been so much safer not to be." He moves his thumb lightly over my lips, and there's something fleeting in his eyes, something fragile: a tiny vulnerable glimmer of a smile that fades as fast as it appeared.

Safer?

I close my eyes. Sean withdraws his thumb and kisses me, tilting my face to his.

There's no such thing as safer. I'm already lost.

* * *

"Thirty-two and a half . . . This way, *this way*. Down — careful, miss!"

"Sorry," I gasp. Rain is striking the side of my face and running down the neck of my coat. Saturated tendrils of hair escape around my hood; my feet squelch in my boots as I jump over the waterlogged trench to the safety of the concrete chapel step. Sean's on the phone, shouting to make himself heard over the pummelling of the rain and the noise of the JCB.

"No . . . no. We can't cut it. We're keeping the door, it's original . . . A locksmith? Uh-huh . . . What? No. No, that's no good. I don't think I can have made myself clear . . . Yes, exactly." He glances up and our gazes meet. He slashes a sharp gesture across his throat with his finger. "No. *No.* Put me on the line to him, then. Yes — now. I don't care. Thanks. Thank you." He covers the bottom half of the phone with his hand. "Livvy, can you go back down to the Hall?" He tosses me the key to the Defender. "See if you can find Graham, or Claire. We really need to get our hands on this door key. Hello?" He uncovers the phone quickly. "Sean Lorchann speaking. Who is this? Hi . . ."

There is no door key. I've already told him what Gordon-Heyers said, that only Clarissa knows where the spare is. There doesn't seem much chance that that will have changed.

"No . . . No! We're not breaking it down. For a start, the wall's more likely to come down than the door is . . ."

I feel my lips twitch. Pissed off, business-like Sean Lorchann is giving me an inappropriate urge to laugh. I leap the trench and scramble over the piles of earth and ripped-up brambles to the car. I feel like a child driving a tank in the Defender; I have to move the seat all the way to the front to reach the pedals. Ryan's BMW is parked on the drive outside the Hall. I run across the gravel and throw down my hood as I reach the porch, rain pouring from my waterproofs. My fist makes a hollow sound on the door.

Nothing.

I pause, overcome by a distinct sense of déjà vu. There's definitely someone there; I can hear voices. Shouting.

"*. . . How can you . . . How can you say that?!*"

"*You used to!*"

"*That's not true!*"

"*You keep telling yourself that.*"

"*We were friends! For years, after you stopped showing up. That was all there was to it! I chose you, Ryan!*"

"*Did you? Or did he just not choose you?*"

"*Ryan!*"

A crash. Thundering feet. Shit. I dive back from the door. Of all the times I could have knocked.

"*Fucking go then! Go! Go, while I sort out our future! Because one of us has to!*"

"*Ryan — Please—!*"

Shit.

I quail and run. Something tells me Graham isn't at home. And this definitely doesn't seem like the right moment to ask Claire about the key. I slam open the cabin door and fall inside; close it behind me and slump against it, gasping.

Katie is sat on the edge of my desk, legs crossed, one hand resting on the engraved barrel of my pen. I come to a dead stop. She's frowning. And instantly, I know. Her hazel eyes meet mine.

"You spent the night with Sean."

"I-I . . ." For a moment, I can't formulate a word. A denial. A confirmation. A question — how can she know? The Defender key dangles as irrefutable evidence from my fingers, and my car's at the Lookout. I gulp in a deep breath, but she speaks first.

"Oh, Livs," she breathes. The crease between her eyebrows deepens. I can't reply. Her expression paralyses me.

"Be careful." She slides from the desk to her feet. "Tell me he's told you? That you know—"

"I know about Sophia." It comes out garbled. A justification: a defence. "If that's what you mean. We've talked about it."

Why am I explaining myself to her? I screw my nails into my palms. The concern in her face is chilling, and genuine. I don't know what to say.

"She was my friend." Katie's voice is quiet. Pained. "Please, Livia. Think about what you're doing. Sean's . . . not safe ground. He's brilliant, but he's fucked up. This whole place is pretty fucked up. It would be better not to get involved."

For some reason, my hands are shaking. I put down the key.

"I'm already involved," I whisper. And it's true. It's never been more true. The fear hits me like a breaking wave. I'm risking my career, I've given up the flat; I'd give him anything, just as Swift wrote. Suddenly my throat's aching. I blink hard.

"Oh, Livia." In a stride she's beside me. I feel her hesitate, and then her arm's around my shoulders, light and uncertain. Her sympathy makes my eyes sting with unwelcome tears.

"Don't," I tell her, between my teeth. "Don't say it. I'm not her."

"What?" She lowers her arm. "What do you mean?"

"Sophia." I make myself release my breath. "I'm not Sophia."

"No." Katie pauses. Her eyes scour my face. "No, you're not."

"Tell me. About her."

"I don't know." Her frown reinstates itself. Her lips have pressed tightly together, too.

"Katie."

"I don't . . ." She shakes her head. "No. I don't want to talk about her. Sean's told you the bit that matters."

"It's important." I swallow. "Please. You said she was your friend."

"As much as Sophia was friends with anyone." Katie sits back down on the edge of the desk again, and fiddles with my pen. "There's not much to tell. She didn't talk much about herself. It took a long time even to find out a little bit about her."

I sit down too.

"Even a little bit?" I persist.

I'm going to try and tell you the truth. Will you turn the pages, if I do? Even if there aren't any heroes?

"She came here from uni. She really seemed like she needed someone to confide in." Katie's voice is very soft. "I think she was an only child, and she had an unhappy past. Her father was in prison. And . . ." She hesitates.

"And?" My mouth is dry. And she bought razor blades to cut her arms, *and she was in love with Sean*. I bite my lip, hard.

"And she'd had a baby . . . really young."

Oh. I feel the breath rush from my lungs.

"She had a child?"

Katie's lips are set, grim. She shakes her head. "Not when she came here."

My stomach drops. Her father was in prison. She had a baby. *When I was seventeen years old, I killed my—*

"I spent a lot of time with her, but she never really spoke about it." Katie shrugs. "She was the same age as my sister. I tried to get her to come out, do things, live beyond whatever had happened before. It was such a waste . . . I asked her to read at the wedding. Laura — my sister — isn't going to get back from Australia to do it. She said she would." Katie raises her eyebrows. The residual dread in her earnest gaze is inescapable. "And then she disappeared. Two weeks later. Just when she'd started to open up. We'd talked about her father; I'd even persuaded her to write to him — I thought it might help. But she wouldn't talk about Sean. She was . . . hung up on him. Head over heels. Completely. And terrified that he was going to send her away."

Which he was. I catch myself biting my lip again and make myself release it.

"I never asked her any more. Whether . . ." Katie pauses. "But she changed. Over the last few weeks, she changed. She'd lost focus, on everything else . . ."

Words. Words that frighten me. Captivated. Consumed . . .

"I . . ." My voice is strangled. "I have to go."

"Livia." Katie's gaze is level, sharp. "Please, just be careful. It's not worth it. It's not worth getting hurt."

I nod, speechless. Does she have any idea? What if I were to say the same thing to her?

But Craig isn't going to hurt her. Deliberately or unintentionally. Craig doesn't have a reputation, a track record, a hunger for control, a dead intern . . .

I almost slam my fingers in the door as it bangs behind me. The key. I try to focus, breathing hard.

Ryan's car has gone from the drive. I try the door to the Hall first, but there's no answer. I stand for seconds, minutes, staring up at the towering and decrepit three storeys, crenulations, the peeling paint on the sash windows. Sean's right. Its potential now is in renovation and subdivision, not restoration. Five million. I squint at its elevation, picturing the insides, and remember what Niklavs said about neglect. He's not wrong. Another twenty years and the place will be a ruin. It stands a better chance with a developer, or the National Trust.

I start back across the gravel, remembering that Sean's still waiting. He'll be expecting me back, or at least a phone call. Goodness knows how long I've already been. Too long.

I debate briefly whether to walk or take the Defender to the Gatehouse, and decide on the former. I don't need Ryan or Claire questioning Sean's new-found confidence in me. The side gate is open, and I pick my way tentatively through the carefully lined-up toy cars and diggers. Claire's in the conservatory, hanging clothes on a line; she jumps as I tap on the glass.

Come in, she mouths at me through the window. I let myself in through the kitchen and kick off my boots.

"Hi, Livs." She's standing on a step-stool, trying to fasten socks onto the dipping clothes line left-handed. She seems more flustered than usual, and I'm suddenly uncomfortable, aware of what I overheard.

"Did you try to call? I'm sorry, my phone's died. One second." She pins the last sock and the line jolts, a pair of Fin's jeans falling off the other end and landing in heap. I pick them up and shake them out.

"Sorry." She steps down from the stool to take them from me.

"It's okay. I didn't . . ." I trail off. Her right sleeve has fallen back, revealing an angry-looking swelling over her forearm, alarming shades of purple and yellow.

"Oh." Claire sees me looking. She shakes back her sleeve to examine the injury herself. "Crap, that looks bad, doesn't it? I was on the trampoline with Fin and I fell. Do you think I should get it looked at?"

I glance out at the barely relenting rain. The trampoline's slick with it. Wherever Fin is, he's not out there anymore.

"Um." My frown is worthy of Katie. "Yeah. You probably should."

"I just haven't had chance to think about it. Fin only did a half-day today, and I didn't want to take him with me — he spends enough time in hospitals as it is."

"I can watch him for a bit," I say, without thinking. "You really should get it checked."

"Do you think so?" She lays the jeans over the side of the empty laundry basket. "If I go now, while Ryan's still out, I mean—" She flushes.

"I really don't mind keeping an eye on Fin until he's back." I follow her into the kitchen. "Honestly. You should go."

"Are you sure?" Her eyes dart from me to the trail of Lego that leads into the hall. "You came down for something, though? Sean must need you back?"

"I'll call him. I only came to find out about the key. For the chapel," I qualify quickly. "Sean doesn't want to damage the original door; he was sure Graham said there's a spare—"

"I don't know anything about a key," Claire cuts across me, voice sharp. "He should wait and talk to Dad."

"O . . . okay." I'm taken aback.

"I don't even know if he wants it opening, to be honest." She moves to pick up her phone from the kitchen table. "Anyway, he's taken Mum to Exeter to see her consultant. He really doesn't need troubling with it just now."

"Right." I finger my phone, bemused. "Uhm . . ." I glance at her wrist. "Will you be okay to drive?"

"I'm fine, Livs. Thanks. I'm sure it's nothing, anyway. I'll call you if it looks like it's going to take long. Fin's upstairs with the iPad."

"No worries." I nod my understanding. "You go."

"Thanks." The edge to her voice has gone. She flashes me a grateful smile. I wait until the glare of her headlights fades from the granite before I go upstairs.

Sean's phone is engaged. I text him instead, and pause on the last step. Fin's bedroom door is open, and an iPad on the floor is playing cartoons with no sound. I tiptoe in and look around at the smooth bedspread and unnaturally tidy toybox.

"Fin?" I call softly.

Nothing. I tiptoe out again, and try the spare room. There's a thud. I spin round to see Fin cross the landing, the thick curtains falling back over the windowsill behind him.

"Oh," I breathe out my surprise. "Hi, Fin. I was looking for you. Mum's just had to go out." I'm telling him what he already knows; the landing windows both look over the drive. "She won't be very long."

He nods placidly. No smiles today. Maybe today's a no-touching day. I hesitate.

"Are you okay?"

He nods.

"Would you like to do anything?"

A pause. He regards me for a second, then disappears into the bedroom. Moments later, he's back. He presses the book into my hands.

"*Peter Pan.*" I smile. "Have you been reading it without me?"

He shakes his head.

"Oh." I bite my lip. "You waited for me?"

Fin nods. He points at the stairs, and we descend together. I let him run ahead, and watch as he builds a throne of cushions on the end of the sofa. He takes my sleeve to lead me to it, then curls himself into a ball beside me as I sit down.

"Where had we got to?" I ask. He points. Saturday morning seems like a very long time ago now. We read almost ten chapters, sitting in the conservatory with the rain drumming on the roof, while Claire and Ryan were shopping. Sean had still been in Oxford. I'd never been more glad of a way to pass the time.

"That far?" I check the page. Fin does too, and turns forwards one to the next picture.

"Peter raised the cup. No time for words now; time for deeds; and with one of her lightning movements Tink got between his lips and the draught, and drained it to the dregs.

"'Why, Tink, how dare you drink my medicine?' But she didn't answer. Already she was reeling in the air. 'It was poisoned, Peter,' she told him softly; 'and now I'm going to be dead.'"

I pause. Beside me, Fin has jolted upright, his face pale. He touches his index finger to the picture. I carry on, quickly.

"Every moment her light was growing fainter; and Peter knew that if it went out she would be no more. Her voice was so low that at first he couldn't make out what she said.

But then he made it out. She was saying that she thought she could get well again if children believed in fairies.

"Peter flung out his arms. There were no children there, and it was night time; but he addressed all who might be dreaming of Neverland. 'Do you believe?' he cried. 'If you believe, clap your hands; don't let Tink die.'"

Silence. Fin's still staring at the picture. For a horrible moment, I think he's going to cry; he's motionless, lips trembling. I touch his shoulder. He turns.

"Can you clap, Fin?" I whisper. His dark eyes are wide with dismay.

"It's okay. We can save Tink." I put down the book. "Clap your hands. Like this."

I clap softly. Fin falters, arms hugged around his chest. I carry on. Very slowly, he joins in. Our timid applause is absorbed by the silence of the sitting room. I reach to turn the page.

"See?" I show him. "Already, Tink was saved. First her voice grew strong, then she popped out of bed, then she was flashing through the room—"

I break off. The unmistakable slam of a car door echoes outside. Seconds later, the front door opens. Fin slides from the nest of cushions, and pads out into the hall.

"Hi, buddy!" A thump and a scuffle of keys. Ryan's boots are loud on the wooden floor. "What're you up to? Where's Mum?" He appears in the sitting-room doorway, and does a double-take.

"Oh, hey Livs. What's the happs? I think Sean was looking for you." He pauses, scans the rest of the room. "Where's Claire?"

"Oh." I stand hastily. "Hi. Um . . . she's gone to get her arm checked out. She fell on the trampoline with Fin."

"Shit." Ryan's face creases with concern. "Why didn't she call me? Is she okay? Are you all right, buddy?" He touches the tumble of blond hair that's appeared under his arm. Fin ducks quickly out of his reach to retrieve *Peter Pan* from the sofa and carries it protectively back in the direction of his room.

"I think he's fine," I murmur. There's a loaded silence. Ryan shakes his head.

"You'd better get going. Seriously, Livs; I owe you again. I actually can't remember what we did without you." He reaches over to give me a friendly, bone-crushing hug. "If you speak to Kris, tell him I'm on for the fourth. I'll give him a call tomorrow."

"Sure."

"I'd better call Claire." He pulls out his phone to dial. I give an awkward wave and beat my retreat. It's too late to worry about how much work I've missed. I set off at a jog, eyes screwed up against the driving rain, and arrive at the cabin at an ungainly, sodden run. My clothes from Friday morning's meetings are still folded neatly under my desk, and I pull out my slightly creased skirt and crumpled tights, infinitely glad of my own disorganisation. I kick off my wellies and hide in the back room to peel off my wet jeans and change into the dry clothes. I can't suppress the vague hope that no one will want me back on site, now it's got so late. I check my phone. Nothing from Sean. I cross the mezzanine, and stop at the top of the stairs with a sudden lurch of anxiety to check my outbox. Surely he's got my message?

"Good to see you, Frost."

I start. Drop the phone.

"Where have you been?" His eyebrows lift. His clothes are damp. He reaches around me to tug the band from my dishevelled hair, and leans close to whisper, his lips against my temple, "I was starting to think you'd taken Katelyn's advice and made a run for it."

"Oh," I exhale. "No . . ." I bite back my smile. "I'm a fast runner. I would have been much further away by now."

"So I've heard," he remarks dryly.

"Claire didn't have the key."

"I gathered. They've dug half the foundations while you've been gone."

"Graham's taken Clarissa somewhere . . . Exeter . . . Claire said to wait until he's back."

"Claire would have us wait until hell freezes over," he murmurs. "Come on."

"Where are we going?" My voice sounds husky. His hand is an inch behind my waist, tantalizingly not touching. Not quite.

"Home."

"Now?" I glance at the clock and double-take. Five. *Shit* . . . the landlord . . . I snatch up my phone. I've missed a call. I dial back, but it goes to voicemail. Sean pulls it gently from my hand and slides it into his back pocket.

"Now." His voice is low.

I turn. "Why the rush?"

Sean stops. He's one step above me on the stairs, immersed in the shadows of the black clouds through the skylight.

"Because I really hate waiting." His eyes don't leave my face. "You want to drive?" he asks, and I suddenly realise that I still have his key.

I've never concentrated so hard on the road in my life. I can feel him watching my every movement, brows low, eyes smoky-dark. The last hundred yards of the track fall away in front of us, and I slow the Defender to a careful halt, pulling on the handbrake with both hands. A smile plays over Sean's lips, boyish, wistful somehow. I climb down onto the stone chips.

He unlocks the door and locks it again behind us. His gaze travels from my kicked-off shoes to the creases in my blouse.

"You forgot your coat," he mutters. I glance at his mud-flecked jeans.

"You forgot your suit," I retort.

His eyebrows flicker. In a single stride he's on top of me, one knee of his crisp Levi's detaining me pointedly against the doorframe.

"Is that a criticism, Frost?" He pushes his hands through my hair, letting the damp locks flow between his fingers. "You know I don't take criticism well."

"Oh, no." I back, upright, into the frame. "I wouldn't dare criticise you." I can feel his lips, taste them, right against mine. I can't look at anything else. He kisses me slowly, his teeth tugging deliberately at my lower lip.

"This." His voice is rough; his fingers curl against my scalp to pin me, motionless. "This is . . . not good . . ." He's breathing hard. "I'm not good for you." He draws me with him; his mouth moves against my ear, planting delicate kisses along my earlobe, the corner of my jaw, my neck, until I'm gasping and off balance.

"But I fucking want to be."

"You . . . you are—" I clutch at the collar of his shirt, hot, light-headed with desire. "You are—" I wrestle with the buttons and he struggles out of it, casts it aside as my back collides with the kitchen counter. He pulls my blouse off over my head without undoing it, and then his hands are on me, inside my camisole, travelling over my skirt: fervent, impatient. I reach out to unfasten his jeans, and he grabs my hand and pushes me backwards, his other hand closing in the ends of my hair, pulling gently, relentlessly, so that my face is turned to his and his eyes fix mine, intent Ivory Black. He doesn't look away; he hitches up my skirt, our gazes lock, wordless, urgent—

The phone vibrates before it rings, the sound echoing across the kitchen. My phone, in his pocket. I freeze. Sean fumbles to silence it and tosses it onto the stone worktop. It rings again straight away.

"Fuck." He snatches it up. I can see the name on the screen in his hand, backlit. *Kris Frost.*

Something cold jolts in my chest. At six in the evening. Monday night. Monday night is First Fifteens. He never calls on Mondays. Sean pauses, his finger over the touchscreen.

"Wait," I exhale. I slide free and take the phone as he holds it out to me. I stumble a few steps away.

"Hello?" I breathe.

"Livs." Kris's voice at the other end sounds wrong. Painfully soft. It's the A&E voice. The voice from the abyss. A chill runs down my spine.

"Livs, I think you'd better turn on the news."

"What?"

"The six o'clock news." His words are quiet, strained. "Just put it on."

I falter. Sean's watching me, brows lowered, a frown darkening his face. He retrieves his shirt and crosses the floor to join me, silently questioning. I pick up the TV remote.

"Judith, from Westminster, thank you.

"Next, the father of a toddler who drowned three years ago after falling from his family's yacht in the English Channel, has died in what are described as 'suspicious' circumstances following a light aircraft crash in Hampshire. The plane, in which Tom Rainworth — son of Michael Rainworth, multimillionaire CEO of the leading British yacht manufacturer, Rivent — was flying alone, came down in a field near Andover shortly before eight p.m. on Wednesday. No one else was injured in the incident. Police and the Air Accident Investigations Branch are working together to establish the cause of the crash, although there has already been public speculation. This recent video, taken by a family acquaintance, shows Rainworth, who had previously received treatment for depression and drink-related problems following the death of his son Toby in 2019, aggressive and apparently disturbed at a function only hours before the crash."

I feel for the edge of the sofa. Sit down without looking and keep my eyes glued to the wall-mounted flatscreen. Dimly, distantly, the voice is just audible over the background noise and static. Slurred, scrambled but sickeningly familiar. The view pixelates, angles and loses focus.

"*Get out of my way!*"

The phone falls into my lap. I don't dare to touch anything. I stare at the television screen, straining my ears to make it out.

"*Out of my way! You can't stop me! He's not dead! He can't be! Get off me! I'm going to find him! I'm going to find my—*"

The scuffle of noise and motion heralds the clip cutting out, flipping instead to a hazy reproduction of a family photo that I've already seen a thousand too many times. A sailor suit. Honey and starlight. I stare, mute.

"One close source has told reporters that he is 'saddened' but 'not deeply shocked' by news of Rainworth's death. Police have declined comment at this stage, and a spokesperson for the family tonight stated 'Tom's family are in pieces. We simply ask that we might be left to face this second devastating bereavement with respect and priv—'"

I dig my finger into the remote. The phone slides and lands on the floor with a clatter, Kris's voice spilling tinnily from the speaker for a moment more before it cuts to dial tone.

Honey and starlight. I gaze at the empty screen, numb. Honey and starlight. I've known Tom Rainworth since I was eleven years old.

"Livia?" Sean's voice is quiet, concerned. I get to my feet.

"I . . ." I trail off. I can't think of anything to say. Sean stoops to pick up the phone.

"Livvy." He stays at a distance. Follows a few paces behind me as I walk through to the bedroom, legs shaky, and kneel beside my still-packed suitcase. I rest my hands on the lid. Sean puts down the phone and sits beside me, silent. I flip open the case and draw the zip of the inside top pocket.

Best friends always. A wooden cat, a photo frame. The dust-jacket. I pause. The day that *Mercy's Child* was launched was the last day Hannah Rainworth spoke to me. I suck in a slow breath. And I still haven't read it. After all this time.

I trace the outline of the blackbird. The tagline on the front cover: the one that struck the last, fatal blow to our relationship. The only friend that ever really knew me. The only other person who'd been there, in the empty cabin, that night.

A missing child,
a lost past,
a broken heart.

And now Tom Rainworth's dead. Just like Toby. Just like my father. What's the sense in hating, when it turns out we all have so little time? I hug the book-jacket to my chest, thinking of Finbar clapping his hands. Thinking of Sophia Swift, locking the door and writing her last letter. *A broken heart.* Her journal, hidden inside my father's cover. The story that wakes you, sobbing, sweating . . .

Praying for it to end?

I let out my breath in a rush.

The book. I need to read the book.

CHAPTER 23

It's been less than a week, but it feels like a lifetime. The flat is a shell, abandoned and cold, like a museum of Livia before. There's a letter in my pigeon hole, starting to gather dust. And even though I know it's only my imagination, all I can smell as I close the door is the faint lingering stench of death. The landlord is due in ten minutes. After a couple of days of phone tennis, we managed to rearrange. I can't see it taking long.

I open the wardrobe. Flick through the empty coat-hangers. There's not much left; most of my clothes are at the Lookout. I just hadn't foreseen needing a dress for a funeral when I packed my bags.

My mother called last night. Her voice on the phone sounded weird, the background noise unfamiliar. The uncomfortable truth is, I've never stayed in her new flat in Manchester. Not even for a night. I haven't spoken to her since January, the day before I moved to Porthtrevelen. Text messages are easier, less awkward. You don't have to worry about the tone of your voice, and what it might give away. It's enough contact to be contact. Little enough not to hurt anyone.

My first instinct had been to ignore the phone. Let it ring out. WhatsApp her later, under the pretence of missing the call. But Sean's lowered eyebrows suggested disapproval, so I snatched it up at the last second, took it outside and paced the same short stretch of granite in the brisk sea breeze as we talked. It was a pretext of funeral arrangements, with an underlying tremor. I had no idea what to say other than that I'll go. I really don't want to go. To stand in another crematorium for another life that's ended far too early, rasp out a few choice words of condolence, and try not to meet Hannah Rainworth's eye for an hour or two while her family crumbles into the depths of another tragedy. What else is there to say?

There isn't much choice. My tickets are booked. My train leaves at three. Kris is going to pick me up from the station in Canterbury. It'll be nearly midnight by the time I get in; all I'll need is a dress and an overnight bag.

I wonder who went to Sophia Swift's funeral. Were there friends, somewhere in her troubled past? An extended family? Katie said her father was in prison. Did he go? Can you get out of prison for your child's funeral? I have no idea. Did Katie go? Or Sean? I haven't asked, and I'm not sure that I want to know.

A shiver runs down my spine. Why *Mercy's Child*? Why did she hide her journal inside *Mercy's Child*? A coincidence. That's all it *can* be. I jerk the dress from its hanger and fold it over my arm. But if I've got the dust-jacket, where's rest of the book? I frown out of the window at the deserted street. Did it go, with the rest of her possessions, when the place got emptied? Or is it still here, somewhere?

There aren't many places to look. The drawers of the dressing table, the kitchen units, under the bath, on top of the boiler. I check every place I can think of, but there's nothing.

I move through the kitchen to close the other blind, shutting out the warbling wind. I don't know when I'll be back. Never, if Sean has any say over it. But I'm at least going to have to empty the place and clean. And I haven't mentioned it to the landlord yet. Somehow, I feel I owe it to Niklavs to tell him first.

The knock at the door is right on time. I check through the peephole before I open it. Simon is older than I expected from his voice, thin and nervy. I'm not sure I even know his second name. His eyes seem to dart in all directions except at my face as I stand back to let him in. There's grey stubble on his sharp chin and his cheeks are hollow. He looks positively stressed. Which makes two of us.

"Thanks, thanks Livia." He walks right by me into the flat, glancing tensely from wall to wall. "It won't take . . . won't be long. Do you mind if I take pictures?"

"Err . . ." I hesitate. Is it normal to take pictures?

"Just of the erm . . . fixtures. You know." He pulls out a decrepit-looking phone and snaps a picture of the mirrors. Then the bed. The blind. I hover by the door, slightly uneasy.

"Is everything . . . okay?" I shuffle my overnight bag closer to my feet.

"Fine . . . fine." He barely glances back. Snap, snap, the kitchen cupboards, the fridge. He strolls to the other end of the kitchen and stops by the easel in the window. A little lurch of anxiety and indignation stirs me from my acceptance.

"Sorry." I catch him up. "Is this really necessary?"

"Oh. Yes. Sorry. All done." He drops the phone back into the pocket of his slightly shabby suit. "Thanks."

"Okay." I make myself exhale. It's not his fault. I guess my mind's already on the train, travelling at a hundred miles per hour back towards the Rainworths and every memory of the Solent. "Did you need to see the bathroom, and uhm . . ." I try to pull myself back. "The heating?"

"Oh, yes." There's a brief look of uncertainty on Simon's face. "The bathroom."

An awkward pause. He drums his fingers against his suit pocket. When, at last, he moves, he walks right past it. I falter. All at once, I feel a little queasy. I follow him a few paces behind.

"It's um." I'm frowning. "In here."

"Of course." He backtracks, nodding, and I take a wary step away. A chill has crept like ice across my skin. This is *his* flat . . . right? I watch him walk inside. He's out again as quickly as he went in, no pictures this time.

"Great. Brilliant. Thank you." He backs out and closes the door hurriedly. "All fine. Thanks."

There's something familiar about his eyes. Unnerving, vacuous eyes. Isn't there? How can there be? I stare at him, trying not to give way to an irrational feeling of panic. I finger my phone in my pocket. I don't want him to check the heating. I want him to leave. Right now. Because I suddenly don't believe that he even knows where the boiler is.

"Actually, if you're finished, I need to go out." I speak so quickly that the words are garbled. "A . . . a train to catch." I seize on the overnight bag. I stumble to the door and open it for him before he even has chance to reply. "If that's okay."

"Right." His gaze snaps away from the bathroom door to alight briefly on my face. "Yes, of course."

There's a chasm of silence.

"You mentioned the boiler." His eyes dart back along the kitchen cupboards.

"Yes. No . . ." I flounder. "It's er . . . intermittent. Maybe an engineer would be better?"

"Oh. Yes." Relief seems to fall over his angular face. "Good idea. I'll get someone to call you."

"Perfect." I gulp. "Thanks."

The chasm grows wider. I wait, my fingers tightening involuntarily on the door.

"A . . . er . . . a pleasure to meet you . . . Livia. Stay safe."

He's out through the door. I shut it behind him without ceremony and fight a disproportionate urge to lock it. *Stay safe?* My heart is pounding and the chill hasn't faded. It seems to have sunk in, bone-deep. I'm shivering. I wait long enough to be sure he's gone, throw on my coat from the end of the bed and pick up my bag and dress.

Niklavs isn't in. I knock twice and try the door before I give up and go outside to put my things in my car. The tabby cat's winding around the lamp-post across the street; it bolts as I approach it and dives for the open window. I watch it go in, with a growing feeling of unease. Where *is* Niklavs? Surely he can't have got far on crutches? I follow the cat at a distance and stand on tiptoe to peer through the glass. What if he *is* there, and he's not answering? What if—

"Door is easier."

I spin in alarm.

Niklavs swings himself along the decline of the cobbles from the promenade with astonishing speed.

"To get in. Door is easier." He balances the crutches to pull a key from the pocket of his corduroys.

"Um," I falter. "Yeah." I can't quite meet his eye. "I guess it is."

"Unless you wish to walk with me?" His shrewd blue gaze narrows. "I was thinking of making trip into town."

I eye the plaster-cast. "You were?"

"I am not invalid." He raises his eyebrows. "You are coming?"

I hesitate.

"Okay." I nod. "Just let me . . ." I wave the dress in the vague direction of my car. Niklavs inclines his head. I jog over and throw the dress and bag onto the back seat, running a few steps to catch him up.

"You are going somewhere?" He jerks his head at the car. I bite my lip. Time for the whole truth, half the truth, or nothing near the truth?

"Yeah." I nod again. "A funeral."

"I am sorry." He falls into stride beside me, the crutches clicking on the uneven paving. "It is today?"

"Tomorrow. I'm going straight from work."

"You are not at job this morning?"

"No, I . . ." I hesitate. "I took the morning off. To get sorted."

To meet the landlord. Sean gave me the morning off so that I could tie things up and give my notice. Which isn't quite what I did. I clear my throat.

"Actually—"

"I was not completely honest with you, Livia." Niklavs speaks across me suddenly. I glance up, surprised and uncertain. His brows have drawn together. He's looking at the road, just like I was.

"About Graham Gordon-Heyers and his Hall. I have thought great deal. Why I have not told you? Because I am stubborn old man. No other better reason." He glares at the crutches as we navigate down the kerb. "I am hypocrite. I tell you to talk of trouble in confidence, and I do not follow own advice." He shakes his head.

"You . . ." I frown. "You know you can talk to me." My voice sounds thick. I clear my throat. Crap. How can I tell him now? How can I leave? I swallow. We've reached the edge of town, where the first few art galleries and curiosity shops cluster with unmet aspiration for the high street, like ambitious children. Niklavs slows to a halt.

"I said I knew him once. Graham." He transfers the crutches to one hand, and bends to examine one of the window boxes on the shopfront, where a smattering of daffodils have pushed their way between the spring crocuses: a splash of colour amidst the grey. *Garden of the Year 2006*. I realise I'm holding my breath.

"After time on boats ended, my work was Trethallyan. That is truth. At beginning, we were small team. Graham Gordon-Heyers was a good man — good employer. Eventually, cost of maintenance was too high. But I stay on, as caretaker, grounds and buildings. So when I said I did not know it, it was lie. I know Trethallyan well. Heart was there, for long time."

"Why did you leave?" It's a whisper. I gaze studiously at the paving stones, at the moss growing between the cracks.

Niklavs' face darkens.

"You have heard, perhaps, of burglary." He straightens one of the daffodils with a weathered finger. "If it is still spoken of."

"Yeah . . ." I chew my lip. "I've . . . heard about it."

"You heard, then, that they suspect involvement of someone who knew Hall well."

"But they didn't prove anything." I look up fiercely. "That's what I heard."

"Did not stop them sacking him. Man who worked for family for twenty-three years. Who considered himself as friend."

Oh, shit.

"Niklavs." I face him, appalled. "Why didn't you tell them? Why don't you go to Gordon-Heyers? Talk to him? You said he's a good man. He'd listen, I'm sure he w—"

"Because sometimes there is truth a person does not want to hear." He rearranges the crutches, and pivots around.

"Him and wife were out of country. I was first to discover. There was no window broken, or door. No locks damaged. How, then, was there burglary at all? I sleep on site all night, and I see no one, hear nothing . . . except argument. Argument that I should not have heard, I think."

"What?" I squint up at him against the drizzle. "What argument?"

"About child."

"Wh—"

"Excuse me."

I jump, violently. I didn't even hear anyone behind us.

"I think you dropped something."

The girl's auburn hair falls over her face. She reaches to push it back with one hand and holds something out. But I barely see. I'm frozen, for a split second, scanning her forearms for scars. Trying to make out the colour of her eyes.

Beside us, the church bells chime eleven. I hear my own breath in.

"It's yours?" She thrusts it at me and I take it wordlessly. It's not. But it is. The Arrow receipt. My phone number. Someone has drawn a tiny bird in the corner. Niklavs? My head is throbbing. No. I swallow.

"Thanks," I mumble.

"I thought it looked important." She shrugs, and the spell breaks. Her eyes are blue, and her hair is dyed. The air escapes my lungs in a rush. Before I can formulate a reply, she's gone.

Niklavs has halted on his crutches a few paces ahead. I jog to catch him up, trying not to notice how shaky I am.

"What time you are back to work?" The moment's gone. I can't help the feeling that he's taking the opportunity to change the subject.

"Not for a bit." I shrug. I've told Sean I'll be back by midday. "What did you need from town?"

"Walk, and company." His bushy brows lift. "How about you?"

I turn to look at him, not sure whether to be perplexed or amused. "Nothing," I say. "It was you that wanted to come into town."

A smile glistens in Niklavs' sharp eyes. "Ah yes." He nods. "It was."

"Actually." I glance at the shop we're passing, something occurring to me. "I could do with something to read on the train."

The bell on the door jangles as I push it. I tiptoe inside through the muted maze of floor-to-ceiling bookcases. Niklavs is out of sight almost immediately, lost amongst maps and travel memoirs. The wooden floor creaks as I seek out *Fiction A-Z*.

"Can I help you?"

A woman has materialised from the darkness, wearing jogging bottoms and an enormous *Ramones* t-shirt that's stretched over her sizeable chest.

"Oh . . . uhm . . ." I stumble. "A book. I was looking for a book . . ."

She gazes at me, nonplussed. What a stupid thing to say, Livia. A book. No shit.

"Frost," I add hastily. "A R Frost. *Mercy's Child*? Do you have it?"

"A R Frost is here." She squeezes past me to show me, her index finger picking out an orange and grey graduated spine that I recognise straight away. "I've only got *Fellrunner* in at the moment. You're the second person today to ask. I can get it on order."

"Um . . ." I chew my lip. "Okay. Thanks. I'll come back."

I make a pretence of browsing some of the other titles on my way out. The glossy trendy-covered bestseller pile, the bargain bin by the door. Niklavs is waiting outside.

"You have not bought book," he observes.

"No." I watch the rubber ends of his crutches make purchase on the pavement. "I couldn't find what I was looking for."

What makes a story? What's in a book that makes you turn the pages? Keeps you up all night, makes you late for work . . .

"What kind of book you want? I have few English books at home. You are welcome to borrow."

I flush. "Oh, no. It's okay. Thanks, though. You know . . ." I glance at my watchless wrist, suddenly awkward. "I should probably get back."

"Mm-hmm." Niklavs doesn't look convinced.

"Do you need to . . . I mean . . ."

"I will stay in town." There's something astute in his smile. "I am sure I will find errand or two to run. You must go. Architect is waiting for you, I expect."

I don't miss the slightest flicker of his brows. If he only knew. I fight back a fresh, unbidden image of candlelight on sea-washed wood and skin. The velvet press of fabric covering my eyes, supple fingers securing it, travelling over my cheek to touch my lips. *Breathe, Livvy Frost.* I exhale sharply.

"I expect so," I mumble.

"*Drošs ceļojums*. Have safe journey, Livia."

"Thanks." I watch him wheel around on the crutches. *What kind of book*? Would he know? Would he know about Sophia Swift's kind of book? No. But there's someone else who might.

* * *

Katie's Mini is parked on the driveway at Trethallyan and I pull in beside it, decelerating to an abrupt halt. The Defender isn't there. Luck, or fate? My pulse is slightly too fast as I slip between the rhododendrons, my tread light on the path.

When Sophia hid her journal, she meant for someone to find it. And that someone couldn't have been me.

A veil of drizzle is clinging to my hair; I pause to look in the window under the pretence of tying it back. She's alone. I flip my phone onto airplane mode. It seems like a long time since I first came to this door with Ryan. Longer than three months. I open it.

Katie looks up. I catch sight of the plans on her laptop screen for a split second before she closes it. Plans that look suspiciously like the land registry documents for Trethallyan.

"Hey," I venture.

"Hey, Livs." She pushes the laptop aside. I hesitate.

"I'm still trying to write up the survey for Ryan," she explains, even though I haven't asked. "I meant to get it finished before today. I was hoping you'd be in, before I left."

"It's your last day." It strikes me suddenly. The first of April. Less than a week until my birthday. Tomorrow is Tom Rainworth's funeral. And Saturday's the wedding.

"Yeah." Katie nods. The pause is an upstroke. A pen in mid-air, not quite committed to paper.

"I'm glad you can come on Saturday," she says at last.

I nod. "Me too."

Silence. I wet my lips nervously.

"Katie . . ."

"Mh-hmm?"

"I want to talk about Sophia. I know you don't want to," I carry on quickly. "But it's important." I swallow. Somewhere outside, a bird takes flight in a flurry of wings and panic. I glance up, but there's no one there.

"I won't ask again, after this. I promise. I just . . . Did she seem like . . . Before she died, did she seem like she wanted to tell you anything? Like she . . ." I tail off.

"I don't understand why you're so interested." Katie shakes her head. She rises to her feet. "But no." She assesses me across the desk. "I don't think so. Sophia had secrets

— that much was obvious. But she wasn't crazy, if that's what you're asking. It's what everyone said, in the end. She wasn't . . . *okay*. I know that. But there was more to it than that. She was afraid, Livia. She was scared."

"Of something in her past?" I raise my eyes. We regard each other for a moment.

"I'm not sure that it *was* in the past." Katie's voice is very quiet.

What is it she's trying to say? I draw in a measured breath. What else — who else — could Sophia have been afraid of? She couldn't be suggesting . . .

Not safe ground . . .

I curl my fists inside my pockets. She's wrong. Whatever she thinks. She can't know. She hasn't seen the journal. She can't have. Even if Sophia meant for her to; even if she tried . . .

"Katie . . ." I falter. "Did she . . . Did Sophia ever give you anything?"

"Huh?"

"You know, like . . . gifts. Or . . . books, or anything?"

Katie regards me from beneath lowered brows. "Why?"

"Oh." I shrug, not quite meeting her gaze. "I just . . . wondered."

"She lent me a book." Katie's eyes don't leave my face. "Once."

Oh. A chill runs along my spine. "Do you still have it?"

"Yes." Katie folds her arms across her chest. "Are you going to tell me what's going on, Livs?"

"Nothing." I swallow. I can see she isn't fooled. "Nothing, really. What . . . what book is it?"

Katie's eyes narrow. "She lent me her copy of *Mercy's Child*. A few days before she died. But you already knew that, didn't you?"

Yes. My heart is thundering against my ribcage. I already knew.

"That's why you're asking, isn't it?"

Holy shit. I try to breathe slowly.

"I . . ." I curl my fingernails into my palms. "I wondered if I could borrow it."

"Livs, what—"

"I've . . . been wanting to read it."

"And you don't have a copy of your own?" Katie raises her eyebrows at me, disbelieving.

I shake my head. "Not here."

For a split second more, Katie stares at me. "You can borrow it if you want to." Her eyebrows lift tellingly. "But the ending's missing. Ripped out. I finished up downloading it from Amazon just for the last two pages."

Ripped out. I dig my fingers deeper into the flesh of my palms. The end of the book. Just like the journal . . . Why? What had it meant to her?

"Livia, are you sure you're alright?"

"I'm fine." My voice doesn't sound fine. "Thanks . . . thanks for talking." I fumble for my boots under my desk, and struggle into them. There's a stretching silence. I zip up my coat. Start for the door.

"I'll uh . . . I'd better . . ."

"I'll see you on Saturday, Livs." Katie's voice has softened. "Look after yourself."

I nod, mute. Outside, it's starting to rain again. It's hard to remember what the chapel looked like without rain, and its surrounding radius of mud. Hard to imagine that in a few more days we'll be ready. That we've ordered the oak frame.

At first, I can't make him out. I scan the footings, the remaining huddle of soaked contractors, the rain pooling on the concrete and block-work. He's there, hi-vis tied around his waist, hard-hat dangling jauntily from his hand, in a way that only he could carry off. And suddenly my mouth is dry, and all of the contractors' rapt attention seems fixed on the two of us: my stumbling halt, Sean's languid smile.

"Frost," he says.

"Hi." I clear my throat. Try to look serious. Business-like. His dark gaze burns with amusement.

"I'm glad to see you made it." He's been on site all day. On closer inspection, I see that his coat and shirt collar are drenched, his wet hair standing on end from the unconscious backwards thrust of his hand. "We're nearly done here. I was about to head down."

"Have you heard from Oakstill?"

"A week Tuesday, they think. Earliest." He plunges his free hand into his pocket.

"And the door?"

"Carl Williamson thinks he can do it, but he's away until the end of next week."

"I guess there's no point in taking it off until he can do something with it." I glance at the rusty hinges, the sturdy, unyielding lock. Graham Gordon-Heyers has only made it back from Exeter for one day all week. It somehow hasn't seemed the right time to press the issue of the key. Claire's driving the A30 almost every day with her arm in plaster — it turned out to be fractured — and Ryan seems to be everywhere else: checking in on the building work, balancing the ever-dwindling Trethallyan finances, making the school run in the relentless winds and April downpours. Only Fin seems oblivious, a flicker of white-gold light between the worried frowns and shadows, and I can't help wondering how many bedtime tears are stored, in secret, behind his outward silence.

"Are you okay?" Sean's soft voice makes me jump. I turn back, surprised at the question.

"Fine." The most overused of lies. I've never heard Claire say she isn't fine. Or Ryan. Or Graham. Or my father; my father was never not fine, even on the day he died.

"What time's your train?"

I check my phone. "In an hour."

"I'll give you a lift."

"No, it's okay." I fiddle with the phone cover. "I can drive — I'll leave my car at the station. You have to work."

"Fuck work." His fingers are over the middle of my back, skimming lightly to the nape of my neck. I gasp.

"I—" My gaze darts nervously to the contractors.

"I'll drive you." It isn't a question. I duck free, my cheeks on fire. Sean's eyes don't leave my face.

"Come on."

* * *

The minutes are gone before I realise the need to clutch at them. I leave my boots in the Defender, and he insists on carrying my bag onto the platform, even though it isn't heavy. The train's an old one, a squealing protest of brakes and aged groaning chassis that loses momentum at the last second to glide to a serpentine halt in front of us. Sean hands me my bag. We're the only people on the platform: an interlude show for two carriages of bored, watching faces. He leans forward to whisper.

"Are you sure you're going to be okay by yourself?" His hand cups my cheek. I frown.

"Of course I will."

Of course. Why, then, is my throat hurting so much?

"Good." He lets go of my cheek, his fingers brushing my lips. "Call me when you get there. I don't care what time it is."

"I will." I nod, jaw clenched.

"Promise?"

"I promise."

"Fuck, Frost, you make it hard to say goodbye." His teeth are gritted, too. "Get on the train, before I make you miss it."

It's over in seconds. The lingering by the filmy, scratched windows. The search for the reservation ticket in the carriage full of itchy empty seats. I sit down and curl my fingers through the strap of my bag, blinking furiously.

Goodbye. That's what this is all about, isn't it? Goodbyes. The ones that don't get said in time. Tom Rainworth, Sophia Swift, Toby, Dad. How many more will there have to be? How do we weather them? I lay my head against the prickly headrest, and close my eyes.

* * *

"We have come here today to remember before God our brother Tom. To give thanks for his life; to commend him to God our merciful redeemer and judge; to commit his body to be cremated, and to comfort one another in our grief . . ."

Yeah. I tighten my grip on the hymn book. Comfort. On one side of me, Kristopher is fiddling with the cuff buttons of his shirt. His tie knot is loose, lopsided. He never wears a suit. On the other side of me, my mother is keeping up appearances for the social circle she has never belonged to, but always wished she did. Right from the day of the *c* word she changed. Since my father died, she's reinvented herself entirely. She's started wearing make-up and dresses a size too tight, and holding cocktail nights instead of coffee mornings. She doesn't wear her wedding ring anymore.

We've never gone back. Barely touched. Barely spoken, since the funeral. It's my fault; I know it is. I didn't let her back in. She's tried, more than once. But I couldn't forgive her for the fact that she didn't love him enough. Enough to see it through to the bitter end. That during the weeks of intractable pain and waking nightmares, she spent more time with her ladies' group than at his bedside. That she ran away. She was his world, but in the end she hadn't loved him as much as he loved her. She hadn't loved him as much as I did. And when she cried, at his funeral, and not a single tear would grace my cheeks, it was too late. The distance had already established itself in our every stilted gesture and unspoken word.

I blink and look back up. The morbidly too-upbeat music that means something to someone has finally faded. Kris is still fiddling with his cuff button. I want to grab his arm and stop him, but my days as authoritative older sister are over. I push my hands into the pockets of my black coat. The chapel is cold. The priest is talking in a slow, lulling duotone.

". . . And now these three remain: faith, hope and love. But the greatest of these is love. Well, Tom was defined by love and generosity. The overwhelming feeling from his family and co-workers was that Tom was a man who loved. Indeed, so great was his love, that when he and Leanna were unable to . . ."

I glance away, not able to keep looking at the front, where Leanna is supporting herself against the seat beside her, one hand on her undeniably distended belly. She isn't crying, but the pallor in her face is unendurable. I let my gaze travel over the other seats and faces, deliberately avoiding Hannah's. The room's packed; they've had to leave the side doors open. I scan over them, then stop dead.

Sean Lorchann's suit is crisp black and immaculate, a jet tie-pin glinting in his charcoal tie as it catches the light. He isn't fiddling with his shirt cuffs. He's absolutely still. Astute, silent. Our eyes meet. I almost let go of the hymn book and fumble to save it, catching my sleeve on the service sheet and making it swish to the floor. I crouch down, face aflame.

"Tom was a devoted father. A colleague from the HR department at Rivent, where Tom worked for his own father for eight years, described how never a day went by without a mention of Toby. When Toby's life was tragically cut short in 2019, after—"

No, no, no. I don't want to hear it. I grit my teeth and try to think of something else. The oak frame, the locked door. The crash of waves. Rain on—

No. I turn. Sean hasn't moved. His brows flicker as he sees me looking. I suck in a deep breath, and Kris turns to look at me. Too late, I feel the line of his sight follow mine. I sense him stiffen.

". . . Now, let us pray. When I say *Lord Hear Us*, the response is *Lord, Graciously Hear Us.*

"Almighty God, we give you thanks for Tom and Toby. We thank you that whe—"

Oak frames. Picture windows. Prussian Blue and Davy's Grey. I bow my head. I have my own prayers; I pray them every night, in the dark. Like Sophia Swift, with her rosary beads. *She told me God would forgive me. But what's the point, if you can't forgive yourself?* My mother sniffs loudly beside me. Kris has turned back, tight-lipped and angry, his blue eyes burning into the side of my head. I stare at the service sheet. Line by line, second by second; it'll be over, eventually.

It is. I don't look up as the curtains close. As Leanna Rainworth bolts from her seat and out of the chapel, followed by her mother-in-law, a step behind. I only look up as the filing from seats starts, and I trail behind Kris out onto the paved terrace, littered with floral tributes and handwritten notes with messages that aren't heartfelt because nobody knows what to say. There's a milling silence that evolves into a low hum of sympathy. *Such a beautiful service. Lovely hymns.* The crowd begins to shift and fragment. I have the sudden urge to make a break for it, like Leanna, but Kris is stuck to me like a shadow. Perhaps it's because of the Dad thing, or the Toby thing. But I can't help noticing the stubborn set of his mouth, and thinking it's more likely to be the Sean thing.

"Livia, sweetheart." My mother, also, is adhering like glue. She touches my shoulder. "We should go and speak to Meredith and Michael."

We should? I swallow. We should.

"Uh-huh." I duck free of her hand. I can't see him, but I can feel him. At a watchful distance. Observing every movement. I follow my mother across the terrace.

Hannah is standing with her parents, her arm through Meredith's. It's hard to tell who's supporting who. Her waterfall of blonde hair half covers her face, and behind it her cheeks are the gaunt echo of tearstains that mine should have been, but never were. Not for Toby. Not for my father. Not for anyone. Not until the neglected gravel paths and unkempt rhododendrons of Trethallyan.

Hannah Rainworth. My oldest friend, who hates me because I'm my father's daughter. Like the cards and notes, I can't think what to say. My mother and Meredith hug stiffly, and Michael Rainworth holds out his hand to thank us for coming. I shake it, then Meredith's. By the time I get to Hannah, she's walked away, the heels of her shoes striking smartly on the paving slabs.

I drift beside my mother with the ranks of well-wishers towards the car park, where everyone is hovering awkwardly because no one wants to be the first to leave.

"I had no idea she was expecting."

My mother's voice makes me start. I turn.

"Leanna." My mother folds her handkerchief into her palm. "What would you say she is? Six, seven months?"

"I have no idea, Mum," I mumble.

"They always told her she couldn't . . . I mean, it wouldn't be possible, apart from egg donation . . . and Tom was always utterly against it, because it was *much* too dangerous—"

"Mum, really." I speak between my teeth. "I don't think now's the ti—"

"Meredith always said it would tip him over the edge—"

"*Mother*," I hiss. She falls silent. Kris is looking at me sideways, the accusation ready to burst from his lips.

I extract myself. "I have to find a toilet. I'll see you at the car."

I almost run across the terrace. The queue for the two cramped cubicles is half a dozen people long, and I stand in line, trying not to jiggle. My jaw is clenched so hard that my head's starting to ache. By the time I come out of the cubicle, the room has emptied, and I stand in front of the mirror for a good ten minutes fixing my hair and checking my eyes, as if I'd worn make-up that could have got smudged by the tears I haven't cried. I fasten my coat, and slip outside onto the terrace in the hope that everyone will have gone, or at least no one will notice.

". . . please. Stay away from my sister."

Kris's voice carries unmistakably through the flower arrangements. I dodge behind the door.

"That'll be difficult, Kristopher. She works for me."

"She doesn't need someone like you." Kris's voice is sharp. "I've heard about you. Oh yeah, fucking *all* about you, and the things you like to do with your so-called *girlfriends*."

Oh, shit. I roll my hands into my sleeves.

"Really." Sean is as unshakeably smooth as ever; I can sense my brother bristling under his uncompromising dark stare. Kris has never taken well to being patronised.

"It doesn't add up to me, Kristopher. That on the one hand you purport to know her so well. Yet on the other, you talk about her like she's weak, vulnerable — like she doesn't know her own mind."

"Oh, and *you* do? Is that i—"

"The Livia in there isn't weak. She's talented, audacious, strong. She outshines me — everyone — by a long way. I don't know what the deal is with you . . . fuck, I don't even really care. Livia can decide for herself."

"Who *are* you?" Kris's voice rises, heated. "You don't know anything. Anything at all. You have no idea. She's clearly told you *nothing*. Where she was this time last year . . . how much less 'strong' she looked in a hospital bed, eighteen months ago, when they held her down to put the feeding tube down her nose. You have no fucking *clue* where she's come from! No fucking clue at all!"

There's a painful pause. I feel myself shrink into the doorway. No. How can he? How can he do this to me? I can hear the realisation in Sean's silence.

"Perhaps," he replies at last. "But perhaps *you* have no idea where she is now. Perhaps she's stronger than either of us, for having come through it. Has that occurred to you? Has it occurred to you that maybe what she needs most is a little bit of trust?"

"It's not *her* I don't trust."

"Then that makes two of us."

"You should get out of here. She'll be out in a minute. You're not welcome here."

"Why don't we both wait, Kristopher, and I'll ask her myself?"

"Fuck you," Kris growls. I hear the soles of his shoes squeak on the concrete. I grind my nails into the palms of my hands. Three . . . two . . . one. I push open the door.

"Kris," I murmur. They both turn e. "Sean." I stop in my tracks. The raw intensity of his gaze takes me utterly off guard. For a moment, the world stands still.

"Livvy," he breathes at last. I feel Kris draw himself up to full height.

"Kris, go take Mum to the wake. Please. Sean and I will see you there."

I see him try to formulate a protest, and fail. He shakes his head. He doesn't even reply; he swings around the end post of the terrace and jumps the low wall to the car park, striding away across the tarmac.

Silence.

"So . . ." I venture at last.

"So." Sean's gaze gives nothing away. I take a deep breath, my chest crammed with a hundred words that I can't put together. I clear my throat.

"Why . . . Why are you here?"

He doesn't miss a beat. His eyes hold mine, level, intent.

"Because you are."

Oh. I swallow. What else was he going to say? Suddenly my mouth is dry.

"Do you know where we need to go?" He tugs his jacket sleeves straight. I blink up at him. He must have driven all day to get here. There isn't a single crease in his suit or shirt. His dark eyes are still focussed on my face.

"Yeah," I exhale. "Cathedral House. In the city. For three. I have the postcode."

"It's three now. Shall we go?"

"I . . ." I falter. "I really don't want to go to the wake."

Sean's eyebrows lift.

"No one's going to thank you — or me — if you do a disappearing act."

"No." I stare at my feet. At my much too polished black high-heeled shoes. I hate heels. My toes are already a world of pain.

"What were you planning to do?" His eyes narrow a fraction.

"Get there. Slip away." I study the patent leather. "It's not far from the station."

"You don't need to go to the station anymore," he points out.

"It's a seven-hour drive to Porthtrevelen." I pull my coat around me, trying to avoid his scrutiny.

"I know," he remarks dryly. "I just came that way."

"Sean . . ." I look up. There's no point in trying to argue with him. The conviction in his dark, molten eyes swamps me. I let go of my coat, and his fingers slip through mine, his thumb tracing a path from my palm to the inside of my wrist that makes me stiffen with sudden, carnal need.

"Come on," he murmurs.

* * *

The hotel is high-end and ultra-modern, all silvers, blacks and creams with echoing polished stone floors, and mirrors everywhere. I hate mirrors. I focus assiduously on not seeing my reflection, and try not to turn an ankle in my stupid shoes as we navigate the ice-rink-smooth floors. The function room is vast, a whole wall of tiered tables set out with food — more food than I can imagine even the couple of hundred funeral mourners being able to eat. I can't help pondering the way that people turn out for the dead. I'm pretty sure I don't know two hundred people to invite, if I were to throw a party. Strange, then, how people materialise from the woodwork when you die.

Morbid, Livia. I teeter across the room towards the tables, with Sean half a step behind me and still not touching me, not quite. There were a lot of people at my father's funeral, too. People I had no idea even existed. Literary types, people from London, a whole side of his existence I'd never known.

Everyone else is already indulging; chatting, eating. Drinking, which somehow doesn't seem appropriate given the circumstances of Tom Rainworth's demise. I take a tea plate and load it with two quarter sandwiches, which I have no intention of eating. I couldn't feel less hungry. I accept a wine glass from Sean, and grip it with cold fingers.

"You know her?"

"Huh?" I glance up at him, startled. Follow his line of sight to the far corner, where a board of photos and a memory book are propped up on a white-clothed table. Hannah Rainworth's grey-green eyes corrode for a split second more into my face. Then she sees me looking, and her head snaps around to look the other way.

"I did once."

"Right." His arm moves closer into my waist. Still not touching. *Just touch me.* I'm rigid, trembling. *You're here. Why don't you?*

"Livia, sweetheart. There you are. I didn't know if you were here . . . I was completely confused; Kristopher said. . . Oh."

Shit. I close my eyes.

"This must be . . . must be . . ."

"Sean," I exhale. "Mum, this is Sean. My uh . . ."

"Mentor. Mrs Frost, it's nice to meet you. Sean Lorchann."

Sean Lorchann, architect. For fuck's sake. They're shaking hands. I'm not sure if I want to open my eyes again or not. Not.

"It's lovely to meet you, Sean. It must have been a long way out of your way to come here, just to drive Livia back. Although I must say I'm glad she's not getting the train. I did try to persuade her to stay another night at the Travelodge with Kristopher and me. Do you know what time that train was due in? Ridiculously late. And after—"

"Mother." There's no choice. I cut in before she can get any further.

"Livia." She turns her attention back on me. "Have you spoken to Hannah yet?"

"No." I grind my teeth.

"I'm sorry." Sean takes a step sideways. "Please, excuse me just for a moment." He touches my mother's arm lightly, and flashes her a gut-churningly insincere smile. I watch, disbelieving, as he disappears into the milling horde of people.

You were strong for them, Livvy. For all of them, after Toby died. What did my father know? What did he know about it? *Everyone said how strong you were.* Strong, hiding behind the wheelie bins in the cemetery car park with Hannah Rainworth's head cradled in my lap. Without a single word to say to console her. I hadn't been strong. I'd been guilty. Clueless. Just as I am now.

"You really ought to speak to her." There's a note of reproach in my mother's voice.

Ought to? Like my mother *ought* to have sat with my father while he rambled and sweated. While he died?

"She doesn't want to speak to me." I put down my wine.

"This isn't still about the boo—"

"It doesn't matter, Mum." I shake my head. "Leave it. Her brother's dead. It's bad enough for her that we're even here."

"Michael insisted we came. You know how close he was to y—"

"Yes," I breathe. "I know."

"Livia."

I start.

"My apologies." Velvet-smooth, catlike, Sean slides back in beside us. "I'm afraid something urgent has come up." Something urgent? I frown. Did his phone ring? I didn't hear it. "Was there anyone else you needed to see before we go?"

Kristopher. I scan the crowd, then shelve the idea. Perhaps I don't need to see Kris just now.

"No," I reply. "No one."

"It's been a pleasure to meet you, Mrs Frost." Sean holds out his hand again, and grasps my mother's firmly. I feel her protest thaw in the face of his charm. "Sorry to drag Livia away so soon. Perhaps you'll visit Porthtrevelen at some point and see her project?"

My project? My head snaps up. But he's looking the other way.

"You have a project?" My mother's voice has softened. And for a moment, there in her eyes is the old Mum, the one that I baked brownies with on Saturday mornings and cried to about hopeless teenage crushes and cat-fights. The one that helped me obsessively cut out pictures from *Country Home* and *Exterior Face*, and saved them for my scrapbook.

I swallow. "Yeah," I whisper.

"I'd like to see it," she says.

I pause. "I'd . . . like that too," I lie. "Love you, Mum."

"I love you too, sweetheart."

What's with the glint of tears in her eyes? I move hastily away, suddenly terrified that she might hug me.

"Bye, Mum."

The foyer is surprisingly quiet. I traverse the polished floor more quickly than I did the first time, and stop by the reception desk.

I turn to Sean. "Where are we going?" He jerks his head, and I follow him as he strides to the lifts and punches the call button.

"You haven't eaten anything," he points out. The doors open, and he steps back to let me go first. I pause.

"No."

"Did you have breakfast? Lunch?"

"Um . . ." I direct my attention quickly to the glowing outlines of the lift buttons. "Which floor?"

"Two." We ride the rest of the way in silence. I can see his reflection in the mirrored panels. More mirrors. I find myself studying the profile of the back of his suit in triplicate. We step out onto plush grey carpet; I match his strides to where rows of tiny starry lights mark out the edges of three descending steps. The chink and clink of cutlery on fine china betrays our destination before I even see the sign. Sean holds open the door to the almost-empty restaurant.

"You need to eat." It isn't a question. A waiter arrives to escort us to a table. I sit, and Sean takes the seat opposite. And, finally, his skin touches mine, a dance of his fingertips across my knuckles, the momentary pressure of his legs against mine as he pulls in his chair. I catch my breath.

"Here?" I croak.

"I have a room." His voice gives nothing away.

I raise my eyes to his face. Sean folds his arms, and my pulse skips. His eyes meet mine.

"Since when?" I ask, a whisper.

"Five minutes ago when I booked it at reception."

I pick up a menu, and pretend to look at it. "How much did *that* cost?"

"A lot less than I would have paid, right now," he says darkly. Already the crematorium, my mother, Hannah Rainworth, the argument with Kris, are fading from my mind. Desire is pooling in my abdomen instead, hot and forbidden. I grip the menu tightly.

"I saw you and Kris talking."

There's a pause. Sean doesn't reply. I lower the menu to look at him.

"I got the impression he doesn't really like you."

"He doesn't." A wry smile plays at the corner of Sean's mouth. "But I suggested to him that perhaps he needs to credit you with a little trust."

I swallow. The low conversation in the restaurant around us seems to have dwindled into nothing. I drop my gaze.

"I'm not sure that I've done much in the past to earn his trust," I whisper.

Sean's smile fades. He reaches out to take the menu. I don't stop him. He tugs it gently from my hands.

"Have *I* earned your trust, Livia?" His voice is very soft. Serious. "How much do you trust me?"

How much? I look up, incapable of reply. How much? More than I should. More than I trust anyone. My body is trembling, tense and waiting; my heart breaking rhythm in mutiny against my ribs. I don't say it. I watch him read it from my eyes. From the breath I draw between my lips, from the smallest tremor of my fingers as I reach with all the control I can muster to pick up the slim ivory reservation card from the centre of the tablecloth. He booked the table, too.

I order at his example and eat at his insistence, although barely; the food is rich, composed to perfection, a symphony that falls on deaf ears. I can't taste anything. Anything except the prickle of nerves, the citrus tang of anticipation, the smoky aftertaste of longing. He orders coffee instead of dessert and sips it slowly while I nibble an after-dinner mint. After dinner . . . it isn't even after six. Golden sunshine is still spilling through the windows in apologetic puddles as we climb the wide staircase to the third floor. The door closes behind us with a click.

"Livvy," he growls.

I grab his arms, push his jacket from his shoulders, stumble as he pulls me into him, my dress cascading downwards and pouring over our shoes. The sunlight through the heavy voile curtains is the colour of embers, the bedcovers white in a modern black four-poster with no canopy. We bypass it, kicking off our shoes on the bathroom tiles. His shirt is damp with sweat; he pulls me into the vast shower with him and turns it on, and the deluge of hot water drenches us both instantly, driving my hair into my eyes. The designer cotton is sticking to his chest. Very deliberately he stands back to undo his cufflinks and reaches around the gleaming glass screen to lay them beside the sink, watching me struggle out of my sodden tights as the steam blossoms around us. He peels off his shirt and I hear the ring of his belt-buckle on the tiles. Then he strides forward, a single swift movement, and pushes his hands back through my hair to take my mouth with his.

"Do you try intentionally to drive me out of my mind?" His teeth tug at my lower lip. "Or does it just come naturally to you?"

My breathing is ragged and shallow; the tiles are slick and slippery under my feet. Sean seizes one of the miniature branded bottles from the shelf behind me and pours its perfumed contents into his hand.

"Still trust me?" He turns me away from him, his lips against the nape of my neck.

"Yes," I gasp.

"Good."

The shampoo is cold. He moves slowly, kneading, caressing, teasing it through every tangled, sodden lock of my hair. And maybe he *is* bad for me. Maybe Kris is right. Or maybe, just maybe, there's a chance we can both find our Eden — if not our redemption — in the things we try to deny ourselves.

I take the soap when he's finished. Smooth it over his skin, crush it through his wet jet hair until he catches my wrists to stop me. He turns off the shower. His eyes on mine are endlessly dark.

The towels are small, and faintly abrasive from over-washing. The bedroom's warm. Two white robes hang on the back of the door; Sean moves to lift one from its hook. His free hand cups my cheek, lifting my chin to kiss me again.

"Oh, Livvy," he breathes. "Do you have any idea how much I need you?"

My arms are trembling. His voice is low, a jagged murmur against my ear.

"All you have to say is stop," he breathes. "Remember that."

I do remember, briefly. But thought gives way to colour, a consuming dance of shadow and of fire. I'm only sensation, with his fist wound tight in my damp hair to turn my face towards him, his lips capturing mine. I'm Gold Ochre, Crimson and Carmine, shot through with darkness: Winsor Violet and Perylene Black; his, in every way he wants me.

He lets go of my hair. His fingers weave through mine as he takes me. Like the sea dancing with the land, the lust has got too strong, and we'll destroy ourselves before we refuse it.

"Livia . . ." he chokes out, and the word is harsh and reverent.

For a second we're both still. Trembling, entwined, locked in the urgent ache of physical relief.

I open my eyes. The silence is intense, his expression raw and suddenly unguarded. He bows his head to kiss me, our mouths salty with sweat, and the repressed tremor in his hands is enough to break my heart.

Finally, he gets up to hang our wet clothes over the towel rail. My overnight bag is at the foot of the bed beside his; someone must have brought them to the room ahead of us. I retrieve the robe and slide to my feet to check. Definitely mine. I pad to the window and part the curtains to look down into the road below. The street lights are on. My mother and Kris's car has gone.

"Why didn't you tell me? About what you went through?"

I turn around, startled. Sean is watching me from a distance.

"What do you mean?"

"Kris told me."

There's no room for pretence. I wrap the robe around me, all at once glad that it covers me from neck to ankles.

"I . . ." I hesitate. Fight my way through the rewind of stop-motion images, clinic scales, gowns and masks, tape measures, tubes, Elastoplast. Calories on cardboard, Wollaton Park. Speed equals distance over time.

I swallow. "I didn't want you to look at me like that. Like everyone else does. Like I . . . Like I'm weak. Broken."

His feet make no sound on the carpeted floor. He reaches me in a few strides, his face clouded.

"Oh, Livvy." He lifts the unruly spirals of hair back from my cheek to tuck them behind my ear, presses his lips to my forehead. I can hear his breathing, slow and not quite even. "How could you have imagined I'd think that?"

"I didn't . . . I just . . ." I look at the floor. At the chipped nail varnish on my toes.

"Look at me." He lifts my chin with two fingers. "We all have scars. Some are just buried deeper than others. The things you've defeated only make you more beautiful, more incredible. Don't you see that?"

Defeated. If only he knew. I avoid his eyes. There's no such thing as defeat. There are days when the voice is quieter, subdued. Days, whole weeks — even months — when the walls I've built around that dark, bottomless pool of thoughts are strong enough to contain it. But there's no defeat. All it takes is one wayward idea. One skipped meal. One second's weakness . . .

"No one . . ." I speak between clenched teeth. "No one gets to find this out, okay? No one gets to know this. This is the past. This isn't me anymore."

He releases my chin, straightens the robe instead, drawing it tightly around me before he lets me go. He moves away, picks up the duvet; I watch as he remakes the bed: folding back the covers with such precision that, for a split second, I can't help but think about Fin's much-too-tidy bedroom and the Spider-Man bedspread without a single crease.

"But it was?" His question startles me. I glance up.

"Was what?"

"You. It isn't you anymore . . . but it was, once?"

I close my eyes.

"It . . ." The truth. He's right; there's no solace in the truth. "It always could have been. I . . ." I pause. "It wasn't. Not quite. But then Dad got ill. Things were . . . And then . . ." I move to the bed, too. Run my fingernails over the wooden post, studying the grain. Steeling myself. "Then there was the Rainworths' ruby wedding, 2019." The ninth of August, a date that will never erase itself from my mind. "I was best friends with their daughter. Hannah Rainworth . . . the girl you saw at the wake. Tom Rainworth's sister . . ." My nails bite into the wood; I grip it hard. "And . . . and . . ."

"The kid that died," Sean interjects softly.

"I was there." I raise my eyes to his. "I was there, that night . . . I was there. I . . . should have checked on him." I let go of the bedpost. Screw my fingers into my palms, where they can't shake. Where they can't touch anything to reinforce the memory; the creaking panelled door. The ring of metal around the porthole.

"Livvy . . ."

"He was crying," I carry on before I can lose momentum, before my courage can desert me. The words are tumbling out in the wrong order, garbled and illogical. "I was supposed to get Hannah, and I couldn't find her. I couldn't find her . . . I should just have just gone myself. I should have gone straight to him. And I didn't. I didn't. And when I did, he was gone. Gone. I . . . I didn't go down in time. He was . . . he was . . ."

"Fuck," he breathes. "Livvy—"

"They never even found his body." I forgot about the nausea. How strong it can get, how quickly. I try to force it back: the taste of champagne. "The coastguard. Lifeboats. They searched all night. Only his blanket in the sea. Some fabric from his pyjamas a few weeks later, on a beach on the Isle of Wight . . ."

"You didn't want to look after Fin." Sean sits slowly on the edge of the bed, eyes dark with realisation.

"How could I? Whatever they said, I was responsible. Partly, at least. I mean, it was nothing to do with me — it wasn't my fault — they all said that. Everyone said that, that it wasn't my fault. But it was. Because if I'd gone straight down. If I'd gone to him . . ."

I can't breathe it away. The nausea. I'd learned how to breathe it away. Slowly, not too deep, or it gets worse. I can already feel the prickling in my lips, my fingertips. I sit down, too.

"Then, six months later, Dad died. And I . . . I don't know. I just wanted to carry on. If I kept busy enough, if I didn't let it in . . . I went back to uni, and it was . . . it was the only thing left that I felt like I could control. It was so . . . real. Clean, somehow. The emptiness. I don't . . ." I scrunch the bedcovers in my hands. "I don't think I could make you understand. And I . . . I wouldn't want you to, anyway."

"I might understand better than you realise, Livia." Sean's voice is achingly soft.

"What . . . do you mean?" I pause, remembering dinner with Ryan, and the argument at the cove. Remembering

Claire, the seat by the overgrown pond: *Sean's never spoken about it at all.* And something shifts. A sudden, irrefutable certainty. I let go of the duvet.

"You're talking about your mum?"

"Like I said." He stands up abruptly. "We all have scars."

The conversation's over. In an instant, the darkness has fallen over his face. I let out my breath. Sean crosses the floor to draw the curtains; I watch the way he moves, the way he breathes. And I think of ruby balloons and kissing in the rain. Of the girl in the dandelion stems, dancing and dancing. Of sandcastles, and a lonely little brown-haired boy with umber eyes who won't let people in.

I never cried for Toby Rainworth. I dash a fierce hand across my cheeks. Never for myself, not even for my father. So how is it that in the twilight, stripped to the soul, it's this man that takes my tears and makes them his? *Sean Lorchann, architect.* This man. The one I can't want. The one whispered warning. The man that tried everything he could think of not to love me.

CHAPTER 24

My body is prickling with sweat. The covers are on the floor. Whatever woke me is impossible to place, but my heart's thumping, and I can't quite catch my breath in the heavy blanket of darkness. I can hear cars, brakes. Nottingham traffic. The crescendo of a bike racing down Castle Boulevard—

No. I sit up, disorientated. I'm on the wrong side of the bed. The orange glow of street lights is from a window, not a skylight; the faintest chill of a breeze breaks in with the Doppler shift of another car. The air is stuffy, conditioned, hotel-room air. Not Nottingham. I can hear the blood in my ears. A hotel room. Greys and blacks and mirrors. Bathrobes. I swing my legs out of bed.

Sean Lorchann is by the window. The floor-length silver curtains are parted a few inches, the draped voile behind them lifting in the draught. The window is open a crack; his hand is still on the lever, white-knuckled. I stop. He's half in shadow, obscured by the fall of the curtain, his back and shoulders tense and glistening with sweat. I stand still. He doesn't move.

"Sean . . ."

He spins round to face me. He's breathing fast, deep shuddering breaths. Panic grips my gut.

"Sean?" I cross the floor to join him. For a moment, he doesn't reply. I reach out to touch him, and withdraw my hand quickly. His skin is cold. How long has he been there?

"What is it?" My pulse has accelerated again. "What's wrong?"

"Nothing." The roughness in his voice startles me. I step back, unnerved.

"A dream," he clarifies. He lets the curtains drop, plunging us into shadow.

"What dream?" I'm emboldened by tiredness. I slip my arms around his waist. Feel every tight, hard muscle of his abdomen, the sheen of sweat on his skin. I wet my lips.

"What dream?"

"The same dream." His fists are still clenched. "The same dream as every other night." He breaks away from me. "Except now, when I open the door, it's not her."

Not her? I frown up at him.

"It's not her." His teeth are gritted. "I break the lock, I open it, and I go in, and find her. Hanging there, just hanging there . . . but it isn't her." His gaze is a black hole, endless with dread "It isn't her. It's you."

"Oh." I suck in a sharp breath.

"It's you . . ." He closes his eyes. Opens them again. "*You*. And I can't . . . I can't . . ."

"It's a dream," I whisper. "Just a—"

"What if it isn't?" He rounds on me. "What if it *isn't*? Jesus Christ." His fingers clench in his hair, pulling it in handfuls. "Who fucking showers before they hang themselves?"

"Sean . . ." I try to be rational, but I'm sick and dizzy with sleep.

"No." He shakes his head. His mouth is a stubborn line. "No. That place. You can't . . . I won't . . ." He releases his hands and I watch his fingers uncurl. "Don't go back there. If I have to beg you, Livia, I will. Fuck, I'll move everything myself. Wherever you want me to take it, just not there."

"It's a month's notice." My voice is a croak. "That's all."

I swallow. Look up at his earnest, impassioned eyes. A month. I'll call the estate agent in the morning. First thing. I'll find a way to explain to Niklavs somehow, dodge the questions at work. Even if I have to take a room elsewhere.

"I won't," I add, under my breath. "I won't spend another night there."

"I need you to promise." It's soft, painful. Sean moves to hold me, his lips brushing my temple; the words make something ache deep in my chest.

"I promise." I respond without thinking. Without hesitation. Of course I promise. I'd promise him anything . . . Swift's words are seared in my mind, impossible to erase.

Anything.

* * *

"I said I'd have Fin tonight." Sean turns to look at me, snapping me abruptly out of my reverie. The roads are gridlocked; we're going nowhere. "Are you okay with that?"

"Sure." I glance up. I'm not even sure what I've been thinking about.

"I thought we could take him and Max down to Clandine Cove." Finally, we're moving. Sean takes off the handbrake, and the Defender crawls into second gear.

"We." I squint against the clear April sunshine, uncertain. "You want me to come?"

"Yes." His eyes are warmed by something I can't name. Amusement, sincerity. "I want you to come. They're away for the night. I said I'd stay."

As if that makes it better. My cheeks are smarting.

"What . . ." I stumble over the question. "But . . ."

"Fin likes you. He trusts you. And he's not exactly going to tell anyone, is he?"

"I guess not." I fiddle with a thread on my sleeve. We ride for a while in silence.

"Is Max at Ryan and Claire's?"

"He's at the Hall."

"With Graham?"

"Mm-hmm."

Picturing it evokes a painful memory of Tess and Dad.

"Does Fin like him?"

"More than he likes most people." A wry smile plays on Sean's lips. There's a distinct hint of irony in the way he says it. His hand is on the gearstick between us and I have the sudden unbidden urge to reach out and touch it.

"With Fin . . ." I start, then trail off. "Was he . . . Did he always . . . Has he never . . . ?"

"He can talk." Sean's voice is quiet. "If that's what you're asking."

Oh. It is, and I'm not prepared for the answer. I falter, unnerved by the look on his face.

"I know he can." He's looking straight ahead out of the windscreen, not at me. "He has bad dreams."

Silence. I don't know what to say. Sean shakes his head. "You think that's going to help them? Any of them?"

"I . . ." I turn to look at him. *I didn't speak much.* The brown-haired boy. The ethereal nephew. I realise I'm frowning.

"You mean, he can—"

"I've heard him. When he was alone. Ryan and Claire were out late. One night, not long after they moved back. I stayed with him. He has bad dreams. He called out, when he was waking up. He can talk. He's just chosen not to."

"You think . . . ?" I scour his face, unsure how to read the flicker of darkness in his expression.

"My mother died when I was five, Livia. I didn't speak for a year. Whatever his reason, he'll talk when he's ready."

And there it is — just like that. Bare and matter-of-fact. Half of the pieces fall instantly into place. The rest still don't fit; like two jigsaws, not one, that've accidentally been scrambled together. I realise I'm biting my lip.

"Was it . . . something in Dubai?" I venture. "The move?"

"Who's to know?" His shrug is stilted, somehow. "He sees a psychologist, a speech therapist, whoever else they think will help. I'm sure they intend to get to the bottom of it."

"But *you* don't think they will?"

"I think he's made a decision and we should respect it." His voice is quiet. "He's a bright kid. He communicates when he needs to."

"He was a baby when they moved there, wasn't he?"

"Mm. Not much more." He indicates to change lanes. "He was nearly two."

"Was he talking then?"

"I don't know." He shrugs again. "I was in Norway, finishing my research project. I saw him when he was about a year old — Ryan was still working weekdays in the office at Lorchann McLeod, then. They were going to a wedding and couldn't take him with them. My father and I had him for four days. He was saying words — car, mostly." He shrugged. "Just starting to walk."

I open my mouth, then close it again quickly, biting back my next question. Sean's face has darkened, some memory or regret that I've stumbled upon without meaning to. What was it he said about scars? I look at my hands. Isn't there a point in time when they need un-burying? I'm not sure.

"He's special to you. I mean . . ." I fold my hands in my lap. "Not just as a nephew. Isn't he? It's more."

Silence. I shoot a sideways glance at his face. At his low brows and the stubborn set of his lips, and the hint of vulnerability in his guardedness that I've never noticed, until today.

"He reminds you of yourself." It slips out before I can curtail it. The only thought in my mind. *Troubled . . . Different.* But they aren't *so* different, are they? I think of Makaton, Lego, Lost Boys. Sean's jaw clenches, unclenches. For a long time, he doesn't say anything at all. He tightens his grip on the wheel.

"He's not me." His expression has hardened. "He's not mine."

"No," I breathe. There's an edge to his voice that unsettles me.

"But I feel like I could help him." He turns to me suddenly. "In ways that they don't. Can't. They don't understand him."

"But you do?"

"I might." He looks back out of the windscreen.

He has bad dreams. And he's not the only one. I swallow, study the profile of his shoulders again, tense and aching, just like in the stifled darkness of 2.00 a.m. A dream. *I don't let people in.* I hesitate.

"Sean . . ." I whisper. He glances back.

"What?"

"Just . . ." I pause. "Not all memories are scars. But if they are . . . you don't always have to bury them, right?"

"Right." He nods. But there's no agreement in his eyes as he looks away. Only an aching certainty that, somehow, no number of words or promises will ever quite undo.

* * *

"Second to the right!" I'm breathless, panting. The fresh April air burns the base of my lungs. "And straight on 'til morning!"

Fin, apparently tireless, has scrambled up onto his third successive seaweed-covered rock. He puts out his arms and wobbles. I smile, stoop to roll up the bottoms of the legs of my jeans. Fin hops neatly to the next rock and raises a hand to point.

"Is that Neverland?" I start across the wet sand after him, little ice-cold wavelets lapping at my bare feet. We cast off our shoes long ago, at the top of the cove, along with Max's lead and Sean's coat. Neither Max nor Sean are in sight now, although every so often an excited yelp or Sean's low whistle carries on the wind from the clifftop.

Fin nods. An impish grin spreads over his face.

"Come on, then." I smile. Fin lifts his arms, and takes an almighty leap down from the last rock. Shards of water explode everywhere, shattering like glass and reflecting the evening sunshine in a thousand directions as they scatter.

He's standing calf deep in water, immobile, a look of pure terror on his face. The tide must have crept further in than either of us realised; shallow waves are breaking gently around his legs. He looks down; I see his small shoulders heave and shudder as he looks at the water rolling over his bare feet. His mouth opens a fraction. For a split second, I think he's going to call out, even whisper his distress.

But he doesn't. At the last moment he seems to remember, and his jaw clenches tight. I hurry to his aid.

"Fin?" I hold out a hand to him, uncertain. To touch or not to touch? He raises huge eyes to my face.

"Are you okay?" I wade in beside him. The salt water is bone-achingly cold; it soaks my rolled jeans in an instant. Fin looks at the dark splodges spreading through the denim, then back at his own saturated trousers. He lifts one foot gingerly, then the other, watching the swirl of sand as a wave tumbles in around our legs. And, like a dispersing storm, his expression clears. I see the tension evaporate from him. He lifts his foot higher. Then, before I can react, he stamps it into the next breaking wave, and we're both drenched from head to toe. I gasp, splutter.

"Finbar Lorchann!" I dash the water from my eyes, disorientated.

Suddenly, Fin's laughing. Silent, paroxysmal giggles that hijack his breathing and flush his pale face with colour. He raises his left foot, dripping, and I dart away before he has the chance to bring it down.

"No way!" I'm laughing too, gasping. "Don't you dare!" I break into an unbalanced run, leaping over the wavelets to get out of his range. Fin hesitates, and then sets off in hot pursuit, ploughing through the edge of the tide. He catches me up at the other end of the glistening strip of beach, and I jog backwards onto the white-gold sand, flicking back my damp hair from my eyes.

"That really wasn't very kind!" I try to sound stern, but my irrepressible smile renders the reprimand completely null and void. Fin grins. He tugs at his coat, watching the droplets roll over his front and into his trousers.

"We're soaked!" I gaze woefully at my shrunken jeans and clinging hoody. Fin closes one eye and squints up at me, appraising. He takes three more jumps up the sand, and then launches himself in the direction of the rocks, leaving a triplet of sets of footprints in his wake that fill slowly with water as I watch. I move to dry myself and pull on my socks and boots, listening to the little hollow splashes of Fin dropping pebbles into the rock pools, his spiky tuft of blond hair sticking up between the rocks. My thoughts drift to the flat, and the promise I still haven't acted on. There's no way I'm calling Simon. But I don't have the number for the estate agent; it's on my fridge and I'll have to go back for it. It's too late, today. It's Friday afternoon — the office will be closed by now. There's no point in bringing it up.

I finish tying my laces and pause, unnerved by the sudden silence. The splashes have stopped. I straighten. Fin's hair has vanished.

"Fin?" A cold fist tightens in my chest. "*Finbar*?"

He's gone. It's all I can think. All I can process. The sea is sucking at the shore, hungry, and the noise is so familiar — *lapping, beckoning* — that I can't move. Can't breathe—

The first clap echoes off the cliff face, cutting through the burbling semi-silence, and I don't even realise what it is. Not until the next one, the next: slow, mournful applause that reverberates around the rocks. A chill runs down my neck.

"Fin?!" I stumble forwards, seized with shivers. "Fin, are you okay? *Fin*?" I'm scrambling over seaweed and abrasive granite.

I come to a sudden stop.

He's crouched down, still clapping, his hands raw with cold. His small body is hunched over, so that I almost can't make out what he's looking at. There in the puddles of salt water is a seagull. It's huge; even dead and bedraggled it must be half as big as him. Its one intact wing is sprawled on the sand, trampled and bloodied, its body a macabre mound of feathers that are starting to smell. *Do you believe?* I realise, suddenly. *If you believe, clap your hands. Don't let her die.*

"Fin," I whisper. "I think it's too late."

He doesn't relent. He stands up slowly, palms still clasped tightly together.

"You don't need to clap anymore." I swallow. "I know you've done your best. But he's . . . really . . ." I waver. "We were too late. He died before you found him. I'm sorry."

Finbar looks up. He shakes his head vehemently. I pause. "Shall we go and find Max and Uncle Sean?"

Another shake of the head. I regard him, helpless.

"Maybe we can bury him?" I look back at the seagull. So does Fin. I touch his shoulder without thinking. He's cold and shivering, too.

"I'm sorry he's dead. It's good that you tried."

He nods, once. I steel myself, regretting the offer almost immediately. It's going to have to be a burial in situ; not even Fin's desolate dark stare is going to persuade me to pick the rotting carcass up. I glance around for something to use beside my bare hands. The fact is, the tide will claim the gull by sunset.

The brief funeral is a silent affair; I can't think of any fitting words of send-off. By the time we're done, with a covering of white shells sown by Fin like seeds over the top of the makeshift grave, Sean's silhouette is growing larger at the other end of the beach. Within seconds Max is upon us, butting his way between us to lick Finbar's hand.

We walk back to Trethallyan, shadows long, with Fin on Sean's shoulders and Max at our heels. I wrap the leather leash around my hand, overly conscious of its smell, lost in thoughts of where we started: fool's gold and the view of the Witch's Cat. The Gatehouse is aglow with low sunshine; we eat supper in the conservatory, watching the sunset, and Sean carries a sleeping, mop-haired Fin to bed as I clear up. *Not me. Not mine.* But the way he holds him, the stubborn pout, playful smile, silence — if you didn't know, it wouldn't be hard to get the wrong idea altogether.

I creep to the spare room like a fugitive. Like the rest of the house, it's airy, all designer fabrics, oak floorboards and expensive rugs. I draw the curtains and shove my overnight bag under the side of the bed. Something falls out from the other side with a crash. I tiptoe around to put it back, and stop.

A box of paperwork The lid has come off, knocked askew by my bag. And in the corner of the box is a key.

I stoop to pick it up, a strange feeling in the pit of my stomach. It's old: dull heavy iron with a heart-shaped ring. I turn it in my hands. There's a name inscribed in the top curve: J Wright & Son. I trace it with my fingernail. J Wright & Son. The name of the locksmith in 1921.

The key to the chapel. It has to be. My mouth is suddenly dry. The spare key. The one that everyone thinks is lost. Except it isn't lost. It's here, under the spare bed with the bags of old pillows in a box of paper marked *shredding.*

Why would Claire have hidden it? Does she know it's here? How could she not? She's made up the bed, and the writing on the storage box is hers. I flip up the duvet, and frown into the shadows. There's nothing else there. Nothing it could have been caught up in; nothing except the paper that doesn't quite fit its box. Morbidly curious, I take out the top sheet.

Mrs Claire Lorchann

Overcoming Depression — The Cognitive Behavioural Approach.

Avoiding Avoidance. From Red to Green: Pathways Through Anxiety.

Call Samaritans — No Names, No Pressure, No Judgement. We're here for you. Any time.

Huh? I can feel the frown furrowing my forehead. I really need to stop looking. It's obviously private.

But I can't. I thumb through another few sheets, hands shaking.

Clinic Date 18/12/2021
Dear Parent or Guardian,
RE: Finbar Lorchann D.O.B 06/08/2017

I was sorry not to see Finbar for his appointment in the Children's Development Centre today . . .

12th January 2022

I hope this letter finds you well. An appointment was arranged for Finbar at Children's Speech and Language Therapy. I am sorry that you were unable to attend . . .

09/02/2022

I am sorry that you and Finbar were unable to keep your appointment at the tier 2 assessment today. Please contact the Child and Adolescent Mental Health Services hub on the number below if a further appointment is required.

Clinic Date 25/02/2022

. . . as Finbar has now missed three appointments at the Children's Development Centre, I will assume that he is well and our follow-up is no longer required. I have therefore discharged you back into the care of your general practitioner.

Yours sincerely,
Dr M Staniforth
Consultant Community Paediatrician
Checked and signed electronically to avoid delay.

A psychologist. A speech therapist. *He spends enough time in hospitals* . . . I rise to my feet, tremulous. But he doesn't, does he? He hasn't been. Not to a single one. I'm vaguely nauseated. Claire's been lying. To me. To Sean . . . To Ryan? I stare at the letters. She told Ryan they were going, and he believed her; I was there. Does *anyone* know? Does anyone know the truth? And *why*? It doesn't make sense. I push the paper quickly back under the bed and let the duvet drop into place.

What should I do? Tell someone? Sean? Ryan? Or confront her myself? I shudder. No. How can I? Neither she nor Ryan can ever find out I've been here. I wrap my arms around my chest, starting to shiver.

"Livvy?"

I spin, slipping the key into my jeans pocket.

"There you are." Sean's smile is soft, his eyes hungry. "I didn't hear you come upstairs. Fin's asleep."

"That's good." I murmur. I try to drag my gaze away from the shadows under the bed.

"Sean—" I start. Stop. I can't do it. I can't say it. *Is it my secret, or someone else's?* The realisation is ice cold. Sophia Swift knew. Or she suspected. *There's a darkness here that I can't get away from. No matter how hard I try . . .*

"What?"

"Nothing." I swallow. "Are you still going tomorrow?"

"To the wedding?" His gaze levels on my face.

"Mm."

"I hadn't decided. I wasn't expecting an invitation. Are you?"

"I told Katie I would."

"In that case," he lifts the jet necklace from my throat to look at it, "I'd better make sure my suit's dry."

"You don't have to . . ."

"I know." He smiles darkly. "Weddings aren't really my scene. They tend to attract trouble. But I seem to remember you're quite the expert at that yourself."

"At . . . at what?" I feel myself frown.

"Attracting trouble." He lays down the necklace, warm against my skin. For a moment there's silence.

"Come on." He jerks his head towards the door. "We should go downstairs."

I follow him onto the landing. Push my hand into my pocket and turn the key in my fingers. Haunted. That's what

Claire said. I descend the stairs, chilled by the thought of an open window and a face in the shadows. Haunted.

But what kind of ghost needs a key?

* * *

Gulls circle the cliffs like wraiths in the early-morning light, their desolate cries echoing over the sheer drop behind me. The key fits. I knew all along that it would. It rattles loosely, and has to be angled upwards to engage, but the clunk of acceptance, the sideways turn, the lack of ivy around the age-clouded lock provide irrefutable confirmation. My curiosity, piqued and unusually confident, has dispatched the tiny voice in my subconscious that still whispers its doubts. The door's open. What more reason do I need?

Eight thirty. I left Sean and Fin eating breakfast, and drove here under a clear sky. The gravel is wet with last night's rain. I pick my way back to it over the muddy trenches, open the car door and rummage in the glovebox for my torch. I don't have long. Ryan and Claire will be home soon, and Sean will get back to the Lookout to find I'm not there. The wedding's at one, and the drive to Land's End will take most of an hour. I won't have long to get ready.

I lock the car and jog back to the chapel, heart beating hard. The key clunks a second time as I turn it the rest of the way. I stop, listening to the silence.

The latch is heavy, operated by a tarnished metal ring. The hinges are out of alignment but surprisingly devoid of rust, and open silently. I shoulder the door. Ease myself around it and through the narrow open gap. Click on the torch.

It looks different. I blink. My memory must be hazy, at best, but the place has changed. The broken chairs have been moved to one side, under the window I broke in through, leaving scuff marks in the dust. And there are footprints — footprints that aren't mine — visible in the broad beam of the torch.

I glance around, unsettled. At the overturned font, and the timber cross. It didn't occur to me before, but it's in the wrong place. I haven't frequented many churches or chapels, but I'm pretty sure the font should be at the back. Beside it, in front of the cross, there's a kneeler cushion on the floor, cross-stitched with an illegible date and the words *He is Risen.* I follow the blurred-out footsteps to it, and crouch to pick it up. It's dusty too. But not dusty enough. Neither is the floor underneath.

I put it aside. A melee of finger-marks define an edge that I wouldn't have noticed, if the cushion hadn't drawn my attention: the black outline of a square cut into the boards.

I breathe out slowly. The vault. It has to be. Hadn't Gordon-Heyers said it was filled in? I scrabble for the corners with my nails. *A darkness here* . . . I lift the trapdoor.

The space underneath is small, and empty. A pit of earth — filled in, just as Gordon-Heyers had said, with only a shallow hole left between the rubble and soil and the boards — perhaps enough room for a large child or a small adult to curl up inside, little more. I prop up the hatch with my left hand and reach with my right for the torch, making shadows dance across the hole, and something catches the light. There's something there, just out of reach.

I kneel forwards, gripping the torch between my knees, the shaft of light not quite steady. Plastic? No, metallic; it glints as the torch moves. I push my hand inside, and my fingers hit something soft and unexpected. Fabric. I feel around its limits, beaded edges . . . a zip. It's a bag. A suitcase — the kind with wheels and an extending handle — caked with dust and dirt. The zip's rusty and the handle's stuck. It's unsettlingly heavy. I waver. Do I really want to do this? Do I have to . . .

Yes. I curl my frozen toes inside my boots and manhandle the case out onto the floor. But suddenly I'm too afraid to open it. My thoughts are swamped by nauseating flashbacks to the post-watershed crime dramas that my mother used to watch incessantly in my early teens. Murders. Serial killers. I jam my chattering teeth together and sit back, squeezing my eyes closed for a moment. What do I think I'm going to find? A body? Dismembered limbs?

I open them again. *Get real, Livia.* There are no murderers at Trethallyan, no villains and no corpses. Just miserable, manipulative secrets and a whole lot of questions without answers. I'm far more likely to find letters than body parts.

Aren't I? I listen to the mournful repetitive pleas of the gulls outside, and the rush of my own breath. Tentatively, I tug the zipper. It doesn't budge. For a moment, I'm worried it might snap off. I squash the bulging lid, and try again.

Clothes.

I pick up the torch, and squint into the case in confusion, almost disappointment. It's full of clothes. Folded clothes. Women's clothes: a dress, cardigans, jeans, underwear. And more. I feel to the edge of the case. A child's things — baby clothes; I shake the items out one at a time: vests with poppers, little t-shirts, dungarees. There's a plastic packet shoved down one side. Nappies.

"What?" My whisper is loud in the silence. "Who . . ." I trail off. Stare, perplexed. Nothing makes sense. None of it. I sit back on my heels. The sun is shining through the Virgin Mary, casting a strange wash of muted colours that run into each other on the dirty floorboards. I stand up, legs numb. The gulls have moved on. My attention falls back on the kneeler. Someone's been coming here. Praying here. The same person who's hidden their belongings under the floorboards? I'm not sure.

I need to put the key back. I wet my lips nervously and crouch to repack the suitcase. It won't go unmissed for long. Sooner or later, Claire — or whoever's hidden it — will notice it's gone. I need to find a way to get it back into the spare room without anyone realising.

But what happens when we build on the chapel? None of this will stay hidden then. I lower the bag of clothes back into its tomb, brush the dislodged dirt from the floor back over it, trying to scuff out any evidence of my discovery. I straighten, uneasy. It's hard not to think about what Sean said: *Claire would have us wait until hell freezes over*. Perhaps he's more right than he realises.

Sean. The thought jogs my sense of urgency. I pull out my phone. Half nine.

Shit.

"I have to go," I whisper to no one. To the dead spiders in their skeleton-webs. I seize the torch, gripping it harder than I need to, and close the door behind me with a crash that echoes off the cliff-faces. I glance reflexively over my shoulder. No Graham Gordon-Heyers to catch me in the act today. I drop the latch, lock the door and stuff the key into my pocket.

I don't come across a single car on the road back to the Lookout, and I take the winding lanes at uncharacteristic speed. The house is invisible from above as I swing around the corner and onto the track. Too late, I notice the cars in the drive. I pull to one side and decelerate to an abrupt stop.

I can see them both through the bay window as I get out of the car. Sean is spot-lit in profile by the sunshine; their voices reach me even through the tempered glass. I freeze.

"So how long? Tell me!" Ryan's muffled voice isn't quite a shout. "How long? How long have you been fucking your intern?"

"There's nothing like jumping to conclusions, is there?"

"It doesn't take much jumping, Sean! You disappear off the face of the earth, and it turns out it's because you've followed her halfway across the country for a night in some swanky five-star hotel. So much for 'keeping things professional'!"

"That's none of your business."

"It *is* my business. And Graham's business. And our father's busine—"

"I'd like you to leave."

"Does she know?"

"What?"

"Oh, come on, Sean . . ."

"I'm not having this conversation."

"You'll have to, sooner or later . . ."

"You think I don't know that? I don't need *you* to tell me." They shift, their silhouettes blending into shadow.

"Don't fuck it up, Sean. That's all." Ryan's voice nears the door. I slip out of sight around the corner as it opens. Ryan strides to the BMW, jerking open the door. I watch him pull away, tugging at his seatbelt as he reverses at expert speed up the gravel and disappears onto the main road.

My hands are shaking. I stand for a moment, wavering between realisation and panic. He knows. Of course he knows; it was inevitable that someone would find out. How could we think we'd keep it secret, when it's written all over every unspoken word?

But if he knows . . . then who else does? Suddenly I feel sick. It's like he said. Graham, Charles, Peter . . . I press an unsteady hand to my forehead. It's only a matter of time. And then what? I can't imagine that there'll be any kind of job waiting for me at Lorchann McLeod once they find out. If they even let me finish my time at Trethallyan. I slump back against the reclaimed stone wall. *Shit.* I rub my forehead. Shit.

It's warm inside the Lookout, and the shower is on. I let myself in in silence and shut myself in the bedroom to change. My dress is hanging from the curtain rail; I step into it and struggle with the zip, then attempt to tame the hopeless wavy tresses of my hair with curling irons, cursing aloud as I catch my fingers. I have to put on my make-up in my chipped compact mirror, which is a challenge in itself, although I'm secretly glad not to be preparing in front of Sophia Swift's mirror. I root through my meagre supplies for mascara, and find a kohl pencil instead. I contemplate it for a moment, thinking about the red-haired girl in the photos and her painted-on face, then put it to one side. I'm not her. I'm not even like her. I find the mascara and apply a coat, blinking at the zoomed-in segment of my reflection in the mirror, and finish fastening my hair.

I pause. The bathroom door is open. The sound of the shower has stopped. I lay down the mirror. Sean is leaning against the doorframe, arms folded, a navy-blue towel wrapped around his waist. I have no idea how long he's been there. I slip my feet into my shoes and stand up. In an instant, I've forgotten about the chapel, and the letters. He's regarding me in silence. I flatten my skirt.

"Is everything okay?"

He nods, still silent. I reach down to buckle the ankle straps of my shoes, unnerved by his stare. There's a sharp new dark grey suit hanging on the wardrobe door; he plucks it from its hanger to dress, and I watch him fasten the stiff buttons of his painfully crisp white shirt one at a time and secure the jet cufflinks. Jet. I put a hand to my throat, a tiny frown creasing my forehead. Since when has he started wearing jet?

"We should go." Sean moves to pick up the collection of items from the foot of the bed: wallet, keys, an unmarked silver envelope. He pushes them into his pocket as I pick up my clutch bag. I follow him to the door. The wind picks at my newly-curled hair, whisking it instantly across my face. I raise a hand to tidy it back.

"Why so quiet?" I venture.

Sean pauses beside the car door. "Because I have no desire to go to this wedding." His eyes smoulder on mine. I swallow.

"You don't?"

"No." He opens the door and holds it for me. "I'd much rather keep you here." His fingers skate my bare shoulder-blades, revealed by the low back of my dress. "Shall we?"

* * *

The hotel is spectacular, the breeze chilly as we hurry across the imposing courtyard and into reception. The stairway to the upstairs function room is wide and sweeping, adorned with ivory bows. The room's smaller than I expected, set out with chairs for the ceremony and decorated simply with cream and dusky-pink roses. There's a string quartet seated beside the window at the far end, bordering an unspoilt view over the Atlantic towards the Isles of Scilly. We're almost the last to arrive, and we file into seats near the back only moments before the quartet starts playing.

Katie looks every bit as perfect as I've imagined she would; the breathless hush as the quartet strikes up Pachelbel's Canon speaks a thousand words, but none as profoundly as the radiance in her cheeks. The ceremony isn't long: it's simple and beautifully put together. I'm surprised by the smarting in my eyes as Katie hiccups her way through her vows, and the room erupts into applause at the first painfully chaste kiss, and the second, less reserved, one. I can't look at Sean. Can't turn my head, and risk that he might catch sight of the sensibilities that have escaped, unchecked, in my expression. He doesn't seem to have moved for a long time, either, as finally the bows dance back across the violin strings. His arm against mine has been rigid with tension, or impatience, from beginning to end. *Trying not to love you.* For some reason my throat aches as we're directed outside onto the terrace for champagne.

The wind has picked up. I shiver as Sean sidesteps, caught up in handshakes and small talk, and scan the crowd fruitlessly for a familiar face. Ryan and Claire must be here somewhere. And Fin . . . My teeth are chattering. I move away from Sean, suddenly conscious of watching eyes. I don't need to add any fuel to Ryan's already flaming suspicion.

It's so cold. I close my eyes for a moment, trying to repress my shivers. When I open them again, the French doors to the ballroom are open, and everyone is moving inside. There's a table plan just inside the door, and I stop to study it. Table six. Between Claire Lorchann and someone called Rachel — one of the school friends, perhaps. My brow furrows. Finbar is sandwiched in an extra chair between Ryan and Claire. But no Sean. I scour the sheet again. I only spot his name on the third run-through, on the furthest table in the corner, among names I don't recognise. I glance up as I make my way inside. He's already reached his place, fingers drumming lightly on the back of his gold and ivory-ribboned chair; our eyes meet and his brows lower a fraction in mock consternation. I watch as he sits.

"Livia."

I turn around. Claire's beside me. Next to her, Ryan is pulling out a chair for Fin to clamber onto, all bony elbows and knees.

"Oh, hi!" I gulp. There's an awkward pause as Ryan scoots Fin's chair closer to the table. I try not to think about the key.

"Your dress is lovely," I tell her, searching desperately for something to break the silence. Finally Claire smiles.

"Thanks."

She sits, and I follow suit. Ryan is busy attaching Fin's napkin to the front of his immaculate herringbone waistcoat, not looking at me. I remember with a lurch his conversation with Sean at the Lookout. Has he realised I was there? I wet my lips nervously. The buzz of chatter around us has amplified. The other school friends have taken their places, their conversation indiscernible. A pianist is playing the baby grand in the corner.

"I heard you had to go to a funeral." Claire has picked up one of the table favours to examine it. "I hope it wasn't anyone close?"

"Uh . . ." I falter. There's something odd in the way she asks. A lack of her normal, dimpled warmth. I scold myself. She's talking about a funeral, and her own mother's dying in hospital. She and Ryan must both be exhausted.

"Not really." I shrug. "A family friend."

"Oh, I'm sorry." She lays down the favour.

"Don't be." I shake my head. "Really." Another pause. I glance down and then back up again, sensing Finbar's gaze on my face.

"Hi, Fin." I lift a hand to sign. He signs back, a glimmer of a grin playing impishly over his lips. Ryan smiles politely.

"Hey, Livs."

Do I imagine the slightest shift in his expression? Maybe I'm just getting paranoid. It takes every ounce of my willpower not to look back at Sean's table.

"Wine?" Ryan holds out the bottle of white. I nod, and he fills the glass.

"Thanks."

"I went up to the chapel on Thursday. Things are looking good."

"Yeah. A little behind schedule but it's coming along." The piano music has stopped. The ring of a glass pierces the hum of conversation as Ryan opens his mouth to reply, and we both fall silent.

The speeches are long, a string of had-to-be-theres, and in-jokes that I'm not party to. I twist my arms behind my back, trying to listen, winding my fingers through the knot of the chair ribbon. Despite my better judgement I look back across the room, straight into the sultry darkness of Sean's eyes. I see his gaze dart to the ribbon and then up again. My mouth is dry.

I'm significantly lacking in appetite by the time the food arrives. Once or twice I glance at Fin, to catch him expertly disposing of meat and vegetables into his paper party bag, in place of the crayons and trinkets that are now strewn across the white tablecloth. I slip out once the cake's cut, mumbling an excuse, and make my way to the windswept terrace. A few pinprick stars are fighting their way through the broken cloud. There's a group of people smoking; I apologise my way through their midst to descend the stone steps, and stand looking out over the dark water. I don't know anyone except the Lorchanns. And something about Claire's surface-only smile is making me uncomfortable.

Somewhere inside, another spoon tinkles against a glass. I glance up and realise the smokers have gone. The ballroom has fallen silent as I ascend the steps and creep back through the half-open fire-door. The main lights have been extinguished and the slow rhythmic revolution of a disco ball casts chequered patterns across the floor. *Ladies and gentlemen, the first dance.* Everyone's taking photos. I melt backwards into the shadows, watching. Watching the glow of happiness wash away the fleeting embarrassment from Katie's face. Watching Craig's arms around her, light and gentle, watching the way her hands lock behind his neck, and her head fits under his chin in their perfectly practised exposition of newlywed bliss. Something in my chest aches dully; I curl my fingers into my palms, letting my gaze lose focus until the squares of coloured light become shifting shards and the band drowns out the discourse of my subconscious.

"I was starting to wonder if you'd left without me."

My hands jerk involuntarily; I half turn. He's a shadow too, jet cufflinks glittering as they catch in the movement of the lights. His lips are on my hair.

"I get the impression that someone's been doing everything in their power to keep me away from you tonight." It's a whisper. "It seems like your brother's not the only person that doesn't want me anywhere near you."

"Sean . . ." I shoot an anxious glance over the room. Fin is exploring the jungle of chair legs under the pushed-back tables. A few couples have gravitated onto the dancefloor, swaying in careful rhythm to the raw-voiced acoustic cover. An Elvis song. *Can't help falling in love.* I scrunch my fingernails tighter into my palms and try to imagine the kind of scathing conversation I'd have with Kris, if he was here, at the vomit-inducing sentimentality. But Kris isn't here. Kris isn't speaking to me. And the ache in my chest has redoubled. I uncurl my fists and fold my arms over it, as if I can cover the void.

Sean's hand touches my waist. I freeze. He steps backwards, the shadows falling across his face.

"Would you like to dance?" he asks.

"What?" The word drops from my lips unchecked.

"Would you like to dance?" Something wicked glimmers on his lips. A smile. Sean Lorchann is smiling. I scan the room, panicked. Ryan, Claire, Katie. Here. They'll all see. If they haven't already seen. I stumble over my own feet as he steers me forwards.

"I . . . can't dance," I gasp.

"I can." His lips are against my cheek, darkly amused.

I don't argue. He reaches to tuck my hair behind my ear, drawing me with him until we're in the middle of the floor and his hands are on my waist, lightly protective.

"I don't care who sees, Livvy." He's read my mind. "I don't care who knows. I want you to be mine."

"I—"

"Always." His eyes are on mine, focussed, deadly serious. Dark with intent. Adrenaline spikes through my bloodstream, breathless exhilaration, fear; some unnameable emotion that swells in my chest so that I can't breathe out. His hands close on my hips, pulling me gently into him; his lips touch mine, and in a fleeting moment I realise what he's doing. No more questions. No more sideways looks or snide suggestions. We're dancing together, and the possessive press of his hand in the small of my back is an assertion, a warning, to anyone that might have doubted him. *A bad choice* . . .

Under the tables, Fin has come to a stop, his arms wrapped around his knees. He's watching us, his pointed face solemn, dark eyes alight. If walls have ears . . . I've always had the feeling that Finbar Lorchann knows more than he lets on.

I glance over my shoulder at the glass doors, where our reflections drift like one fluid form, Sean's fingers spanning my back, my hair dropping out of its updo in unruly rebellion. *Always.* A shiver runs down my spine. There's something in his expression that terrifies me.

The last few guitar chords linger to a close. People start to applaud, then to move, and the music changes. I flounder, in search of the new tempo. Sean leans forwards to press his mouth to my ear.

"I want to leave."

"Now?" I glance at the band, at the rapidly filling dancefloor.

"Now."

"Okay," I breathe.

We should probably say our goodbyes, but we don't. We steal unnoticed out through the double doors and navigate the corridor to reception in vigilant silence. I wait in taut-muscled anticipation as Sean hands over his ticket and the valet goes to fetch the car.

"Excuse me."

I spin around. The receptionist has come out from behind her desk.

"Miss Livia Frost?"

I gape at her for a moment, taken by surprise.

"Yes," I manage finally.

"I have a package for you." She reaches around the counter.

"Oh." I accept it before I can formulate a question. "Thank you."

Sean's eyebrows flicker upwards, but he doesn't ask.

"You're welcome. Have a safe journey."

The outside air hits my face in a blast. The valet holds open the car door, and I climb in, fumbling with the Jiffy bag. Even before I prise it open, I know what's inside. I draw the book out just far enough to see the top corner of its hardback cover. A cover without a dust-jacket. I shove it back in and reseal the half-sticky glue with shaking hands. *Not now.* My heart is beating a drumroll against my ribs. Not now.

* * *

It takes forty-five minutes to get back. The motion of the sea plays across the windows of the Lookout like a cinema screen. I leave the book on the hall table with my bag and keys. Sean locks the door.

If there's a feature presentation after the seascape previews then it's a mute one: a silent movie with no soundtrack, a dance to the rhythm of heartbeats and hungry bright eyes, leather and fool's gold. And maybe I've never believed in predestiny, ivory ribbons, soft-focus fiction romance. But nothing here is in soft focus — how can it be? Sean Lorchann's shadow is too sharp-edged for fiction. There aren't enough words.

Even if there were, I wouldn't keep reading. It isn't the fight, the passion, the pain. I just don't want to get to the ending. I want there to be no last page. No fade out. No rolling credits. I want it frozen in time instead, like a painting where the darkness has spilled from the colour chart onto the page. Where the oils have dried, and nothing will ever erase them.

CHAPTER 25

Red and yellow and pink and green . . .

She is dancing, a fairy-child, a daughter of night time. Her hair is blackbird dark, her skin is the white moon; the breeze of a summer-night's dream touches it, snatching away her lisping song.

Orange and purple and blue . . .

Turning and turning, all by herself, she circles faster, so that the stars blur in her eyes. He watches her, from the sidelines of mowed grass and picket fence. His tiny daughter, a whirlwind of elbows and organza skirt. He has no idea. No idea how little time is left. No idea that he's about to blink. That when he opens his eyes again, she'll be gone.

I can sing a rainbow, sing a rainbow, sing a rainbow . . .

"Mercy," he calls back towards the house. "Mercy?"

There is no reply. He hesitates, torn between the end of the song, and the call of his wife's silence.

"Mercy?" Reluctantly, he ascends the steps towards the kitchen door. A pair of Tallullah's shoes are discarded at the top, miniature white ballet shoes with butterflies on the straps. He throws a last protective glance at his barefoot child, and plunges inside for the briefest of moments.

I can sing a rainbow, sing a rainbow . . .
"Sing a rainbow too."

I lay down the book. The dressing table is covered in a film of dust. Up close, the edges of the mirror are tarnished. The silence in thirty-one Sunnyside is cold and paused mid-breath. I stare at the opening page for a moment longer — Chapter One — then flip to the back. Katie was right. There's no ending.

Outside, the Sunday-morning church bells are ringing. The rugby game will only just have started. I have time — almost an hour — to finish this before Sean gets back to the Lookout. Somehow, it has to be here. In her room. My room. The place we've inhabited in parallel times, in alternative realities.

I trace my finger over the ragged edges where the pages have been plucked from their roots. Just like the journal, just like Finbar's story-book, someone has torn them out, and I still can't fathom why.

I close the book and run my hands over its hard covers. The dust-jacket is creased from being in my suitcase; I smooth it out to fit it back where it belongs. Blackbirds . . . swifts. What am I missing?

It's only as I slide it over the back cover that I feel the indentation under my thumb, the etching of letters in the cardboard underneath. I freeze.

It's her writing. I fold back the glossy paper. Of course it is. Very tiny, almost small enough to miss. She tried. I swallow hard. Whatever the ending says, she tried to tell someone. A cry for help? She gave the book to Katie, a few days before she died . . .

Look in the mirror.
IN THE MIRROR.

I frown at myself. *In the mirror*? I stare, without comprehension, at the army of my own reflection, teetering on the verge of understanding but not quite able to make the pieces fit.

Look in the mirror.

Sometimes I see reflections in that mirror. And they're not mine . . .

For a split second, the images blur. And there, instead, I can see her: auburn hair long and straight, lips harlot red, mouthing something — a name, a word . . . ? I don't believe in ghosts.

Look in the mirror. I hold it up to obscure her face. IN THE MIRROR.

Look in the . . .

In the mirror.

Oh, shit.

I drop the book. Fumble to sweep the dressing table clear, and kneel up on top of it, feeling all around the tarnished edges of the glass. The frame is weighty and deep: thick heavy mahogany, chipped in places and sticky with age and grime. I scrabble along the top edge with my fingers. Nothing.

I jump down, feet thudding on the floorboards, and with a screech of protesting wooden legs, I pull the dressing table out from wall. The brown paper covering the back of the mirror is thick with dust and cobwebs. But the masking tape around it is new.

There's a Stanley knife by the easel. I'm trembling from head to foot. I fetch it.

In the mirror . . . I suck in a deep breath between my teeth.

Then I draw the blade across the paper.

The first sheet hits the floor end on, with a soft thwack. The rest cascade over it: pages and pages of jumbled notepaper lined faintly in blue and covered — every inch — with writing. Sophia Swift's writing, in bold blue ink. I crash back to reality with a jolt. There's a few residual pieces stuck in the backing paper. I pull out the top one, and the others flutter free and fall at my feet.

I told you that I've done something bad. Something terrible. Something I know I should never have done. It's worse than you think. I feel so sick, so used. He knew

My eyes scan the page in my hand. Suddenly I'm light-headed. I back away and sit down on the edge of the bare bed. The rest of the paper settles like snow under the dressing table as I read it, re-read it.

He knew I wouldn't be able to refuse him.

The ringing in my ears is deafening.

I was in love, and he knew. He knew how desperate I'd been, how unhappy . . . and he did it anyway. And I let him, because I wanted it . . . I wanted it so badly, or I thought I did. It was so easy the first time. In the cabin, after everyone had gone. So right. I thought that perhaps . . . But I know now it could never be that way.

In the cabin? What does she mean, in the cabin? My lips are numb. It's about Sean; she's writing about Sean . . . I stare, blank.

I'm so alone. So confused. The only people I thought were friends in this place have turned out to be enemies, apart from you. I know you'll be repulsed by me. I'm repulsed by myself. By the truth. It wasn't just once. I should have drawn a line, but I didn't. I can't. I can't stop myself from running back to him. And every time I hate it — I hate myself — a little more . . .

Hate what? I'm breathing fast, too fast. My fingertips are tingling. *Hate what? What do you mean?* I want to scream at her in the mirror, but she's gone. *What did you do?*

In the cabin.

No. I stand up, so quickly that for a second my vision blacks. I sway. It's not true. He tried to support her. Tried to put a stop to it. He told me. Told me all about her. Didn't he?

There's no solace in the truth, Livia.

No.

I stuff it into my pocket and stumble to the dressing table. My palms are clammy with sweat. No. He would have told me. He wouldn't have lied to me. Would he? Why would he have lied?

Because I wanted it . . . I wanted it so badly, or I thought I did . . .

There's an odd, metallic taste in my mouth. I drop to my knees to scoop up the rest of the paper. I'm cold, shaking. That's not it. It's not true. It can't be. He wouldn't lie. *Then why don't you ask him?* the voice at the back of my mind is taunting me. *Go right back and ask him. Go on . . .*

"Shut up!" I slam the stack of paper onto the dressing table. An uncomprehending sob jams in my throat, stuck fast so that I can't get a breath in past it. I don't want it to add up. But it's irrefutable. Katie's warnings. Ryan's disapproval. Thirteen backwards. *Don't go back.* The things he said himself. Why doesn't he want me to come here? Because he knows I'll find out; because it's too close to the mark . . .

I lurch upright. Snatch up my keys and blunder to the door, leaving everything behind. How could he? How could he have lied? It takes me two attempts to start the car. I accelerate over the cobbles, almost skidding at the corner with the main road.

"Fine." I grip the wheel with both hands. I'm talking to myself. To the boots and hard-hat in my passenger seat. "I will."

I'll ask him. To explain. There'll be an explanation. And, it occurs to me, I don't really care what it is. If he can tell me the truth, whatever it is, then there's nothing to forgive. If he loves me enough to be honest with me, then the other possibility can't be true: that Katie was right, that he's pretty good at getting what he wants from people . . .

I dash a hand across my eyes, furious at myself. I can't think it. How can I think it?

"No." I turn without indicating, bumping over the track so fast that the bottom of the car grinds out on a pothole. The Defender's in the drive . . . He's already back. Adrenaline bursts in my gut. I kill the engine, open the car door and stop, paralysed.

I can't do it.

I have to.

I slam the car door behind me. Try to restore a facade of normality. There's an explanation, however hard it might be to hear. I just need to get it over with.

I push open the door. It's light in the hall. Quiet. Surreally normal. I walk inside and falter, drinking in a deep breath, two, three. The bedroom door opens.

"Livvy?"

I turn to look at him. All the words rush into my head at once, flooding out my thoughts: *He knew I wouldn't be able to refuse him . . . It wasn't just once . . . In the cabin, after everyone had gone . . .*

I feel sick.

"Tell me," I breathe.

"What?" Confusion crosses his face, a hood that falls almost instantly over his dark eyes. His hair is wet from showering; the back of his t-shirt's damp and his arms are bare. I see them tense in apprehension. "Livvy, wh—"

"Tell me!" Suddenly I'm shouting. "Tell me about Sophia Swift! *All* about her! Tell me everything. The parts you didn't tell me about before . . ."

He's come to a halt.

"Livia . . ." A shadow creeps over his expression, darkening his frown. "I don't understand. What do you mean? There's nothing else to tell."

"You were friends?"

"Yes."

"But it wasn't *just* that, was it?"

"I told you. I—"

"No!" Panic has gripped my gut. Realisation. He isn't going to tell me. He's going to lie. It's just like Katie said.

"No!" I jerk the page from my pocket with a flourish. "You told me lots of things! And I don't know if *any* of them were true!"

"Livvy . . . ?" He's frozen, uncomprehending, his eyes fixed on my face. Sobs have invaded my chest; I hiccup, trying to choke them back.

"Tell me!" I barely recognise my own voice. "Tell me about her! Tell me *all* about her! Tell me about in the cabin! Was it good? Was it easy?" My breaths are jagged, rapid. I can't stop. "Did she . . . *Did she believe you*? Like I . . . Like *I* b-believed you?" The sob breaks out: one that releases the tide, and it's too late. I pull myself upright, and the deluge shakes me from head to foot. I want to turn tail and run, so that he can't see. To not look back, never look back, but I can't look away from him. From the bewildered rage in his endlessly dark eyes, as if he can still sell me his denial.

"I never touched Sophia, Livvy!" Sean's face twists. "What are you saying?! What are you t—"

"You *know* what I'm talking about!"

"*What?* Livia . . ." He's breathing hard, pushing his hands back through his dark hair, gripping fistfuls of it in his agitation. "What I told you was the truth! There *was* nothing else. It's like I said. She was obsessed, I tried to . . . to stop her. To send her away . . . There was never anything between—"

"That's not what *she* says!"

"What?" his voice falls, a whisper. I face him, quaking.

"That's not . . . what sh-she says." I'm whispering too. The notepaper is crumpled in my hands. "I h-have to go. Can you p-pass me my case?"

"No." He exhales. "Livvy . . ."

"Please." I square my shoulders. "It's under the bed. I'll come back for the rest. Or you can drop it at the cabin."

"Don't." He still hasn't moved. "Don't do this. Livia . . ."

"I'd like my case." The pain in my throat is unbearable. He regards me, motionless, for a split second more. Fury, desperation, burn in his eyes. Then he wheels around. I fight not to flinch as he kicks open the bedroom door, zips up the suitcase and swings it out.

"Thanks." My voice sounds strange. The warm, firm grip of his fingers over mine as he passes it to me sends a bolt of agony through me. I turn to go.

"It was Katelyn?"

His snarl stops me in my tracks.

"It was, wasn't it?! I don't know what her problem is with me . . . or why the fuck you'd believe her over me." His fists clench. "She doesn't know what happened with Sophia. She—"

"It wasn't Katie." I grip the case harder.

"What?"

"*I* know what happened with Sophia. I've read everything. All I needed was the truth. I thought . . . I thought you . . ." The sobs have gained a stranglehold. "I . . . I thought I-I . . . B-but . . ." I can't do it. Not for a second longer. I start towards the door.

"Wait!" He moves to block me. "No! Livvy!" He tries to catch my arm, but I wrench it away. "Don't do this! Don't—"

I shake my head, blind. Blunder past him, out into the hall. I hear his fists collide with the table instead, the sweep of flesh across wood, the smash of a Scotch glass hitting the tiles, like dreams shattering. I fumble with the door, burst out into pouring rain and almost collide with the front wing of the BMW. I dart round it and break into a run.

"Livia?" The car door has opened; Ryan leaps out, voice sharp with concern. "Livia, are you okay?"

I don't stop. I keep running until I'm at my own car door. I wrench it open and fling the case inside, my hands stiff and non-compliant, frozen to the bone. It's only as I start the engine that I see the wayward sheet of paper flap up from the gravel and stick itself to Ryan's back wheel, Sophia's writing bleeding down the page in the relentless onslaught of the rain.

It's too late. I reverse onto the track, sob after sob rising in my throat. I drive until I can't see anymore, then I pull into the seafront car park at the edge of town, where Claire parked on my first day.

"*Why*?" I breathe it into my scrunched hands. "*Why, why* . . ."

I curl forwards in my seat, pressing my fists to my eyes so hard that it hurts. Tears are running down my wrists and soaking my sleeves. The sobs are transitioning from disbelief to despair. What have I done? My hard-hat and boots are watching me from the footwell, spattered with half-dried Trethallyan mud. I can't go back. How can I go back? I screw my eyes tightly closed. Everything's drifting apart at the seams: Trethallyan, the chapel, Lorchann McLeod. I've sacrificed it all for the one thing it turns out I can't have.

How can he not know? I've never loved anyone. Not like this. I've surrendered everything to him, inside and out, until there's nothing left. Done things I would never have done, shared things I've never shared with anyone. And all along, all along . . .

It's cold in the car. My body has grown rigid with shivering. And suddenly, I want to go home. More than anything. I curl up tighter, screwing my sleeves into my hands. Real home. Not Sunnyside. Not Nottingham. Home, to my father's study, where under the desk there's room for a small child to sit and hide from the world. Home, to woodsmoke and stewing apples, a time when dreams were innocent.

But it's gone. It's been gone for a long time. I've closed my eyes, pretended not to notice the hole, but now the emptiness is inside me and I just can't block it out.

My phone's ringing. I sit up slowly, dizzy and blurry-eyed. I pull it from my pocket and turn it off, then slump back, stare blankly at the windscreen. I need to go. Back to the flat. I can't stay here.

I park a little way along the road. Creep inside, avoid the stairs that creak. The last thing I want is for Niklavs to hear me, to come to investigate. I deadlock the door behind me and don't turn on the light. I put down the suitcase, push the dressing table back against the wall, unfold my coverless duvet and sit down with it draped it around my shoulders. In the mirror. The answer was there the whole time. Right in front of me.

I stand up. The journal's in my suitcase. I move to fetch it, somehow numb. What else am I going to do? It's as though I've been bound to this moment, right from the start. Right from the very first page.

> *I'm going to try and tell you the truth, I think. Will you turn the pages, if I do? Even if it's not great, or good. My truth? Even if there aren't any heroes?*

I turn to the back. Pick up the torn pages and try to piece one back in, matching up the ragged edges. There are so many . . .

I get a pencil from the easel. Frown down at the disorder, eyes aching. It's like a jigsaw, without a picture for reference. One by one, I fit them back, numbering each as I find it. Minutes stretch to hours, day to evening, until at last I sit back, stiff and shivering. The heating isn't working. I'd forgotten. I pull the duvet tighter around me. So this is it. However unpalatable. The one promise I've stuck to. Not to abandon her.

> *My name is Sophia Swift. And when I was seventeen years old, I killed my*

Heart in my mouth, I hold up the next page.

> *own son.*
>
> *I sentenced him to death. It was my fault. It's always been my fault.*
>
> *It's time I told you a story. The one about the girl in the dandelion stems. It's the story of how she forgot to dance.*
>
> *It's easy to believe in the wrong thing. The wrong person. It turns out, it's the one thing I'm best at. She was fifteen, and she believed in so many things. Things she didn't*

have experience of, like people believe in science, or superstition. She had no idea, not really. Until she wasn't the girl at all, anymore. Until the bird and the butterflies had flown away, and the grass suddenly wasn't tall enough to hide in. When she found out about her baby, her world changed. She wanted him, more than anything. She just didn't know how.

That's how her mother persuaded her not to go through with the abortion. She said the only thing that mattered was to do the right thing for him. That God would forgive everything else.

It hurt. Every second of it hurt. Until the memory of the grass and the bird were gone altogether. She couldn't dance anymore. She could barely walk. She could hardly stand up, for being sick. She had to give up everything. Those months were the darkest. Alone, no one knew how alone. Alone except from his tiny life inside her. There were days when she couldn't wake up, couldn't sleep. Days when the razor was all that kept her going, training for the pain. She longed to do more. But anything else would have hurt the baby. Pills. Ending it. She couldn't hurt the baby.

She'd sit, and feel him move, to remind herself. She bought a set of white mittens, a hat and socks, such tiny socks. She learned to sew: a blanket, all in white because she didn't know who or what he'd be, and she stitched her initial into the corner, because this was all he'd have to remember her by.

She met the parents. The real parents. The ones that would take this little life, and shape it. Teach it to smile, to walk, to talk, to love . . . to ride a bike, read novels, and play the clarinet badly. She spent months preparing for the moment that they'd take him. That moment when she'd become truly empty. They said they'd love him. Look after him like he was theirs. They couldn't have children of their own. They even wanted her to choose a name for him. His name. The most important gift of a whole lifetime.

I didn't even put him in their arms. I put him into the arms of a stranger. It was six weeks early, the night he came. I had no idea what was happening. I was bleeding. The doctor said they had to get him out. It was all over so fast. I couldn't even see. And then he was screaming, and they gave him to me to hold. To me. Because he was mine . . . And just for a moment, just for a moment, I didn't want to let him go . . .

But I did let him go. I let him go. I could have saved him, and I didn't. I gave him away.

It's easy to believe in the wrong thing. I kept trying to believe he was better off. With everything they could give him, like my mother told me. She knew her — the woman who would love him instead of me — from work, her colleague's daughter. They had everything except the child they wanted. Family, money, a beautiful home. He would be doted on. Want for nothing. And I had nothing . . . except the child they wanted.

And now he's dead. The night I found out, it was like I died too. Like the last little spark of light went out. And I couldn't tell a soul. His name was my secret. No one would ever know. No one would ever know what I'd done.

For so long. For so long, I tried to pretend. I'm not pretending anymore.

I had to go back. To before. I already had half a plan, a desperate hope. I hated university. How could I bear it, the frivolous disregard for innocence? My mother found me the internship. She had no idea. No idea. But as soon as I saw where it was, I knew. I had to take it. I had to come here. I thought that somehow, I could find a way back. Alter the course we'd taken. Change everything. It didn't work out that way.

Who could have foreseen the way it worked out? It's like a destiny, an ever-recurring circle. To love a man who will never love me. Until it destroys me.

Maybe it won't be long.

To love. To love a man who will never love me. The pain lances through me without warning. How can I have made the same mistake? I pull my knees up and hug them to my chest, as if I can cover the aching rift that's opened inside me. All I can think about is dancing, that last dark, tender dance. How can I let it go? If I could give back the knowledge, disregard it . . . but no. Our stories are already too close: the same flat, the same job, the same man . . .

Except Sophia Swift's story ended. Here, in this room.

28/08/2021

It's been a long time. I thought I'd reconciled myself to the truth. But the truth is never that easy. I didn't see it coming. After everything. After so long, I'd stopped believing in this moment. Now here it is, right in front of me: the living, breathing picture of the life I should have led. Right here, in Porthtrevelen. I thought I was over this, beyond it. Maybe I thought that if I loved someone else hard enough, this couldn't touch me.

I barely recognised them. Faces to photographs. Yet I feel like I know everything about them.

I wanted so much to go back. Now I can't go forward. How do I weather this, how do I desist? His eyes on me are more than I can bear. I know that in them, I'll never be what he was to me. And yet I'm drawn in. I can't keep away. I can't keep from trying to show him.

Can he know what I'm guilty of? What happened to our child? Can he know the direction my life has taken? I want to tell him. I want him to know. I need to talk to him. How can't I? He deserves to know the truth.

This isn't how I thought it would be. I don't know what to do. My mother was wrong. God never forgave me. No one did. What do I do? Where do I go from here?

I prayed tonight. But I don't know what for. Who for.
And I don't know who's going to answer.

05/09/21

We talked. I didn't even have to try. All week, I'd been dreading it. Trying to think how. To find the courage.

But he found me. Down by the stable block. And we talked. It was so much easier than I ever imagined it would be. So much more natural. Like nothing ever changed at all. Even though everything's changed.

I'm so confused. I don't even know what I want anymore. What I should want. What I can want . . .

01/10/2021

I've done something awful.

I let it happen. I walked into it.

It started out so surreptitiously. Talking. More talking. We'd been talking a lot. I'd forgotten how easy he is to talk to, the way he has of making me open up.

He told me that history is history. That I'm a beautiful, independent woman, and I can make up my own mind. I pretended like I didn't know what he was suggesting. But I did. I did . . .

I close my eyes. *Bad choice, Livvy Frost.* I know what comes next. The words that dissolved against the wheel of Ryan's BMW: *I told you that I've done something bad. Something terrible . . . It wasn't just once. And every time I hate it — I hate myself — a little more . . .*

How do I come back from this? How can I? How do I stop? I've taken the wrong fork in the road. It's the only thing that wipes out the guilt. Makes me feel alive. When I'm with him, I don't remember. I don't have to remember . . .

He doesn't love me. I know that.

But he wants me. And there's something powerful about being wanted. Being desired. Toeing that fine, indistinct line between intimacy and hurt. I wrote once about choosing between the pleasure and the pain. But I'm starting to understand that they're the same. They're both the same. The only difference is in your perception.

If I shut off my thoughts, it's pleasure. If I don't look at him. It doesn't have to matter. If I close my eyes, I can imagine what I want.

Afterwards, he'll tell me I'm beautiful. And he still doesn't love me. He never did. But I can be beautiful for a few moments more. I can be beautiful, until the pleasure starts to hurt more than the pain ever did. Until I have to let it back in, the shameful, miserable truth.

I told you there're no heroes. If I was a hero, I'd be better than this. I wish I was.

28/10/2021

Claire Lorchann asked me to babysit today.

Claire Lorchann. I felt like I was walking into an enemy camp.

I don't know why I'm so afraid of her. I think it's her perfection. Her crocodile smile.

I think it's because she's beautiful, and I'm not.

I think it's because I think she knows.

She's never said a word. But it's in her face. The way she speaks. She hates me, and it's in her eyes.

I chose you, Ryan!

Did you? Or did he just not choose you?

Slowly but surely, more pieces are starting to fit. My head aches like it might burst. Claire. I remember the way her expression changed when she spoke about him. They were children together. Apart from Ryan, she knows him better than anyone. And she hated Sophia. And now she hates me . . .

I didn't know what to do. What to say. So I've agreed. I'm going, tomorrow night. They've moved into the Gatehouse, her and Finbar and Ryan. I can't even imagine how wrong it's going to feel. How sordid. How exposed. Like she's watching me. Looking right through me.

Nausea is swelling from the pit of my stomach. But I can't stop reading. Nothing can be worse than what I've already read. If I can get to the end, it can all be over . . .

today could be over . . . I'll never have to think about it again. The look in his eyes when I confronted him, the slam of his hand against the table.

But will I ever live a second when I don't remember? And what about tomorrow when I have to go back to Trethallyan, what then?

29/10/2021

I don't want to do this anymore. I want out.

You're the only person I can tell. It's all a mess, a squalid, tangled mess. But it's not that. It's worse. There's something under the surface, something much more sinister than the sordid sex and the lies.

I can't get out. I'm too far in. And I'm realising I'm afraid of him. I'm afraid.

I never realised it before. But I am. I'm afraid. I always was. Everyone is. On the surface, you wouldn't know, you'd never comprehend . . .

I have to go. I'm supposed to be at the Gatehouse now. I can't escape it. I've made a mistake. A mistake in coming here. A mistake in loving the wrong man . . . I need to take it back, but I can't. I'm in over my head, and my feet don't touch the bottom.

I have to go. I'll write later. I'll explain.

29/10

God, what have I done?

This moment changes everything. Everything I ever conceived that I knew. Everything I believed about myself. It's a lie.

I must have known it the whole time. In my heart, I must have. How couldn't I? What kind of person would it make me if I hadn't?

We were alone tonight. We were finally alone. I held him in my arms, like a baby. I held him in my arms, and for a moment, I didn't want to let him go. And I knew. Suddenly I was sure. I don't know why. I don't know why I ever looked, what possessed me, ever even to imagine . . .

Oh, God. I don't know what to do.

I'm so afraid. I never truly thought he'd hurt me. But this changes everything. If he finds out, if he finds out that I know—

"Know what?" My whisper is harsh, broken. I don't dare to look up, because I know she'll be there. There, in the mirror, where she's always been. Know what? What did she find out? The memory of Katie's words resounds in my head, impossible to shut out. *Not safe ground.*

Everyone's told me to be careful. Right from the beginning. Niklavs, Katie, even Kris. They've all said it. What have they all seen that I haven't?

There was more to it. She was afraid, Livia. She was scared.

She was. She was terrified. I stand up with such force that my chair falls with a crash. But it can't be because of him. It can't. The pain in his eyes, the nightmares — they were real. There's something else. There must be something else. I want so badly for there to be some other explanation. An exoneration. I want his fists against my door. I want him to walk right in and tell me, however bad it is, because it can't be as bad as she's suggesting. It can't be.

With trembling hands, I shove the journal and its pages into the dressing-table drawer. Where it belongs; where it should have stayed. I can't look at the mirror. I pull out fresh bedsheets and throw the first one I find over the mirror. Draw the curtains, make the bed and huddle in it, waiting. Waiting.

Come back, Livvy Frost . . .

The pain is unbearable. I double over around it and tighten my arms over my head, as if doing so might hold me together.

I want you to be mine. Always.

Always. If that's how long I have to stay like this, I will. Sobbing, sweating, praying for it to end.

I slide under the covers.

* * *

"Red, I'm sorry."

"Don't be sorry." He touches a hand to her waxy forehead. It's cold. Like ice, colder than a living, breathing being should be.

"Mercy," he whispers.

Time's up. This time he knows it. This time, he recognises the measure of the seconds. He's fighting himself not to show it, and it aches, a pain that must be visible no matter how he tries. There are tears on the bedsheet and Mercy isn't weeping.

"Ssh. My love." She's touching him. But he doesn't feel her hand. He feels the sharp fleeting feet of a bird taking flight. If he'd known it was possible to die of a broken heart, he would have done so himself, long ago.

Five a.m. and sleep hasn't come. Or if it did, it was transitory. The bed is damp with sweat. Sophia's bed. I clutch my father's book in my hands and try to obliterate my thoughts with his words. But the images are too strong. My bed. My bathroom. How long was she there . . . ?

Of course I can't sleep. To have imagined that I could was ridiculous. I get up and open the curtains. Watch the sun rise. The slow light is an inundation of clinically cold relief.

I pace the floor until six, listening for the sound of Niklavs' alarm clock through the floor, but it never comes. The church bells toll instead, and I pause by the window, staring at the puddles and the odd passer-by in the street. I'm going to have to go to work.

Time ticks inexorably down. I sit still, as though my lack of motion might stop it. I ignore the chime for seven.

Seven-thirty sends a lurch of nausea through me so powerful that I actually stumble to the bathroom and heave, my empty stomach producing nothing but bile.

He hasn't come. I've maintained a strange equilibrium in the silence, and now I'm out of time.

I put on my shirt, chinos, ankle boots; brush my hair without looking at my reflection. I'm in my car, hands too unsteady to get the key in the ignition, by the time I realise that my already sweat-damp clothes are the same that I wore the first day I met him.

I park outside the Hall. The Defender isn't there. There are no cars in the drive at all, but the lights in the cabin are on. I spend a disproportionately long time on the path, touching the wet leaves of the rhododendrons, trying to ground myself. My phone buzzes in my pocket, and for a dizzying moment I think it's him. It's not.

"Hello, is that Livia Frost?"

"Hi?" I whisper. "Yes?"

"It's Rory, from Peninsula. The estate agent."

"Oh." I wet my lips. My brain isn't working. "Hi."

"Hi, Livia, sorry to bother you this morning. I was just calling to see if we could pencil in a time for a property check."

"A . . ." I blink. "Oh. What?"

"A property inspection. It's done as a matter of course, nothing urgent. If you're happy, you don't have to be home. Or we can arrange a time you can be there. Whatever you'd prefer."

"Wait." I frown at the rhododendrons. "I've already . . . Simon's already been in."

"Simon?"

"Yeah. The landlord."

"The . . . ? No, no, twenty-nine to thirty-three are owned by a Mrs Amisha Dhar."

"It . . . *what*?"

"We handle any visits. We'd know if anyone had been in."

I have the sudden urge to be sick again. My ears are ringing faintly.

"Right." I stare, crazed, at the rhododendrons. "I . . . uh . . . Can I . . . can I get back to you?"

"Sure. If you can call me back on this number, that would be brilliant."

"Yeah." I take a steadying gulp of cold air. "Yeah. Sure."

"Thanks, Livia. I look forward to hearing from you. Bye."

"Bye . . ." I lower the phone. A property check. My head's aching. I don't have the mental capacity to process it. I stumble the last few steps along the path to the cabin door.

Please, God.

He's not there. Claire Lorchann is on the mezzanine, her long-sleeved jersey dress immaculate, her half-up, half-down hairdo twisted into an elegant knot. She turns around slowly. I freeze.

There isn't a lick of make-up on her perfect face. And no hint of a smile. I can't move. She doesn't either. We stand in absolute silence. *Like she's watching me. Looking right through me.* I'm paralysed. What does she know?

Why is she here?

Who was Simon and why did he force his way into my flat?

At last she takes a step and my muscles tense in readiness. Then I realise that in her hand there's nothing more than a piece of folded paper, and that her eyes aren't on me at all; they're on her bag, which is propped against Sean's desk, next to where I'm standing.

"Sorry, Livia." She descends the steps. Moves past me, her expression blank, just focussing on the bag. She pushes the piece of paper into it and hangs it over her shoulder. "I have to go to the hospital. Mother's had another stroke."

'Oh . . .' I exhale in a rush. "I'm so sorry."

She shakes her head, mouth tight. Then she's gone, the door sealing itself in her wake.

I stand for a moment in the hush, horrible guilt creeping over me. What's the matter with me? Am I going crazy?

Sean isn't here. I don't know what I expected. The relief is unspeakable, and yet the realisation only seems to open the rift inside me wider, gaping and raw. If he isn't here, then where is he? I have no idea what I should do. Today. Tomorrow. The next day. Maybe there won't be a next day. My throat feels tight. Maybe that's the decision he's expecting me to make. Not to come back.

I lower my satchel, gazing around at the empty desks. The plans are still on the drawing board. My eyes are smarting. Strange, the way you stop seeing a place once you've come to know it. The familiar details have faded into insignificance. I let out my breath. Pick up my satchel and push open the door. I'm not sure why it feels like goodbye.

I walk to the chapel. Slowly, taking in every millimetre of the view as I go. The colours have changed; there are blossoms in some of the trees and daffodils cluster in the over-long grass. An orange plastic fence flutters at the height of the cliff, guarding the drop. The sky has cleared; the sea's blue, almost like the picture postcards should have been. But there's no remedy in the tints and hues. I don't name a single one. I walk to the tune of my own silence.

The wind is howling on the edge as I pick my way over the granite ridges, thinking of Armageddon. Its buffeting fills my ears and makes my skin burn. Perhaps there'll be no house with a view anyway, if Clarissa Gordon-Heyers dies today. Perhaps none of us will ever find our Helvellyn.

I pause, the rise and fall of human intonation reaching me suddenly. My gut contracts.

"Look, Dad, I just need to know if it's possible. Feasible. Tonight. Yes. I know it's sudden. Yeah. It's the only option. I—"

His voice. Private school, Russell Group with a hint of Gaelic twang. Pain stabs in my chest. For a long, lingering second, I can't make myself move.

"Yes. Yes. In Oxford? Yeah, I can do that. How soon? You can make that work . . . ? A hundred percent sure. I just have to know. One way or the other. She's—"

I recoil, as if the words have physically struck me. *Oxford. The only option.* I grab at the gorse stems, barbs sinking into my hand. Oxford. *If you wanted to go, I couldn't have stopped you.* He isn't just expecting me not to come back. He's already arranged it.

I stumble and run, jarring my ankles in the rabbit holes and ruts. I think, briefly, about going back to the cabin, leaving a note. For who? Katie's not coming back. Claire's gone to the hospital. I head for my car instead. Maybe I don't want anyone to find me. Maybe I don't want anyone to know. I park in the empty space outside Sunnyside, and the seagulls supervise me back as far as the front step. Two or three sleek black feathers drift in the hallway as I open the door; there was a time when I'd have picked them up, but not today. More litter the stairs, softer ones, downier, lifting and scattering with the draught as I reach number thirty-one and stop, feeling sick.

The bird's right against the foot of my door. I take an abrupt step backwards, convulsed by a shudder of revulsion. Its glassy eye is half-closed, its neck snapped at an unnatural angle. I try to remind myself that Niklavs has a cat. A cat that can catch things and climb in through open windows. A cat that can make the simplest silence seem haunted . . .

I push it aside with my foot and let myself in, dropping everything in disarray on the kitchen side keys, phone, satchel. The phone buzzes, its screen fading slowly as the door closes behind me. I move in a daze to pick it up, the unfamiliar number burning itself into the backlight.

Somehow, I already know.

I swipe the message open.

GET OUT OF HERE. BEFORE IT'S TOO LATE.
GET OUT, BLACKBIRD.
GET OUT

CHAPTER 26

> *I have to carry on like normal. That's all. Make everyone believe nothing's changed. Like I don't know . . . Just until I can figure out what to do. Until I figure out where to go. Where can I go?*
>
> *I've got to get away from here. I've got to get out.*

Get out, Blackbird. Get out . . .

> *Why would anyone believe me? No one will. I can't talk to anyone. I have nothing. No one. No way to prove it. But I know.*
>
> *And I'm so afraid.*

She wasn't crazy, if that's what you're asking. It's what everyone said, in the end. She wasn't okay. I know that. But there was more to it than that. She was afraid, Livia. She was scared.

> *If I hide this . . . if I leave it behind, just in case . . . I'll come back for it. If I'm okay, I'll come back for it. That's a promise.*
>
> *So . . . if you've found it? Then I haven't. I haven't come back. And I need you to—*

Wait—

There's someone here, now. Outside the door.

I think I'm out of time.

It's too late to explain. But you have to believe me. He's mine, I know he is, he always has been. Promise me you'll help him. He doesn't belong here. Neither of us do. It's too late for me. But help him, please. Help to

"Help to what?" My voice cracks, desiccated with underuse. I wet my lips. Help to what? I'm trembling. I've been trembling for twenty-four hours; my body aches with it and my head is pounding. I haven't eaten. I'm not even sure when I last had something to drink. I run the cold tap, letting the water flow through my fingers, and fill a glass.

I'm not Sophia Swift. I can't lose my mind over this. She's dead. She can't be sending me messages.

So who is?

Get out.

Who knows? Nobody. *Mercy's Child* is still beside the bed. I sit down heavily, trace the outline of the blackbird on the cover. No one knows that. Who can know that?

I pick up my phone. *Get out.* Maybe they're right. My fingers shake as I rap my passcode into the touchscreen, so fast that it takes me three attempts to get it right. I find Kris's number and pause, his miniature picture staring out of the screen at me. What am I going to say?

I swallow painfully. I don't have to say anything. Just tell him I'm visiting. Worry about the rest later . . .

I press to call him and pace the floor as it rings: four, five, six rings. It cuts out abruptly. What? I lower it, stare at it. Try again, but it goes straight to voicemail. I drop it onto the kitchen side and brace myself against the sink, taking a few steadying breaths. It doesn't matter. I can just set off. Call him on the way. Or Jen, my housemate. Even if she's let my old room, I'm sure she'll let me sleep on her floor.

My suitcase is turned out all over the floor, an eruption of creased clothes. I select the bare minimum and push them into an overnight bag with a toothbrush and my phone charger. It doesn't have to be for long. It certainly isn't permanent. Just long enough to get my head together. To get out of Sophia Swift's flat.

There's a certain irony to it. He was so desperate for me to leave, and it turns out he was right, in all the wrong ways. *Thirteen, backwards.* I try not to think of his eyes, but they haunt my every step as I empty the fridge and draw the blinds.

The vibration of my phone makes me jump. The sound resonates through the empty cups on the kitchen side, setting my teeth on edge. I grab it.

Ryan Lorchann. I falter. I was expecting Kris. I waver with the phone mid-air, torn over whether to answer, and what I might say.

"Hello?"

"Livs." He sounds relieved. "Thank goodness you're there. You . . . is it a good time? I mean . . ."

He means the driveway, at the Lookout. Nearly running me over because I threw myself full pelt into his bonnet. I grip the phone tightly.

"Yeah. It's uh, it's fine. Is everything okay?"

"Not really." Traffic noise and sirens blast past him in the background. His voice is fading in and out. "Clarissa's really poorly. I'm still in Exeter with Claire and Graham."

"Oh." I'm not really sure what to say. I blink and try to focus, not quite grasping why this involves me.

"I've tried everyone, but Sean's gone to Oxford, the cleaning lady's not picking up . . . I wasn't sure who else to call . . ."

"Fin's at school?" The light switch clicks. I readjust the phone under my chin.

"Yeah. They can hang onto him 'til four, but we're not going to be back. Graham's . . . not good. Not good at all. And I don't want to leave Claire . . ."

"No. No, of course not. I can get him. It's fine."

"Are you sure?" I hear him exhale. "I didn't want to ask, after everything . . . You're sure?"

"Of course I'm sure." The emphasis in my voice surprises even me. "I'll sort Fin. Don't worry about it."

No, no. The voice in the back of my mind is raging. I'm supposed to be leaving. What am I doing?

"Be as long as you need to." I'm still talking, despite the battle raging in my head. "And tell Claire not to worry."

It doesn't matter. I won't be in the flat. I'll be safe in the Gatehouse, until they get back. Just me and Fin. And I'll be able to put the key to the chapel back, before anyone realises it's missing. I can leave afterwards, or first thing in the morning. They need my help. I know what it's like: the valley of the shadow of death. How unpredictable. How dark, and seemingly endless. Of course I'll do what I can. How could it even be a question?

"Livs, I don't know how to thank you."

"You don't need to thank me." I loosen my hold on the phone. For some reason, my fingers are slippery with sweat. "Go. You need to be with Claire. Call me if there's anything else."

"I will. Thank you, Livia. I'll ring school and let them know. There's a key to the Gatehouse at the cabin, in my desk drawer. Give the little guy a big hug for me."

"Sure."

A muffled bluster of movement, then the line goes dead. I hang up. It'll be safer to leave in the morning, anyway. After I've rested, slept. It's not like Sean's going to come here looking for me. The empty ache in my chest has expanded again, suffocating. I fix my gaze on the stack of old paintings. I lived a hundred waking dreams last night, of his fist against the door, his hands in my hair. *Come back.*

Does he know what he's done to me? Does he have any idea? That he's made me love him and now I can't stop; I can't stop, and the pain's going to destroy me, like paper buckling in an open flame.

It's spitting with rain. I pull my waterproof from the back of the door and something falls from the peg under it, folding itself silently at my feet. I stoop and stop, immobilised by the wave of beach-hut bodywash and sea salt. I press the hoody to my face and drink it in desperately, the last lingering traces of his presence.

If I go back . . . Forgiven, not forgotten . . .

No. I have forgotten. I've forgotten *Oxford, the only option.* I let the hoody fall. Snatch up my raincoat and push my arms into the sleeves.

I feel like an imposter outside the primary school, hovering on the periphery of parental chat and playdate arrangements. Fin's an outsider too; he squeezes silently out beside the doorframe as his teacher calls across to check my name, then stops in the way so that half a dozen other children fall over him and then have to recalculate their courses in a chattering swarm around him. He stoops to pick something up, then carries on as if nothing happened, drowned in his over-sized blue cagoule.

"Finbar." I duck and weave my way through the jam of parents and school uniforms. "Fin!"

He looks up. He doesn't smile. A little frown flits across his pale forehead. His twiggy fingers drift to the emblazoned rainbow on the breast of his coat.

"Hey, Fin." I crouch down. Suddenly the press of people seems distant. As if there's only the two of us, and the unspoken words in the sentence that I haven't finished. I'm not sure how much to try and explain. He holds out his book bag. I take it without saying anything. I don't touch him; he doesn't take my proffered hand. We walk to the car and he clambers in and does up his own seatbelt. Nearly five years old. I gaze in the driver's mirror at his reflection. He doesn't look nearly five. Out of all of the children in the playground, he was easily the smallest. His hands are lost in the sleeves of his cagoule, and his trousers are turned up over his Velcro shoes.

"Did you have a good day?" I glance in the mirror at him again as we pull away. He nods.

"That's good." I find myself checking and double checking the road with burning eyes. My sleep deprivation must be catching up with me.

"Mum and Dad might be late home." I wrack my brain for the right phrasing. The right words. Ones he'll understand. His dark eyes are fixed on me; I can sense them without looking. Who am I kidding? He understands everything. Better than I do, probably. "They're at the hospital with Grandad and Grandma. They have to stay there for a bit, because Grandma's really sick, and Grandad's sad."

Sad. I glance in the mirror again to see him sign. There's a pause. Then he points at me. *Sad.* He lifts tentative wings to gesture. Blackbird. Sad. It's a question.

"A little," I admit. My voice sounds stifled. I try to clear my throat, but I can't. My jaw hurts unreasonably as I turn into the driveway, and park in the shelter of the trees. We fetch the spare key from the cabin and Fin waits as I unlock the door, then shrugs off his cagoule, scampers upstairs and disappears. I stand in the hallway, shivering. I can't banish the memory: the last time I was here, Max capering around Sean's legs, the taste of salt in our stolen kisses. I grip the book bag tightly.

I barely notice Fin come back downstairs. Not until his light touch on my arm startles me from my thoughts. I look down. He's holding something out to me. A paper windmill, all the colours of the rainbow. Tears leap, unbidden, to my eyes.

Happy. He pushes it into my hand, and signs at me. Happy. I clutch it tight.

"Thanks, Fin," I whisper. He brushes a finger over the blades so that they turn. Then he dematerialises into the shadows, soft-footed and solitary. I dash a hand across my eyes.

The chapel key. I try to pull myself together and go upstairs. It drops easily back into the corner of the shredding box. I push the crate under the bed and stare at it for long seconds before I go back down.

Fin's sat at the table drawing by the time I go through to the kitchen. I cook dinner for both of us, deliberately not watching the meticulous motions of his pencil. For some reason the sound of the lead on the paper unsettles me. After a few minutes, as if he's sensed it, he picks up the paper and takes it upstairs, returning empty-handed. I dish up the food, and we both pick our fish fingers apart in wary silence.

Eventually, I give up on the meal. I leave the dishes on the table and follow him through to the sitting room. Fin tries one sofa and then the other, fidgeting anxiously on the cushions before he gets up again and comes to tug at my sleeve.

"I'm okay," I reassure him. "What do you want to do?"

The words leave my mouth before their familiarity hits me. The image of the bucket and spade, two architects building sandcastles, is so vivid that for a moment I can't breathe. How can it have gone so wrong? How can it be over so fast? I close my eyes. Think of an advancing tide. Dying sunshine.

Fin has let go of my sleeve. He points at the TV.

"You want it on?" I move to try and decipher the controller for the vast HD screen. Fin picks up a DVD box from the coffee table. *Peter Pan*. I breathe an inward sigh of relief. *Peter Pan*, without me having to risk trying to read it to him. I open the DVD player and he puts the disc in and sits on the floor in front of it. At first, I watch with him. But there's something about the dark flicker of the Darlings' nursery that, for the first time, disturbs me. I stare, troubled, as the young dark-eyed Pan entices Wendy from her bed, the blatant and cunning charms of childlike innocence.

"But where do you live mostly now?"

"With the boys. The lost boys."

"Who are they?"

"They are the children who fall out of their perambulators when the nurse is looking the other way."

I'm starting to shiver, although it isn't cold. I pull my knees tighter against my chest. The children are out of the window, soaring, dipping, skimming the tops of the waves. I close my eyes and try not to look. Fin is gazing, rapt. It's half an hour before he moves, retreating from the clash of pirate swords to seek safety with me on the sofa. His small hand clutches my sleeve tightly as the story unfolds, through mermaids and Indians, swashbuckling and poisoned medicine. His eyes are wide with horror as Hook makes his capture, and Wendy walks, trembling, out onto the plank—

No. He shakes his head vehemently. Jumps down from the sofa with a thud. Before I can try to comfort him, he's gone. I hear his feet on the stairs. I don't know whether to follow him or not. The screen erupts in a burst of music and sword-fighting; I slide to my feet too and pause the DVD. I give him a couple of minutes and then go up after him. I halt on the landing. I was almost expecting him to be hiding, upset, afraid. But he isn't. There's no trace of tears on his cheeks; he's seated at the desk in his bedroom drawing, face tight with concentration.

I tiptoe back downstairs and stop the film. Flick channels to try and fill the emptiness. *At eight, has Daniel taken on more than he can handle in Noman's Town? But first, coming up after the break, find out if your home is reaching its full potential, in D—*

NCIS! Lower your weapon!

. . . now the weather, with Tom Davis.

A weather warning is in place for the South West and parts of Wales and the West Midlands, following predictions of huge storms to hit the region in the next forty-ei—

I turn it off. Stare at the blank screen for seconds, minutes, my chin resting on my hands. My legs are trembling with tension. I get up and walk the length of the living room, losing the battle not to pace. The floorboards creak gently under my feet. I go into the snug and turn on the light. I deliberately don't look at the windows. I look at the bookcases instead, scanning them. I've always found the smell of books comforting.

But not tonight. I run my fingers along the mismatched spines, my gaze flashing over the assortment of names, titles, dustcovers. Something's wrong.

I must have caught sight of it out of the corner of my eye; it registers in my subconscious before my thoughts catch up. I pause. There's a book in the bin. Its paperback covers are open, the pages splayed, crushed. I read the title upside down, even though I already know what it is. The bright eye of the blackbird is creased in the broken spine. I stoop to take it out, frowning.

Mercy's Child. The book that Claire Lorchann said she's never read. The book that, it turns out, everyone is reading.

I smooth it out. Open it to the back. There are no pages missing in this copy. It's all there. Every word.

A R Frost. 429

The door of the interrogation room closes. He hears Harrison's footsteps recede outside.

"You should have a lawyer," he says flatly.

She lowers her face.

"It's okay." She shrugs, and the end of her braid falls over her shoulder, starting to come undone.

He watches her breathe, little, tremulous breaths. She's barely more than a child. Eighteen or nineteen years old. Her hooded sweat-top is loose on her elfin frame. Pain and sympathy are twisting his gut into knots. She is biting her lip.

"At least let me get you a drink," he says gruffly.

She looks up. "I'm okay, Detective Inspector."

There's a calm detachment in her voice that chills him. Guileless acceptance.

"Red," he tells her. "You should call me Red."

For a moment there's silence. How many more hours? Watching the questions tear into her is breaking him. He scrapes his chair forwards, tormented, making her start.

"Tell me. While he's not here." For a moment, he's tempted to reach out and turn off the recorder.

"What?" A little frown creases between her wide eyes before she lowers them, hastily, to the table-top.

"You're hiding something."

She shakes her head.

"Why won't you tell the truth? I'm going to have to charge you. Don't you understand? You'll get thirty years for murder. Twenty-five, if you're lucky. Who are you protecting?"

There's a pause. Aching. He can feel it in his chest. She's biting her lip again.

"You," she breathes finally.

The silence is resounding. Red's muscles lock. He can't move.

"What?"

She closes her eyes. Turns her palms into the table and spreads out her fingers. Pale fingers, moon white.

"I did it."

"I don't believe you."

"I know. I'm glad." Her lips press together, glistening wet. "I want you to think I didn't. I want you always to think I didn't."

"I don't understand." The feeling in his chest is unbearable: crushing, constricting pain. "Who are you?"

"Don't you know?"

"No." The pain is getting worse. "How . . . How could I? How could I know you?"

"Oh," she murmurs. "I hoped . . ." She folds her trembling fingers, and tails off. Her breath escapes. A release, somehow.

"How do you know me?" Red sits forward in his chair. The pain fades abruptly, leaving something else. Fear. Fear? But he hasn't been afraid for fifteen years.

"I don't." She shakes her head, and it's barely a whisper. "I never had the chance."

She unfolds her hands again and slips off her sweat-top. For the first time, he sees her arms, thin, graceful arms that make him think of swans and lakes, and organza shoes. The breeze of a summer-night's dream.

He swallows. There's a burn on the inside of her wrist — transverse, one inch. He stares dully, remembering the picture in the squad room. The profile. An exact match.

"I had to." At last, she raises her eyes to his, earnest. "I had to do it. I tried to think of another way, but there

wasn't one. And . . . when it came to it, it . . . it was easier . . . easier than I thought . . ."

Tears are gathering in her lashes. Dripping, soundlessly, onto the table. He wants to stop the recording. He wants to stop it, or stop her, but he knows he can't do either. He has to listen, as she keeps talking, the words spilling out of her, not so much a confession as a deliverance.

A R Frost. 431

"That's it," she concludes, and her gaze drops to her hands and her ballet-dancer arms. "I'm sorry. You don't have to ask any more questions."

But he does. He does have to ask.

"What did you hope I—"

His voice fades in his throat.

She has risen to her feet, light as a bird, dark hair dropping out of its braid as she turns away. A daughter of night time. She's whispering.

No. Singing.

Red and yellow and pink and green . . .

He's about to blink. He's about to blink. And when he opens his eyes again—

I start. Drop the book. The sound from upstairs pierces me like a bullet.

"Fin?" I whisper.

The gentle smack of flesh on flesh. A slow, desolate crescendo. Clapping.

He's clapping.

Suddenly, the blood has drained from my cheeks. The house, the silence, seem frozen in time. *Clap your hands . . . Don't let her die . . .*

I don't want to move. The chill is creeping through me from my extremities inwards, the certainty. I turn around.

It's like I already know. The inevitability to my movements is painful, reality slowed to nonsense as I mount the first step, the next, the last; as I round the corner onto the landing and push open his bedroom door with a sick feeling in my stomach.

Get out of here. Before it's too late.

The Spider-Man clock has stopped; its second hand shudders in melancholy ticking protest. Fin has pushed his chair away from the desk and stood up. He has his back to me. His slow clap measures out the rhythm of my steps.

"Fin, are you okay?"

No answer. I look over his shoulder at his drawing.

Clap your hands.

My mouth tastes acidic. He's lined up the pencils beside the picture, a perfectly ordered rainbow.

Don't let her die—

At last he stops clapping and raises his face to mine.

"What have you drawn?" I pretend to inspect it for the first time. But I've already seen. Already taken in every millimetre of the green blob body, red-line arms and legs, yellow hair on a circle face with brown eyes. Of the light blue scribbles, coloured right over the top.

"Is he a boy?" I point to the red.

Fin nods.

"Peter Pan?"

He shakes his head.

"Is that water?" I show him the light blue. There's a momentary pause. Then a nod.

I force an uneasy smile. "That's really good, Fin. Is the boy you?"

Behind us, the door has drifted closed on its hinges. It latches itself with a gentle click. Fin climbs back onto the chair, straightening the last pencil on the desk, an unused black with a sharp, pointed tip. He traces his fingers over the blue scribbles.

"Why are you in the water?" I touch the light blue, too.

Fin freezes. I feel his small body stiffen, and quickly withdraw my hand. He shakes his head fiercely.

"Is it your reflection?" I'm not sure why all at once I'm whispering. "Like we saw at the beach?"

Nothing.

"A reflection . . ." I try again. "Like in a mirror?"

Sometimes I see reflections in that mirror . . .

Fin's hands close around the edges of the piece of paper. He picks it up and holds it to his chest for a moment. Then he lays it down again, smoothing it out carefully on the table-top.

He shakes his head. *No.*

"It's *not* a reflection?" An inexplicable chill runs down the back of my neck.

No. He's still shaking his head.

"It's not you?"

No.

I swallow.

"Fin. If it's not you, then who . . ." I frown down at the drawing, strangely sickened. "*Who's in the water?*"

Somewhere above us the hands of the stopped clock clunk heavily into the silence.

I think I'm out of time.

Agonisingly slowly, Fin picks up the pencil. The lead scratches into the paper.

T . . . o

And suddenly, I'm holding my breath.

b

"Fin?" My lips are numb. "Fin . . ."

y

He doesn't move. He's staring at the page. At the wobbly curves and lines of the name he's written, the pencil still upright and trembling at its conclusion.

Toby.

With a sudden, startling crack, the lead snaps, sending a spray of shattered graphite across the paper. The pencil falls onto the desk and rolls. Hits the floor, and keeps going. He doesn't seem to notice. His hand is still closed around the empty air, a death-grasp, white-knuckled and motionless, his gaze vacant. And there on the table, underneath his picture, is the missing page of the Thomas book, and his sheet of drawings from the kitchen. But they aren't drawings. They're letters. The same four letters, over and over and over again . . .

"Fin." My pulse is deafening. "Fin?"

He doesn't respond. Doesn't stir. I take hold of his arms, panic gripping my throat.

"Fin!"

Nothing. I hold his small shoulders tightly, comprehension not quite dawning past the ringing in my ears. Toby the Tram Engine. *He doesn't. Fin doesn't speak* . . .

Silence. Three years of silence . . .

"*Toby*?" I whisper.

Abruptly, he looks up. His strange, unclouded, depthless eyes meet mine. And then, in a voice as clear and pure and definite as the note of a bell, Finbar speaks.

"Toby's dead," he says.

CHAPTER 27

"Toby's dead." He's still looking at me. Staring, unblinking. "He fell in the water."

The floor seems to have dropped away from under my feet. I put out a hand to steady myself, feel my fingernails bite into the wooden desk.

"Sometimes," Finbar slides from the chair to his feet; his unearthly gaze doesn't leave mine, wide and serious, "I have a dream about Toby."

I can't respond. All I can do is gaze, sickened, at his rumpled golden hair and milk-pale skin, at honey and starlight. It isn't possible — can't be — I take a step back and almost trip on the edge of the rug. Honey and starlight. I'm disorientated, dazed; rain is battering the window glass, a gust of wind that throbs and echoes around the outside of the house. I take another step away. Reach to open the door.

Get out. Before it's too late—

"Livia."

I hear my own gasp in. My hands close on empty air.

The door's already open.

Ryan Lorchann's silhouette fills most of the doorway. His hands are buried in his pockets. There's fresh mud on his shoes, and his clothes are flecked with rain. I didn't hear the front door. The car. His feet on the stairs. I stand immobilised in his shadow as he withdraws his hands from his pockets and smiles.

"There you are." He's looking directly at me. I try to respond, and something incomprehensible passes my lips.

"Livia?" The smile fades, replaced by a look of concern. "Livia, are you okay?"

"I uh . . ." Suddenly I find my voice. "Yeah . . . I . . ." I swallow. "Just not . . . feeling well. I think, I . . ."

"Finbar." Ryan speaks past me, as if it's the most normal thing in the world. "Can you get your PJs on, buddy, and get into bed?" It's so quiet, so reassuring, that I blink in confusion. He turns back. "Livs, come downstairs. Can I get you a drink or something? You don't look too good." He supervises me onto the stairs. His hand on my shoulder is warm and heavy. "Thank you — so much — for coming. Has he been all right?"

"It's okay. Yeah. He was . . . fine. I . . ." I grip the banister as we reach the hall. "I think I just need to get home."

"Yeah." Ryan nods slowly. "Yeah. Of course. Are you all right to drive? Do you want me to run you back?"

"No, it's fine." I waver. I need my coat. My bag. My bag's in the car. I seek out my raincoat from the hooks behind the door, bewildered; terrified.

"Are you sure you don't want a lift?" An earnest frown furrows his forehead. "You look awful."

"I'll be alright," I croak. "Thanks."

"Then at least let me know you get back in one piece. Text me when you get there, okay?"

"Yeah."

"Promise?"

"I promise." I don't even stop to get my coat on. I flee with my arms half-tangled in the sleeves, fumbling with the door and running, off balance, across the drive. I bundle my coat into the passenger seat, spinning the wheels on the gravel as I reverse and floor it back past the Hall towards the main road.

But I don't quite get as far as the road. White noise is reverberating in my ears, the odd emergent word. *Afraid . . . I'm so afraid . . .*

Get out, Blackbird . . .

I swerve to a halt in the conifer trees beyond the gates. Snatch my bag from underneath my bundled coat and tip its contents onto the seat. The journal splays open on the upholstery, spilling the paper-clipped severed pages. I scoop them back together and pause, mind racing. Turn off the engine.

Shaky, sick, I put on the coat and zip it up. I'm glad of the cover of the darkness as I feel my way out of the car and try to close the door without a sound. Not wanting to risk opening the gates, I squeeze myself between the thick growth of the bushes instead, thorns and branches snagging at my hair and clothes until I emerge onto the weedy gravel. Every inch seems to shift and crunch mutinously as I tiptoe over it, and slip between the rhododendrons to the cabin. I feel in my pocket for my keys. My hands are unsteady as I unlock the door; I close it behind me and hesitate, not quite wanting to turn on the light. Instead, I light my way with the torch on my phone, like a thief. My work laptop is in my desk drawer. The brightness of its screen hurts my eyes. I stare at the logon page. *frostl.*

What if . . .

I click the trackpad, my fingers hovering painfully over the keys.

swifts

I type it slowly, a letter at a time. I need a password. Perhaps she'd never changed it? I type the same letters into the second box and hit enter. Incorrect. Shit. I curl my hands into fists. Is it far-fetched even to imagine that this had been hers? I'm assuming that her laptop wasn't taken away after she died. Or that her account hasn't been deleted. But, somehow I'm sure . . .

I swallow. What else. What else, if I'm right? The journal. A clue. A sign . . . *As I come to close, I can't help thinking that I should probably sign and date.*

I suck a sharp breath in.

Apus apus.

I rap it into the keyboard. Hit enter and close my eyes, barely daring to look.

I open them again. The screen has brightened. *LMLA.* I suddenly realise I'm holding my breath. *Swifts.* She's still here. The back of my neck prickles with the realisation. I've logged into Sophia Swift's laptop.

I stare at it for seconds, a minute, maybe more. What next? My hand is frozen over the trackpad.

And then, out of nowhere, it's there. The bird. The bird from back at the beginning — not imagined after all — there, on the screen: black-brown, sharp-billed, with sickle-shaped wings and a short, forked tail. A swift. My ears are ringing. I slash a finger over the trackpad, and it disappears. A screen-saver. I let out my breath. Her screensaver.

The desktop is blank. But there has to be something, somewhere. If whoever set it up hasn't wiped her account altogether, I can't imagine they'll have gone to the trouble of completely erasing her files.

It's instinct that makes me open the recycle bin. Whether it's her cover, or someone else's, it's transparent. It takes a few minutes to restore all the files, and I find myself glancing up over the glare of the screen at the darkness outside. At least with the lights off, I can still make out what or who is outside the glass. A shudder runs along my spine.

It's done. The first folder has restored to the desktop. I double tap, and a list of files fills the page. They're images. I pull my chair closer to the desk, scrutinising the file names. 1034494_101n.jpg 1034494_101n.jpg . . . I squint, trying to make sense of it. Fifty-six items. I click on the first.

Claire's flawless dimpled smile looks like an advert from a magazine, with one of Ryan's arms encircling her and the other steadying Fin on his broad shoulders. The brilliant blue ocean and iconic skyscrapers in the backdrop don't look like anywhere in the UK. I scroll through to the next one. Claire again, a younger Claire in a zip-up hoody, with a babe in arms. I still don't really understand. The next one, a toddling child with a baby-walker and dimples like his mum, which I've never noticed before. More and more. Picture after picture. I flick from one to the next, to the next—

I freeze.

Not Claire. Or Fin. I recoil, gripping the edges of my chair. Tom and Leanna Rainworth are locked in an artificial studio embrace, while their sailor-suited toddler plays with a red toy yacht in the brilliant white foreground, his molten midnight-brown eyes turned entreatingly on the camera. Toby Rainworth.

How . . . The acidic taste in my mouth is making me feel sick. How would she have got these? And why? The next one, the one after, they're all the same photo-shoot. And then there are baby pictures. White mittens, knitted blankets and muslin cloths. I scroll through them faster, sweat breaking on my upper lip. I don't understand. I don't *want* to understand . . .

I reach the end abruptly. It won't let me click any further. The last file isn't a picture: *document3.docx*. Fear and expectation stab in my gut. More journal? Another letter—

No. A page of browser links.

What?

CHILD DROWNS IN SOLENT HARBOUR
Saturday 18 August 18.36 BST
Home» News» UK»
MILLIONAIRE'S GRANDSON MISSING FROM YACHT
Philanthropist's 20-month-old grandchild presumed drowned after anniversary celebration ends in tragedy.
www.facebook.com/photo.php?fbid=1030&set=t.54297&type=3s88&thx

Facebook. I haven't been on Facebook for months. I've barely used it since Dad died, other than to message Hannah and keep tabs on a few old school friends, and since the *Mercy's Child* fiasco I haven't logged on at all. It never even occurred to me that Sophia Swift might have a Facebook page. I touch a finger to the trackpad.

A Facebook page, yes.

But it isn't Sophia Swift's. I stare, dazed. It's a photo, from an album of mobile uploads full of faces even more familiar than the high-resolution Rainworth photo-shoot.

The name at the top of the page is Kris Frost.

The picture is of me.

"What . . . ?" Bile has risen in my throat. I let the cursor hover over the tag, *Livia Frost*, click through to my own disappointingly neglected profile: *Studies Architecture at the University of Nottingham.* I hit the back button, uncomprehending.

Swing-dancing. Ruby lights and balloons. Rivent. *A yacht. An actual yacht.* A picture of me. Me.

And there, in the background beside me, his face lit unmistakably by the festoon lights, is Ryan Lorchann.

His old colleagues from Rivent . . .

Rivent. Michael Rainworth's company. Tom and Ryan both worked for Rivent . . .

"Fuck . . ." I'm clutching at my hair, gazing, half-witted. "Oh, fuck."

It wasn't from the interview. The instant dazzling-smiled familiarity. It wasn't from the interview that I recognised Ryan.

I grab the laptop and lurch to my feet.

The rhododendrons are an ambush of shadows, flapping and roaring in the wind; rain blows into my eyes as I flee wildly for my car. It's only as I get to the door that I realise I forgot to lock it; I dive in and then look behind me, gripped by sudden terror, to check the back seats. There's no one there. I grind the gears in my haste to pull away. By the time I'm on the coast road, the rain is an onslaught. I can barely see through the wipers on full pelt. Sunnyside is a river, a torrent of water and litter pounding over the cobbles. I'm soaked before I even reach the steps.

I deadlock the flat door and put on the chain. Peel off my raincoat and slump back dizzily, a headache pounding behind my eyes.

The flat's empty.

Right?

I'm too afraid to listen. Too afraid to look. I flick on all the lights to prove it to myself and turn on the shower to fill the silence, trying to drive it back: the ever-closing circle of darkness. I need to get warm. To calm down. To think. *Think.* I strip and shower, watching the suds spiral around the blocked drain.

Toby Rainworth. Peter Pan . . . *the children who fall out of their perambulators when the nurse is looking the other way.*

Who are the Lost Boys?

It's too late to explain. But you have to believe me. He's mine, I know he is, he always has been. Promise me you'll help him. He doesn't belong here. Neither of us do. It's too late for me. But help him, please. Help to—

Help to

But what if it *isn't* help to?

I grab my robe from the back of the door and huddle in it, shivering. The dust-jacket. *Mercy's Child.* Why *Mercy's Child*? It can't be a coincidence. There are too many coincidences. *Mercy's Child*: the one book of my father's that I've never read.

My bare feet leave wet prints on the floorboards. I sit down in front of the mirror and pull off the sheet. Smooth the glossy paper cover over the spine of the book. Why did she choose *Mercy's Child*? I turn it over. Stare, as if for the first time, at the back.

A missing child,
A lost past,
A broken heart.
And one survivor.

Oh, shit.

Just for a moment, I didn't want to let him go . . . Leanna. Leanna Rainworth couldn't *have* a child of her own . . .

I stand up so quickly that the girl in the mirror pales and separates in two. I blink hard as she swims and converges, her auburn hair glowing darkly in the artificial light, her black kohl eyeliner smudged with tears and her eyes red-rimmed with exhaustion. *Get out, Blackbird.* Her lips form the words, the glass the only barrier that separates my world from hers. *Get out.*

I've lost my mind. I must have.

"No!" I swipe out. "No . . ."

It falls and shatters, a myriad of broken shards glinting up at me as they spread themselves across the floor. I teeter, off balance. The splintered glass surrounds me like a sea. I stop, trembling.

There, in the broken mess of the end pane, is one last piece of paper. I crouch down, deafened by the ringing in my ears. The last page. It's the very last page.

A R Frost. 436

And as I lay, at the border of sleep, all I could think about was Mercy, and the words that had passed her lips as she found her place with God.

She isn't here.

I'd misunderstood, at the time. For all those years, I always thought she'd meant here — this room, our room. But she hadn't. She hadn't meant here. She'd meant there.

Mercy had reached the place where sick people go, and children when their stars stop shining.

And Tallullah wasn't there.

It wasn't help to.

It was help To. *Help To.* I fumble for the journal, forgetting about the glass.

Help Toby.

I know. And I'm so afraid.

"Oh my God." I wrestle my phone from the pocket of my discarded jeans. My hands are shaking too much to dial. "Oh my God. Oh God. Oh my God."

Kris Frost. I hit the number and clutch the phone to my ear, numb.

"Come on," I'm whispering. "Come on, come on . . ."

"*The phone you are calling is out of range or turned off. Please try again later.*"

"No," I hiss. "No, come *on* . . ."

I try again. Nothing. Panic is starting to invade my chest. Katie's number is just above Kris's. I scroll up and try to pull myself together as it dials.

"*You have reached* . . . Katie. *Please leave your message after the—*"

"No!" I jab a finger into the screen, gasping. Where is everyone? Midnight, already. Sweat has broken on my upper lip.

I dial the last number without looking. The anticipation of his voice makes my muscles clench, my pulse quicken. Desperate tears prick my eyes. It doesn't matter, whatever happened, the things that were said. None of it matters. I just need him to answer. I just need to tell him. He needs to know . . .

He doesn't know. He *can't* know—

"Please . . ." My voice sounds cracked, unfamiliar. "Come on . . ."

It's ringing, ringing. Just his voice. If I can only hear his voice, it'll be okay. I know it will. Somehow.

"Sean," I whisper. "Please . . ."

Ringing. Still ringing. He isn't picking up.

"*Please*," I choke. But there's no answer. Just a pure tone bleep that obliterates my thoughts.

I drop the phone.

Sophia. This was exactly what happened to her. Exactly how the journal ended. Alone. Panicking. Cut off. I pace the length of the room, breathing hard. Niklavs. I could go to Niklavs. Stay in his flat, instead of mine. But how will I explain? Where can I even start? It's the middle of the night. I sit down heavily on the side of the bed, gripping the journal with both hands. I try to be rational. I'm safe. Behind a locked door. Things will be different in the morning. I can go to Niklavs in the morning.

I open the journal. Gaze stupidly at the pages. Flip to the inside front cover, and then to the back. I've never really looked at the back cover. I was distracted by the page of *Mercy's Child* folded against it.

I've certainly never looked hard enough to notice the ghost of the letters blotted in blue fountain-pen ink onto the faintly flower-printed cardboard.

Blotted from what? I dash a hand across my eyes, frowning. There isn't anything at the back. There are still missing pages, at least two that I've never found the counterparts to; their paper stubs still protrude from the binding. But I knew that. She must have used pages for other things. Messages. Notes. She wrote her suicide note on one.

Her suicide note. Realisation dawns dully. It's still folded in my suitcase — I've not unpacked. I draw it out. Line it up against the back-most stub of paper, but it doesn't fit. The second to back. I chew my lip. It still doesn't. How can it not fit?

My eyes are tired. I blink, hard. The fine blue lines don't match up . . . the widest is at the bottom, not the top. I release my breath in a rush. It's upside down. She must have turned the book over. Used it from the back, as if the last page was the first.

Sure enough, the edges appose perfectly. Like a jigsaw puzzle. A lock and key. But not at the very back. The note fits on the second stub.

Which means . . .

I falter.

Which means that the writing imprinted on the inside of the cover isn't from the note. It's from something else. Something after the note.

No. My mind is working sluggishly. Not after the note. If the book was upside down when she wrote it, then she *started* at the back page. There was something *before* the note.

Painfully slowly, I kneel down. One pane of the mirror has survived the fall. I pick it out of the broken mess and lean it tentatively upright. Then I hold the book up to the glass to read the reversed characters.

It's faint. Patchy. But decipherable.

His name.

Sean,

This isn't the way I wanted to do this. But I have to tell you that I'm leaving.

By the time you get this letter, I'll be gone. I wish I could have explained. I want you to know that I'm thankful for everything I learned from you.

Once this is over, I'll find a way to tell you properly. If you can still bear to speak to me once the truth is out, once I'm safe and all's said and done. I'll call you. Or something.

In the meantime, there's a book. I lent it to Katie, but I need you to read it. I need you to read every word. Right to the very last page. Right to the back. In a roundabout way, it explains almost everything. Please read it. I want you to know. I need you to know. The truth. About me. About my son. About why I have to do this. I know

Something before the note. There was another page. My ears are ringing, the pure tone of the phone cut-off, but louder. A first page. I lay out the note beside it on the glass.

what's about to happen will hurt you. I hope you'll forgive me. I tried. I tried to think of a better way. But I wasn't strong enough. One day, you'll understand. One day, you'll understand everything.

Thank you for believing in me. I know that was all it was. I know you could never have loved me. Not really. But — for a time, at least — you made my sun rise.

I'm sorry that it has to fall.

I'm sorry, for everything.

Goodbye, Sean.

Sophia

I know what's about to happen will hurt you.

It completes the sentence. A second page. What Sean found was a second page. They're one and the same letter.

Suddenly the context has shifted completely. I'm motionless, paralysed by the realisation. By the writing in the mirror. *I'll call you.* Who writes 'I'll call you' in a suicide note? It might have been a goodbye, but it wasn't a suicide letter. *Who showers before they hang themselves?*

Sophia Swift wasn't planning to die.

There's someone here now. Outside the door.
I think I'm out of time.

The rap of a fist splits the silence on cue. I drop the book, terror sharp in my mouth. I can almost hear them breathing: whoever's there. The shift of feet at the bottom of the door.

Another knock—

CHAPTER 28

It's morning. The shadows in the hallway are long, bathed in the light of a red sky. A shepherd's warning. His footfalls slow. It seems a long time since he's been here. Ahead of him, the old man is surprisingly agile on the stairs. He knows something's wrong. Who is he kidding? They both do. There's an animosity in the silence, a reluctant acknowledgement that, in this, they're united, despite their mutual suspicion. He alights the last step.

Thirteen backwards. The instant, bizarre thought had struck him the first time he came here. 31. The old man stops.

"I knock yesterday, last night. Again this morning. Nothing."

"We should try again." The reflected sun winks at him from the metallic numbers. Her car's still here. Where else would she be? He raps firmly on the wood. Nothing stirs. He pauses. He knocks again, hard, the sound so loud that it echoes around the hallway and someone on the next floor opens their door.

Nothing. Beside him, the old man's jaw has clenched tight.

"Does anyone have a key?" he hears himself ask. The tension in his voice is barely disguised. "Do you know if she left a spare?"

The old man shakes his head. "Not with me or neighbour. With letting agent, perhaps. In Redruth."

"Shit." His hands close in his hair; he clutches it in fistfuls. What was it she'd said? He couldn't even remember. "*Shit.*"

Silence. They both stare at the door. He lowers his hands.

"Stand back," he mutters.

"What?"

"Get back."

"*Jēzus Kristus* . . ."

His foot strikes the lock with a resounding crash and the crunch of splintering wood. He staggers, then kicks again, once, twice. He takes a step backwards, steels himself. Then his shoulder contacts the door instead, and in one go it caves, sending him stumbling into the middle of the room.

She isn't there.

But she is. He's too late.

The bathroom door is half open. It's her feet he sees first. The paint on her toenails, revolving slowly, a half turn. He retches before he can repress the reflex. There's something on the floor. Fallen from her half-curled hand.

"Fuck," he chokes. A sob of terror bottlenecks in his throat. "Oh fuck. Oh fuck, no . . ."

* * *

Sean Lorchann closes his eyes. Opens them. Forces a breath in. The bathroom is empty. The tap is dripping. The flashback takes its time to disperse, the images slowly erasing themselves from the blank tiles. He backtracks, not able to feel the relief, back to the broken glass and torn paper, a snowstorm of chaos over the unmade bed and the floorboards. The door creaks on its hinges. The Latvian isn't far behind him, just like in the replays. Except this time, there was a key. And this time, the flat's deserted.

"Fuck." He spins on the spot. "*Fuck.*" He stares around at the blank walls, the clothes hung over the cold radiators, the wet towel thrown over the foot of the bed. He stoops to touch it. Wet. It's still wet.

"You are satisfied?" The Latvian is in the doorway, lips pursed behind his bushy beard.

"No." He shakes his head. Raises his hands to grip his hair, and lets it go again. "No. She's not here. Where is she?" He spins back. "Where is she?" He can hear the note of despair rising in his voice. "She's not fucking here!"

"I tell you." The Latvian folds his arms across his chest. "She is awake all of night, lights on. Perhaps she go for run, as usual. Or, if she has sense, she already leaves this forsaken place."

"Her car's here." It sounds like a broken record. The same conversation, over again. Panic is closing around his chest, totally irrational. He sees it suddenly: "The window's open. Why would she leave the window open?"

Rain is blasting in over the easel and spattering onto the stack of canvases. That picture, replicated in a dozen disturbing forms: the circle of sea through a porthole, rain and darkness. He remembers them, from before. They aren't easy to forget.

"This is last time I break into this room." The Latvian's voice cuts through the air like a whip. "I do not know how you persuade me to do this. You, and me. One time is too many. Whatever thing you—"

"No!" Sean flings the canvases down. Strides the length of the room in desperation. Broken glass. It is — was — a mirror. There's still one pane intact, propped against the bed. And something beside it. He crouches and snatches it up.

> *what's about to happen will hurt you. I hope you'll forgive me. I tried. I tried to think of a better way. But I wasn't strong enough*

"Shit," he gasps. "*Shit.*"

I'm sorry that it has to fall.
I'm sorry, for everything.
Goodbye, Sean.

She's gone.

* * *

I climbed out of the dormitory window once, at school, to find Hannah when she didn't come back from a date in town. I'd been stronger and nimbler then than I was today, in the breaking Porthtrevelen light with the church bells ringing. Five. Run time. The idea crept over me as I crouched against the kitchen cabinets, as far away as I could get from any external line of sight. I don't know how long I was hiding — long enough that I couldn't make out if the shadow on the other side of the door was still there.

At first I was too cramped and stiff to move. Too terrified of attracting unwanted attention from the other side of the door. My head was light as I backed against the kitchen cabinets and slid upright. Then, deafened by the sound of my own breath, I put on my running gear. Eased open the bottom sash of the misted-up window behind the easel, my fingerprints smearing in the condensation. There was no one in the street. I watched for a long time, to be sure. Then I climbed out.

I'm tiring now. I've outpaced myself. I've never run the cliff route to Trethallyan from here, only the part from the Lookout, and Sean's not at the Lookout. He's in Oxford, and he's not picking up my calls, and the only person who can do this is me.

My Lycra is soaked. I make myself focus on my footfalls. Find the rhythm. *Breathe in, lengthen the stride, out.*

The path has narrowed: the descent beckons. My feet thunder hollowly on the path. There's hail mixed in with the rain, stinging my cheeks; the tide has been in and it's turning, the waves are churning over the white-gold beach and seething hungrily in their reach for the rocks. Somehow, the bitter, drenching wind is bringing clarity to my thoughts.

If Fin is Toby, then where is Finbar?

I need proof.

The chapel is a flickering mirage through the rain. I jog the last ascent, dreamlike, watching the wind tear through the brambles and rip at the orange fence, tugging it in crackling, fluttering protest from the few steel posts that are still standing. I don't know how, but I'm sure. A suitcase full of baby clothes. I know where Finbar Lorchann is.

I leap across the trenches, between the heaps of earth and slaughtered brambles. The render abrades my hands as I pull myself up to the window; the board is still loose. I swing my feet through the gap and drop inside, prepared this time for the fall, to land softly in the dust. I make straight for the font, the cross. The kneeler, the trapdoor, *the darkness*. But it's not dark. It's lighter than before. The weeping Virgin casts an oddly coloured glow over me as I get my fingernails under the edge and lift.

Empty.

It's empty. I feel the heave of my breath in my chest. The suitcase isn't there.

I'm not sure what it is that alerts me. A sound. The tiniest sound.

He's standing in the semi-darkness. Alone, a tiny wraith, a shadow, the child that fell out of the perambulator when everyone was looking the other way.

"Fin," I breathe.

He turns, as though he's heard me. Raises his arms: wings, like a bird—

Are you afraid, Frost?

"Fin . . . ?" I stumble numbly to my feet.

He hasn't moved. He's frightened. I can see it in the stiffness of his posture and, as I get closer, in his wide, uncomprehending eyes. I waver.

"*Fin,*" I whisper. "*Fin . . . ?*"

Then darkness explodes across my vision.

I stagger, trying to stay upright, the room around me returning in fragments. The door is open, just a crack, but enough. Of course it's open. How else would he have got in? Through the Carmine mist, his white face and mop of gold hair drift into two. I reel upright, forwards. Something hot is running down my neck.

"Hail Mary, full of grace . . ."

I clutch at my hair, dazed. Pull my hand away. It's blood. My hand is covered in blood.

"The Lord is with thee." Claire Lorchann's chant is a faint monotone She's gripping the steel fencepost with both hands.

Fin?

"Blessed art thou among women, and blessed is the fruit of thy womb, Jesus. Holy Mary, Mother of God, pray for us sinners now and at the hour of our death. Amen. Hail Mary, full of grace, the Lord is with thee . . ."

He darts past her, towards the daylight, then stops as if held back by some invisible force, cowering against the door.

"Holy Mary, Mother of God—"

"Claire," I rasp.

The fencepost trembles in her hands. Both of her arms are shaking. There's a bruise across her face, a weal, angry blue and red; her eye is bloodshot and swollen almost closed.

"He's mine."

I can see her lips moving, but I barely recognise her voice.

"*Mine. He's mine.*" At last, she lowers the post. Her knuckles are white around the rusted steel. "Whatever you say, he's *my* baby. Mine! You can't change that! You can't—"

"Claire?" I feel so sick. I blink desperately. Her face keeps dividing and reconverging, out of focus in the dim light, until I don't know which of the erratic swaying images is hers. "What—"

I could plead ignorance. Plead it, but there's no point; we're past a point of reason. The wildness in her eyes is grief and fear.

"It's a lie! He's mine! Whatever they told you, they're lying!"

"Claire . . ." I put out my arms, appeasing, surrendering. "It's okay. I know. I know. I believe you." It's oddly easy to lie with the trapdoor behind me somewhere in the gloom, and a steel bar glinting over my head. "I believe y—"

"No!" she screams, and the sound splinters through me. "No! You don't! But it was an accident! An accident that he died . . . I would never have hurt him. Never have . . . *never* . . ."

An accident. That he died. I open my mouth, but no sound emerges. An accident.

"Finbar . . ."

"F-Finbar died! He's d-dead! I k-killed him! I was trying to save him; all I wanted was to get us away, get us out . . .

"After Sean went away, after Mother and Daddy went to Montreal, things got so bad. He'd never been like that before. Ryan. So . . . so angry. The tiniest h-h-things . . . He always said sorry. H-h-he didn't m-mean to, he didn't kn-know what he was d-doing. But he did know, h-h-he *did* know . . . Th-the first time I ended up in hospital, I thought it would s-stop. He was broken up. H-he said he loved me, so . . . *much* . . . He just needed a chance . . . I wanted to give him a chance . . ."

Ryan. Oh, God. I stare, horrified, at the colours of the bruise over her cheek. Remembering: *I was on the trampoline with Fin and I fell.* Remembering the marks under her scarf, the clothes that never exposed any skin.

"It didn't. H-h-it didn't stop. It only got worse. I got . . . I got so sc-scared of him. H-h-I wanted to leave. But he told me if I d-did, he'd take Finbar. He'd t-take Finbar — they'd never let *me* have him, because of the depression, the m-medication . . . I couldn't let him take him. I c-*couldn't* . . . My baby boy . . .

"But that m-morning, he hit me in front of Fin. He knocked him over and he cut his face. And it made me realise I — I couldn't let it carry on. It was one thing to hurt me, but if he hurt F-Finbar . . .

"I thought of a plan. I p-packed a bag, and I hid it in the chapel. I ordered a cab to meet us, here, at three in the m-morning. I g-gave . . ."

There's something crazed in her eyes, something desperate. I search the darkness for Fin, but he's gone. Sweat is stinging my lip, my underarms. I have to keep her calm. If I can just keep her calm . . .

"I g-gave F-Finbar. One of . . . one of my s-sleeping tablets. I just w-wanted . . . wanted to be s-sure he'd stay asleep. I never thought . . . never th-thought . . ."

Oh, God. I want to close my eyes, so that I won't have to see it in her face.

"I put . . . p-put him to bed. Stayed up with R-Ryan and h-had a drink. It was only s-supposed to keep him asleep. I couldn't risk him w-waking up before we g-got to the taxi. I needed to . . . be able . . . t-to carry him . . . to c-carry . . . h-him . . ."

No, no. Oh no. I can't look away from her. From the fencepost, her ashen face, her quaking hands. I take an unsteady step backwards.

"After Ryan was asleep, I went to get him from his cot. But he was . . . h-h-so still. So . . . s-still . . . He wasn't . . . wasn't . . . breathing. Just still, for such a long, long time . . . and c-cold. Freezing c-cold, no m-matter how tightly . . . t-tightly I h-held him."

"Claire . . ." I exhale. "No . . ."

Temazepam 20mg in the bathroom cabinet. *An accident.*

"Please," I breathe. "Put it down. I can help you. We can find a way out of this. Let . . . let me help you. I know . . . I know you didn't mean to h—"

"I wanted . . . w-wanted to get h-help . . . but . . . but I c-couldn't! He said everyone would know! What I'd d-done. He said I'd go to prison! If I c-called . . . if I ever told . . . about a-anything . . . *anything*. I had to stay quiet. He said he'd help me if I kept q-quiet. If I kept my mouth shut. He'd look after me . . .

"He said he knew what to do. He called Rivent that morning, and accepted the t-transfer. We told everyone we were l-leaving. Booked tickets, p-packed everything. He even sold off some of D-Daddy's things, to pay. We were supposed to t-tell everyone that we'd left already, to make it look like a break-in. But we didn't leave. He made me wait at the H-Hall. I didn't know where he'd gone, he just said he'd . . . h-he'd s-sort everything. I was so . . . s-scared . . .

"It was four in the morning when he c-came back. I thought he'd brought him b-back. He'd brought him back to l-life, it c-couldn't have happened, he wasn't d-dead. He looked . . . so much . . . like . . . my . . . my little boy . . ."

Her sobs are giddying. I clutch at my head. I can't keep up.

"My little boy . . . Just like . . . just like . . . it had never . . . n-never happened . . . nothing had . . . e-ever . . . He was mine. Ours. It was all like . . . l-like it had been a bad . . . b-bad d-dream . . . I th-thought . . ."

Sometimes, I have a dream about Toby . . .

"He didn't belong to th-them anyway, he wasn't theirs! He wasn't anyone's! His own *m-mother* didn't want him! But *I* wanted him. I needed him. *I* l-loved him. *I* love him!

"So you see, he *is* mine. He's mine. And no one . . . n-no one's going to ch-change that. I can't l-let you! I *w-won't!*"

She's turning the metal unsteadily in her hands, like a soul possessed. I can see the pulse at her temple. The tremor in her arms. She's between me and the door.

"Claire." I whisper. "I know. I know how much you love him. I—"

"It was Ryan's idea to send the advert to your tutor. It was only s-supposed to be f-finding out . . . what you'd seen . . . I didn't know. I didn't *know,* I swear. I didn't know this is what he meant. I didn't know what he did to Sophia! I never wanted to hurt you . . ."

"Then don't," I choke. "Don't—"

We've reached the wall, the stacked carcasses of the chairs. The stained glass is above me, bleeding filtered light like tears across her swollen face.

"But it's better this way. It's better if . . . if it's me, than . . . than if *he* finds you. I'm sorry."

It wasn't her at the door to my flat.

Sophia didn't kill herself.

"Claire—" I plead. "Please. Just—"

"I'm sorry," she sobs. "I'm sorry . . ."

I take another step back. One last step, one too many, into the jagged arms of the broken chairs, and it sends me sprawling. She swings. Like a strange mime-dance, I see myself duck sideways, see my arm fling across my face, see the uncontrolled arc of the rusted steel through the air—

To die . . . To die would be an awfully big adventure . . .

The first hit buckles my knees.

And on the second, the stars turn black.

CHAPTER 29

2021

> *Thank you for believing in me. I know that was all it was. I know you could never have loved me. Not really. But — for a time, at least — you made my sun rise.*

She sat back. Her hand ached from writing. She'd been gripping the pen so hard that the tip of her finger had turned white. Not long, now. She glanced at her watch. An hour. She leaned forward again. Blotted the ink from her forefinger on her robe.

How to finish it? She bit the end of the pen, a shudder of nerves running through her. There was so much still left to say. But now wasn't the time. Otherwise she'd be risking that he — or someone else — would find it before she got far enough away.

She levelled the pen. Her heart was beating hard.

> *I'm sorry that it has to fall.*
> *I'm sorry, for everything.*
> *Goodbye, Sean.*
> *Sophia*

She flapped the cover of the diary over before the ink had dried, so that she wouldn't have to see what she'd written. Searched her bag for the envelopes she'd bought and wrote his name on one with a flourish. Then she opened the diary and ripped out the pages. Slid them into the envelope and paused, listening to the silence.

Fifty minutes. Her train was at ten. It seemed better than taking the car; no one would realise she was gone, for a while at least. Sophia stood up. She needed to get ready. The taxi driver was going to phone her from the end of the road when he arrived. Her bag was packed. She just needed to get dressed. Her clothes were folded over the back of the chair, her railcard tucked in a pocket with her facemask. She checked it, rechecked it. Forty-five minutes. There was time yet.

She sat down again. She'd decided what to do with the diary. It was just a case of trying to get the last few words of explanation onto the paper. It seemed morbid, somehow. But there needed to be a failsafe. She picked up the pen.

If I hide this . . . if I leave it behind, just in case . . .

I'll come back for it. If I'm okay, I'll come back for it. That's a promise.

So . . . if you've found it? Then I haven't. I haven't come back. And I need you to—

The knock at the door made her start so violently that she dropped the pen. Ink splattered onto the wooden floor like blood. She picked it up, adrenaline coursing through her.

There's someone here, now. Outside the door.
I think I'm out of time.

Another knock. She caught her breath. Sped up, the writing deteriorating into almost illegible scrawl.

It's too late to explain. But you have to believe me. He's mine, I know he is, he always has been. Promise me you'll help him. He doesn't belong here. Neither of us do. It's too late for me. But help him, please. Help To

"Sophia?"

She froze. Lowered the pen.

"Shit," she whispered.

"Soph, I can hear you in there. Aren't you going to let me in?"

She closed her eyes, tried to breathe.

"One second," she called. Her voice sounded sing-songy. Fake.

The mirror. She'd peeled the paper back already, exposed the space inside. With shaking hands, she fumbled to tear the rest of the pages out of the diary. But they were tough, stronger than they should have been.

"*Shit,*" she hissed. "*Shit!*"

"Soph?"

"I'm coming!" In desperation, she snatched up what she'd got. Stuffed it behind the brown backing paper and plastered the tape over the join. She shoved the dressing table back against the wall, and rammed the masking tape into her bag. The diary. The rest of the diary. She wavered, seized by indecision.

"Soph, what are you even *doing* in there? C'mon. I just thought we could talk—"

"Sorry!" She scanned the table-top, panicking. *Mercy's Child.* She still had the book-jacket. Without thinking she wrapped the diary in the glossy paper. Tugged open the desk drawer and threw it inside. Then she stumbled to the door.

She stopped. Fear had stolen her voice. She gripped the latch, trying to be rational. He didn't know that she knew. There was no reason why he should. She drew back the chain and flipped up the latch.

"Soph." He smiled as she opened the door. His dazzling, winning smile. There was a bottle under his arm. Merlot. A far cry from the old days in his car. Her tastes had changed. The world had changed, since then.

"Hey, Soph." He walked right in. The door closed and he moved to embrace her, reaching past her to put the bottle down on the kitchen side. She felt herself stiffen.

"What's the matter?" He released her, pushed her to arm's length.

"Nothing." She shook her head.

"Where've you been? Sean said you weren't at work." The backs of his fingers brushed her cheek, warm and rough. She swallowed painfully.

"Nowhere. Here." She shrugged. "I'm fine." She extracted herself from his hold.

"Thanks for helping out last night." He moved casually to examine the items on the desk. Her phone, the pen. The envelope—

Shit, the envelope.

"What's this?" He stopped. Picked it up. She spun, wordless. His fingers had found the edge of the paper inside.

"It's nothing." Her voice was tremulous. "Leave it."

"To Sean . . . ?" He drew it out, smile suddenly gone. She couldn't stop him. Her spine was rigid with fear. His eyes scanned downwards. Narrowed.

"Sophia, what have you done?"

"I'm leaving." She snatched it from him, but he caught her hand.

"No. Wait. Let me read it."

"It's not *for* you, Ryan. No—" He had twisted it away, holding it out of reach. She swiped for it, desperate. "Give it back. Ryan—"

"You're . . ." He had reached the second page, his gaze scrolling to the bottom and back up again quickly. He frowned. "No, Sophia. Don't. Don't do this." He turned to her suddenly, his voice soft, regretful, and she took a step back, wrongfooted by his calm. "It's us. Me and you. We can make this work. Look . . ." He slid the letter into his pocket. "I brought a bottle over. I thought we could sit down and have a drink. Talk about it."

"There's nothing to talk about." She took another step away, towards the kitchen. Tried to process it. To think . . .

"Then let's just have a drink." He shrugged. His eyes were on her face, earnest. Persuasive. She shook her head.

To think. She needed to think. Fast . . .

"I need to go and . . . and get dressed."

"No you don't."

"Ryan . . ."

"You look fine, Sophia." The heat of his gaze washed over her, stopping her in her tracks. "You look . . . good." He moved towards her. His fingers brushed her cheek, her lips. And it struck her in a jolt. She was going to have to pretend. Whatever he was doing, she was going to have to play along. To feign ignorance. Until she could work out the next move . . .

She slipped out under his arm.

"Okay." She didn't have to make her voice breathy, didn't have to will the blush into her cheeks. Her palms were sweating as she took two glasses from the cupboard and passed him the bottle to open.

He smiled again, and this time it was the knowing, sultry smile of the car park at Sandford Lane as he filled both glasses and sat down on the end of the desk. She turned hers in her fingers then noticed him watching. The sip burned her lips and became a gulp under his scrutiny. He drank, too, and put down his glass.

"Here."

He unfolded something from his pocket. For a disorientating second she thought he was giving back the letter. She took another gulp of wine, desperately trying to look relaxed.

"I brought you something. For old times' sake." He grinned, his voice liquid and warm, like the Merlot. He slid the pen and the phone away and tipped the contents out onto the desk.

She felt herself freeze. Watched as he divided it out and stooped to inhale his own line as calmly as if he were lighting a cigarette.

"You know I don't do this anymore."

"But you know it'll feel good." It was soft, coaxing, an undertone. He pushed himself to his feet. Came closer, his hands on her waist, his mouth against her ear. "Don't you?"

"I don't know," she wavered.

"C'mon, Soph. It's *us*. It's always been us . . ."

She stared down at it. Weighing it up. Willing herself. If she played the part, did what he wanted, told him what he wanted to hear . . . If she . . .

"I was wrong, Soph. Wrong to ever let you go." He moved against her, so close that she could feel him through the robe. Her throat constricted, heart beating fast for all the wrong reasons. She half turned.

"One time," she whispered. Glanced up at him through her lashes, and hoped he wouldn't see the fear in her eyes. "Just one more time." She realised her lip was between her teeth, and made herself release it. "It's no worse for you than a smoke, right?"

He laughed under his breath.

He still had hold of her waist as she leaned down and sniffed, let the once familiar bitterness hit the back of her nose and work its way into her senses. It would be over soon. If she could ride it out. She just had to ride it out.

"Hey. That's better." His voice was against her neck, lips moving over her skin. "I missed you, you know. You were right. You're good for me. Don't leave now . . ."

"Ryan," she mumbled. "Stop it. Stop—"

"Come on." His hands closed around her arms, drawing her in. In, like she had always been drawn in; always, since she was fifteen years old—

"No," she whispered.

"Sophia," he murmured it against her hair, the lullaby of a lie that she still wasn't quite immune to. "Don't do this. Don't leave. We can figure this out." His hands were on her shoulders, her arms, untying the robe. "We can figure everything out."

Fear was giving way to something else: molten, breathless.

"Ryan . . ." she inhaled.

"You know what you do to me . . ." His touch burned her elbows, scorched trails of fire down her forearms. "Don't you realise?" His lips were on her neck, his knee forcing her gently off balance. The bed creaked. The skin of his fingers was rough and enticing as he pulled her arms behind her back and slid the cord belt out of the robe, letting it fall open, the sound of his voice swamping her like the tide.

"Don't you realise, Sophia?" he breathed, and his mouth was against hers. "What you've done?"

And for a moment, she didn't. She didn't realise. His kiss was slow and sure; his lips parting, persuading, until her body was loose and compliant in his hold, until she was ready to believe him.

Until he slid the cord around her neck.

Panic rose in her throat. She wrenched her hands free, tried to grab it, to loosen it. But her fingers were weak, their scrabbling futile as his hand twisted the cord and his knee forced her legs apart. There was a rushing in her ears, a baby crying somewhere, the noise growing louder and louder, obliterating everything except the memory, the way the whole world had changed that first second that Toby cried. She felt her muscles twitch, slacken, like they weren't her muscles at all. Felt him lower himself onto her as she retched and struggled, saliva spilling from her mouth.

"Ryan . . ." She could barely recognise the splutter of her own voice. "Stop. Please . . . *Please* . . ."

And she was back in his flat, in the dark, her head slammed against the headboard, fireworks popping in front of her eyes, his voice raw with rage: *get on the fucking bed.* And for some reason, all she could think about was the school tie wrapped around his fingers, and how it had been a mistake. A sob escaped her numb lips as he finished and pulled away. As he put another twist in the fabric. Dragged her to her feet and pocketed her phone from the dressing table—

His whisper against her ear was a kiss goodbye.

"It's over, Sophia."

CHAPTER 30

2022

It sounds like somebody crying. The shuddering, sobbing moan of grief, unanswered. I can't place it. Everything is dark. I don't know where it's coming from, who it is. I try to call out in response but my mouth is dry, filled with dust.

After a while there is an answer. A slow, arrhythmic tap. A finger. A fist? My eyes are already open, so why can't I see? The pain in my head is unbearable.

I *can* see. I'm just not concentrating hard enough. I frown, blink. Broken chairs. Damp plaster. A timber cross. The roof is leaking; the droplets catch the colours of the weeping Virgin and glisten as they fall, shattering into a thousand shards as they strike the wooden floor. *Tap . . . tap*, there's no rhythm to it. A torture of unpredictability. I watch them, trying to pick out reality from mirage. Darkness from light. Closing my eyes doesn't help; I can't distinguish how it's darker when I open them and lighter when they're shut: shimmering sunlight, roofbeams. Architects building sandcastles. Cerulean Blue and Raw Umber, a slowly revolving dance. *I want to learn. What? Everything.*

I'm in the chapel. I try to remember why he sent me here. Was he here?

I sit up. Pain pounds in my head, a migraine. No. There's blood, all over the floor. Rain running into my eyes. I wipe them, and realise. Not rain.

The weeping Virgin. Claire Lorchann. *Hail Mary, full of grace.* The images flash across my vision. Finbar. I stumble to my feet.

Claire . . . But she's gone. I'd be able to hear if anyone was left. The whisper of breath, the heave of a stifled sob. There's nothing. Nothing except the inconsolable wind and the rain dripping through the broken roof tiles. She's gone. And Fin?

I want to feel relief, but I can't. *He's dead! I killed him* . . .

Gone.

My muscles seem to lack substance. I'm suddenly aware of the nauseating pain in my arm. I flex my fingers and for a second everything swims. Steel, flesh, bone. My knees are jelly as I use my left hand to feel my way through the carcasses of the chairs to the wall. Along the wall. It gets darker the further I get, which doesn't seem right. The light was coming from the door. I almost fall, blind and disorientated, in the debris at my feet. The door.

It's shut. There *is* no light. I twist the handle. Tug at it, trying to fight back a wave of panic. Locked. She locked it.

I have to get out. This single thought brings clarity. I pull myself back along the wall. The window. I have to get to the window. But how will I climb? I slump against the sloughy plaster.

My phone. The relief is cool and dizzying. I free it from my pocket, fumble to unlock it, my fingers shaking. Sean. My left-handed swiping is uncoordinated, clumsy. *Sean.*

There's no signal.

The light of the screen is dazzling. I stare at it, dazed.

But there's something else. Outside. Not just the wind. I strain my ears to make it out. An engine. A car door. He's already found me. Hope leaps, wild, in my chest.

"Sean?" I whisper. It's cracked, barely audible. "*Sean?*"

The scrunch of feet. An abrupt halt. The scrabble of a key in a hundred-year-old lock.

A key . . .

I drop the phone.

Sean doesn't have a key.

Somehow, I run, the tang of blood choking off my breath. There's nowhere to go. The key rattles in the door, putting up a fight. The wind has dropped. All that's left is the steady drip of water onto the trapdoor . . . *the trapdoor.*

I scrabble with my fingers for the edges, pull it up. The space isn't big enough. I won't be able to shut it. I cram myself in, breathing in rapid, thready sobs. Further — please, further — I curl into the earth, gasping. *Please.*

The key turns.

I hear the footfalls on the wood. Then silence.

My breath, loud, *it's too loud* . . . I squeeze my arms around myself, trying to stifle it. Trying to edge myself further into the void. Don't make a sound. *Idanthrene. Ochre. Davy's Grey.* The footsteps have started again.

Ryan Lorchann's voice is soft.

"Clever trick. I liked it. Getting him to write his name. You couldn't have timed it any better, could you?"

Another step, another. Slow. Measured.

"What to do about it was the question. Until she decided to take matters into her own hands, my beautiful, deranged, wonderful wife. So now she tells me we're good; that she's already done it for me . . . Another dead intern on Sean's watch . . ."

Indanthrene. Ochre . . .

I screw my eyes tight shut. Clamp my teeth over my shuddering intake of breath. He's speaking in a stage whisper.

"There's just one problem. Because dead people can't hide, can they, Livs?"

Winsor Violet, Perylene Black. He's moving the carcasses of the chairs, scraping them over the floor. Coming closer. *Phthalo Turquoise.* Another breath; *in, lengthen, out . . .*

"Dead people can't play games."

Payne's Grey. I have to stay still. There's no space. No air. *Charcoal.* Every instinct in my body says move. Further in. *Further in*, get away from the trapdoor, further, *further*, into the darkness, where he won't find you . . . My feet grope desperately against the soil, looking for an opening. For anything other than earth and stone and—

Plastic?

It gives without warning, brittle, jagged, my trainer punching straight through, and fabric entangles my feet.

I stifle the scream. Swallow it, but I can't, I can't . . . even blind, with no light, just a wrapped sheet, I know what it is. I retch, heave—

The footsteps stop.

Better me . . . than if he finds you. There's a faint ringing in my ears.

Light flashes through the cracks of the trapdoor, penetrating around the edges. I recoil. But it's too late.

It opens easily, crashes back on its hinges. The beam of the torch falls directly onto my face. And Ryan Lorchann's steel-hard gaze meets mine, a chill smile at the corner of his lips.

I hear the sound in my throat. Cracked, suffocated.

He grabs a handful of my hair and jerks my head backwards.

"Five minutes." He's crouched down. "I was on that boat for less than five fucking minutes, and some little fuck of a kid managed to take a picture . . ."

"No!" I try to scream, but his finger and thumb are gripping my chin, forcing my mouth shut. I thrash, uncomprehending . . . A picture. Some kid took a picture. *Kris . . . He's done something to Kris . . .*

"And now it turns out *she'd* been writing out her fucking confessions."

"Sophia." My lips form the name, soundless.

"You thought she meant Sean, didn't you?" The chill smile flits back across his lips.

"Sean wasn't interested in Sophia, Livs. She wasn't looking for *Sean.*"

"She — she knew . . ." It's strangled. Barely audible. "She knew about Toby . . . she knew what you'd done! He was hers. And you took him—"

"I *took* him?" A bitter laugh spills from Ryan's lips. "No." He's shaking his head. "He's *my* son, Livia. He *is* my son."

"*Livvy!*"

He lets go. The voice is not quite imminent. It could be a thousand miles away, or a hundred yards. Reverberating with the wind, buffeted by the squalls of rain.

"*Livvy* . . . ?"

Tears spring to my eyes, of relief, of renewed terror. *No,* I whisper.

Ryan's foot slams into me.

All of the breath seems to leave my body. Vomit scorches my throat and burns the back of my nose as I fold around the pain, gasping. Curling into the dirt . . .

The hinges screech in protest. Then his weight is on the trapdoor, forcing it down. Down, the darkness. Like the closing circle of a porthole. I'm too weak to struggle anymore. Too weak to remember . . . *0.7 mm. Intertwined fingers and sweat on skin. Restraint, surrender. The things we try to deny ourselves . . .*

Now do you understand?

Always.

"Ryan? Ryan. Thank fuck! Is she here? Livia? Have you seen Livia?" I can hear his feet on the floor, his words, raw with relief.

Sean! I scream. But my throat is swollen, soundless. *Sean, no!*

"Is she here?"

I raise my arm. Try to strike the wood. *No. Oh God, no.*

The pause is excruciating.

"That's . . . her phone."

I can hear it. The dawning comprehension.

"What the fuck . . . Ryan? Where is she? What's going on?"

"Sean!" This time as I scream it, the sound registers. Shrill with terror. With certainty.

"*Livvy?*"

I sob, panic, slam myself upwards into the door with everything I have left. It doesn't move. Doesn't give a millimetre. Beyond it, his shout is of rage and pain. Feet stagger across the floor, sending a shower of grit into my eyes.

"Livvy!"

More footfalls, scuffling, panting. His voice sounds strange, thick.

"It was *you . . . Sophia . . .*"

But I don't hear the answer. Another sound hits home first. A sickening sound, a sound that silences my prayers and makes my blood run cold. The swing of steel. The crunch of metal on unresisting flesh and bone.

"Sean!" I'm screaming, screaming again. Hammering at the trapdoor with anything I can move, my hands, elbows, oblivious to the pain.

The cry is shrill: a piercing, unearthly sound that chills me to the core.

And everything stops.

Fin. *Toby.*

My voice has given out. My hands are raw. I try to kick instead, but there's nothing left. Nothing. I can barely raise my hand to strike, and when I do it's too weak to be audible. I can't hear anything anymore. Only the blood in my own ears, my own rasping breaths, scream after silent scream. And then silence.

Tears are trickling backwards, running hot and relentless into my ears. The sobs grip my chest. Beyond the wooden ceiling of Finbar's grave there's nothing. No movement. No sound at all. And I wait. I wait so long that my legs grow numb, that the tears turn cold. I don't even know what I'm waiting for. To die? *An awfully big adventure.* And Sean? My eyes are squeezed tightly closed. Sean?

I can't open them.

You'd better not start doubting.

But it's over. I know it, somewhere deep in my gut. That it's too late. I already know the soft, slow tread of feet across the floor. The scrape of stone on wood, heavy and resistant: slow motion. I remember. I remember everything. Rain on window glass, festoon lights. Yes, I remember slow motion.

This time, the light isn't as bright. A flicker, darting across me and away. The illusion of a face, not the one I expect; one with angular hollow cheeks, staring eyes. The voice is unfamiliar, low.

Urgent.

"Quick, get out. Can you get out?"

I try to blink away the dust, the shards of piercing light that abrade my eyes.

"Can you get up?" His hand is outstretched, wet with rain, sinewy and shaking. I don't take it. A sharp chin, greying stubble.

"Simon . . . ?" I'm dazed. Sick.

He shakes his head.

"Giles. Giles Stanley. Can you get out? Can you stand?" His eyes flit to the doorway, where rain is blowing in, illuminated in the light from his phone. He returns it to my face, dazzling me.

Stanley?

"Livia." He's on his knees, reaching to grasp my hands, insistent. "Please, *quickly*."

"Sean," I rasp. But I let him take my hands. "Where's Sean?"

He's not here. There's only the two of us. Giles's gaze flicks back toward the door. It returns to me, but not quickly enough. I've seen. Seen the trail he followed. The spatters of dark, sticky blood in the dust.

"Sean . . ." My throat is raw, torn. I'm scrambling out, backwards, onto my elbows. Staggering to my feet, my legs almost giving way. He makes as if to stop me, but I blunder out of his reach, starting to sob. Starting to run, off balance. "Fin?"

I'm at the door. I can feel it, at last, the burst of wind and rain against my face, cold and real. I gulp it in, grab the doorframe to keep myself from falling. Swing around it, out; *I have to get out.* I have to find them.

My feet are on mud and broken brambles.

And the rest of me collides full-force with Ryan Lorchann's immovable, drenched chest.

He catches my arm mid-air, pulling me up short. His fingers bite into my skin. I raise my eyes, stupor-slow. And then he twists, and a different kind of scream tears itself from my lungs. I feel my body slacken, limp, at the crack of bone. Feel my feet disconnect from the ground. A dull reflection flashes across my eyes before I register it: steel in daylight, nonsensical and fractured.

Then Ryan staggers, a look of disbelief crossing his perfectly masculine face, as Giles Stanley twists the knife from his abdomen and plunges it into his neck instead.

I feel the blood hit my forehead, a hot, livid spatter. Ryan's hands splay open. I fall, choke, gag, tasting metal. For a fleeting, stomach-dropping moment, I think he's going to keep coming. His boots skid in the dust.

Then his body crumples.

I lurch backwards. Blood is in my mouth, my eyes — I can't breathe through it — it fills my nostrils, hot and suffocating.

"*It's okay. You're all right. You're okay—*"

I can hear someone breathing; rapid, thready, ineffectual breaths. Then I realise they're in time with the shudder of my own chest.

"Come on, Livia. I've got you—"

Giles's hands are around my elbows. Drawing me away. Holding me up. I'm not sure which.

"I've got you. You're okay."

"*No!*" Sound returns; I'm screaming, hysterical, trying to claw my way free. Blood: hot, slick blood. I can taste it; I'm slipping in it, the smell of iron and terror. The knife is still in Ryan Lorchann's neck. I gag.

"He ruined my daughter. She was my little girl. And he destroyed her."

"No . . . *no* . . ." The fight is ebbing from my body. "*No* . . ."

"Come on." He's pulling me, half carrying me. Over the trenches, between the bracken, away from the door, the knife, the blood. Holding me, as the rain and wind take us, until the words turn to sobs, until the fight is gone. The tide is over the beach; the orange fence has torn free, lost to the wind. The soil at the cliff edge is crumbled, a single clump of grass dangling hopelessly as it contemplates its fate.

Sean. The burst of wind hits me like the shockwave of a detonation; the force of it knocks me headlong. Giles lets me go, and I stumble to the drop. I can see it. In the water. The taste in my mouth is Ivory Black and ashen. A flash of darkness, a rainbow; everything has lost its definition, everything except the water and something blue. *Something blue.* Floating, rippling with the hungry currents, swirling as it's sucked away.

"No—" I moan. "*No.*"

My gaze travels downwards. Down in time to see the cagoule fold in on itself. For a second, just a second, the embroidered rainbow breaks the surface, saltwater soaking through the stitches, darkening, fading . . . I stumble. And then I run, half fall, scrambling down what's left of the descent, over the rocks, to where the sand should have been, white-gold and perfect. The sea tears at my legs, colder than anything before, than anything I've ever imagined.

"Fin!" I shriek. "Fin!" My cry is tiny, insignificant over the spray, white noise.

"FIN!" It gives out, becomes a sob; another, rising and hopeless. "Sean . . ." I try to kick off my shoes. To take another step forwards. To follow them. But it's too late to follow them. Too late, like I always have been. The cagoule has succumbed to its destiny. They're gone.

"Livia."

"*No.*" I grit my teeth. Block it out. The nightmare. The landlord who can't find the bathroom. The stranger who knows my name. The man who's always been there in the shadows, the trees, the periphery of my vision. In the hallway at Sunnyside, in the Gatehouse's drive. The man who's reaching for me with the rain diluting Ryan Lorchann's blood on his arms. The man with Sophia Swift's eyes.

"Livia." He's on the shore. "I'm sorry. I'm so sorry. I was too late. I was too late. I'm so sorry—"

"Get away from me!" I can hear my voice from a thousand miles away, shrieking, breaking, and I can't stop it. "Keep away!"

"There's help now. Come on." He's wading into the water; I can hear the waves hitting his legs. "They're here to help you. Come on. Please. It's not safe. Come back. For Sophia."

I snap around.

There are people on the rocks. Two figures, three. Hi-vis jackets. Grab-bags. *There's help now.* All the breath seems to have left my body.

"*What?*" I whisper.

"For Sophia." His eyes are hollow.

I turn to face him.

"I need you to come back for Sophia. To tell them the truth."

There are more people now. Uniforms. Lights.

"They know what I've done. I called them."

For Sophia.

"She phoned me. The day before she died. She'd never called me before. Not in seven years."

Tears are sliding, silent and helpless over my cheeks.

"She wanted to meet me. She said she understood now. That no matter what I'd done, I must still have loved her. That I wouldn't have given up on her, because a parent doesn't give up on a child, even when they screw up, even when they leave them. That they think about them all the time. That they'd do anything — anything — to protect them. She was right."

"Sir. Put your hands where we can see them and turn around."

He doesn't flinch. He lifts his hands, palms outwards, raises them at his sides. But his gaze doesn't leave my face.

"The last thing she said . . . She said the strangest thing. She said . . . just for a moment, she didn't want to let him go. I didn't understand. But he was hers, wasn't he? That was the truth she wanted to tell me. The child. Finbar. He was hers."

Finbar. The pain lances through me. Finbar. Toby Rainworth. A child who belonged to everybody and nobody. I have no reply. No words.

"*Sir.* Now, please. Place your hands on your head and turn around."

"Tell them," he says.

Then he turns away. I falter, numb. Numb, as he starts to walk, the waves sucking at his trouser legs. As they turn him against the rocks and cuff his hands behind his back.

There are hands reaching for me, too: a circle of faces, like when I came round on the ground in Wollaton Park and opened my eyes to the truth of my self-destruction.

"No." I shake my head. "*No . . .*"

The rain is merciless, hitting in sheets, assault after bitterly cold assault. A string of sobs rises from deep in my gut, violent and irrepressible. All I can remember is what she wrote about the rips — the death under the water, the skeletons on the rocks — as I start to stumble away from them, all of them, along the edge of the waves. Everything is cold. So very cold. I stagger to a stop.

There are blue lights on the track. So many lights. I can see them in array from where I stand as I turn full circle, the throb of a helicopter spiralling louder in my ears.

Now do you understand?

I sway, clinging to the numbness. But the lights are too real to shut out. The noise. The dull, gnawing comprehension. There's so much rain. I let it run into my eyes, so that everything drifts, ill-defined. Horizon, clouds. The place where the sea meets the sky, where once there was a rainbow. And for a split second, I can see him: there at the water's edge. Jeans surprisingly worn, their denim soft and frayed. The strong, unsmiling set of his jaw, the low flicker of his brows, the blaze of excitement in his raw-umber eyes.

I bury my fingernails in my palms, trying to breathe.

Self-sabotage, Livvy Frost.

"Over there!"

"Oh my God. Get the paediatric grab bag—"

I try to blink away the picture. But it won't go. His face, the light of the fractured dawn on his skin, the black, sultry certainty in his eyes. It loses focus, fades . . . sharpens, white with cold. Grim and shivering—

To breathe. To breathe; I've forgotten how . . .

"Get them to recall helimed—"

There, at the water's edge. His whole body's shaking, teeth chattering in his clenched jaw. And in his arms, in his arms—

It looks like a doll. A mannequin, child-sized and limp, marble skin and lips painted blue-grey . . . until its head rolls backwards, and Toby Rainworth's unseeing eyes stare into mine.

Water is streaming from his mouth and nose, pouring into his sodden dark-honey hair; his limbs spill lifeless, one once-closed fist curling open. And then they're running past me, running in, someone taking his head, laying him out on the ground. And I can't see anymore, can't see anything except movement, chaos, a mask, orange blocks—

"One. Two. Three. Four. Five."

I watch from a thousand miles away as Sean collapses to his knees.

I want to learn.

"Heart rate's less than fifty."

What?

"Start compressions."

Everything.

"Fourteen, fifteen—"

"Stand clear . . ."

Toby's dead. He fell in the water.

My breath is lodged in my throat. It won't move up or down. My body won't respond, motionless, meaningless. And this time there's no circle, no porthole, no scream splintering the darkness. Just silence, the blur of motion; the eventuality that, after everything, it was impossible to change. The truth in the end is the same.

The boy who never grew up.

My tears spill over.

"One."

A fist, squeezing an inflatable bag. A tube, taped between dusky lips.

"Two."

A faltering rhythm, a heartbeat. *Do you believe?* A final drumroll. A falling curtain. The last page of a novel, ripped out and cast into the dust. *If you believe, clap your hands* . . .

I can't. Panic grips my throat. I can't.

Don't let him die.

I can. What else is left? The impact echoes off the cliffs, the ring of flesh on flesh, palm on palm, the sound of hardback falling onto paper, blotting out the print. Everything's dark, receding. The beat of a bird's wings. The ring of applause, cut off.

If you believe.

Of course I believe. Somehow, deep down, I've always believed. In Sophia Swift, in Toby Rainworth, in the things we try to deny ourselves. In the tiny child turning and turning in the dandelion stems, a whirlwind of elbows and ethereal eyes: a twilight child who doesn't have a name or a face anymore, or a place, or even a time. Only a dance — no one else's dance — and a whispered song, all the colours of the rainbow.

CHAPTER 31

2023

There's ice on all the pavements, patches of delicate lace that are melting where the sun is starting to lick at the shadows. The trees are clinging desperately to the tatters of their autumn splendour; they wear them proudly, like once-glorious ballgowns that have turned to rags in the November wind.

Sean looks uncomfortably cramped in the driver's seat of my new car. My trusty three-door has finally given up its struggle after an eleven-month retirement in the Oxford city streets. It was never quite the same after the Cornish cliffs.

I shift the gift bag between my feet. The months have slipped by unnoticed; the first frost took both of us by surprise, and now there is already a smattering of premature Christmas lights illuminating the streets. We slow to a halt and Sean kills the engine.

I miss it. I suppose I always knew I would. There was never really a moment of decision, never a final wrench. We were, and then we weren't; the house at Trethallyan Edge was finished and there was no reason left to stay. No number of seagulls or ghosts could drown out the call of reality.

He turns. "Shall we?" For a second, I don't reply. I study the shadow in his eyes, the one that has never quite been banished. He reaches to tidy back my non-compliant hair, and the warm graze of his thumb exiles the memory. We're both holding our breath.

"Come on." Sean jerks his head. I scoop up the present and open the car door.

The house is a brand-new clone — albeit luxurious — in an expansion of upper-middle-class Britain on the outskirts of Tunbridge Wells. It has a postage-stamp garden and an eye-watering price tag. There are no Christmas lights here, but there are balloons on the gatepost, a red and a yellow bobbing with the breeze and four burst carcasses that didn't weather the cold.

Sean holds open the gate for me, and we make our way along the path. I ring the bell and stand back, listening for the tumult of motion within. Sure enough, it crescendos closer. A latch clicks.

"Livia!" Leanna reaches out an arm to hug me, planting a kiss in the air beside my ear. "Come in."

Her gaze flickers to Sean. She doesn't quite extend the welcome embrace to him. Like Kris, she still has distrust in her eyes, even after all this time. Kris, who it turns out had suffered no worse a fate than losing his phone in Rescue Rooms and passing out in somebody's kitchen after a twenty-eight-nil win against Keele. I'm still not sure what Ryan intended. The alumni game that never happened still nags at the back of my mind some nights, when the darkness is bigger than the silence.

My chain of thought is broken. A mop-headed toddler in a pinafore dress has tumbled into my knees and is clinging to the hem of my coat. I reach down tentatively to rescue the child's pink headband from in front of her eyes.

"Sorry!" Leanna swoops to intervene, propping the baby on her hip. "It's Livia, Rose. And Uncle Sean. Say Livia?"

"Lever," Rose obliges, then wriggles to get down. Leanna lets her go, and she totters off in the direction of the sitting room. I shrug out of my coat. Sean is standing very still, a tell-tale sign that he is just as uncomfortable as Leanna.

"Come through — would you like a drink, both of you? I've just made coffee. Let me fetch it."

The heated tiles are warm under my feet. Sean follows me along the hallway into the sitting room. We stop.

Rose has sat down on the floor, legs splayed, to dismantle a little building made of Duplo. And there he is. Rumpled starlight hair and moon-white skin. He jumps up from in front of her, still clutching the house he's been building. He's got tall, and it takes me by surprise.

For a moment, he stands motionless. His red lips are slightly parted. I half expect him to hug his arms around his chest, but he doesn't. Very carefully, he puts down the house.

Then he's running. His arms lock around Sean's waist with such force that it knocks them both off balance. I look on in silence, blinking fiercely. Neither of them speaks. Eventually, Toby lets go. He steps back, and I watch his hands shape a symbol. After a beat, Sean's move in reply.

"Coffee?" Leanna has appeared in the doorway behind us. I hasten aside, dashing a hand quickly over my eyes as she sets down the tray. I clear a stack of scrunched silver paper and boxes of paints off the sofa to sit beside her.

"Birthday presents," she explains. She isn't looking at me. We're both watching the exchange of shapes and signs. There's something intense and beautiful in the unspoken interaction. A world that neither of us inhabits.

"We're having fireworks this evening," she says at last. I can feel her tension relenting, even as we watch. "Once it's dark. Won't you stay until then?"

"I'm sorry, we can't." I shake my head. Part of me would love to. A larger part of me baulks at the very suggestion of another Rainworth family gathering. "We have to get going. We've got a long drive."

She nods. We fall silent, and I take a coffee. There are cards all along the mantelpiece, and strung around the mirror over the hearth. *6 Today. Birthday Boy.*

As if he's felt me looking, Toby turns. A broad smile creeps over his lips.

"Blackbird," he says.

One word. One word, and in it the world might have ended, or begun. I gape at him, in role-reversed silence, warmth prickling from my scalp to my spine. This time, there's no disguising my tears; they spring to attention before they're repressible. I daren't even blink for fear of them overflowing onto my cheeks.

"Happy birthday, Toby," I whisper. The present is still in its gift bag at my feet. He takes Sean by the hand and brings him to examine it, pushing back the chequered paper to look inside, then closes it again with meticulous care.

"Don't be sad." His voice is pure and melodious. Hearing it seems so wrong. He lets go of Sean's hand.

"I'm not sad." I laugh through the tears, and he frowns at me for a moment, perplexed by the contradiction. There's something very reminiscent of Sean in his critical dark stare. He turns on his heel without warning and disappears out into the hall. Seconds later, he returns, concealing something behind his back.

"It's for you." He produces it with a flourish. "I made it."

Something has expanded in my chest, irrepressible and impossible to breathe against. I take the wooden stem of the windmill without a word. Touch my finger to the sugar-paper, and spin the blades on their brass split-pin. And for just a moment, the reflection watching me from the mirror isn't mine at all. She's a girl with auburn hair and indiscernible eyes, and she's smiling.

* * *

There's a pattern to everything, if you look for it. The falling of a leaf, or the way that a raindrop tracks on glass. The misting of your breath, the gathering of clouds above an autumn sunset. The pattern of the sea is different. It doesn't last long enough to capture or commit to mind. It moves on, like time, washes clean and forgets.

There are things I won't forget. Things I promised not to. There are other things that I'd do anything to lose to the tides of time: the inside of the children's intensive care unit, the police interview room, the witness stand. Claire Lorchann has been charged with manslaughter and attempted murder; I'd like to forget that, but I can't. I'd like to forget the trapdoor. The strike of raw hands against ungiving wood. The suffocating darkness. No one but Toby Rainworth knows what happened between Ryan and Sean that day. And I don't think anyone else ever will.

From Sunnyside, the sea is unusually calm this afternoon. The street is unchanged. Time here has its own pattern. It's very quiet — all I can hear is the tide. Sean has stopped the car engine to wait for me; I mount the step and remember that I need to look for the buzzer, then notice that the outer door is ajar. I push it with my foot and tiptoe into the shadows. The door to 29a is shut. I knock.

I've wondered, often. I wrote a card, after we rented the apartment in Oxford, but I never got one back.

The door opens. I blink in surprise and take a step back. Radiohead spills around the high-buttoned, skinny-jeaned occupant, who is regarding me over a beard that is far too big for his youthful face. The dissonant melody pulses loudly enough in my ears that I can't quite hear his greeting.

"I'm sorry?" I start. "I'm . . ." I falter. I can't help noticing that the flat behind him is all wrong. The threadbare carpet is gone. So is the fireside chair. The mantelpiece houses nothing except a Banksy print propped against the wall. The music is hypnotic, somehow.

"I . . . I'm looking for Niklavs."

"Who?" He looks nonplussed.

"Niklavs. Niklavs . . ." I search, desperately, and suddenly realise that I never knew his second name. "Niklavs. He lives — lived, here."

"Umm?" He lolls against the doorframe, apparently deep in thought. "You mean the old guy?"

"Not that old," I manage through my teeth.

"I guess he must have . . . moved on." He pulls a comic face. "I mean, man . . . I hope—"

He must catch sight of the look on my face. His expression changes.

"Sorry. I just mean, he didn't leave an address to send stuff on." He takes his hands out of his pockets and stands to size me up. "Hey, d'you want to come in or something?"

"No . . ." I retreat. "Thanks. Thanks anyway."

No address. The irony of it smarts painfully in the backs of my eyes. No forwarding address. I climb back into the car.

"That was quick." Sean unfolds his arms and pushes himself upright in the driver's seat. I don't reply. I can't quite think what to say. I nod instead, and fix my eyes on the familiar cobbles as we pull away.

We don't pass a single car on the coast road. It's warmer here than it was in Oxford. The late afternoon sun is disintegrating on the horizon over the sea. It marks out the silhouettes of the half-bare trees, and casts a long shadow from the signboard beside the road. *For Sale.* We turn in past it. *Public auction 01/12/2023.*

The drive is bumpier than ever, rutted with tyre tracks, and my car doesn't handle it well. I brace myself against the dashboard as mud splatters the windscreen. There are more boards by the gate. Sean lowers the window to tap the code into the keypad, but it doesn't work. He presses the call button instead.

"Hello?" The voice through the intercom is hard to understand, thick with static, but I think it says something about Gordon-Heyers. Sean frowns as he gives our names. In reply, the gates groan open and we roll onto the gravel.

Someone has weeded the drive, trimmed the rhododendrons — even cleaned the windows. The Hall really is for sale. I gaze up at it with an uncomfortable lump in my throat as we climb the steps together and Sean raps on the door. I'm not sure that I've ever seen him hesitate, but he's hesitant now. We both stand back.

Bolts scrape, metal on metal, and the door opens with a clatter. A pair of shrewd eyes regards us from the gloom.

"What is it I tell you? Forty years, and I never leave. It seems you, also, not capable to stay away."

"Wh-what . . ." I stammer.

He steps forwards from the darkness, the low sun falling across his crinkled blue eyes.

"*Niklavs—*" I exhale.

Within a couple of strides, he's outside. His arms close around me in a bear-hug almost strong enough to lift my feet off the floor, despite the deepened creases in his weathered face. He smells of salt, spirits, strong coffee. He lowers me carefully, and I become suddenly aware of Sean's raised eyebrows. Niklavs grins.

"Is good to see you, Livia."

I extract myself, smiling helplessly.

"It's good to see you too."

"But you have wrong house, I think." Niklavs pushes me to arm's length. "If you come here looking for Graham." His gaze travels with calm perception from me to Sean. "He has not lived in Hall for several months."

"But . . ." For a beat, I'm confused. "You're . . ."

"Lending hand with estate." His grin hasn't faded. "For what efforts are worth. I move here to help him. I can show you place he will be. But I think perhaps you find way well enough by yourself."

Well enough? From the corner of my eye, I see Sean shake his head. Well enough that none of us has to look where we're going. We traverse the grounds on foot, and I'm flooded with a sudden rush of memories I didn't even realise I'd amassed: the police cordons, the day they carried Finbar Lorchann's remains from the vault. The revisions and planning amendments, watching the JCB take its first bite of the chapel walls — it was over so fast — shards of the weeping Virgin glistening amongst the ruins of the brick and render. The lightning strikes over the sea the day the oak frame finally arrived . . . Walking away, that last night, alone in the December darkness when the workmen had all gone and there was nothing left in the picture windows except a quiet sense of unfulfilled expectation.

There was a time when I knew every line and angle of this place, every recess and prominence, but it looks different now that it's inhabited. A year on, and all the windows at the front have curtains. There are new additions: a driveway, a fence, a name carved into a slate plaque. I come to a halt, eyes stinging. *Helvellyn.*

There's a strip of garden that borders the cliff edge, turfed and trimmed in startling contrast to the wild, unconquered array of gorse and bracken around it. The figure standing there is stooped low. For a moment, I think he's alone. Then I realise that what he's leaning on is a wheelchair. He stands in placid silence, his arms folded across the handgrips, and past them I can see the faint bob of white hair illuminated against the sunset.

Clarissa loves the sunset.

I can't bring myself to go any further. To intrude on something so intimate. I turn back, instead, and look up by accident, straight into the blaze of unsmiling emotion in Sean Lorchann's dark eyes.

His hands capture mine, his forefinger and thumb toying lightly with the band around my ring-finger. I found the box on the floor of number 31 Sunnyside while he was still keeping vigil in children's intensive care. The box had the name of an Oxford jeweller inside its lid. I was alone, and I didn't say a word to the silence. I knew, even then as I put it on, that people would say it was a mistake.

My gaze drifts back to the figures on the clifftop. I watch in silence as Graham Gordon-Heyers manoeuvres the wheelchair.

"All he ever wanted," Sean's whisper startles me, "was to give her the world. Don't you see?"

Do I see? I look up at the shadows in Sean's face. There's a wry smile on his lips that makes my heart hurt. The sun is almost gone. Gordon-Heyers is pushing the chair back towards the gable end. Even Niklavs has slipped away, unnoticed. We're alone. Alone, at Helvellyn, watching the darkness creep across the sky. Watching the colours fade: red, yellow, pink and green. And it occurs to me I'll never have an answer for Sophia Swift. I'll never be able to tell her what it was in the story. What had made me turn the pages. Her story. My father's story. *Mercy's Child.* He'd tried to write the truth for me, in the spaces between the print. And all that time I'd misunderstood.

He had reached the place where sick people go, and children when their stars stop shining.

And Toby wasn't there.

THE END

THE JOFFE BOOKS STORY

We began in 2014 when Jasper agreed to publish his mum's much-rejected romance novel and it became a bestseller.

Since then we've grown into the largest independent publisher in the UK. We're extremely proud to publish some of the very best writers in the world, including Joy Ellis, Faith Martin, Caro Ramsay, Helen Forrester, Simon Brett and Robert Goddard. Everyone at Joffe Books loves reading and we never forget that it all begins with the magic of an author telling a story.

We are proud to publish talented first-time authors, as well as established writers whose books we love introducing to a new generation of readers.

We have been shortlisted for Independent Publisher of the Year at the British Book Awards three times, in 2020, 2021 and 2022, and for the Diversity and Inclusivity Award at the Independent Publishing Awards in 2022.

We built this company with your help, and we love to hear from you, so please email us about absolutely anything bookish at feedback@joffebooks.com

If you want to receive free books every Friday and hear about all our new releases, join our mailing list: www.joffebooks.com/contact

And when you tell your friends about us, just remember: it's pronounced Joffe as in coffee or toffee!

ALSO BY ELEONOR SAMUEL

STANDALONES
THE NANNY
THE CORNISH DIARY

www.ingramcontent.com/pod-product-compliance
Lightning Source LLC
LaVergne TN
LVHW041053080826
845145LV00007B/1554

* 9 7 8 1 8 3 5 2 6 0 1 8 0 *